# FREE *Fall*

KHUSHI T. SAHA

*Dedicated to all you romantics out there ... who are secretly—
but not so secretly—dirty girls.*

PRESENT DAY
new york, new york

## CHAPTER 1

꒐

"Forty bucks?" Chrissy gasped under her breath, her fingers carefully caressing the delicate petals. Smooth and pristine white, with no visible blemishes, the daisies smiled cheerfully back at her—was she imagining it, or were they mocking her?

She crouched at floor level where the cramped flower shop displayed the cheapest blooms. The price's sticker shock almost knocked her back onto her soaked butt as sweat trickled down the side of her face. She swiped it away and took a deep breath, almost choking on the thick humidity in the air. It was a tangle of varying scented blooms and balminess, only magnifying the place's heady, sticky quality.

"So help me, Miley, I love you, but I *cannot* buy myself flowers. Not right now anyway." She sadly put the bunch back in its place, giving it one last longing look.

The gentle pitter-patter outside sounded like the rain was letting up. Sure enough, when she glanced through the window, there was a drizzle; a contrast to the harsh splatter on concrete that assaulted the city only moments ago—the reason why

1

Chrissy had ducked inside the nearest shop for shelter. Seeing as it was a flower shop, her current unhappy mood brightened significantly, only to be dashed to smithereens by the price of the daisies—her favorite.

It made sense that daisies were her favorite. She was an otherwise positive, bubbly person, except that lately, life was dishing her a less desirable meal. In a nutshell, she was broke in one of the most expensive cities in the world, and it was more than complicated trying to figure out her problems.

A cheery face popped into view above her.

"I know what you mean," the bright-eyed salesgirl said. "Miley Cyrus gets it when it comes to relationships. I just saw her at the Barclays Center. Did you go?" Chrissy would have answered "no," if the girl let her, but she kept talking. "But I think she might be a touch out of it when it comes to inflation and the economy." She reached a hand down to her. "Need a help up?"

"Thanks, I got it," Chrissy said, waving the girl's hand away, her tone chipper as she smiled at the other woman.

She stood up on her own, trying unsuccessfully to brush the creases that had managed to set along the front of her trench coat. "I guess it's the message we should be listening to. We deserve to treat ourselves in some shape or form." She blew her bangs out of her eyes. "Do we really need a man in our lives to complete us?"

The other woman raised a brow skeptically, and Chrissy hastily backtracked. "Or a woman, or *any* kind of living, breathing being we can just lie on top of at the end of the day?"

The other girl chuckled and Chrissy laughed, too. She always tried to keep a positive attitude, no matter what life threw at her—the whole 'when life gives you lemons mumbo-jumbo' was kind of her thing.

She continued. "I should count my lucky stars I can't afford them. I'm saving up for a new umbrella." She joked, though inwardly she cursed herself and her need to rush out that morning, as she pictured her umbrella in its stand right by the front door of her apartment.

She peered out the window again and at the dark skies above. Grey clouds hung low and bloated against the sea of skyscrapers. But it did appear as though the heavy early spring showers were on pause for the moment.

*Gotta love New York at the end of March.* It was a wet, chilly mess most days, but it was worth it when the sun stayed out, unlike that day.

Glancing at her watch, she jolted, realizing she had ten minutes to make to the meeting she'd been dreading all week (attorneys had never been her favorite kind of people). And given there were at least fifteen more blocks to walk to the office amid the teeming midtown lunch crowd, she'd need to haul ass.

She hurried to the door.

"Stay dry!" she called out to the nice salesgirl, but she'd vanished to the back of the store. Chrissy ended up waving to the stern elderly florist, now behind the counter, giving her a testy look.

She grabbed a free city paper from the newsstand beside the entrance for some cover in case the rain started again, ducked into the crowd of people outside, and walked hastily toward her destination. Her shoes squelched hideously with each step, but she kept pushing through the throng of moving limbs while dodging pointy umbrella parts that vied to take her eye out.

The rain decided to beat down again just as she glanced up to see she was at 33<sup>rd</sup> Street and Park Avenue. With just a few more blocks to go, she picked up her pace, running the rest of the way, though the pavement was slick.

She arrived at her destination out of breath, just as her newspaper turned to mush. She tossed it in the trashcan on the sidewalk and panted, pushing quickly through the heavy revolving doors.

Her first step was tricky, though, as she proceeded to slide on the marble floor. Usually, her balance was quick, like a cat with nine lives, and she could right herself immediately if she happened to trip—intense dance training most of her life would do that to a person. But the marble floor had other ideas. Shiny and slippery from the rain outside, with not a heavy-duty office building doormat in sight, Chrissy's feet flew out from under her. How ironic. Do they want a lawsuit on their hands? she thought as she went down.

"*Shi--ugarrrrrr!*" she squealed, landing with a loud thud—this time definitely on her butt. Her friends would be proud though, at her attempt to curb her overuse of foul language—which admittedly was a lot.

The doorman stood frozen. The look of horror on his face would've made her chuckle if she wasn't so worried about being late. He snapped out of it as her struggles to get up became apparent and he hurried over.

"Ma'am," he said apologetically, lifting her like a rag doll with beefy hands under her arms. "Ma'am, I apologize. The rugs got all soaked and the replacements haven't arrived from basement storage yet." He stood back, wringing his hands while Chrissy tried to sort herself out. She gingerly rubbed her behind and winced. She'd have an ugly bruise there, no question.

Pushing her damp bangs back out of her eyes and squaring her shoulders, she took in the concerned look of the elderly doorman.

"Ma'am?" he asked again, this time taking his doorman cap off and rubbing his bald head. "Are you all right?"

"First of all, I am *not* a ma'am," she said, a little miffed to be called that at having just turned twenty-eight a few weeks ago. She flashed him a huge grin though, because she could tell he felt terrible. "And second, my butt might be bruised, but I think my ego needs an ambulance."

"Ma'am—er, Miss?" He stepped toward her, arms out to catch her in case she collapsed, his eyes bulging again. "You want me to call an ambulance?"

She fluttered her hands and shook her head, making her damp shoulder-length, strawberry-blonde hair stick against her cheeks. "I'm kidding. I'm fine ... really." She assured him. "But, I'm running late and need to get to an appointment." She rushed on.

"Which floor?" he asked, relieved she wasn't making a fuss about taking a tumble.

"Um ... I'm not sure. I need the attorney's offices of Meyer, Meyer, Chin-Donahue, and Lang," she said confidently, having no choice but to memorize the partners' names. They'd been running through her mind all week leading up to her appointment.

The doorman rushed over to the three electronic turnstiles at the other end of the high-domed foyer. He swiped the key card attached to his belt and the metal blades swished open to the elevator banks sitting behind them.

"You want the fortieth floor," he said.

"Thank you!" She half ran, half walked through, trying not

to slip again. "You're a gem." She remarked as she passed him. The older man's face pinkened and he smiled in return.

Her anxiety decided to kick it up a notch just as the elevator arrived, her esophagus closing up as though she'd unsuccessfully swallowed cotton balls. She coughed and cleared her throat, getting past it while entering the elevator and punching the button for the fortieth floor. As she rode up, she gave herself a pep talk.

"He'll be nice (hopefully), and not a bastard like every other lawyer out there. He's Mariam's cousin for crying out loud. How much of a dirtbag could he be?"

Did she feel bad about lumping all attorneys into the negative pile? Maybe just a little, because they couldn't all be terrible, could they? Just that one she'd dated who'd had red flags from the get-go, but still left her to rot in love jail moping for weeks when he broke it off. She'd finally seen the light and realized she was better off without his lying ass.

And then there was that one who'd given her mother a hell of a time when she'd taken over a small rug store operation when Chrissy had been tiny. He'd been a wicked bad man; she'd been sure of it back then, remembering the all-dark clothes he wore and his giant-like stature. Though she could be misremembering—she tended to let her imagination get the best of her, and she'd been around five years old at the time. But what she did remember vividly was how that ogre had made her mother—a confident and sharp-witted Russian woman with grit who'd recently immigrated from the motherland—quake in her heels whenever he came around. Was he even a legal man of the law? That whole scenario had always felt creepy to Chrissy and the man had disappeared from their lives a few years later.

She shook her head putting her thoughts back in order.

Regardless, of the awful behavior of the others, *this* lawyer she was meeting today was legit. Her friend, Mariam, couldn't speak more highly of him … except for that one flaw she'd warned about, but being his cousin, she'd brushed it off as a sign of his success.

Chrissy stared at her reflection in the shiny gold doors, barely recognizing herself. She was still getting used to her naturally reddish blonde hair, having stopped dying it a golden blonde months ago. And, her appearance was more than rumpled. Her carefully put-together hair and makeup, not to mention donning the most professional-looking pencil skirt and white button-down she owned, were all for naught. Her previously, and painstakingly straightened hair was now curling back to its natural waves, with a good amount of frizz. The black liner carefully drawn to perfect cat eyes on her lids had pooled into smudges around her rims. She quickly rummaged around for a tissue in her bag to wipe the smears away. She'd just managed to look less raccoon-like when the doors slid open to the fortieth floor with a loud ding.

Bold, glossy lettering shone under cool fluorescent lights behind the receptionist's desk, listing off the partners of the firm: Meyer, Meyer, Chin-Donahue, and Lang. The office was sleek and silver, with touches of grey upholstery. She carefully walked up to the receptionist and waited while the smart-looking young man in a crisp grey suit and tie (nearly the same color as the décor) held up a long finger as he took call after call that lit up the phone system.

When her fingers began to drum impatiently on the desk, he finally looked up and gave her a pleasantly bland look. "How may I help you, today?"

"Hi. I'm here to see Aariv Abbas." She unconsciously

smoothed her hair down, as the man's curious eyes darted around her face, a hint of a frown between his brows.

"Mr. Abbas? And you are…?"

"Oh. Duh." She smiled apologetically. "Chrissy Smyth, both names with a 'y,'" she said as cheerfully as she could. "I have an appointment, I promise." She assured him, trying for cheeky and flirty, aware that she was running more than late.

The young man nodded expressionlessly and clicked his mouse, turning his attention to the enormous, sleek computer screen on his desk. From where she was standing, Chrissy saw a calendar pop up that was chock-full of appointments. Each attorney's name and corresponding meetings were color-coded to tell whose meeting was whose and when. It made her eyes cross just staring at it.

"Let's see. Chrissy Smyth with 'y's.' Chrissy … Smyth … with … 'y's.' Hmm, where did he put you?" His eyes darted around the calendar. "Ah ha. You have the fifteen minutes Mr. Abbas reserves for his lunch break. Actually," he glanced at the tiny digital clock in the corner of his screen, "you're already five minutes late." The receptionist tried to keep a straight face, but the "oh shit" was written all across the downward spread of his lips and the slight click of his tongue. "Mr. Abbas expects punctuality. His 'on-time' is five minutes early."

"Super," Chrissy said, her bright demeanor masking her agitation. Could this day get any worse? And who booked only fifteen minutes for a lunch break, unless you were a masochist in the making?

She glanced at his key card lying beside the keyboard, reading his name. "Todd, is it?" She gave him her most winning smile. "Can you just let him know I'm here? What with the crappy weather and all—things were running a bit behind schedule. He should understand." This was no lie. The 7 train, from Long Island City, Queens into Manhattan had been supremely backed-up with the rain. It was one of the things she could rely on—the MTA being reliably late due to bad weather —and which she could always use as an excuse every time she arrived tardy to either of her two jobs in the city.

She put her hands in prayer, giving the receptionist a pleading look while widening her eyes. She needed this meeting. It'd been delayed by weeks, then months after her good friend, Mariam, had mentioned her attorney cousin back over the holidays, and that he might be willing to meet with her. The situation at her mother's rug company was going from bad to worse and she needed some legal advice—specifically *free* legal advice because she didn't have the money to pay anyone, and this guy seemed to be ok with meeting with her for a free consultation to start with. Who knew, maybe he'd be noble enough to take her case on with no charge. She just had to play nice and not let her emotions get the best of her.

"Sure," the receptionist said politely. Then she distinctly heard him mutter under his breath, as he picked up his phone receiver. "It's your funeral."

"Great!" she said brightly. Then she sighed a mournful, "great" to herself.

This Aariv Abbas was starting to sound like the jack-hole she'd predicted.

## THREE MONTHS AGO

"He's a nice guy ... once you get to know him," Mariam told her over the phone. They'd finally connected after the holiday craze and New Year's celebrations.

Chrissy was more than grateful that Mariam had found time for her, what with her romantic drama involving her mega-hot English boyfriend and his crazy family in London. Thankfully it'd all worked out between those two, and they were finally rightfully together, happy, and *engaged*! That last part she couldn't even handle as both Mariam and her man were allergic to relationships—by choice—before meeting each other. Of course, Chrissy was happy for her, but she was just slightly envious. Chrissy's only allergy in life was to good men. She seemed to pick up the shitty ones each and every time, like a virus aimed only at her. All of her friends were in new or serious relationships at this point in their lives. Chrissy tried to remain upbeat about it because her perfect partner had to be around the next corner. But her dating record of meeting men who dumped her out of the blue or joined the seminary (the story her most recent ex had fed her and which she knew was crap, but had given him points for creativity) was at least a mile long.

"Okay," Chrissy said unsure of what Mariam was trying to convey. "Like, what does that even mean?"

"Oh—well, Chris, he'll help you. I'm sure of it. But he needs to meet you first, to make sure he can even advise you."

Chrissy rolled her eyes and stirred the broccoli and cheddar soup she'd heated up for lunch absentmindedly. "Great. He wants to suss me out and make sure my situation is dire enough so that it's worth his while—"

"Well, yeah." Mariam interrupted unapologetically. "I'm not trying to make you feel bad. He's a busy guy, and a talented attorney trying to make partner. And he's particular about certain things. He wants to make sure it's worth *both* of your times."

Chrissy continued stirring the lukewarm soup that was beginning to look more like orange sludge.

"And you're sure about meeting with him first before getting the police involved?" Mariam continued.

Invisible needles prickled the base of her neck and sprung up Chrissy's scalp. She pushed her bowl away, and took a deep breath, attempting to shake off the unease she felt at the notion of the police.

"If I can avoid the cops, I will."

She remembered as a child, the hushed tones of her mother and other Russian immigrants discussing the NYPD. Their disgust had been laced with fear toward the abusive treatment some of the small business owners (her mother included) received at the hands of law enforcement as the Russian Mafia had been rampant in the 1990s. Russian-owned enterprises, from the far reaches of Brooklyn's Brighton Beach and Sheepshead Bay to shops in Manhattan, had experienced extortion and smuggling of illegal goods at the hands of the mafia. The police had been intent on ending the illegal activity, which sometimes led to lifeless bodies appearing on the shores of Brooklyn. Though that had been long ago, and as far as Chrissy was concerned, the Russian Mafia hadn't been prevalent in the last decade, the apprehension about the police still stuck with her. She wasn't about to willingly enter any precinct until she had some legal advice first. And who knew? Maybe the lawyer could help her, and she could skip the NYPD altogether.

"So," she said, nibbling on an oyster cracker, steering the conversation back to Mariam's cousin. "What is your cousin particular about?" she asked curiously. Chrissy was also particular about things, like making sure she made time for her friends, family, and herself. Sometimes taking a day to relax at home in comfy pj's while binge-watching all of her favorite shows was her version of self-care. Fitting in mental health days was her jam. Thankfully her boss at the events company thought so, too.

"Hmm … off the top of my head, he's a bona fide overachiever and isn't ashamed of it, works out five days a week, no question, and hates to miss work."

Chrissy was appalled. This guy was a legit grown-up professional, with a heavy dose of type-A thrown in.

"Is he a robot? What if he gets sick? He wouldn't willingly infect his co-workers would he?"

"He never gets sick," Mariam said matter-of-factly.

Chrissy scoffed. "Is he superhuman?" She giggled as Mariam chuckled on the other end, but her friend stopped short when she said, "I'll bet if I tried, I could get him to loosen up."

"Don't you dare go and bat your eyelashes at him, or stick your boobs out for that matter, Chrissy. He's not that type of guy."

Well, that posed a conundrum. Chrissy was known to flirt her way in and out of situations.

"So, he's not into cute women?"

Mariam snorted. "The absolute opposite, Chris. The man is totally in love with all women, trust me. He just chooses not to right now. He's super focused on his career—kind of obsessed actually."

How could someone just choose to put aside their physical needs or attractions? The words spilled out of her mouth before she could curb them. "Sounds a little mental if you ask me. Is he a tight-ass jack-hole trying to be a big shot?"

There were crickets on the other end and she realized she may have over-stepped with her honesty. It had gotten her into hot water before. What was wrong with her? Looking a gift horse in the mouth was bad juju and she needed this guy's help like yesterday.

Before she could make amends, Mariam answered a little testily. "Hey now. That's my favorite cousin you're talking about." She sighed. "I know how he can come across, but he's a good guy and an even better lawyer."

"I'm sorry," Chrissy said with contrition. The last thing she needed to do was offend the person trying to connect her to some help.

"Look, admittedly he's a little stiff around the edges, but he might be able to work with you. Give him a chance. What've you got to lose?"

Dutifully chastised she said, "Nothing. You're right. I'll get in touch with him. Send me his details." She'd donned her usual cheerful mask back on. "And thank you, Mariam."

## PRESENT DAY

*N*ow she was convinced he was a tight-ass jack-hole. "Nope. Can't think like that," she whispered tersely under her breath. She pasted on her most persuasive smile, which was undeniably extremely flirty (or so she'd been told by everyone near and dear to her and a few others who weren't).

She sunk into one of the sleek chrome grey chairs in the waiting area which was just as uncomfortable as it looked. She wiggled her lips and flexed the muscles around her mouth, going for a neutral expression—it was harder than it looked. Chrissy wore the title of 'the flirt' amongst her friends as a badge of honor, using her best feminine wile to maneuver her way in and out of situations. But what was a girl supposed to do when cautioned that her best skill was not going to work here?

Her late mother's voice popped into her head with the familiar mantra she'd always encouraged Chrissy with since putting on a bra for the first time at twelve. The rough smoker's voice, laden with a thick Russian accent, was always there to comfort her (or reprimand her—depending on the situation) in difficult times. "Charm them, *moya* (my) Chrisstika. You can get anything with that face and your charms."

She thoughtfully combed her fingers through her almost dry strands. "Not sure that's going to work this time, Mama," she murmured under her breath.

She squared her shoulders. She could do this. She'd just

been promoted to a managerial role within the events company she worked for. She was smart, she was capable, and professional. She'd make this faux big shot take her seriously, take on her case, and charge her nothing in the process. And by God, if she had to pull out her flirting card, she would, but only as a last-ditch effort.

CHAPTER 2

ર

*a*riv checked the time again, irritation brimming to the surface. He took the last bite of his sandwich and chewed with more ferocity than necessary.

Where was she? He didn't have all fucking day. His calendar was so booked he couldn't even add more meetings if he wanted to. *Shit.* Why did he always make promises that he didn't want to keep? Because he was too good a guy, and his favorite cousin, more like a sister really, had asked him to help. Family was everything in his world.

He tugged the paper napkin from around his collar where it was tucked in bib-like over his pristine Brunello Cucinelli white oxford buttoned-down shirt. He balled it up with his sandwich wrapper and took careful aim at the waste basket he'd pushed across his office to the door. He took his shot. The wad arched high, bounced off the rim, and sunk in, turning his scowl into a grin.

"Yes! Three points, for Abbas!"

He mimicked a crowd cheering with hands waving in the air, then held up an imaginary microphone. "The crowd goes wild, Bill. How does he do it? He's the youngest NBA player drafted right out of high school!" He chuckled to himself. "And a freaking Brownie, Bill."

The grin wiped off his face when he heard the buzzer on his intercom. He leaned over pressing the call button.

"Yes, Terri?" he asked his assistant in a neutral tone.

"Your noon is here."

He looked at the clock again and huffed. It was now 12:08. This didn't bode well. Promptness was a must in every aspect of his life and what he deemed separated the successful from those, well … not successful. And honestly, what the hell could they get done in the seven minutes before he had to meet his next client? He inhaled deeply. For his cousin. He would meet with this person for his favorite cousin, Mariam, and then just turn her away, citing a full schedule. It was the truth anyway, damn it.

"Send her in, Terri. And you may go to lunch now. Take an extra five minutes for yourself, since I kept you here."

"Thank you, Mr. Abbas." Was there a hint of a condescending tone he detected in his assistant's voice? He'd given her extra minutes for fuck's sake. Where was the gratitude for his generosity?

Aariv pulled his silver tie from where he'd flung it over his shoulder while eating and straightened it before smoothing it down. He stood up, walked around his desk, and leaned back on the edge just as he heard a light rap and his door opened before he could respond. A petite woman walked in with a wild halo of reddish-blonde hair circling her head.

Aariv squinted his eyes behind the rims of his square, tortoise-shell glasses, while his forehead frowned mimicking the downturn of his mouth. He crossed his arms over his chest as the woman, more like a soggy girl, calmly shut the door behind her. He was already more than annoyed.

When she turned back around, he pointedly lifted his wrist to stare a little too long at the face of his vintage Cartier watch. Yes, he was determined to show this girl who was boss. But her expression was bland, almost serene, though her wide, plump lips pursed, definitely taking the hint. Then she lifted her chin slightly as if challenging him.

As much as he wanted to laugh in her face because this small woman dared to continue to test him, he rather surprisingly admired her gumption. And despite the wet-cat-dragged-in look, she wasn't bad to look at, with a curvy figure and small waist, only accentuated by the damp trench coat sticking to her. He caught himself and looked away before he stood taller, dismissing that last thought. Clients were always off-limits. But she wasn't going to be his client, he reminded himself, so it wouldn't matter how attractive he found her, now would it? Nor what he could possibly do about it.

"Sorry I'm late," she finally said apologetically, the words tumbling throatily from her. She brushed aside the bangs from her eyes and Aariv stared into a pair of deep dark blue pools. They were wide set against her tawny skin, making them even more bluish-black, like the very depths of the ocean. Something about them tugged at his memory.

As she spoke about train delays and the rain, something akin to familiarity continued to pull at him. He wasn't sure why, because surely he'd never met this person before.

She took a few steps toward him, hand outstretched in greeting and the squish in her black leather heels made him flinch. She winced, her eyes closing momentarily in embarrassment then opened and her face was impassive, though her rounded cheeks reddened.

"Sorry," she said again. "I was sure the sun would stay out from this morning. The rain was totally unexpected. Global warming, am I right?" Her head shook and her eyes rolled. "And of course, I forgot my umbrella …"

Her voice trailed away as she studied him, her hand dropping limply. Her eyes enlarged to almost round cartoonish proportions as her gaze glided over his facial features, his shoulders, his chest, right down to his impeccably shiny brown brogues.

Aariv smoothed his hand down around his chin, ensuring no lunch crumbs clung to his cropped beard. There weren't, but her ink-blue eyes narrowed anyway as they landed on the thin red strand of rope around his wrist. The gold lotus flower amulet attached to it was made of opals and shimmered in the sterile white of the overhead office lights. He realized he hadn't rolled his shirt sleeves down after eating, and the *rakhi*—a good luck charm tied by a sibling on one's wrist to celebrate their bond— was on display. He still wore it, though the Hindu festival of *Raksha Bandhan* had been last summer. Being a tad superstitious made him continue to wear it, even though it was Mariam, his cousin, who performed the ritual (she was the closest thing he had to a sister—or a sibling for that matter), and really, what did he need protecting from?

As he proceeded to roll his shirt sleeves down, buttoning them at the wrist, he chided, "You know what it's like here in early spring. And checking the weather app before you leave usually makes the weather *more* expected—"

"*You!*" she suddenly cried in disbelief, and he glanced up sharply, exasperated at being interrupted. She half smiled, but her confusion overtook her pretty face, as her brows squished together. She took a deep breath and placed a hand over her belly as if to calm herself before spitting out, "It is you, isn't it?" The laugh that escaped her was husky and familiar. "Well, fuc—fudge nuggets. And you're a lawyer, too." She sniffed, shaking her head. "I should've known … *Grumpenstein.*"

That nickname. God, he'd hated it when he first heard it. He hated it just as much now.

He realized why she seemed so familiar. He *had* met her before and at the time, he hadn't been so pleasant—more of an asshole really, though he'd wanted more than anything to end the night with her. Because as much as he hadn't sought it in the first place, the draw to her had been a force he couldn't stop, though there were hundreds of guests that night, and plenty of other more appropriate and available women for him and what he was in search of.

6 MONTHS AGO
an indian wedding
IN NEW JERSEY

# CHAPTER 3

ᕷ

*A*ariv nudged his best friend Zayn on the shoulder … again. This time harder. But the man stood there like a rock, continuing to converse with a distant cousin he recognized at the wedding. His friend was either ignoring him purposefully or just that obtuse because he continued to meander his way politely through the crowd, greeting acquaintances on the manor's large back patio. Cocktail hour was in full swing and everyone chattered loudly over one another, vying to be heard about their take on the wedding ceremony they'd just witnessed.

Just as Zayn began to courteously listen to a group of middle-aged women rave about the bride's outfit, Aariv couldn't take it anymore. He laid a hand on his friend's broad, silk-covered back and forcefully pushed him to a spot at the edge of the patio, well away from the crush of guests and any more bland, eye-glazing wedding talk.

"Jeezus, fuck, man. Cool it," his friend quipped, shaking himself out of Aariv's grip.

"Sorry, Z. I need a break from the meddling biddies." He uttered this quietly and with a pleasant smile, as one of said biddies passed by and nodded at them. Both men put their hands together and slightly bowed their heads to the wrinkled elderly Indian woman.

"*Namaste* (Greetings), Aunty," they said in unison.

She smiled and said something nondescript in greeting and then launched into not being too choosy when in search of a bride. All of the single good ones were getting snatched up.

Aariv thanked her for her advice while Zayn nodded but looked away, hiding his exasperated expression. She smiled and walked on, pleased with her own words of wisdom.

When she was far enough away, his friend pounced on him. "Fake much, Cuz?" Zayn shook the cubes in his drink before taking a sip.

"Shut the hell up. You're not being harassed to meet every single daughter, niece, sister, second cousin by marriage twice removed, or any other eligible woman with all her teeth." Aariv rubbed his hand over his jaw, expecting to feel the sensation of short hairs from the cropped beard he usually wore scratching his palm. The bristling sensation was both familiar and soothing, but for the dozenth time that day, he remembered he'd shaved it off for this occasion. Why? Because he didn't want to look too much like his father who also sported a beard.

"You brought it on yourself, Cuz." Zayn scoffed. "What did you expect? You put yourself out there, asking every Patel, Singh, and Kahn for help in the marriage market." He shook his head.

"Lest you forget, Z, *I* didn't ask. It was my father and Huma Aunty." He grunted, still irritated he'd revealed considering marriage to his father and stepmother given the amount of attention and interest he was receiving that evening. He'd probably have a long list of biodata profiles waiting in his inbox when he got home, and he hadn't even willingly (or actively) given out his email address. The mere mention of the 'm-word' had his parents off to the races, openly discussing prospective brides and handing over his email to anyone in their social circles with an available daughter. All he could do was grin and bear it, even as the regret struck him tenfold.

"Didn't you think about the consequences of your actions?" Zayn teased. This was a familiar mantra between them, but it was usually the other way around, with Aariv on the lecturing end.

"Screw you," Aariv grumbled.

Zayn chuckled and then lifted his chin in the direction of a chubby little woman waving at them from across the patio.

It was his stepmother, Huma Aunty. She was in a silver and baby pink sari, one of her favorites. It was wrapped artistically around her, the folds elegantly draping to the floor, but the material couldn't hide her roundness, and she looked like a cute little dumpling.

Aariv waved back and caught the eye of the big burly man standing next to her. It was Viraj, his father. He wore a silk forest green *sherwani* with ivory accents. The color of the formal Indian suit accentuated his width and height, as well as the growing belly of fat around his midsection that older Indian men of a certain generation without care for health and diet sported. His beard was thick and bushy but well-groomed and the reason Aariv had shaved his own earlier that day. Petty, yes, but did he dislike the man? Also, yes.

He held his father's golden gaze, so like his own, for a beat before turning away from the stern-faced man.

"Bro, does your dad ever look happy? We're at a wedding for fuck's sake," his friend muttered through a fake smile toward his parents after noticing the strained interaction between Aariv and his father. "Anyway, you might as well have a 'marry-me' sticker plastered to your forehead," Zayn continued. "You and your need to get through that list of achievements before forty." He shook his head. "I get wanting to make partner at your law firm, but what's the rush for marriage? All that astrology bullshit will turn you into a zealot, by the way." Zayn raised a thick brow. "And don't blame me if you get stuck with a rando goon for a wife."

"Listen," Aariv said slowly, emphatically, as if he was speaking to a toddler. They'd already argued about this on the way there. "I met with the astrologer because I was curious. He said I'd meet my future while attending a happy occasion. Is that vague? Sure as fuck is. But what's happier than a wedding?" His eyes darted around the crowd, picking out one young Indian woman or another, certain that his bride must be out there in the pool of at least thirty appropriate candidates. "And I doubt any woman here is anything remotely close to a goon." Shit, he hoped so.

The elaborate event was the most talked about occasion of the year, celebrating a well-to-do Indian family's daughter to a wealthy non-Indian businessman with celebrity status. Anyone who was anyone wanted to be invited to the nuptials of Simran Khan and her white fiancé, Marcus Lehigh. Any young woman there was bound to be eligible and in good standing, for the most part. And since hearing the astrologer's verdict about his future, Aariv couldn't help but wonder how extraordinary it would be if he and his future wife met there, on their own terms.

Zayn nodded but then grunted. "That man, by the way, is a legit quack—a fucking *khyapa* (slang for eccentric)." He was referring to the astrologer.

"Z, I know you think your advice is the best advice—"

Zayn nodded. "Of course it is. Dude, I'm basically family. I know you better than myself sometimes—"

"And you know why I had to visit him," he continued insistently. "So, listen to this, the planet Mars' positioning in my seventh house is just right—"

His friend slapped his hands over his ears, closing his eyes and singing tunelessly. "La la la la—I don't want to hear this crap."

Aariv sighed in irritation and plucked a beer out of the assortment of cocktails expertly balanced on a tray from the waiter whizzing by. He didn't understand what the big deal was. Many Indians believed in *Vedic* astrology. Based on ancient Indian teachings involving celestial influences, it'd helped plan futures for thousands of generations before him by setting out a path and plan for believers. And, for certain, Aariv was a planner. He'd led life erring on the side of caution and playing by the rules. He considered himself the good, Indian son, who had a successful career as an attorney and always thought about his family first. And though this role made him feel a little tense at times, it was just the way things were done.

Sure, in the past, like Zayn, he'd considered astrologers full of crap and then some. Foretelling the future? Yeah right. But lately, he needed not only the organization of his list of rules— his own carefully laid out life plans that he contrived as a teenager about to embark on a new life in the US—but the guidance of someone deigned to see the future in some way, shape, or form. His *dadi* (grandmother on his father's side) had been a firm believer as well, so he was more than familiar with it. She'd lived for the monthly phone call from her trusted astrologer back in India until the day she died.

It was his most recent visit back to India to see his father that made him feel more urgent about checking off his list of to-do's. As a thirty-six-year-old single man, he must be wanting for a wife, surely. Huma Aunty had lamented over their morning *chai* that he needed a good woman to organize his household (never mind that he'd been living on his own for over a decade pretty sufficiently). And he'd need children one day, because what was the purpose of life if one didn't have offspring? He'd laughed, and at Huma's hurt expression, he'd quickly said, "*Bas* (enough). Sure. I'll consider it." But who was he kidding? He should've known that as soon as his parents got any hint of a green light, they were in full bride-hunting mode.

And when his father had looked up at him from silently reading the news on his iPad and stated that he saw so much of himself in his son when he'd been that age, Aariv knew he had to do something to change the course he'd already started. He had to make sure he was as unlike the arrogant, gambling drunkard, as he could be. So he was now starting to enlist any help he could get, matchmakers and astrologers alike. He'd seek out a witch doctor next if he had to because he wasn't so sure an arranged marriage was going to work for him considering the nature of his father and Huma's arranged marriage—not speaking to one another for most of their existence together, and when they did, constant bickering as their mode of communication was not how Aariv envisioned his future. Granted his father was a condescending ass and bickering was the only way to discuss anything with him, but still, it wasn't something anyone would willingly jump into if they had any sort of choice.

He tilted his head back and chugged the beer. The effervescence of the crisp liquid perked his senses, while the alcohol slithered warmly throughout his body. He automatically felt relaxed in a matter of seconds. This was his second beer that evening. He didn't normally over-imbibe, or at least, hadn't in a long time due to his work schedule and more importantly professional goals. Making a partner at his law firm was his focus so in the last few months, hadn't the time for carousing with buddies. Personally, this was a good thing. He tended to enjoy alcohol a little too much to the point of dulled senses and judgment. It was a family trait, given his father was a raging over-imbiber. So, work was a great excuse to not spiral out of control.

His friend watched him guzzle his beer and a grin spread across his face. "Aari! I like seeing you like this. You haven't been in party mode in a while." Zayn saluted him with his whisky, tilted his shaggy head back, and swallowed the liquid in one swig.

"This is it for me. Just needed to take the edge off." He glanced around impatiently; aware he was also at the wedding to keep an eye on a family member. "Shit. Where's my cousin?" His eyes trained on every tall, dark-haired woman with a *sari*, *lehnga*, or, other traditional women's Indian garb in a burst of bright colors, beading, and sequence. What had Mariam been wearing? Was it pink? Purple?

"So, did you put in a good word for me?" his friend asked, his own eyes combing the crowded patio, looking for her.

"No way. You know you're total shit," Aariv said offhandedly, finally spotting her talking with her friends—some of the bridesmaids. She was the only one not in the floral fuchsia blouse and full-length skirt combo of the *lehngas* they each wore which made it a little easier to keep tabs on her, so long as she stayed with that bunch. She was dealing with a messy break-up and being at a joyous occasion like a wedding must be like rubbing salt in the wound. He wanted to be there for her, as she'd done for him in the past. She was his favorite cousin, a person he'd vowed to protect, and she him, as children, and lately he hadn't been around, too busy with work, and even other family matters back in India. He needed to make sure she was all right, especially since the best man at this wedding happened to be the fucker who'd screwed it up with her.

"That's no way to speak to the only friend who defended you back in secondary school," Zayn said with a slight frown.

And just like that, the relaxed state from moments ago left Aariv's limbs. The weight of his responsibilities landed heavily on his shoulders again.

He turned to the other man, gritting his teeth, and working his jaw tightly. Why was his friend bringing up the past? It was a subject he kept under lock and key, and meant to stay that way for good.

Zayn side-eyed him, noting his reaction. He exhaled heavily. "Sorry, Cuz. Why are you still so touchy about her? Twenty years, man. Twenty years since it happened. If you're still hung up, I don't know, maybe you need to reach out to her—"

Aariv swung around facing his friend almost nose to nose. His hands clenched tightly at his sides. His voice came out strangled when he muttered, "I'm not hung up. And don't *ever* mention her again, Z."

Staring his friend down was kind of absurd since Zayn and he were both equally a few inches above six feet tall; same height, same age—thirty-six—went to the same secondary school together, and came to live in the US around the same time. Hell, the story went that they'd met as toddlers and played under the ancient mango trees of his own grandfather's family compound in West Bengal when Zayn's family had been visiting from abroad. They'd been thrown together again when Zayn moved to India to finish high school as an exchange student (of mixed Indian and Greek cultures, his parents wanted him to be immersed in his Indian side for a bit), and he lived with the only people he knew there—Aariv and his family. They became best friends and their lives mirrored each other's in some fashion, except for that one awful incident concerning a girl named Leila when they were eighteen, and the fact that Aariv pursued law, whereas Zayn dove into the shiny, psychotic world as restauranter and personal chef.

A slight warm touch at his elbow made him snap out of it, and he spun around. The top of a blond head just tickled his lips. He took a step back and looked down to see who it was so he could tell them to get lost. He had a verbal thrashing he needed to continue and hated being interrupted.

A girl with shining dark blue eyes stared up at him, batting thick, long lashes delicately, like butterfly wings flitting upon rosy petals that were her smooth, round cheeks. A small smile curved her full pink-hued lips, with a hint of a dimple on each side. The sudden thought passed through his mind that her lips looked like juicy berries that begged to be sucked on, but that he shouldn't be thinking that about a girl, barely a woman it seemed, like her.

It took him a few moments until he realized she wasn't a girl at all, though her rounded cheeks made her look quite young at first glance. She was certainly a young woman with full curves, despite her petite stature. Her smile, now wider, was both flirtatious and infectious, and her dimples, now deeper, were the perfect parenthesis around her mouth, accentuating a pretty face.

While she leaned into him, the initial irritation from being interrupted as he gave his friend a much-deserved verbal beating slipped away. The corners of his mouth began to lift automatically in reaction to the joy reflected on her face. He felt … disarmed, and relaxed, almost as though he'd guzzled another beer.

"Well there's a nice smile," she commented cheekily, her voice lower, throatier than he expected, as she bumped him lightly with her elbow. It was sexy and sweet, kind of like her. He immediately frowned at his thoughts and turned away, a voice in his head telling him that he didn't deserve to flirt and have fun. She still stood there though, so close behind him that the warmth of her body radiated through the ivory silk fabric of his *kurta* (knee-length tunic) and matching silk pants.

He turned back to give her his full attention, not exactly sure what had come over him because really, he should just ignore her as he did lately when any woman came on to him. But he couldn't help noticing again how attractive she was. Her tan skin glowed from either the revelry, the deep pink of her *lehenga*, or both, but whatever it was, she seemed lit up from within and if he was being honest with himself, she was hard to ignore.

He told himself he was just being polite, as he listened to her tease him and his friend about two handsome men being so serious on a joyous occasion, and he couldn't help but study her a little more closely. Golden blonde hair was pulled back into a complicated hairdo, with a few wavy tendrils shaped like loopy S's framing her face. Her full lips were plump, the bottom even tauntingly plumper, just asking to be bitten. She noticed his appraisal and she sucked that ripe bottom lip into her mouth while raising a well-shaped eyebrow tauntingly, an unspoken offer passing between them.

As she tipped her head to one side, the large gold discs of her earrings swung in her lobes, making the tiny jewels dotted within twinkle merrily. His eyes automatically roamed down the column of her slim, almost swanlike neck, searching for the matching necklace she'd no doubt be wearing as most fancy, Indian jewelry came as a matching earring and necklace set. But instead, there was a simple gold cross with a deep wine-red ruby studded in the center, hanging off a thin gold chain. The modest ornament nestled between the two perfect top curves of her smooth breasts which were exposed by the neckline of her top.

"So," she spoke again, and his eyes snapped back to her face. "Can I ask, because the maid of honor who, by the way, is a total bossy bitch and I'm not even sure how the bride is best friends with that bogus British snob—but don't tell anyone I said so," she said this last part in a faux whisper behind her small hand. Aariv chuckled because it was kind of true. The maid of honor, Bettina, lived in England now with her English-Indian husband. She'd grown up in Connecticut, alongside her best friend, the bride, Simran, and yet, the first month she came back to visit as a married woman, everyone noticed her sporting a slight British accent. Almost two years later, it was full-on posh sounding as if she'd lived there amongst the aristocrats all her life.

Her small hand landed on his arm comfortably, as she giggled huskily, while heat filtered through the thin material of his sleeve to his skin again. "Anyway, she said it was our duty as bridesmaids to welcome guests and make sure everyone is having a good time." She gave them both a dazzling smile, but her gaze locked on his a little longer. "Shouldn't you be celebrating, socializing, or dancing … maybe with me?"

She fiddled with the cross at her cleavage as she waited for an answer, and Aariv noticed again how dark blue her eyes were, almost like bejeweled sapphires. The shapes were naturally cat-like, the outer edges just slightly slanted higher than the inner corners.

At the word 'bridesmaids' his eyes quickly scanned down her figure. He hadn't realized she was a bridesmaid but upon closer inspection of her outfit—yep it was the same as the others. It looked better than great on her—sexy and demure all at the same time, with flashes of bare skin at her mid-drift and the full floor-length skirt molding to her hips before flaring wide to the floor.

The right words to tell her to get lost seemed to have taken a wrong turn in his brain, and it was around this time that Aariv realized he was attracted to this woman. Attracted not just by her appearance—she was uniquely striking—but by her attitude which seemed fun-going and flippant right off the bat, a complete contrast to him. And when her upper body started stirring side to side in sync with the upbeat Indian music the DJ had started up only moments ago, he let himself watch her, feeling a hunger stir up within him that matched the tempo of her sensuality. And she wanted to be watched, too. She unabashedly let her arms loose and moved them along with her body—toned limbs that moved wide in hypnotic waves.

Her movements got more obvious and he noticed the lines of her ab muscles jump and flex under the smooth golden skin of her torso. As a self-proclaimed gym rat himself, Aariv appreciated this. She was athletic, too, and that was a complete turn-on.

"See something interesting?" she asked, leaning into him, the top of her head just brushing his mouth again, and he caught a hint of something fresh and botanical in her hair. Then she moved away, and Aariv found himself almost following as she stepped back and murmured a sassy apology, because the scent was kind of addicting, unearthing long-forgotten memories of … what he couldn't quite recall. But it reminded him of something and not unpleasant. And if she could see his dick starting to rise at half-mast, she'd know exactly how interested he was. Fuck. He cleared his throat, trying to also clear his head. He hadn't gotten laid in … fuck, how long had it been? Too long, he thought, if he couldn't even remember and his body was reacting this way.

She giggled at his astonished expression, and his eyes landed on those cute dimples again. "You look like you've seen a ghost," she murmured, her full lips blooming wide again.

*Yeah, the ghost of a man who wanted to screw a good-looking, fun, and sexy woman with a wildness he hadn't felt in ages.*

A throaty laugh escaped her, and with her mouth open he saw her teeth were pearly white and straight, for the most part. Her right incisor nearest her top center teeth was slightly misaligned. Some might call her snaggle-toothed, but she seemed to own it, only adding to her charm.

Aariv ran a hand over his chin. Regardless of how cute and sexy she was, he was in no mood to entertain her behavior. He was here for another purpose altogether and needed to keep his focus. He shook off the ghost of getting-laid-Aariv and it disappeared in a puff of disappointment.

"Excuse me, but we're in the middle of something," he said

curtly, trying to be polite. He gestured between himself and Zayn.

"Oh come on. Don't be such a crank," she said good-naturedly, waving a small hand in the air, and the stack of delicate glittery pink bangles clicked in agreement along her forearm.

"What?" he asked, standing up straighter, taken aback. The tell-tale irritation of being told he was a stick in the mud as a child came back to him. So what if he was a rule follower? What was wrong with that? But more importantly, this woman was hitting a nerve—the one where he was more interested in her than he should be. Confused momentarily as she wasn't Indian and, therefore shouldn't even cause a blip on his radar, but yet his radar frequencies—not to mention his lust—were on high alert.

"You heard her, Cranks," Zayn said with a chuckle behind him, and Aariv almost forgot he was there. "Sorry for my buddy's shitty behavior. He's having one of his … moments." And his friend dared to roll his eyes and shrug.

"Moments?" the girl asked curiously, raising an eyebrow at him. "Are you ok? Do you need medical attention … or any other kind of attention?" She batted her eyes again slowly. How old *was* she? She was a bridesmaid, yes, but she had the effect of looking like a girl one minute, and a woman the next.

"Cuz. You hear that?" Zayn flicked him in the chest. "She wants to know if you need some attention. Lady, you've come to the right place. This guy could use—"

"Cut it out," Aariv said between his teeth, stopping his friend with a sharp slice of a hand in the air. Zayn rolled his eyes again.

Suddenly her soft hands were on him, grabbing the one he

waved in the air, and he physically felt something. The stirring in his crotch was nothing new. She was a pretty woman with a hot body and he hadn't gotten any in months. He was thankful for the looseness of his silk ivory tunic because it hid how quickly his arousal had flared up. He'd never be able to live that down in front of Zayn. But it was something other than the thickening of his dick, too.

Her fingertips brushed over the amulet he wore on his wrist, tied on with a thin red rope and they were rougher than he expected—her fingers. With a thoughtful expression, she studied the lotus flower made up of delicate opal stones. And for some reason, he let her, because what he was feeling was a surprise in its sort of weightlessness, as if the struggles of the past few minutes, the past few hours, days, weeks, and even months didn't matter. Just this girl and her soothing energy.

CHAPTER 4

8

"It's unique," Chrissy murmured, and she meant it, with not a hint of the flirt from before in her tone. She traced the opals with her fingertips. "Opals are some of my favorite stones. I think they get a bad rap as being old-fashioned. But I love them. I like to think of them as good luck."

The gems on his bracelet charm shone and changed in hue as she moved his wrist first one way, and then the other, her eyes following them. She looked up and caught his hazel stare, the fiery seriousness almost singeing her. Dear lord, a man this intense could melt her into a puddle, and here he was, giving her his full attention. She hoped she wasn't obviously panting in front of him, making a fool out of herself. The man was attractive, no question, but there was something else about him, a mysteriousness—an austerity that she inherently wanted to get under and chip away at. Admittedly, she'd zeroed in on him from the get-go. Even from afar, she'd noticed his thick, swooped-back black hair and strong square jawline. Her stare had followed him since the ceremony had ended. How could it not? He was the definition of godliness, with confidence and authority in his strong wide stance she could smell from across the room. And when they'd been ordered by the bride's best friend—the bossy maid of honor—to mingle with the guests, she knew who she'd be focusing on.

In truth, Chrissy wasn't shy about going after what she wanted. She didn't "wait for the weather by the sea," as her mother used to say, an old Russian proverb that referred to her daughter's boldness (which sometimes bordered on rashness). Sometimes she was successful in her endeavors, and sometimes she wasn't. But what was life without making a few mistakes in the pursuit of what one wanted? And what Chrissy wanted right now was to experience this strong, manly man. It'd been ages since she'd been with anyone and the thought of him up against her, maybe lying on top of her, was becoming a consuming need.

His hands radiated with heat. They were large, with long elegant fingers. She noted the dusting of black hair around his wrist that no doubt went up his arms underneath the ivory silk of his Indian suit. She shivered and she felt her nipples harden. Something about a man and his 'man hair' always gave her goosebumps. It was just so virile, and quite frankly, got her all worked up. She shimmied her hips a little toward him like one magnet attracted to another.

This close, it was damn near impossible not to ogle as she really took inventory of him. The breadth of his broad shoulders and his height—check and check. Beautiful hazel green eyes that might see into the depths of her soul—check. High sculpted cheekbones in an arrestingly handsome face that she could probably stare at for hours if given the chance—check. Looking for all the world like a beautifully bronzed skin Super-man—

bingo. And that confidence of his that she thought she'd smelled from across the room? It was a heady mix of pine and something else woody and warm—never a bad combination in her opinion.

But something seemed to transform in him now. What started as a striking smile that lit up his angry face (yes, she'd known he and his buddy were sharing heated words) had turned into disbelief at her mention of socializing and dancing. And now, as she still held his warm hand, she felt it curl in hers as he tugged away. The energy between them changed; something in him changed. The openness, the breath he seemed to hold until she spoke, expelled almost harshly out of him, and his face closed back up into the stiff mask from before.

*What just happened?*

"Move on," he said abruptly and turned his broad back on her in dismissal.

Wait, did having a recent bad dating streak somehow exude a negative aura around a person (aka herself)? Did it make her repulsive? Or was what her friend, Mariam, who had literally only moments ago described these successful Indian guys here tonight as only wanting a good Indian woman, completely accurate? She hadn't believed her but now…

*Like … seriously?!*

"Wait, what's happening?" she asked, trying to keep it light and tease the nice, interested guy back out of him.

He huffed, turning only halfway back, and grunted over his shoulder. "I'm not looking to hook up."

His abrupt comment startled her so much that she huffed in return and stomped—actually stomped—her foot in irritation.

"Um, how dare you. What makes you think I would even *let* you near me like that?" Honestly, she might have, if it had gone that way. What else did she have to look forward to tonight as a single bridesmaid, aside from the good food and dancing? And she'd thought there was a spark between them. Was she imagining it? No, she wasn't that delusional, though her friends, and even her mother when she'd been alive, always said she had her head in the clouds. Something had passed between them; she'd seen it in his eyes before he turned back into an angry grump. She shivered again. She didn't even know him, and his behavior bordered on a split personality disorder, but she still found him hot.

*You are desperate, aren't you?*

Now he turned fully back and crossed his arms over his chest. He looked down at her and his gorgeous grin returned, but it was marred by the coolness in his eyes which were more pale green than hazel now.

"You're trying to tell me you weren't coming on to me just now?"

Her jaw dropped open. The audacity of this man! How rude.

"How rude!" she exclaimed because she couldn't think of anything else to say.

He chuckled and it was a deeply masculine sound that had her knees going a little noodle-like under her. She eyed his broad chest as it reverberated with it. Cripes, the man was more than in shape. She could make out the firm ridges of his pecs under the thin material—she was right at eye-level with his chest, how could she not—and the bulge of his biceps which threatened to rip the seams of his shirt's delicate fabric. What would it feel like to have *those* arms wrapped around her? But, it figured that the only man she was attracted to happened to be a big fat a-hole. That seemed to be her MO lately.

"Well, I wouldn't give you the time of day if you chased me

around this party … naked," she said, lifting her chin. Well, this was embarrassing. Her cheeks must be on fire—it felt like she needed to run ice cubes up and down the flames licking her skin.

"Who would be naked, you, or him, or both?" his friend said jovially. "I could get behind that—"

"Yeah, keep telling that to your horny little self." The hunky a-hole cut in, ignoring his friend. The smirk he gave her was sexy, hot; hotter than hot. But oh man, the guy was giving major hater vibes, and she'd give anything to punch him in that sexy mouth.

"What the hell, man?" his friend said in shock. "Apologize to her."

"I won't," Indian Superman said firmly. "I'm not here to entertain possibly drunk and horny bridesmaids."

Something in Chrissy crumbled just a little inside. She swallowed the ball rising in her throat and looked up at him furiously.

"Whatever, *Grumpenstein.* Sad that you're here. Just your presence is bringing me down right about now," she quipped, fanning her heated face, and tossing her head in satisfaction that she wasn't tongue-tied after all. "You should leave before you ruin *everyone's* evening!"

And miraculously something in the cranky man's demeanor softened. His arms dropped from his chest and he reached a hand out as if he was going to touch her, but it hovered inches away.

She looked at his hand, the one with the red-roped bracelet tied around it as he spoke, his voice gentle and gruff, a complete contrast to his mocking tone before.

"I apologize. I don't know what came over me." He dropped

his hand and sighed heavily. "I'm having a day … a week … hell, a year."

She looked up at him suspiciously, not sure about this sudden turn of demeanor. He was either an absolute mystery, or giving her a complete mindfuck.

"That sucks," she finally said with conviction. No matter how bad one's life was going, being a complete jack-ass was never the answer—at least, that wasn't how she did things.

She studied him. Something had deflated that macho asshole so much so she could tell he spoke the truth by the earnestness in his bright eyes. She almost wanted to reach over and push the thick lock of black hair that had fallen across his forehead.

"Now I feel sorry for you, and I don't even know you."

"Look." He pushed the fallen lock back and combed his fingers through his hair. "I don't need your sympathy. I just need you to know that I'm generally not … like this."

His friend coughed behind him and she heard a distinct "bullshit."

She covered her mouth with her hand, hiding her smile. Thank goodness for the funny friend because she wouldn't have had the nerve to say, "Well, too bad. You *do* have my sympathy because acting hostile at a happy occasion like this must be exhausting." She turned to leave but threw back over her shoulder. "Just do me a favor, as a bridesmaid with a job to do, try to relax and have a good time."

Then she walked away, shaking her head. Turd bucket to begin with, and then a sad sack in the end. She couldn't tell which was worse, but both scenarios sucked. She'd met less desirable men before, but this man sealed the fact that her choice of men was always shitty. Like, really? Was she just *that* bad at picking them? Apparently so—and that, she realized, was what had crumbled inside her earlier—her will to be positive about ever finding "the one." Was she a romantic? Absolutely and she'd own it 'til she took her last dying breath. But, not everyone was a believer.

Something made her glance back over her shoulder, wanting one last look at the man, and she caught his reserved, stern expression as he talked quickly to his friend … but his eyes were still on her. She jerked her stare away.

Would she consider herself boyfriend-hungry? Perhaps—maybe more than just a little, especially since everyone seemed to be pairing up these days. But no way was she desperate enough to go for a man with multiple personalities. She had enough of her own problems to deal with.

*A*riv couldn't help himself. All evening his mind was on the young woman from before. Something about her—her bold sweetness and her smart bratty mouth before walking away, had awoken something in him.

An unpleasant feeling enclosed his chest sporadically as he thought about the rush of hurt darting across her face when he mocked her. He found himself keeping tabs on her with his eyes glued to her golden halo of hair as she flitted around chatting with friends and laughing.

Before the elaborate dinner buffet, she got up on stage along with the entire bridal party to dance a choreographed Bollywood number for the now-married couple. She made the dance moves look effortless and seemed to lead everyone through the steps as she was placed front and center. She shimmied her hips while waving her arms with careful precision, but made it all look artistically fluid, all while darting flirty looks at the audience, her eyebrows wiggling humorously in tandem. She seemed to crave attention, but not in a bad way. She was a natural performer—that must be why his eyes stayed on her.

When her glance met his during dinner, her smile disappeared, turning into a frown before she swiftly looked away. If she'd stuck her tongue out at him, he wouldn't have been surprised. He might've even chuckled. And now he knew his curiosity was more than mounting for her, which was odd because her type—the overtly flirty and mischievous kind—had never really been his thing. He'd always felt that women like her were more about playing games when it came to their relationship conquests. But he'd be lying if he didn't admit that the uncomfortable feeling inside his chest from before was remorse for the way he'd treated her earlier. The thought crossed his mind that he'd been borderline abusive toward her which wasn't like him. Something about this woman just got to him. Even at that very moment, as he was being introduced to an eligible Indian woman, he sought out the petite woman's perfect form in the bridesmaids' sea of fuchsia which she now seemed to stick closely to.

Once the lavish wedding dinner finished, everyone crammed onto the dance floor, shaking everything they had to the beats the DJ played. And yet again, Aariv looked for her, noting her hair starting to fall, her face gleaming with a sheen of sweat, and yet, she was still the most alluringly sensual woman out there, dancing with abandon alongside her friends.

"Bro, you've been screwing her with your eyes all night. Go fucking dance with her," Zayn hissed before disappearing into the crowd with a woman he'd met at dinner. Before his face got lost in the jumble of people, and before Aariv could protest, he yelled over the revelry, "You owe her for being such a dicktard!"

Had he been that apparent in his obsession with her all night? Jesus. He supposed so. It'd been a long time since a woman had piqued his interest like this. Maybe for once, he wouldn't think and would just do.

Without another thought, he pushed through waving limbs, and bopping bodies and reached her. Her back was toward him, and he stood there watching her momentarily, close enough to be able to slide his body up against her gyrating one. His hands curled into fists beside him, holding him back from letting go.

A thick blonde lock had escaped her hairdo, and trailed down her back like a golden snake, slithering and bouncing as she raised her arms to the hip-hop *raga*. The traditional Indian melodic tune mixed with beats blared from the speakers and thumped through him. He could smell her fresh botanical scent, though the infusion of musty powders and sweat was strong in the throng of people he stood amongst.

Sweat glistened on the skin of her neck, along the exposed skin of her waist, and the small of her back. Dark spots saturated the satin fuchsia material under her arms. And yet, he was still absolutely turned on. He could feel his dick thrumming to attention and it pushed him to sidle up behind her and start moving his body in sync with hers, whether she noticed him or not.

She suddenly twirled with her eyes closed, her mouth opened in laughter and started shaking her ass at her friends. She bumped her head right into his chest and she reached a hand out to steady herself.

Her eyes popped open and he stared into the dark blue of an evening sky, studded with sparkling stars as she looked up at him in astonishment. Her mouth formed a perfect circle as she stopped dancing in her tracks, her small hand burning a print into the center of his chest.

She blinked slowly a few times, probably registering the fact that it was the jerk from before standing in front of her. But instead of pushing him away with distaste, her hand curled on his chest, into the material of his tunic, and pulled him closer, so that her soft full breasts along with her curvy warm hips smashed into him. Her eyes got even larger, no doubt feeling his hardened arousal against her. He rubbed into her warmth, not able to help that physical, animalistic reaction, and he heard a throaty moan escape her full lips.

They danced that way for a few moments, intimately rubbing against each other, their eyes locked, his hands finally clutching her hips, his fingers wrapped around that pert ass. He wanted to get lost in that stare, bury his dick into her heated body and forget the responsibilities in his life for just one enjoyable moment of heated passion.

"What's your name?" he asked softly, leaning down to her while his hand brushed damp strands from her smooth rounded cheek.

"*Now* you want to know?" she asked playfully, a smile starting to appear across her berry-like lips. He was going to kiss that mouth all night long, he thought in anticipation, a smile starting to cross his own lips. And maybe he'd witness those lips wrapped around his cock as he fucked her pretty mouth. He groaned in anticipation and leaned his forehead down on hers.

Something in the corner of his eyes made him glance to his right—a frantic movement trying to gain his attention. It was

Zayn, with an exasperated look on his face. Aariv stood up to his full height and peered in the direction his friend was pointing. He saw his cousin, Mariam, the one he was supposed to be keeping an eye on all evening, dancing sensually with a tall figure in all black on the other side of the dance floor. *Shit.* He wasn't the only one with sex on his mind. And double shit, the man was her ex. He'd completely forgotten about keeping her away from him.

He looked stoically down at the pretty face of the hot-blooded woman in his arms, trying to mask his utter disappointment.

"Damn." He squeezed her waist. "I'm sorry. I have to go."

"What? Wait—"

He let her go, and her fingers grabbed at his wrist.

"You're joking—" she started.

He shook his head and turned away quickly, pulling out of her grasp. She let him leave and he headed back to what he was most known for—family responsibility.

# PRESENT DAY

## new york, new york

# CHAPTER 5

Zariv blinked rapidly behind his lenses as the memory flooded his mind. So this was her—the girl from that night. The one who almost made him shirk his responsibilities in the hopes of a moment of unadulterated passion. Admittedly, the one he couldn't stop thinking about days afterward and still did occasionally when he let himself have some downtime—which only ended up with him jerking off to any details he could remember about her, like the tightness and warmth of her body when she'd been crushed up against him. The deep blue of her eyes looking up at him as he imagined her full lips sucking him off. So, this was Chrissy Smyth. What were the fucking odds? He almost said it out loud, that's how caught off guard he was.

It wasn't as though it was out of the question, he thought, as he swiped his hand over his short beard in consternation. She'd been a bridesmaid; he'd known that fact. But he hadn't connected the dots because he'd been inundated with carting his drunk cousin away before she ended up doing something stupid with her ex (which was pointless, since she was now engaged to the man). And he'd let the idea of the mysterious wedding woman go, not even bothering to ask Mariam about her because he believed the interruption had been a sign—he needed to concentrate on his family and his own goals (including marriage).

*But what the fuck kind of sign was this!?*

Chrissy took a deep breath, her hand still on her stomach, as she glanced around. She pulled the ties of her trench coat, opening it and shrugging it off. She moved to the coat rack in the corner to hang it up before turning back to him. And Aariv couldn't help but drink in all of her movements. Though banal they were, she moved lithely, like a cat—the same as when he'd watched her all night at the wedding. And now, this woman, whom he'd thought he'd lost an opportunity with, happened to waltz back into his life months later, and his attraction to her came back at him like a tidal wave.

He scanned her from head to toe. Her hair was a different color, and shorter. The reddish blonde shone like a new copper penny as she moved about, and he found that the color suited her. The compactness of her petite form—the way the slim black skirt she wore hugged her shapely hips and that tight round ass was hard not to stare and salivate at. What could that curvy little body do in bed?

Pearl buttons marched down the front of her white button-down shirt, a handful undone at the top. The material was sheer—did she know he could see her white bra underneath? He didn't need to see her tits to know she had a nice rack; he already knew from ogling her at the wedding and having their soft fullness pressed up against him.

"Are you done?" she asked, her head cocked to one side. Those lips, so plump, were turned up into a cool smile, with those memorable deep dimples in each cheek. Her wide eyes blinked unhurriedly at him and she looked for all the world like she wanted to do some physical damage, no nice girl from the wedding in sight. "So, I guess there's the answer to your question."

Her blue gaze held his stare, taunting him it seemed. Aariv cleared his throat and looked away. The physical reaction he had to this woman would no doubt make keeping things professional absolute torture. What kind of candidate for partner at one of the most sought out New York law firms openly stared at a client's tits? Forget that part—he'd been there before when he was still green and interning and he'd assisted with a gorgeous divorcee's business dealings. He'd had the luxury of getting to screw that woman after the case had closed out of the office. No harm, no foul. But what kind of attorney daydreamed about fucking their client every which way right off the bat, maybe throwing her on his desk to accomplish it? And to add to that—which was probably the most fucked up part—was also in the market for an Indian wife?

He cleared his throat again, trying to get a hold of his train of thought. "What's that, now?"

He gestured for her to take a seat while he went back around his desk and sat down.

"My name. You asked me what it was right before you … you know…" She waved her hands in the air, laughing, but it sounded forced. "Anyway, it's … well it's good to see you again." She combed a hand through her hair. "And … you're ok. You didn't have a medical emergency, or someone close to you didn't die?"

He leaned back in his high-back cushy office chair, the springs squeaking slightly under him. His elbows rested on the armrests. He cracked his fingers before stapling them, giving Chrissy a serious look as she sat down across from him.

"I apologize for my behavior that evening, Ms. Smyth. A personal matter took me away." She opened her mouth to respond, but he continued, preferring not to rehash that night's events, nor dwell on any 'almosts.' As a potential client now, he had to maintain that crucial fact. "So, how I can help you today?"

Her eyes rounded and she nodded, getting the hint. She crossed one shapely leg over the other and clutched her bag to her. He fixated on her legs. He couldn't help it. They were trim and toned, appearing longer than they surely were in her sheer black stockings.

*Law, boka (idiot),* put your dick away.

He tore his eyes away and looked at his watch. "Seeing as how we have about five—no, scratch that—four minutes left of our appointed meeting time, I'm not sure if we can get through everything."

She eyed him suspiciously, her large blue eyes turning into black slits. "You've already made up your mind not to help me, haven't you?" She was cleverer than he thought.

"I didn't say that." Even if that had been his exact initial decision. But something made him want to hear her out. Maybe he could help her, and then he would be absolved of his shitty behavior from that night. Guilt was what he'd felt when he left her hanging on the dance floor but was forgotten when faced with family duty. But seeing her now brought it all back.

She shifted in her seat and he caught a hint of her cleavage again. Her breasts were two perfect half apricots sitting above her bra, which he now noticed was extremely femininely lacy. Her skin appeared darker against the stark white, and even more naturally browner than your average Caucasian. Was she a mix of something else?

"Listen, I can tell it all to you in a nutshell," she rushed on. "I don't even need sixty seconds." Now she sounded almost desperate. He nodded, trying to make her feel comfortable.

She took a deep breath, her chest heaving against her shirt. Her hands flew around as she spoke and he dragged his gaze to her face.

"My family has a rug store, over in the Oriental Rug District a few blocks from here. It's been in business since we came over from Russia when I was little. Well, not my family—my mom—she raised me—but she's dead now—and the business is mine—which is so weird." She shook her head, her eyes closed as if sorting her thoughts. "But anyway." She continued. "I'm not actively running it. I mean, I'm in the loop, but the manager, Boris, who's been around since I can remember, has been in charge since she died a few years ago. This year, I started to notice things really slowing down. It's a shame; it was my mom's passion before she died. I have a feeling it's because the place isn't up with the times. It's kind of old-school. I mean, it wouldn't kill Boris to consider some of my ideas." She was going off on a tangent, and Aariv should stop her, but the way she got animated about some of her ideas for the shop was kind of mesmerizing. Her eyes were big and shiny blue and she was looking off into the distance, her hands waving around. "I think a nice home goods section would be great, or maybe even something with curated candles. You know people love 'one of kind' things." She air-quoted. "Or maybe offer some Russian snacks and tea? Like in a small café in the front. Though that needs a food license…" Her eyes met his and he wasn't sure what look he was giving her, but she quieted immediately and placed her hands in her lap lacing them tightly. "So, anyway, I assumed the business was going under. We haven't had the best sales in the past few years, even before Mama died. But for some reason, we keep getting—like a shi—like a lot of inventory, and somehow, even though the numbers look *really* bad, we're still in business."

Aariv leaned back in his chair, contemplating. It was interesting, whether from the actual implications of something legally not right or because it involved her, he wasn't sure. But he held back, not wanting to get her hopes up. He did have a current full case load after all.

"And?" he finally asked.

She leaned forward, and the gold cross with the ruby studded in the center escaped from her shirt, dangling on its slim gold chain. He remembered it clearly from months ago. She grasped onto it and worried it with her fingers mindlessly.

"And, I think something shady is going on. Look, I don't have a business degree. I'll be the first to tell you I don't know a single thing about accounting, and numbers give me hives. But," she counted off on her fingers, "rugs keep piling up, Boris keeps meeting with goon types, and, oh yeah, our rent just went up, too. The whole thing just seems fishy." She shook her head, tousling her waves even more around her face. "How are we still in business!?"

"Fishy?" he asked with humor, a smile starting on his lips. He couldn't help it. She was entertaining. "What do you think is happening that's not above board?"

*Bad Aariv,* he admonished himself. Of course, something was up. There was no way something could not be up with commercial rent at an all-time high in the tri-state area. It might not be as bad as she seemed to think it was, but there was unquestionably something … fishy.

"I don't know." Her slim shoulders shrugged. "What if some bad guys are involved? What if Boris' life is in danger—" she gasped loudly. "What if *my* life is in danger?" Her breath became fluttery as she shuddered, closing her eyes again.

"Ms. Smyth, this isn't some episode of *Law & Order*. Your risk of finding yourself at the bottom of the East River is as small as zero," he said sardonically. She seemed to have an overactive imagination, didn't she?

Her eyes popped open, dark azure like a clear night in the West Bengal countryside. "How do you know that?" she asked, her tone rising an octave. "And how would I even find myself at the bottom of the East River? I'd be dead, so I wouldn't even know!"

He sighed, putting his hands up trying to calm her. Here was the thing, it absolutely made for an interesting case if he did find anything out of line or illegal.

"Do you have any evidence that anything is … fishy?"

"What do mean?"

"I mean I need hard evidence if something's going on. And if something *is* going on, you would need to decide what steps you want to take."

"Oh. I guess I'm not there yet, except for what I've witnessed and already told you. You can't do anything with that?" Her eyes were big and hopeful as she sucked her bottom lip into her mouth.

"Nothing I can do," he said a little more harshly than he intended, looking away from her again. Why was she still so sexy to him … after all this time?

*Because you haven't fucked a woman in forever.* It didn't take a genius to figure that one out.

If this case did happen to pan out, it could be a great contender for the partners' dreaded pro bono initiative, which was on everyone's minds lately. The partners wanted to see what more their employees could do for the community—along with what they could do for the company—specifically those who were up to make the next big leap in their careers to partner, like Aariv.

Aariv sunk back into his chair and pondered the woman sitting across from him. Her crossed leg bounced periodically as she clutched the cross around her neck, pulling at the delicate gold chain. Her demeanor seemed so different from the confident sexy woman he'd met briefly ages ago. The one he'd been so fascinated by. It was telling that she was worried about this situation. And it didn't make her less attractive to him. Her vulnerability made him want to find a way to help her.

"Listen, what you need right now is a detective and a damn good accountant," he said firmly. "Or, someone good with numbers, preferably who doesn't get hives when presented with them." He finished drily, earning a small smile from her.

"Uh, okay." She looked up at the ceiling and counted off on her fingers. "I don't know any detectives. And I don't have an accountant."

"You don't have an accountant? Not even a personal one for your taxes?" he asked shocked. Who didn't have an accountant as a young professional living in New York City?

Chrissy's shoulders sagged like sandbags were attached to them. It wasn't enough that the guy couldn't help her right now but that he was also judging her. What nerve.

"Yeah, not everyone is super ... organized with adulting," she said trying not to let her anger rise. God he was making her feel childish. She'd been on pins and needles for the good part of the week in preparation for this meeting, and he was making fun of her. But why should she think he'd be any different than some of the other lawyer jerks she'd met before? How silly of her.

When she'd first entered his office, she hadn't recognized him, at least not immediately with his glasses over those pale, hazel-green eyes and the short beard covering his jaw. The only thing that seemed familiar was that he looked like a bronzed Clark Kent. So striking, so broad-shouldered, with his wavy thick dark hair pushed back from his wide forehead. He had a serious look about him though. He looked like a man who knew his stuff and a man who could possibly save her family's business from who knows what, but something that seemed corrupt, perhaps crime-worthy.

It was his bracelet that gave him away. She'd recognize it anywhere. It was unique, with shining opals that reminded her instantly of a set of beloved Matryoshka dolls her mother had owned. The intricately decorated wooden antiques were a total of seven in all, each one nesting snuggly within the other with Russian opals embedded into the elaborately hand-painted details. Whenever the light changed, the opals took on a new brilliance and color, looking like the bright turquoise of a tropical ocean one minute, and then the shimmery grey of stormy spring skies the next. Chrissy had gotten in trouble once when as a child she'd stolen the smallest doll and put it in the crib of her doll house. She'd needed a baby for her family. Her mother had sternly chastised her and told her they were not for playing. They were family heirlooms, not toys. To which Chrissy had argued innocently that they looked like toys because of their big eyes and round cheeks. And to that, her mother had sent her to her room without dinner. She'd always wondered what happened to them once her mother passed away. She'd never been able to find them.

Seeing that red roped bracelet around his wrist now had completely thrown her. Every ounce of confidence she'd mustered before she walked through his door slid right out of her, replaced by appalled recognition.

As soon as he checked the time on his fancy watch, his handsome features pulled into utter smugness while he spoke about weather forecasts, she knew without a doubt that she was face to face with the turd bucket hot man from the wedding a few months back. The one and the same who'd made her feel both simultaneously childish and hooker-like, and then later, like the most beautiful, sexiest woman in the room. Confusion, the same from that night when he'd abruptly left after almost setting her panties on fire, washed over her again. How was this happening? He was still as gorgeous as ever, and that beard— dear God it took everything in her not to fan herself outright at His Hotness. Her draw to him, the one she felt months ago, was rising within her again. And he was the very same man her friend thought could help her? No way, she thought. But even as she sat in front of him, crossing and uncrossing her leg sporadically, willing her libido to cool it and her panties to stay as dry as the Sahara, she knew it to be the truth.

His gaze remained bland, his demeanor unchanged, as she fidgeted in front of him. How dumb she must seem to him; how silly, with her silly problems. He was a big, successful corporate lawyer for Pete's sake. And from what Mariam had also said, not only was he up for making partner, but was up for it with a firm that held global distinction.

She shook her head at the ridiculous hope she'd held in meeting with him. There was no way a guy like him would even consider little ole' Chrissy Smyth and her meager financial troubles.

"Ugh!" She sighed in disgust, throwing her hands up in the air. "I cannot believe *you're* the lawyer cousin. And why would I think you'd be any different from the grump you clearly were last time?" She didn't mean that. She'd seen a hint of a side of him that hadn't been so grumpy—quite the opposite when his big, hard body had been up against hers. But right now, this was more than awkward as he sat so calmly in front of her, so stern. It was as though the attraction they'd had then was now only one-sided.

She felt her cheeks burn, embarrassment washing over her. She wasn't sure how to save face in front of this hot asshole, but ripping him a new one seemed to be the only way she could get out of there with a little dignity. The humiliation and frustration from that night of being left cold, as if he'd thrown a bucket of icy water on her, was kind of how she was feeling at that very moment, too.

"Excuse me?" Aariv said, leaning forward, placing his hands flat on the desk. One thick brow arched, and a smirk—a *fucking* smirk—tugged at his lips, though he was trying not to show it. Whatever his face wanted to do, she desperately wanted to swipe it off with the back of her hand. He found this all funny, didn't he?

"I mean, you can't help being an asshole, can you?" Her voice had raised a decibel or three, she was aware, but couldn't seem to stop. "You lawyers are all the same, you know that? You act all fucking high and mighty as if everyone else is teeny tiny compared to you and your busy fucking lawyer … things." She waved her hands again, willing them to not flail haphazardly. She was already a bit of a flailer, but this man brought out the worst in her, and right now, she couldn't even find the words to describe anything.

"Hold up a second," Grumpenhunk said, his voice gruff with confusion as he stood up. "Where is this coming from—"

"I think we both know you were never serious about my case in the first place." She stood up, too, and shouldered her purse. Her clothes were stiff and almost dry now, and she smoothed the front of her skirt down self-consciously.

"Ms. Smyth, I am as serious as a practicing attorney can be when I say that you need hard evidence first or this is a waste of everyone's time." His mouth had gone from smirking to a hard straight line.

"Well, I wouldn't want to waste your *precious* time." She nodded, unsure what her next steps should be. She had no resources but probably could find an accountant on the cheap. She'd need to get her hands on the financial books though…

He smirked. "Well if the shoe fits…"

*Jeez, what an ass!*

The office was still as they both eyed one another. His gaze was more charged behind the lenses of his glasses, more brightened in their hazel hue. How could such a jerk always look so yummy? Life just wasn't fair, was it?

Smoothing down the front of her shirt, she realized she'd missed a few buttons at the top of her blouse in her rush out the door that morning. Had she been giving him cleavage the entire time? No, life was definitely not fair.

She looked up and caught him staring at her chest, and that bolstered her confidence, though she didn't want it to. She decided to leave the buttons undone. Let him stare. She had nothing to be ashamed of. Instead, she lifted her chin and walked to the coat rack, snatching her coat off and folding it over her arm.

"Well, thank you for your *time*, Mr. Abbas, and your bit of *advice*. I hope I can return the favor someday." *What the hell was she saying?* As if a guy like him would ever need anything from her.

Aariv came around from behind his desk and folded his arms across his chest. He leaned back casually and crossed one ankle over the other, revealing a flash of bright orange on his socks. She squinted, trying to see the pattern, and hardly believed what she saw … were those fun Knicks socks the grump wore under his clean-cut pants?

Her gaze roamed up his body. She tried not to stare at the way his muscular form practically oozed through his ultra-fine clothes. They fit him like a glove—the crisp button-down shirt and slacks—and probably cost about the same as one month's rent for her studio apartment in Queens.

"So … are we good, Ms. Smyth?" he asked gruffly. Her eyes shot to his face, and he held a hard stare, intimidating for sure, which would make any other person quake in their shoes. But Chrissy was no ordinary person. She was a tough cookie and could figure this out. Her life hadn't always been smooth sailing and she'd gotten this far, hadn't she?

She shot her chin up and nodded.

Aariv adjusted his glasses with a half-smile lifting the corner of his thick lips. "If that's all…?" And now she was sure he thought she was a bona fide idiot. Evidence. Hard Evidence. She'd watched enough crime shows to have known this.

He followed her to the door and reached it before her, opening it. His gaze was direct, and up close she could make out again how charged his eyes were. They were beautiful, lit up with a burning fire as he studied her. Something spun haphazardly at the bottom of her belly. God, he looked great in glasses. Some men couldn't pull it off but, this guy … and she realized his grin had disappeared and the set of his mouth was harsh, no doubt waiting impatiently for her to get out of his sight.

*All right, girl, roll your tongue back in and get the hell out of there.* She felt like he was out of her league in more ways than one.

Her chin raised again of its own volition. "Thank you." She threw him a last look and a confident flick (or so she hoped) of her hair. She glanced at her own Casio gold wristwatch, the one with the stretchy gold band which seemed ironic and chic only moments ago, but now felt cheap. "And would you look at that, 12:15 on the dot." She marched out of his office. She might've been mistaken but she could swear if ever asked later that she heard the hunky lawyer spit out, "brat," just as the door slammed behind her, which made her smile for the rest of the afternoon.

# CHAPTER 6

ↄ

It was late that evening when Aariv finally decided to head home. He'd let his assistant go for the night hours ago, and the janitor had poked his head into his office twice trying to get in and clean.

He grabbed his black pebble-grained leather briefcase, the one his parents had splurged on when he'd graduated from Yale Law School years ago.

"You did it, *Beta* (term of endearment). You picked wisely." Viraj, his father had pronounced after the graduation ceremony and the elaborate celebratory brunch where the man had imbibed more scotch than was necessary for a midday meal. "Forget about being a doctor. Pah! No need to get your hands dirty!" The older man swiped his hand in the air in good riddance. "And engineering … *nah* (no)!" He gave a good Indian head bobble, nodding and shaking it simultaneously, agreeing with himself. "My son is a big hotshot lawyer, now!" He'd clapped Aariv around the shoulder, pulling him in and the younger man smelled his sour whiskey breath. "Now." He'd guided him to an elegantly wrapped gift tied with a huge red bow sitting on the dining table of their hotel suite. "Only successful attorneys carry *this*!" His words slurred and his eyes were red-rimmed as Aariv unwrapped the luxurious briefcase, his stepmother squealing and clapping her hands in the background before Viraj snapped at her to shut up. Aariv had stepped over to her and hugged her, as Huma bobbled her head quickly, but still smiled from ear to ear. The condescending angry behavior her husband always dealt her was overshadowed by her pride in her stepson.

As much as he didn't want to think so then, it was a thoughtful (and useful) gift, and they weren't wrong. Many successful attorneys carried high-end, even fashionable bags in the city, and he did feel a sense of importance with the weight of it in his hand.

He stuffed his laptop along with legal files inside, determined to examine them better at some point later that evening. He hadn't gotten much done that day. Oh, he'd made it through all of his meetings, signed documents, and even rushed to the latest staff meeting, but in terms of reviewing legal data on upcoming cases, he hadn't made much headway. No, his mind was otherwise preoccupied with a pair of angry sapphire eyes and the sexy sway of a nice pert ass encased in a tight black skirt as it sashayed out his door earlier that day.

*Fuck*. Why did he keep thinking about her? What exactly was his problem? All he knew was that as soon as her temper flared, along with her bratty behavior (what the fuck problem did she have with lawyers?), so had his arousal. She was hot. He'd give her that, but completely off-brand for him.

He clicked off his desk lamp and shrugged on his suit jacket as he headed out the door. He was glad he could do this for his cousin, and by doing so, advise Chrissy, too; case closed—no pun intended. So why was she still on his mind?

She'd taken him utterly by surprise with her proud fury albeit a little misguided. How could anyone pursue legal action without evidence? Perhaps he could help her further if she'd be open to him sending her information to a PI friend of his. Tag Underwood was old-school, straight out of a 1980s detective show, trench coat, cigar, and all. The man was in his sixties but as sharp as a tack, retirement still a far-off ideal for him. He owed Aariv a few favors from previous cases and might be open to working with Chrissy.

As he strode toward the elevators, his phone rang. He searched his pockets, locating it and swiping to take the call.

"*Beta*!" The girlish sweet voice of his stepmother cried out on the other end. "How are you? Just leaving the office? You work too hard. Are you eating?"

"Hi, Aunty. I'm great, never been better," he said smoothly though he dreaded her reason for calling. She'd sent over a list of twenty new bridal candidates last week for him to review. Time was of the essence, or so she persisted, and all of the good 'ones' were getting engaged. And Aariv wondered why the elders kept saying that. It was a rush that had no merit to it.

He shifted his phone to the other ear as he shrugged his light overcoat on, pressing the elevator down button. "Up early meditating?" he asked, cutting off the inquiry he knew was coming about it, along with her second most asked-about subject—if he'd yet touched the frozen Indian food that took up his entire freezer space that she'd made the last time she visited. He hadn't. She'd made enough food to feed an army, including painstakingly trying her hand at making *parathas* (layered flaky flatbreads considered the croissant of South Asia). Huma

Aunty's love language, like many South Asians, was to service her loved ones, and she did that by making food. Unfortunately, she hadn't mastered the spice blending technique necessary to create the intricately balanced flavors of their home country. And rather than crack a tooth on her hockey puck like flatbreads and try to stomach her badly seasoned food, Aariv tended to donate everything to a homeless shelter so it wouldn't go to waste. He really did appreciate her efforts but hated lying to her.

Now, the stash of his favorite Indian candies she brought by the suitcase load was a different story. Aariv's sweet tooth would kill him with diabetes one day, no doubt about it—and one of his other reasons for keeping a strict code of gym rat conduct in his regimental schedule.

"*Heh* (yes). You know I like to rise with the birds and welcome the sun." It was 6:30 am in Kolkata, to his 8 pm in New York.

He could almost see her rosy round face grinning lazily with relaxation. It was hard to believe that this sweet woman was his douche of a father's second wife. It seemed that as time went on, his father became shittier, and Huma Aunty became even sweeter.

After his mother had disappeared off the face of the planet it seemed when he'd been just shy of four years old, his father had been arranged to Huma Aunty. And though their stars had aligned as did their astrological signs, he couldn't fathom how their relationship worked. The quibbling that started only a few years into their marriage was now the constant form of communication between them, along with days of silent treatments. And his father's disdain became more and more severe as the years wore on. But Aariv had to hand it to the woman—she took Viraj's shit and turned it into sugary *chai* and he could only admire her for that.

The early morning mediations she was known for occurred on a wide veranda that held an elaborate altar housing the Hindu deities she worshiped. The space was serene and overlooked her gorgeous garden which she tended to almost as religiously as she did her Hindu faith. It wasn't a fluke that her practice began simultaneously with the squabbling. The woman got up early for a little peace as she knew her husband was unpredictable in his sleep habits. One morning might be a normal day when he got up and wordlessly headed to work, while other times might be a late start due to a terrible hangover. Regardless, Huma knew when and where to find a moment of solitude during the day, and what she touted as her way of keeping a positive attitude.

"Have you looked at the new biodata files I sent to you?" She jumped right into topic number one. He could hear her tapping away at her laptop and he smiled warmly. He'd purchased that laptop for her the last time he'd visited because his father had refused to provide a new computer after their old one died. Aariv had set it up and shown her how to use it. Now she was a pro, constantly video calling friends and relatives all over the globe … and sending him file after file of single women's profiles, which he barely looked at before deleting.

Huma Aunty was more like his friend than his mother. When she'd first entered the picture, she'd insisted he call her Huma Aunty rather than *Amma* (mother). She was very in tune with the fact that he was a little boy confused by the disappearance of the woman he knew as his mother. To his father's irritation, she refused to begin their relationship by trying to fill her shoes. To her credit, in Aariv's opinion, she understood that a boy his age would still have memories of his mother, and she didn't want to start on the wrong foot with him.

And so Huma had become more like a friend and confidant, and when his father was in one of his drunken rages, his protector. He loved her fiercely, though she could be a silly hair-brain at times, and downright stubborn in other things, such as ensuring Aariv lived up to his potential, and like now—finding the right woman as his bride. Ever since the wedding they'd attended months ago, she'd been at it like a hunting dog on a strong scent trail.

"Give me a second, Aunty. I'm riding the elevator down. I might lose you."

By the time he stepped out into the lobby, he'd formulated his answer because no, he hadn't reviewed the twenty separate emails and attachments she'd recently sent over. Every few weeks was a new batch because every batch left him uninterested.

It wasn't that the women were unsuitable. Each of them was a successful doctor, lawyer, computer science engineer, or even the new trendier and now acceptable marketing director. They were attractive and no doubt had interesting traits if he got to know them, but something just didn't feel right. Or maybe it was that he was too busy with work, which wasn't a lie. He clocked in an average of fifty to sixty hours a week with a recent entertainment behemoth's litigation case they'd taken on. Lately, it was all hands on deck, including the partners, who seemed to be living at the office these days. And because there was a new partner spot opening up next year, which Aariv wanted, he kind of lived at the office, too.

"Sorry. I haven't had a chance. The partners have us

working long hours on this Turner & Turner case and I've barely had a moment to breathe, but I am eating." He threw in.

He nodded at the doorman as he left the building, gliding through the revolving doors. The air was chilly outside, but refreshing after being stuck in his office all day. He breathed in the cool freshness and the scent of wet concrete after the day's downpour as he made his way in the direction of his apartment. He lived only a few blocks away, in the nearby neighborhood of Murray Hill, close to where his cousin lived as well.

"*Eesh*!" Huma exclaimed, sucking her teeth loudly. "Are you making time for yourself, Aari? You are still playing the basket tasket-ball every week, *nah*?"

He had a weekly pick-up basketball game that he played with the same guys every Sunday. It was his time to relax and let loose, other than working out at the gym every morning which was more of an anxiety release before he started his insane workday at the office.

"I do. And Zayn gives his regards." He chuckled. She thought Zayn was a legit wacko, and had said as much the last time she'd witnessed them play ball. Z had zoomed back and forth on the court, aggressively shouting curse words to anyone who missed the plays he'd set up. She didn't know that Z had been hopped up on pills that morning. Aariv had given him a stern talking to about it.

"*Eesh*!" she exclaimed again, but in a mixture of disgust and concern. "Maybe I should speak to his father about his behavior? You never know with these mixed kids—"

"Nope. Please don't. He's a grown adult and can take care of himself," he said, nipping that unnecessary conversation (that would blow up into a nonexistent issue) in the bud. This is what Indian parents did. They got into the younger generations' business, and if not the younger generations, then any other relative or family friend who must need their help. They meant well, but it usually led to running in circles with no solution in sight and way too much gossiping for Aariv to stomach. "And might I remind you that Mimi is mixed?" he asked.

"I—oh! She's different, *Beta.* She's blood." As if that explanation was obvious and made sense. There was no blood shared between Huma and Mariam, who was the daughter of Aariv's father's sister. "Now," she said going back to her original topic, "please take a look at the biodatas. If you don't, I will put your profile on Dil Mil." She warned. "I am serious, Aari. VIP Elite status, too."

Aariv groaned, pinching the bridge of his nose. Sometimes doing what was expected of one was absolute shit. She'd already threatened him with the popular South Asian dating site before, and elite status was the fast-track version. And she wasn't bluffing. He knew enough about her tenacity that when she believed in something, she'd actually follow through with it one of these days.

"Please don't," he said firmly, brokering no argument. "I'll take a look. I promise."

*L*ater that evening, Aariv pumped iron like the manic beast he always turned into while hitting the gym in his building. If the weights could talk, they'd spill the worst kind of abuse that Aariv's frustrations had led him to inflict on them over the past few years since living there.

Curious as to the list of biodata Huma had sent him, he checked his emails when he got home, just intending to peruse quickly before getting to sitting in front of the TV with his case briefs, leftovers, and ESPN on in the background tuned to NBA highlights.

The first file was an Anisha Devi. It read with the obvious facts such as birthday, birthplace, religion, caste, education, occupation, height, and complexion. He knew they all read like that—but it still made him cringe. Was this how he was supposed to make his decision? Caste, really? He'd never cared about the traditional social group a person was born into in India. Complexion? Why did it matter how light or dark a person was? Everything was so calculated and cold and held nothing that he valued in a person. The question was, what did he value?

His blood boiled when the second profile was of a woman he met when he'd first moved to the US. She lived in New York and was beautiful and successful, no question. She'd had a sort of background presence for him at all of the Indian functions he'd attended but lately hadn't been around much. She was a successful doctor, and surprisingly a widow with a small child of her own. But that wasn't what made him seethe. No, it was because she'd been, and still was as far as he knew, part of a circle of friends who had tirelessly taunted his cousin, Mariam, as teenagers. She, along with her gang of overachievers (ironically like him) had tormented the hell out of her, calling her every negative name describing a person of mixed South Asian and white races that bordered on hate speech. Though their behavior had shaped Mariam into the strong woman she was now, how could he even consider this person? And this was one of the candidates his stepmother presented as ideal? Good

God, she barely knew who he was if she thought this person was an option.

He'd snapped his laptop shut and threw on gym clothes, practically darting down the stairs to the gym.

Now he gripped the rough metal of the free weights, the metallic odor a salty sourness that filled his nostrils with every heavy inhale. The need to become a mindless gym rat was stronger than ever. His sweaty reflection stared back at him, a pained expression mottling his face as he completed his last set of bicep curls. The do-rag he'd tied around his forehead was drenched in sweat and he'd lost his t-shirt a while ago, throwing it in a pile with his gym bag and water bottle.

Having finished, he dropped the weights with a dull thud, his breathing jagged. His muscularly sculpted arms glistened back at him in the mirror as he gave them a flex, while sweat dribbled in rivulets down his chest into the waistband of his sports shorts. He grabbed his water bottle and squirted an electrolyte mixture into his mouth and he felt a brief moment of satisfaction. This he could control, he thought, as he contracted his biceps again.

A message pinged on his phone and he growled, "What the fuck," glad he was the only one in the gym that night. Anyone else would think he was bat-shit crazy, especially if it was Huma or even his father following up with him already. He'd rip them a new one if it was.

He pulled his phone out of his bag and heaved a sigh of relief. It was his cousin.

**"Aari, why didn't you take my friend's case?"**

Damn. Right to the point. He should've known this would get back to Mariam quickly. She and her new circle of friends were thick as thieves lately.

He deflected. **"And how are you, Mimi? Just get back in from London with Lord what's his face?"**

**"Cut the crap. Tell me why you didn't consider Chrissy's case. She also said you were kind of mean."**

Mean?! Of course an obnoxious bratty girl would think that of a serious professional.

He shook his head and texted back, **"I was professional. She was the one who walked out on our meeting."**

He didn't tell her that he'd reserved his fifteen-minute lunch break to advise her. The woman had shown up late after all, what more could he do?

**"I'm sure she had some reason to. You can be overbearing sometimes. You know that, right?"**

Did he know that? Of course he did. But what she thought was overbearing was him being focused. That was just who he was.

**"I was as *nice* and open as possible, Mimi."** Was he gritting his teeth when he texted this? Damn straight he was. He shouldn't have to be nice when all he was doing was his job. **"She was the one who stormed out when I told her I couldn't do anything about her case unless she had her shit together."** Was he going to relay that he'd been slightly patronizing? No, because Chrissy seemed like a woman who needed someone to be a little patronizing and even high-handed. She bordered on being a fantasy-prone. The fact that she'd thought she'd end up murdered had been laughable.

What wasn't laughable was the hard fact of him being a walking boner when it came to Chrissy. That she was the woman he'd almost hooked up with at the wedding. More importantly, seeing her again had awakened an almost uncontrollable desire for her when he should be focusing on other things. He was almost relieved when he found out he couldn't help her.

**"Well, Bossy, how would you feel if you were belittled about something important to you?"**

He guffawed. Well, shit. That was a good point. Great. Now he felt bad.

**"Mimi, she didn't have any hard evidence to even begin talking about a case. There's nothing I could do. Plus she could stand to not let her emotions get carried away. You know, maybe have some patience for the process."**

**"But you could have advised her on what she could do."**

**"Please don't tell me how to do my job."**

**"I will if you don't know how to lawyer."**

That stung and was completely out of left field. But, she usually turned like this when something was going on in her world.

**"What's up, Babe?"** he asked, using the childhood nickname he'd given her a long time ago when she'd been a pink dimpled little kid. She'd reminded him of the movie with the same name about a cute pig on a sheep farm.

His phone rang and he picked up.

"Sorry, Aari," Mariam huffed on a large sigh. "Didn't mean to be a bitch. I'm just exhausted from dealing with my soon-to-be in-laws. They're literally a bunch of twats. Thank goodness we won't be living in the UK once we get married."

"I'm sorry to hear that," he said soberly. "Is there anything I can do to help?

"Not with this. But you can try to find a way to help Chrissy. We're all worried about her."

Aariv had already been thinking about that since the woman had stormed out of his office earlier that day. Why? He had no idea, but he'd already felt the inkling of regret that he couldn't do more after she left.

"Well, I do have a detective buddy who owes me a favor. Maybe I can connect them."

"Yes, *Biya* (male cousin)! That would be so helpful. I don't know if you know this, but she has no family here; no one she can trust like that. Not like what we have."

He didn't know that. He only knew that her immigrant mother had raised her on her own, and then died a few years ago. Now Aariv felt really bad. He had the support of his family, whether here in the US, or India just a phone call away. How would it be to have no one like that?

"I'll make sure it happens," he said with assurance.

"Thank you. Now go take one of your melatonin gummies," she laughed as she said this. "And go to bed. Why are you up so late? I'm the one with jet lag."

He checked the time. It was just approaching half past ten. He hadn't realized how late it was. His usual hard cut-off was ten.

"Well, *Amma* (Mom)," he teased. "I have a lot on my mind. I'm finishing at the gym right now and then heading back for some shut-eye." He started stuffing his things in his bag. "And don't knock the gummies or a great night of sleep." He didn't tell her that the gummies also helped him stay asleep. He had so much going on that sometimes he just stayed away wide-eyed, watching the shadows change in the room from night to early morning.

"The gym? Don't you usually do that at the crack ass of dawn?"

She knew him well. And she was right. He usually started his day at six a.m. sharp (which he'd already done that morning in the form of running on the treadmill and boxing). Then he hit the sauna for twenty minutes at seven, showered, changed, had a light breakfast with coffee, and arrived at work by eight-thirty. He thrived on this routine. But with everything going on lately, he'd gone off the rails and had to visit the gym to burn off some extra jittery energy. Yes, he was a masochist and his body was going to feel it tomorrow.

"Yeah, so what? Quit keeping tabs on me."

"Ok, Cranky."

Jesus, why did everyone think he was cranky, or grumpy? What was wrong with keeping a routine, or even liking to keep in shape?

"I'm going to go before I say something else that's bitchy. I'm around this weekend if you want to grab lunch. We can talk about this marriage situation you've got going on," she said archly.

"And I bet you'll be reserving your bitchiness for that convo," he grumbled. He knew Mariam wasn't being judgmental, but she couldn't understand what he was doing trying to find a bride by being set up. Hell, he was kind of wondering, too.

"You got it."

"Great." He deadpanned. "Let's sync up later in the week. Talk soon."

"Goodnight and you won't regret helping Chrissy. She's really the sweetest and most generous person."

Sweetest person? Were they talking about the same Chrissy Smyth? This was a woman who nicknamed him "Grumpenstein" and got all huffy when he tried to reason with her. But what did it matter? He was finished with her. Let his private investigator buddy handle her.

## CHAPTER 7

9

Chrissy swiped off the last of her thick stage makeup, heaving a deep sigh of relief. Could the day have been any longer? Tired didn't come close to how she felt—more like exhausted by torrential waves pounding down on her, one right after the other with barely any time in between to stand up and regain her balance. Each one was a differing emotion she didn't have time to process as they came on unexpectedly throughout her crazy day.

Hopefully, as it was just approaching midnight, and she'd worked both her day job at the events company, and then gone straight to her night job performing at the club, she could go home, collapse into bed, and fall into a deep slumber. Sleep—an old friend that had alluded her lately. She needed it desperately and preferably dreamless because with so much on her mind, she'd have a night of bad dreams, waking up in a pool of sweat and terror.

"Not at all what you thought my life would be like, huh, Mama?" she said out loud. As the dressing room was empty, she didn't need to feel embarrassed when she spoke to her dead mother in times like this.

Her mother, Natasha Smyth (formally Smyrnov; she'd changed their last name to sound more American) had been a strong-willed, Russian immigrant. She'd singlehandedly raised her daughter in New York City and had run a mostly successful oriental and antiques rug shop.

In this instance, she'd have raised her severely thinned-out brows; lit an extra-long, ultra-light menthol cigarette; and stated loudly on an exhale, "You could have had it all, *Moya* (my in Russian) Chrisstika. But you threw it all away." She'd shake her head, her poofy hair stiff and unmoving, the color dyed to a perfect golden hue which she touched up every few months at a salon in Brighton Beach Brooklyn—a little Russia outside of the mother-land. The beauty ritual was something she dragged Chrissy to do with her, and Chrissy continued with it, even after she died. It was familiar—a piece of her mother she could keep with her. But she'd let it go the previous year because she couldn't afford it anymore, letting her natural reddish hair grow in.

She placed her hands on the small of her back and arched forward. She hadn't thrown it away, she thought firmly, as her muscles cracked loudly along her spine. She'd gone after her own dreams, not her mother's which was that her daughter become a prima ballerina at a world-famous ballet company.

As she stretched, trying to rid herself of the aftermath of the physically taxing day, she reflected on how different her life might've been if she'd decided to continue auditioning for professional ballet companies. She'd have been stuck in the background, dancing with the corps de ballet in some mediocre place in middle America, there was no question.

Because no matter how much she trained, no matter how much she poured her heart into the artistry of ballet, no one could fix her short stature and curvy butt and boobs. One dance director had even commented that her knees were too knobby. As if she could change *that* without going under the knife. Granted, the world of ballet was transforming and views on differing body types (and skin tones!) were expanding (thank you, Misty Copeland!), but there were still unsaid rules about the ideal ballet figure. Chrissy knew herself, and she knew she wouldn't be able to stand not being a soloist at a top-notch theater. After the literal blood, sweat, and tears she'd spent to even achieve the level of skill, confidence, and guts to audition for the best companies around the globe, she'd feel like a failure. To her mother's chagrin, Chrissy had given it exactly one year, though professionals and instructors alike advised that it could take a lot longer to achieve the position one wanted in the dance company of one's dreams. But after 365 days (give or take a few weeks), she'd stopped. Chrissy might be a dreamer and might crave fairy-tale endings, but she wasn't stupid. She wasn't about to become bitter like the former dancer who'd trained her. The older ballerina had blown a knee out during her critical auditioning journey and had never been able to gain her strength back. She ended up in the corps of a company that wasn't on her list to begin with.

No, Chrissy decided to put her efforts into other dreams she had but couldn't pursue because she felt like she had to at least try the ballerina thing for her mother—the woman who'd scrimped and saved to get her daughter the best training. And, it was freeing, surprisingly so, when she'd cast off her leotard and tights, and hung her point shoes up for good. She could go be something of her own making, rather than the little ballerina her mother had started to train when Chrissy was but a toddler.

And look at her now. She was dancing again, though not in the capacity she thought she ever would, but she was appreciating it more than ever. She'd forgotten how much joy she got from performing, and in all, the night had been a good one and she was thankful for that. Being scheduled for two shows, back-to-back meant double the pay and she needed it. Undeniably, her muscles felt over-used, though, and she had to get up bright-eyed and early the next day to do it all over again. Plus, her ass still smarted from the tumble she took earlier, which felt like eons ago.

She grimaced as she thought about that fall; it led to remembering the events of the afternoon. Normally she could brush it aside and move on, but that attorney—that hunky, extremely lick-able, but way too serious for his own good man kept making her stop in her tracks and forget what she was doing. He didn't find her interesting anymore, that was clear, or he wouldn't have let her walk out so easily. And he'd barely cared about her misfortunes or the fact that yes, she really did think she would end at the bottom of the river one of these days with cement shoes on, mob-style.

She put her face into her hands and shook her head. *Stop it, Chrissy, you are totally overreacting.*

She squared her shoulders and looked at herself in the mirror. She had her favorite wig on that night—a dusky lavender bob with sparkles embedded throughout the strands. She loved wearing wigs to perform because it let her be someone else for the night.

Tonight she imagined she was a fairy queen who was also a tempting seductress. One who commanded the audience for the seven minutes she performed. All eyes were on her with awe and hunger as she moved through the sequence of intricate choreography in her scantily clad costume. But her confidence was off. She'd fumbled at the most random moments as Aariv's bright hazel eyes flashed before her, searing her with his serious stare. She couldn't help imagining that he was in the audience, his gaze on her body in her skimpy outfit, watching her with the same desire as the other men out there. And then she imagined it was just him watching her; that she was there performing just for him. At one point amid this fantasy, she'd slipped. It was just for a millisecond, she could've sworn, but she'd missed an important sequence and had to fudge her way through until she got back on to the beat of the music. And then it happened again in her repeat performance later that night!

He was going to be a hard man to forget for the second time, that was certain. Though solemn and arrogant bordering on overbearing, Aariv commanded attention. She'd thought the same thing months ago, and even with his disgusting behavior at first, her opinion had remained. But why couldn't he also be a nice guy? In fact, why did the word "nice" never seem to apply to lawyers? They were saviors in a way, weren't they? And couldn't saviors be nice?

"Yeah, only in the storybooks," she muttered to herself. And in her current situation, she was no Cinderella with a Prince Charming coming to rescue her from possible wicked business dealings. However, she would definitely turn into a pumpkin if she didn't get home and get some rest.

"Great show, tonight, Star," said a scantily dressed voluptuous woman, interrupting her thoughts. She came up to stand behind her and began to touch up her make-up while looking into the mirror that ran along the length of the dressing room.

"Thanks, Desiree," Chrissy said after a beat to the woman, almost forgetting that she had a stage name here at the club.

She tugged off the wig, and shook it, making the sparkles in the strands burst with iridescent shimmer. She combed her fingers through the locks, detangling the twisted strands.

As she worked, she asked the other woman, "You don't think I could've done that last trick a little tighter?"

Desiree looked at her incredulously and stopped mid-lipstick re-application.

"Girl, are you insane? You're the highlight of this stale club's nights." She pointed her dark vampy colored tube of lipstick at her. "Your talent is wasted here. An acrobatic dance performance like yours should be somewhere else; somewhere big; like Cirque de Soleil, or Vegas, you know what I'm saying?"

Chrissy guffawed. She was not *that* talented but appreciated the other woman's positivity.

"Yeah, but then Darius couldn't claim that he has an eye for talent and *real* dance." Her tone was droll and she rolled her eyes. Desiree snorted loudly.

Darius, the club manager didn't realize the core work, arm strength, and creativity it took to be a great pole dancer, like Desiree and some of the other women. His big idea was to turn the club, *Xtasy Unlimited,* into a "classier joint" than it was previously known for by bringing in a more diverse audience earlier in the night. He did this by hiring other acts that veered away from the typical lap dances and stripping and were more palatable to a wider range of people. It was a good idea, but the execution could use a little more thought, because, at the end of the day, he still thought sex was the seller.

Chrissy's act, for instance, consisted of a titillating dance-acrobatic trapeze number. Aerial silk was the technical term, and the performance required stamina, flexibility, and extreme balance while appearing as though it was effortless. Her style was sensual and a little dark, where she used specialist fabrics to tie herself up in choreographed bondage, keeping her attached to a trapeze twenty-five feet above the ground while she moved through a dance number. The wow factor was the free fall to the stage at the end, where she landed with her nose mere inches from the floor. It was thrillingly death-defying, always giving her a major rush. Especially the reaction from the audience as they gasped in horror and then roared in delight.

She'd chosen her stage name, Star, because she knew when she was out there, she was a larger-than-life spectacle, if only for a brief time. It was exhilarating having all of those eyes trained on her, while she played a mysterious, sensual role, one that shone but was full of intrigue, or so she hoped. The fact that Darius was beginning to double-book her meant she was doing something the customers liked.

But, though she had a talented class act, as Darius liked to put it, he still wanted more provocative; more skin showing. He wanted sexier costumes and even pushed his class act girls to entertain the big spenders in the VIP room. The first point Chrissy could agree with; at the end of the day, sex *did* sell. She wore outfits like the one she'd worn tonight—a sheer nude unitard with strategically placed jewels to hide her hoo-ha and nipples. The other "class acts" had similar getups, like the very talented Corinna, aka Coco the Magician, who wore just a top hat, a very fitted blue velvet jacket with coattails as her top, over a tiny glitter bikini bottom, and lace-up black boots.

*Yeah, that's real classy, Darius.*

But the second point was a hard 'no' for her. Entertaining the big spenders meant selling one's body for sex in return for more money and even higher tips. She was strapped for cash but that wasn't worth it to her—it never would be.

"What happened to your butt?" Desiree asked as Chrissy stood up and peeled the unitard from her shoulders.

"Is it that bad? I tried to cover it. I used pancake makeup…" She turned to look at her rear end and saw the faint ugly green and purple smudges still visible under the thick stage makeup concealer. She winced. It'd ballooned and spread completely over her right cheek in a matter of hours. She huffed, still infuriated about the pointless meeting that afternoon with dickhead lawyer man, which had left her bruised … literally.

"Nah, you wouldn't be able to see it in the audience. But I see it now. What happened?" Desiree asked suspiciously. "You working tricks on the side, and some John roughed you up?"

Chrissy choked back a laugh. She shouldn't find it funny. Some of the performers here had to look for that line of work to make ends meet. She didn't know who, as she performed part-time at the club, but had heard the whispers.

"Oh my God, hell no, Desiree. I'll tell you when I'm that desperate to pay rent." She quickly tugged the rest of her unitard off, shaking it out and putting it on a hanger. Completely nude, she searched for her underwear and bra while Desiree waited patiently for an answer. Nothing like the dance and performance world to force one to unabashedly get naked and change in front of others, she mused as she found her underwear in her bag. Nothing phased performers. She continued, "I slipped on wet marble earlier today and *this*," she grabbed her own fleshy, naked butt cheek, grinning, "is where I landed. Pretty great cushion, and doesn't hurt as bad as it looks." She lied. She needed this paycheck and no bruised ass (or ego for that matter) was going to keep her from working.

"Well, you did great tonight, honey. I love it when you're all tied up at the top and then just let yourself fall. It scares the shit out of everybody until you're hanging a few feet off the ground with just your thigh looped up like that. It's pretty hot, too. Gets a lot of the men out there imagining what else they could do to you—or you to them—with that bondage material. And by the way, I saw your tip jar being passed around. It overfloweth tonight."

Chrissy chuckled. "Thanks, Desiree. I'll let those dudes keep imagining. And I hope I get to see some of that extra moolah." They both hooted but the cut that Darius took from their hard-earned pay sucked.

The other woman headed to the door and waved to her. "I'm on. See you later, kid."

"Have a great shift, Desiree. See you tomorrow." She waved back, then finished getting dressed and packing her things up.

As she headed down the stairs toward the back entrance, she passed by the manager's office and stopped, popping her head in.

"Hey, Darius!" she called to the thin, dark-haired man sitting at the desk. He put his cigar down and beckoned her to come in with a long, crooked finger and grin that she could only describe as slimy. Her head prickled as it always did when she was uncomfortable, but she shook it off. He wouldn't do anything to her.

As she walked in she schooled her face to not scrunch up in disgust as she choked on his thick cigar smoke.

"You know that stuff will kill you, right?" She waved a hand in front of her, hoping to get the fumes away from her fresh lungs. She would know. Her mother had died for her love of smoking.

"Everything good in life will kill you." He shot back, chuckling deeply. "We all end up dead one way or the other so what's the harm in enjoying some vices." He leaned back in his chair, contemplating her with his beady eyes. "I have your tips from tonight." He slapped a thick stack of bills sharply against his palm. "It's a lot, girly."

She reached over to take the stack from him, but he pulled away quickly, shaking his head. He peeled about a third of the bills from the top and shoved them into his desk drawer. "A little for the skin off my back."

She snorted; she couldn't help it. Darius had no talent for anything; as if he deserved a big cut like that...

"Whatever, Darius. Can I have my money?" She extended her palm out expectantly.

He rolled her bills up with a quick snap of a rubber band and tossed it at her. "You know, for a girl who wanted a bartender job to begin with, you're doing pretty great here as a dancer. You have a following with some of our VIPs and could be making triple in the VIP room." He stared hard at her as he picked up his cigar and worked his thin lips around it. His glare scanned her body. She was fully dressed in casual jeans, a sweatshirt, and sneakers but his eyes made her feel grossly naked.

"Meaning *you* could make even more," she said curtly as

she put her money away in her bag. She'd count it later. Displaying anything remotely money-hungry would only push Darius' cause harder.

He shrugged but didn't disagree.

"Not interested," she said.

"I hear you've got money troubles," he said nonchalantly, blowing fat smoke rings into the air. "You sure you don't want to try your talents in there? I promise I'll make the men behave."

"Who told you that?" she asked quietly, equally casual. *Stay calm, Chris. Don't show him your cards.*

He smiled behind his scraggly goatee. "A little birdie."

Chrissy scoffed. She should've known that her co-worker, Robyn, would say something. The other woman was also a freshly attained entertainer at the club. They'd recently taken a dance class together to hone their skills and she must have mentioned it in passing to the other woman. Of course, Robyn would mention this tiny tidbit to Darius. She too, was trying to keep him off her back about the VIP room, preferring to keep her act which combined belly dancing and fire strictly professional.

"I think she misheard what I was saying," Chrissy said cooly, as she backed out of his office. "I'll see you tomorrow, Darius."

"The offer could disappear if you don't jump on it," he called after her. "Just think about it."

Thinking about it only made her nauseous. There was no way she would stoop to that level. Taking her clothes off in front of men … she could if she really had to make ends meet. But she'd heard other things were done in the VIP room, and she knew she'd never be able to do that. She needed to keep a line drawn when it came to this gig, she thought firmly as she bounded down the steps to the subway. It was only supposed to be temporary, after all.

# CHAPTER 8

ঠ

In Brooklyn the following Sunday afternoon, Chrissy hugged her friend tight after a morning of their version of therapy—aka detailed discussion of what was going on in their lives over brunch.

"You sure you're all right, Chris?" Antoine asked. They'd left the restaurant and he'd pulled her aside on the sidewalk, while his boyfriend dashed into a corner bodega to grab a few groceries.

The look of concern smooshing up his long, attractive face, was becoming his normal expression when it came to her lately. He pushed his gold, round wire-rimmed glasses up his nose as he stared down at her with big doe-like brown eyes.

She squeezed his elbow. "Yes, my dude. I'm ok. I *will* figure this out even though the hunky attorney denied me."

Earlier, over kimchi egg tacos and bottomless mimosas, where thankfully her friend and his new beau picked up the tab at a new hip brunch spot, she'd run down the facts. Mariam's cousin—the hottie with the nice ass who happened to be the biggest ass at the wedding—had ended up being the lawyer. He'd told her he couldn't help her.

Antoine and his boyfriend were shocked until she revealed that she didn't have hard evidence so there was nothing he could do. It's not that they changed their tune from "team Chrissy" after they heard that all too true fact, but they could see Grumpenstein's side.

"But, I still can't believe Mariam's cousin was that big attractive hunk who almost impregnated you on the dance floor months ago," Antoine said, fanning himself at the mere thought of Aariv as they stood waiting outside the bodega.

"Uh, what? We didn't even come close to doing *that* deed," she reminded him. "He left me all hot and bothered, remember?"

"Oh, girl I do. But anyone that fine could make *me* pregnant just by standing next to him. And you were all up in his business for a scorching minute."

Chrissy didn't need to be reminded, though she knew exactly what Antoine was talking about. Since seeing him at his office last week, her vibrator had been her constant companion. For the first time since she'd gotten the dang thing, she'd needed to replace the batteries. It was weird. He just did things to her; made her feel things—yes, it was horniness—by just thinking about him. But he didn't even *like* her, nor did she him. She had no idea what was wrong with her. Her body seemed to think it was ok to get her jollies off of imagining him doing things to her, though he was off-limits. But really, she just couldn't help wondering what it would be like to be with a man like that. Was he a quiet lover? Did his stoic seriousness extend to the bedroom? Or was he all about the power and became as bossy and patronizing during sex as he was in his office? Did he make women come multiple times or was it a series of small 'o's that led to one big ginormous 'O'?

She'd never admit this to anyone, but she'd never had multiple orgasms before, let alone one with a real man. She'd dated many men, and before that, in her teen years, more like boys. And though they could make her feel good, she'd never experienced a true physical awakening like that; a moment of peak pleasure. She was pretty sure she hadn't had the boneless, raw feeling that some of her friends, like Mariam, had experienced when describing what it was like with her fiancé.

"I'm thankful it's not that easy to get pregnant," she responded a little dryly. She'd be the mother of at least a dozen children if that were the case given her tendency to dirty dance with dudes at clubs.

"I saw him by the way, your last beau faux pas." This change of topic from a man who she confusingly couldn't stop thinking about to a guy she hadn't thought about in ages was a welcome relief.

"What!? Where!?" Chrissy exclaimed, grabbing Antoine's arm. "I knew he wasn't joining a seminary, that lying piece of shit."

"Girl, a few nights ago, at Lush Bar. The dude was part of a grinder sandwich with two chicks all over him. Everyone's mouths were on everyone else's. Couldn't see where one began and one ended. I may be no church mouse, but off to the seminary that boy ain't."

"Well fuck," Chrissy said, though she felt nothing. She was over him and had been for a while.

"Girl, your dating life is a Taylor Swift album," Antoine drawled, shaking his head.

"Not even close, or I'd be rolling in dough," she sighed. "I am not making that mistake again, by the way."

"And which mistake are we talking about? The one where you date a guy clearly on the rebound—yes, he was," Antoine said vehemently as Chrissy protested. "His ex-girlfriend was all he could talk about, remember? And he rescheduled your first date three times, and all last minute, Chris. If he genuinely liked you, he would've given better reasons than just work. And don't tell me you didn't forget about the time you saw him out at Lush, in fact, after one of those cancellations." Antoine rolled his eyes. "Saying it was too late to call you my ass. It wasn't even ten o'clock at night."

"All right! Point taken. I'm horrible at picking them." She shook her head.

"That's not it, Love Bug," Antoine said softly, putting his arm around her. "It's that you can't see the red flags because your glasses are too rosy. You think every man who shows you any attention is your happily ever after."

She looked down at her toes in her favorite white ankle boots. Antoine was right, not to mention Shana and Simran, the others in their group of friends. Chrissy always jumped right into every relationship with gusto, never taking the time to pack a parachute. Over-enthusiasm was her middle name. She'd never been a go-with-the-flow kind of girl. Patience might be a virtue, but it'd never been one of hers.

"I know," she said. "I'm trying to be smarter about my choices in men," she said with a sharp nod of her head.

"Oh, honey." Antoine should his head sympathetically. "That's not the issue. You know what is?"

"No, but I can't wait to find out what you think my issues are."

"You, my little friend, have daddy issues," Antoine said with such seriousness that Chrissy wasn't sure if he meant it or not. When his lip twitched, she knew he was kidding … or was he?

They both burst into laughter.

But Chrissy was the first to say it. "I do think I do, actually. No dad growing up, no father figure…"

"From what it sounds like though, your mom was tough enough to be both your parents," Antoine said hugging her again. "Now, stop jumping in love with every Tom, Dick, or Harry that says 'hello.'"

"I'll try," she grumbled.

"Now tell me what the heck you're going to do about the rug shop. It seems like a lost cause. I say sell the damn thing and get out while you still can."

"It's not a lost cause! And what would my mother say if I just gave up on it now—when the going got tough?" Her mom would tell her that she wasn't trying hard enough to figure it out. Which was why she was going to figure it out, even if it meant doing so on her own. "I have an idea and don't try to change my mind, but I'm going to go all Carmen Sandiego. I need to find out what Boris is hiding."

Antoine's eyes lit up. "Oh, girl, you'd look fire in a red fedora. But be careful."

"Oh for sure. I'll go to the shop when I know he won't be there. Like today. Sunday is a formal day off because it's God's Day." She rolled her eyes. She hadn't been a devout Russian Orthodox since she'd been a small girl and she didn't miss it one bit.

She fingered the gold cross that hung around her neck—the one her mother had gifted her when she turned eighteen. Natasha Smyth prayed that her daughter would turn back to the church after she'd slowly pulled away as a teenager because she just couldn't stomach the religion and the holier-than-thou attitudes of the priests. It always made her stomach roil that the church officiants treated her mother with disdain as she was unmarried and had a child, but always filled the till the best she could.

Antoine pulled her into a bear hug. "Well yeah, be careful for your safety; *of course*. But make sure your fedora is the right shade of rouge red. Nothing says crime like the one to fashion if red clashes on red." He tugged a few of her strawberry blonde strands, a look of mock horror crossing his face.

And she couldn't help it, she burst into giggles. This was why they were best friends. He always pulled her into silly humor bordering on the inappropriate, which was her cup of tea.

"Now tell me again why you won't bring this up with Simran? I'm sure she'd give you an advance in salary if you needed it."

Simran Khan was not only their friend, but their boss, and the owner of the events planning company they both worked for. It was pretty successful, with a string of hot new clients always knocking at their door. But Chrissy just didn't feel right about asking her, and she wanted to prove (to whom, she had no idea —maybe just herself) that she could figure this out on her own.

"Maybe. But I need to get to the bottom of what the hell is going on before I do anything like that. Plus, I have the financial thing under control right now."

"Barely," Antoine murmured under his breath. "You're working too much, Chris. I worry about you."

"Aw, Tone-Tone, that's so sweet," she said, leaning her head on his shoulder. He was the best friend a girl could ever ask for.

Just then his new boyfriend ducked out of the bodega with

two full canvas bags of groceries swung over his wide shoulders.

"Hey, Callum," Chrissy said. "I'm off. Thanks for brunch today. And you two…" She made a 'chef's kiss' gesture. "Are beautiful together. Please, please, please tell me you plan to get married soon, and then decide to have kids. Then each of you will donate sperm so you have two adorable mini-me's of each of you!" She clapped her hands in excitement, bouncing on the balls of her feet. How perfect would that be? She loved a happy ending more than anything in life—when things were tied up in a bow. Life didn't always end up like that, but sometimes, it happened and when it did, it was something to be celebrated.

She looked between the two of them, marveling at the attractiveness of them as a couple. Where Antoine was slight, and tall, with a poetic look about him due to his long face, big eyes, and glasses, Callum was brawny and built and exuded his Scottish heritage. His thick auburn hair was wavy, and his Scottish brogue even wavier making him a complete charmer. Together, the two were so great-looking that she almost had to shield her eyes at their beauty.

Antoine smiled tightly at her and looked like he wanted to strangle her. He mouthed, "Still too new."

They'd just started dating but it was moving fast enough that they were already talking about whose borough they would move in together in—Brooklyn or Queens.

"Aw, thanks, Chrissy," Callum said, putting a thick arm around Antoine and pulling him in tight. The slimmer man relaxed into him. "We'll come to you when we're ready to make that leap, how 'bout that?" He gave her a wink.

"I can't be carrying no babies, but I'm down to give major moral support, and I'd be the best aunt ever!" Callum laughed and so did she, but Antoine stared daggers at her, as he shook his head. That was her indicator to go. She knew her filter barely existed when she met new people. Her brain just formed funny (or so *she* thought) anecdotes and her mouth obligingly said them. 'Classic Chrissy' it was called.

"Ok gotta run. Enjoy the rest of your Sunday!"

As she started walking away Antoine called after her, "Stay Gucci, Girl!"

She looked over her shoulder laughing, as Antoine waved, his other hand clutched in a lover's clasp with Callum.

"I'll try, Dude." She blew him a kiss and grinned back, though she felt more second-hand thrift store lately than anything remotely close to Gucci.

# CHAPTER 9

When she arrived at Natasha's Rug Emporium later that afternoon, she knew her plans were foiled. There was a flurry of unusual activity even though the store wasn't open for business.

She saw a familiar portly man directing an unmarked moving truck as it backed up into the alley. She watched as he indicated where the men should put what looked like rolls upon rolls of tightly packaged rugs in thick clear plastic film.

Incensed, she came up behind the stout man, and said, "Boris, we're getting *another* shipment?"

Boris jumped about a foot in the air and turned around. Sharp, beady eyes stared at her in astonishment, and the saggy pink jowls that were his cheeks quivered.

"*Christikka*, what do you do here on this day of God?" he asked, as if berating her, though his jowls continued to quiver and his top buck teeth got caught on his bottom lip. He chewed at it in his tell-tale sign of worry.

"Give me a break, Boris," she scoffed. "I could ask you the same thing. What the hell is going on?" She waved at the activity in the alley. "We haven't even sold the last fucking shipment that came in."

"Language, my girl." He grunted, as he grabbed her elbow, pulling her aside and out of the alley to the front of the store, well away from the action. His grip was rough and he moved quickly, making her stumble behind him. When he let go, she scowled, rubbing her arm.

"What gives?"

Boris put a finger to his mouth. "Quiet." He looked over her shoulder and peered in the direction of the alley. "Nothing is going on. Why do you need to know everything—"

"Because," she said emphatically. "My name is now on the business documents as owner and—"

"I don't want to get you involved."

"But I am involved. Mama left the business to me." Why was he being so dense?

"I'm protecting you; the way Natasha would have wanted."

"Don't go bringing Mama into this. She would've never allowed this bullshit to happen inside her doors."

Boris looked at the sky and uttered something in Russian. Something about God, and the ghost of Natasha giving him strength, and throwing the revered Russian Orthodox saint, St. Nicholas, in there, too. Chrissy wasn't fluent in the mother-tongue but could understand some of it.

"I need you to leave, *Malyshka* (baby girl in Russian). I will explain everything later."

He pushed her away from the store, in the opposite direction of the alley. "Go, go, go."

"But Boris—"

He turned his back on her as a tall, bald man with a scarred face approached from around the corner and towered over him.

He was dressed in the biggest black leather coat Chrissy had ever seen, due to how large his frame was; not fat, but just really, really big-boned. Aside from wondering how many poor cows it must have taken to make that coat, Chrissy felt like she knew that man.

His gaze scanned behind and over Boris' ashy blond mullet in her direction. For a millisecond her eyes met his black ones and she turned around quickly, an instinct telling her to not look back—even to check on the smaller man. She dashed up the block, scooting through a crosswalk even though there was oncoming traffic.

Seriously, what the F was going on here!? Who was the big leather-wearing guy, and why was Boris keeping her away from everything?

*He's protecting you,* she thought. But from what? Or, from whom?

She pulled out her phone, swiping to the notepad. She needed to keep tabs on all of the strange activity and the dates she knew they occurred; grumpy lawyer wasn't wrong about the hard evidence part. She could start here. As she began to type, her phone buzzed with a text message. Some unknown number. She ignored it, proceeding to jot down everything she'd just witnessed.

She was in the process of trying to remember if she'd ever seen that big man before when her phone buzzed again with the same unknown number. She ignored it again.

But just as she decided to sneak back to the rug shop and see if she could see anything further, her phone buzzed with the same number again. Now she was curious. The day couldn't get any odder, she supposed. She swiped to read it.

**"Hey. Are you around?"** Read the first message.

For some reason, her scalp prickled, and she instinctively looked over her shoulder. No one was watching or following her. But what if that big leather guy had someone tailing her?

The next text read, **"I have something I'd like to run by you."**

Her heart beat faster. She felt cold and her teeth started to chatter. She knew she had to sit down. She plopped down on an empty bus stop bench.

The third text read, **"Hello? You there?"**

Gah! What should she do? She felt a clammy sweat start to break out on her forehead.

A new message buzzed in from the same unknown number. **"Are you purposefully ignoring me?"**

What? How could she ignore someone she didn't even know?

She quickly typed back, **"Wrong number,"** and barely experienced the briefest moment of relief when a response buzzed back immediately.

**"I can't believe you'd hold my behavior against me and over your own family's business. How I acted, though not great that night, had reasons, but solving your family's problems should come before your offended pride."**

*Wait, wait, wait.*

Was this who she thought it was?

*Uh, excusez-moi?*

She'd deleted his contact information after their disastrous meeting days ago.

Suddenly her heart rate picked up even faster, but not because she was scared. Quite the opposite.

*Cool it, Crazy,* she chided herself.

She had to answer. She crossed one leg over the other and

jiggled it in thought. Why was Aariv Abbas reaching out to her right now? And why *did* she feel like she had to answer?

**"Grumpenstein?"** She typed boldly, but then hesitated, hovering over the send button. She finally hit it. But what if it wasn't him? What if it was some eloquently spoken axe murderer who'd somehow found her number?

A terse message answered her worries. **"Who else would it be? And don't call me that."**

Oh crud. The guy was even more cranky over text. She smiled with delight; she couldn't help it.

*A*ariv wasn't into his usual Sunday afternoon pick-up basketball game. He'd received a message from Tag that he'd tried to get a hold of Chrissy but she'd never returned his calls. That didn't bother him so much. She'd already exhibited that she was impatient and prone to fantasizing. Why should he expect her to display any responsible behavior now? He would've shrugged it off if the investigator hadn't mentioned the possible involvement of the US-Russian mob clan, the *Shulaya*. He'd already dealt with an investigation like this before. Chrissy's scenario felt all too familiar with the exploitation of small Eastern European-owned businesses by threatening them with violence if they didn't comply with smuggling goods in and out of the country; anything ranging from cocaine to chocolate.

This was admittedly way bigger and much more dicey than he'd assumed. He had to hand it to Chrissy—her instinct was right on in thinking something shady was going on. So why wasn't she returning Tag's calls to help her? Had something happened to her? Great, now he was starting to let his mind run wild.

It was around this time, as all of these thoughts darted through his mind, that he missed a perfectly easy two-pointer that Zayn had laid out for him, causing his friend to kick him out of the game.

He sat on the benches by the court while the others continued playing and decided to text her. After shooting off his message, her response had been slower than he'd expected. She wasn't necessarily jumping at the chance to communicate with him. If he didn't know any better, he'd think she was purposefully ignoring him.

But after the initial back and forth, her smart-ass text was, **"And to what do I owe this charming line of communication?"**

Aariv grunted. Even over text, this girl got under his skin.

They say that texting is a difficult form of communication as one can misread the other's tone. He sure hoped that what he typed next would get through to her and that this was a no-pleasure convo.

**"Do you still not want free legal advice? I'd highly recommend it for your case, but if you're going to be stubborn about it, I can concentrate on those who want my help."**

**"More of your incredible advice. Aren't I the luckiest girl on the planet? BTW, I'm already acting on your guidance from last time."**

**"You returned Tag Underwood's calls?"**

**"????"**

**"My PI buddy. I gave him your contact information to get in touch with you. Have you finally returned his calls?"**

Dots formed and disappeared for a few seconds until she finally wrote back, "**I thought that was a joke. His name sounds fake. And so does his accent. Is he really from the South? I thought it was spam, or a crank call or something.**"

*What the fuck!?*

"**He's originally from Texas, and who the hell crank calls these days?**"

"**You obviously don't run in my circles.**"

"**OBVIOUSLY.**"

"**Besides, I have it all taken care of. I don't need to hire a detective. You've interrupted my first attempt at a stakeout.**"

Now he knew she must be crazy.

"**I hope that doesn't mean what I think it means ... as in you're trying to investigate on your own?**"

"**You think I can't do it by myself?**"

*Yep.*

"**I didn't say that. But I have a perfectly good investigator who will help you as a favor to me. No charge to you.**"

Those same dots formed and disappeared, now for longer than last time. By God had he done the impossible? Had he rendered her speechless? A grin started to spread across his lips.

"**Why would you do this?**"

"**Why would I try to make sure you had a legit investigator helping you? Oh, I don't know. Maybe because I'm a lawyer and it's my job to help those in need?**"

"**No. Why are you helping me, Smartypants?**"

And at this, Aariv couldn't help laughing outright. Honestly, he hadn't had this much fun texting pretty much ever, and at least she'd given him a nickname he could get behind.

As his fingers flew across the screen, now giving her Tag's information so she could call him back, the niggling thought tapped at him as to why he was being so pushy about this. She was an adult and could take care of herself and make her own decisions. So why was he so intent on following up here?

A shadow passed over him, blocking out the sun. A basketball bounced lazily in front of him, the staccato reverberating around the now-empty court.

"What's wrong with your face?" Zayn asked, continuing to bounce the ball.

Aariv looked up from his screen. "What?" he asked, momentarily confused after having just read Chrissy's last response, saying now she *did* owe him. He would have liked to have given her a smartass response back, no doubt she'd be expecting it, but he just signed off, asking her to reach out if she needed more help with anything.

*Did he just keep their line of communication open?*

"You're smiling. That's a rare occurrence," his friend drawled.

Aariv realized he *was* grinning and his mouth promptly fell as he said, "I'm just confirming something for a client." Not technically true, but his friend didn't need to know that.

"On a Sunday?" Zayn sighed. "Cuz, I don't know where I went wrong with you. You look like you just got a happy ending when it's work that has you all satisfied."

Aariv shook his head. There was no way he'd been smiling like *that* … had he?

"You're delusional," he grumbled.

Now Zayn spun the ball on his pointer finger, paddling it quickly with his other hand.

"Food?" he asked. They usually grabbed a bite after they finished their Sunday games.

"Can't. Have to review my list of brides from Huma."

"Sounds like a blast."

"Tell me about it. She's threatened me with VIP elite status on Dil Mil if I don't get on this."

Zayn started laughing. "Go, Huma Aunty. She may seem harmless, but under that sweet face is a killer shark."

"Don't mess with an Indian woman's process in her quest for the perfect daughter-in-law," Aariv said drily, shaking his head. "Shit could get lethal."

# TWO WEEKS LATER
## a hindu holi celebration
### IN NEW JERSEY

# CHAPTER 10

So

ariv looked around the expanse of plush green grass along the lawn of the manor. The colonial estate sat right on a cliff overlooking a shallow drop down to the sand and the water's edge where a cozy private beach was hidden. He stood at that edge, watching the seagulls dip between the spitting salt sprays from the churning grey Atlantic Ocean.

It was chilly that day, with the sky a hazy blue, but not too bad for the beginning of April. The weather finally lent some warmth into the air and the forecast showed no hint of spring showers. Their hostess thanked Lord Krishna above for such a worthy day to finally celebrate *Holi.* The Hindu Festival of Colors ushered in spring with a big party, food, music, and dancing. She'd had to reschedule her festitvies twice already due to cool and wet conditions.

He turned to look back at the sprawling manor, with slate grey tiles that extended along the pink brick of the house's length making up the wide back patio. It was a place he knew well, where many, many celebrations in their South Asian community had taken place. Priya Acharya—or Pinky Aunty as she was known—was the owner of the home and considered a pillar of their community. She hosted as many parties as she could, having the space and means to do so.

Today would no doubt be as spectacular as any of her other events. The place was already swarming with servers setting up food buffets and bars. The DJ's booth stood empty but was already wired up awaiting the master music maker she'd hired.

There were bubble machines ready to go, the perfect entertainment for the multitude of kids that would come with their parents. She'd had a cricket game set up on one part of the huge lawn, a few badminton nets put up on the other side, and the tennis courts hosted pickleball. The woman had thought of everything. With the white picnic blankets she'd had spread out on various sections of the lawn for people to sit and relax on, it almost felt Great Gatsby-ish.

Two lines of unlit tiki torches marched from the edge of the patio, along the greenery, and downward onto the path of gravel disappearing below. Aariv peered over the shallow ridge and saw that the torches continued to the beach, like a line of sentries leading right up to the water's edge. There were tables set up a good distance from the shore with bolsters in the sand indicating the festivities would move there later. No doubt for the traditional throwing of colored powder, which was the messy but fun part of the celebration unfolding in a literal explosion of colors. Aariv remembered past celebrations when people got extremely raucous as everyone was fair game to be "attacked" with color, even using water balloons and water guns to soak their targets first. He wondered what Pinky Aunty had in store for them later. He'd probably try to duck out earlier if he could, giving the excuse of work so he wouldn't have to partake in the unruliness. But only after he'd finished what he was there for.

Aariv looked back at the house again, at the DJ who'd finally arrived and began to set up his equipment. The last time Aariv had been here was that night months ago when he'd first met Chrissy, unaware of who she was. He distinctly remembered the push and pull of his emotions—not wanting to know her, and then craving to, more so than he could remember wanting something before. He would've never thought in his wildest dreams, that after he walked away, she would pop back into his life (and his mind) and continue to be present whether he desired it or not.

How ironic that he was here now to meet a handful of the top contenders in 'The List' (as Huma had deemed her master compilation of perfect women for Aariv), under the guise of reveling in the Spring festivities. Especially when another woman kept invading his thoughts, and this was where it had all started.

An image suddenly flashed before him, one that darted through, breaking his concentration frequently, randomly, at any given time, like right then. A luscious little body, naked—save for intentionally placed scraps of fabrics that left nothing to the imagination—moving sensually, hypnotically under neon lights and smoke. The eroticism of the way she looked all bound up in fabrics. The way her body practically thrummed while inside the tight bonds, her back arching, her eyes closed, her mouth open as if in ecstasy while the music washed over her, waiting for her escape—

"Aariv!"

The sound of his name made the erotic image vanish. A

smallish woman—the one who owned the voice and the home—made her way to him. Pinky Aunty was not only their hostess from a well-to-do Indian family with money of her own having amassed her elderly dead husband's fortune, but she was also a well-known matchmaker. She'd never remarried and had finally settled, in her older age, after much soul searching and traveling the globe (all the while spending her husband's money) on a career in creating successful marriages. It was hard work, she proclaimed, but she loved it and had a knack for it, considering the recent list of marriages she'd brokered on her resume.

She was his liaison that day. Huma Aunty had come up with the bright idea for her stepson to meet and greet prospective marriage material, as there were a few contenders from the 'The List' who were part of their South Asian community and were also party guests. So, she'd called Pinky directly and had it all arranged. Aariv had a sneaky feeling it was also to keep an eye on him, making sure he was doing what he was supposed to do.

"*Beta*!" she called, her accent an elegant mix of hoity-toity, English, and Indian. "Finally. I asked you to come an hour early to discuss everything."

Aariv refrained from rolling his eyes and opted for shrugging his shoulders. "I had work over the weekend." He did. The Turner & Turner case at work required extra hours from everyone.

She approached him brushing off invisible specks of dust from his tan sports coat. Then she straightened the lapels of his jacket.

"You big lawyers. Always work, work, work." She elegantly bobbed her head, but she didn't sound upset. Rather she sounded extremely happy about that. "You aren't wearing white." She frowned, noting his non-Indian outfit of a pale blue button-down oxford under his tan sports coat and jeans.

"Dry cleaners weren't open this weekend," he said, shrugging again. As if he had time to uphold the dress code for a cultural event that he hadn't even attended in years.

She gave him a suspicious look before she smoothed her features over, letting her head bob as if to say she was letting that go, while she gave him a once over. "Never mind," she said brightly. "You look handsome. Perfect to meet some excellent women."

Aariv tried to mask his irritation, but he grunted nonetheless, grimacing rather than smiling. All of this talk about marriage was driving him batshit crazy, and going at a pace he wasn't ready for. Here he was on a Sunday, missing his weekly basketball game, partaking in a *Bachelor*-like scenario. His mind was so far from it that he felt like he was watching a reality television show unfold before him. He wouldn't be surprised if Pinky had a rose ceremony at the end of the night, forcing him to pick his favorite.

She reached up and tried to button the top three buttons of his shirt. He stepped back.

"Please don't, Pinky Aunty," he said stiffly. All of this manhandling from her was making him feel like a prized bull.

"*Atcha* (ok)," she said, jiggling her head side to side, brushing it off, and continuing to speak.

She was in the process of giving him a breakdown of who he was meeting and their biodata highlights when a figure appeared from the house. She half-ran and half-walked to them, crossing the wide patio and the expanse of the lawn, an all-business swish to the clingy ivory wrap dress she wore.

His eyes were riveted on her; he couldn't help it because whenever this woman was in his vicinity, she was all he could see; all he could think about. Pinky's words sounded more like an annoying mosquito buzzing in his ear as he focused on the woman approaching them. The way the breeze picked up her reddish strands making them dance around her face. The color of her curved cheeks heightened in the wind as she juggled her clipboard and iPad under her arm while tucking her hair behind her ears.

He sensed that the older woman knew he wasn't listening because she stopped talking and glanced over to see what had caught his attention. Now they both watched Chrissy approach them, hurried and out of breath, all self-conscious smiles, her eyes focused on her clipboard. Did the older woman know his gaze was fixated on the perfect rounded globes of the younger woman's tits as they bounced deliciously in response to the bounce in her step? As she came closer, he noticed that her nipples were delectably hardened like they always seemed to be and he licked his lips involuntarily. Her hips swayed side to side and had no right looking so sexy in the knee-length skirt of her dress.

What was she doing here, he thought? Why was she always where he was, distracting him? But he couldn't help feeling some of his irritation slip away as she finally stopped in front of them and noticed him.

Her eyes widened into deep cerulean orbs, but a grin spread across her face, her cute dimples on display. Then she laughed huskily in surprise. He felt himself smiling, relaxing in reaction.

"Oh! It's you … *again*," she teased breathlessly.

Aariv felt his blood thump in his ears and was sure his libido had woken up from the snooze it thought it was going to take during what he assumed would be an uneventful afternoon.

"Hey," he said, upbeat for the first time that day. "How've you been?"

She focused on his chin, her cheeks reddening even more. She slowly batted her eyes and licked her pink full lips.

"I'm great." Her sparkling eyes met his. "You?" she said demurely, glancing hesitantly at Pinky, whose stare darted sharply between them, a suspicious cast to her face.

"Do you two know each other?" The older woman cut in, though the answer was obvious.

Aariv stopped himself from rolling his eyes, instead looking at a flock of extremely loud seagulls coming dangerously close to the buffet table on the patio. The silver chaffing dishes were already laid out with food, but thankfully their covers were on. The servers shooed them away haphazardly with arms waving.

He grunted, about to come up with some inane answer when Chrissy spoke.

"We do," she said. "You know I work for Simran—the reason I'm here, of course—but through her I met Mariam Abbas, Aariv's cousin—"

"I know who Mariam is," Pinky said abruptly, a slight curl to her upper lip.

"Oh, right. So I have this problem—a financial problem with my family's business that I went to Aariv for. I needed some legal advice…"

As Chrissy explained the nature of their acquaintance to Pinky, Aariv's mind wandered back to when he'd last seen her; the fact that they kept running into each other, and how every time made him fall a little more under her spell. Knowing enough about Chrissy's personality now, she probably had no idea how much time he spent thinking about her, what she did to him, and how often his hand was on his cock as he imagined being with her. Part of him wondered why this kept happening and the other part wondered why he was fighting this feeling so much.

ONE WEEK AGO
new york, new york

## CHAPTER 11

$$\backsim\backsim$$

ariv sat at the bar of a nondescript entertainment club. He fingered his beer bottle, idly tearing the label off as he looked around the joint.

He swiveled on his bar stool to check out the place. Why had he let himself be talked into ending up there that night, he wondered, as he searched for his cousin and her friends.

There was a stage at the far end of the tired-looking black and purple velvet-covered room. It was everywhere—the velvet —from the tufted walls in a checkered pattern to the black and purple velvet cushioned chairs at the cocktail tables surrounding the space. And every one of them was surprisingly full with people watching the act that was currently on stage in rapt attention.

A night out, he thought, echoing his cousin from their conversation earlier that day. He just needed to relax and enjoy a night out. It had been too long.

## EARLIER THAT DAY

They were just finishing a quick lunch together at a favored bistro in midtown. Mariam waved her hand to the waiter for the check and the sparkling blue on her finger caught his eye.

"He finally put a ring on it, I see." He grabbed her hand to take a better look at her engagement ring. Just like Mariam not to flaunt it, he mused. A rich blue sapphire sat between two diamonds on her ring finger. He couldn't help but think that the color was similar to a pair of eyes he'd been trying not to think about since seeing the titillating person they belonged to a week ago in his office. "Wow, Mimi. You'd think it'd be bigger given he's a lord and shit," Aariv teased. It was a nice size and understated, not too flashy, just like his cousin's style.

"Shut up," Mariam quipped, pulling her hand away. But her face pinkened and she smiled glancing at her ring. "It was a family heirloom." She sighed. "Isn't that just so…" She paused, and took a deep breath, her eyes … dreamy.

Aariv scoffed. Seeing his usually cool and confidently collected cousin in love was kind of strange. She became all wistful and soft … and more emotional than he was used to with her.

"Second hand? Not very original? You're definitely a keeper?" he offered.

"Romantic, Aari. Sheesh," she said, her lip curling up.

"Ah." He nodded chuckling. "That was my next guess."

He whipped out his credit card as soon as the bill arrived. She slapped her hand over his on the table. This was their thing —fighting over who paid for meals.

"Don't even think about it, Mimi. Huma Aunty thinks I need to be more gracious if I'm going to find my bride."

Mariam scowled and lifted her hand off of his.

"That's ridiculous and you know it. You're a great guy as is. Any of those women on that list would be happy to marry you."

They remained quiet as he signed the credit card slip and he waited, aware of what was coming.

"So … this list—" She paused with hesitation, perhaps testing the waters.

"Go ahead," he said, taking a sip of his coffee, and waiting patiently for her opinion.

"It's ridiculous, too."

"Tell me why you think it's so ridiculous. I'm a grown man in need of a wife, aren't I? And I'm shit at finding 'the one.'" He air-quoted.

Mariam snorted. "Well you'll find one—as in a bride, but I don't think she'll be 'the one.'" She fiddled with her ring. "And you know what? You don't even try, Aari. You're all about short-term relationships. When things get too serious you break it off. I can't remember the last time I met one of your girlfriends." She stopped to think. "Oh wait, that one time when you forgot I was coming over with bagels and some Georgia, or Genevieve came to the door in just your *genji* (undershirt)." Mariam started chuckling, noticing how uncomfortable he was, shifting in his chair.

"It was Gina," he said curtly, looking away to adjust his watch and the red rope of his *rakhi* bracelet.

"She was sweet, and pretty. What happened to her?"

Aariv let out a strangled grunt and grumbled, "She wanted me to meet her parents."

Mariam's brows shot up. "See! You can't get close to anyone."

"What's your point, Mimi? You're only proving that I need help in finding a wife."

"But then what? Will you lead a cordial life … like your stepmom and dad?" She asked this last part quietly. "That can't be what you're meant for. You're a good guy. And that kind of life…" She trailed off, folding and unfolding her napkin.

"Sucks?" He filled in.

"Yeah." She agreed.

"Mimi, I'm not meant for romance and ooey-gooey nonsense."

Mariam made a face, scrunching up her features. "You make love sound so childish. It's not, you know. It only makes you stronger in life." When he didn't answer she went on. "There was a time you didn't think love was 'ooey-gooey nonsense.'" She air quoted.

The fact that she was boldly bringing up his first and only love, Leila, whom he never spoke about, indicated she meant business.

"I was an actual child then, so it doesn't count."

"You were eighteen—"

"A child."

"But you felt it. You would've run away to the ends of the earth with her."

"Except that I was a dumb teenager who thought our love could overcome her strict Muslim family's rules. That they would be fine with her marrying a boy from a Hindu family."

He swallowed hard, that moment etched into his memory

when he realized that duty to one's family—the responsibility to uphold the family reputation—was a stronghold that couldn't be broached, no matter the force of love and commitment.

What had happened was something he would never forgive himself for. He'd fallen for Leila Majid, a quiet girl in his class during his last year of secondary school. She was nice to everyone, but her light brown eyes lit up whenever they were in the same group for class projects. She had a gentle nature but was extremely smart and something about her made him fall for her.

They started seeing each other outside of school when they knew they would be somewhere with a group of the same friends—at the local snack shop after school or kicking the soccer ball around at the park. But the two of them would go somewhere quiet and just talk. What the topics were, he couldn't remember exactly, but they ranged from everything about the school's cricket team to family life to future dreams. They both wanted to leave India and go either to the US or England. He didn't know what he wanted to do but she knew she wanted to be a nurse.

Slowly, as they continued to see one another like this, their talks became bolder, as did their actions. They spoke about a future with each other as they kissed and embraced, and Aariv remembered falling hard. He was only eighteen but she was his future, he was certain of it. They started sneaking out of their homes to be together.

But they hadn't counted on her family being extremely prying, and they both should've known better. She was the eldest daughter in a very traditional Muslim home. They no doubt already had plans for her that weren't her own. Her sneaking off wasn't something they could afford to turn a blind eye to. Her reputation was on the line, as was their family honor.

They'd gone to the movies one afternoon. He'd convinced her to skip classes. He was so high on love, so on top of the world, that he took that chance. He'd also had the encouragement of his new best friend, Zayn, who was the American exchange student living in his house for the past year. His friend's positivity, Americanism, and ideals were rubbing off on him, and he believed anything was possible.

The matinee was some old Bollywood film that was running during off hours. He bought their tickets and had a bag of her favorite Indian snacks with him. When she ducked out of the *tuk-tuk* (bike taxi), her look of apprehension transformed into a smile when she saw him. But it quickly turned into fear as two men emerged from behind him and rushed at her. One of them pulled her by her headscarf, nearly ripping it from her hair, and the other turned to him, threatening him to stay away from good Muslim girls, before punching him in the gut. From the ground, wheezing for breath, he watched as they hauled her into the backseat of a car that had been idling on the curb which he hadn't noticed. They drove off, and he never heard from Leila Majid again.

Talk around the school was that she'd been sent off to marry an older distant cousin somewhere in the Middle East who was possibly mean and abusive. Her life looked nothing like what they had discussed together.

Aariv never forgave himself. His silly and naïve actions had pushed a sweet and gentle person to a future she never wanted. He could only assume that she was living her life in a miserable way now. He'd been sent away to America to manage the care of his grandmother during the height of the gossip. And that was that.

"I know you think you don't deserve love in your life, but you do, Aari," Mariam continued, grabbing his hand, and squeezing. "Sheesh," she said when he pulled his hand away. "You're so tense, *Biya*. How long has it been since you went out and had a good time?"

He looked at her skeptically. Was she really asking him about the last time he'd screwed a woman?

Mariam snorted. "Not like that. I mean, honestly, sex *does* help, but I mean just be out with friends and have a few beers."

Aariv sat back in his chair and thought about it. "There were a few work functions," he said, trying to recall. "And that time Z and I went to Atlantic City a few months ago … wait, when was that?"

"Oh my God, if you have to think about it, it's been way too long. You're coming out with me and my friends tonight."

He smirked, telling her to leave it. But she insisted and he decided what the hell. If he was being really honest with himself, he did need a night out. Zayn, his usual going-out buddy, was busy managing catering for a huge medical conference coming up at Rockefeller Center and they hadn't been able to sync up their schedules to hang out.

So, he agreed just as it occurred to him that he might see Chrissy that evening and he felt a spark of something deep in his chest. Was it anticipation? He wasn't sure, but it didn't feel like irritation. He decided it had to do with his curiosity about how it was going with Tag and her investigation.

"Will *all* of your friends be there?" he asked nonchalantly as they left the restaurant.

"I think so, why?" she asked as she started walking toward the subway.

"Just curious." He shrugged his shoulders and stuffed his hands in his suit pants pockets.

"Don't worry. There'll be plenty of other people there so you won't have to talk to Chrissy. I know you think she's annoying," Mariam said over her shoulder.

"Great." Relief was evident in his tone. But was it because he would get to see her, or that he wouldn't be alone with her? He couldn't tell.

So, here he was, at some mediocre nightclub that turned into a strip club later, meeting Mariam and her friends. It was a last-minute change in location due to everyone's availability, but, it made no difference to him. He didn't need somewhere fancy to let loose, and he wasn't trying to score chicks. He was just there to let off some steam. He *had* been stressed lately, and it wasn't work that was the only contributing factor. *That* he knew how to handle. It was an overarching feeling of dread whenever he saw Huma Aunty's name scroll across his screen when his phone buzzed. Under the guise of checking up on him, their conversation inevitably turned to finding out where his head was with The List. He knew he couldn't deflect her for long, but he just wasn't into it. He tried to view it like a mundane work task, something that had to get done, but he always got sidetracked when he opened the files. It was like he had some phobia.

*Shit.*

Did he have a phobia of marriage? He might.

He needed to not think about that tonight so he got comfortable with his back up against the glossy bar's counter, and focused on the performance currently on stage. A scantily clad woman was performing unexceptional magic tricks up there. She kept messing up; at that moment a white rabbit leaped up from its hiding place rather than the top hat on her head. She laughed and guffawed with the audience and Aariv realized that this was her skill—messing up the tricks on purpose but in a charming, even sexy, and entertaining way. He, like the rest of the audience, chuckled with her and clapped and finally gave a hearty round of applause when she finished. When her tip jar came around, he was more than happy to throw a twenty in.

As the lights came up, he caught his cousin Mariam's eye at one of the crowded tables with her friends. She lifted her hand and waved, urging him to come join them. There was no way he was going to jam himself into that small table with three other people so he shook his head and indicated he would stay where he was.

He turned back around to the bartender to order another beer, but not before he took in that Chrissy wasn't sitting at the table. She'd mentioned more people joining them later when she'd texted the location change from a dive bar to the club. Maybe Chrissy was one of those late shows.

Relief again washed over him. Now he knew he didn't want to see her. Any interaction with her would only mount his attraction for her. But he did glance at his watch. It was just a little after ten at night. Would it be weird if he texted her right then, just to find out how things were shaping up with the investigation?

He pulled at the beer set before him and took his phone out of his pocket, finding their last conversation.

**"Well now I owe you, don't I?"** Had been her last text. He pondered it briefly. Had she meant it as cheeky or was she being serious?

The dirty thought came to mind that he wouldn't be opposed to her doing things he'd only imagined with her, in return for his help.

*Bad Aariv.*

**"How are things going with the PI?"** He quickly typed, then put his phone back in his pocket, turning back around.

He caught his cousin's questioning eyes and he raised his beer to her, grinning. She smiled back and turned to the stage just as the lights dimmed, satisfied that he was ok alone at the bar.

"Please welcome to the stage, our Star of Xtasy!" A voice announced over the speakers as smoke plumed from the stage and laser beams cris-crossed overhead in a fantastical light show.

How fucking cheesy, Aariv mused, as he pulled on his beer.

He focused on the stage as long white curtains lowered down through the smoke and bursts of bright lights, so that one end brushed the floor, while the other remained attached somewhere above. A large swing framed by the two swaths of fabric lowered, too, stopping at least fifteen feet above the ground.

On that swing sat a figure. Her back faced the audience, her arms spread wide to grasp the chains that held her seat up.

She had glossy fire-engine red hair, the long strands falling around her shoulders in a half-up and half-down style, and trailing down her back. As the lights hit her, illuminating her figure, she started to sway side to side in tempo to the upbeat music blaring on the sound system.

"Do you ever feel, like a plastic bag..." The familiar words sang, as *Firework*, an older Katy Perry song, played.

Yelps and whistles came from the audience and they were coming from Mariam's table. Did they know the performer?

The woman stood up, continuing to sway, undulating her hips side to side sensually. Her costume appeared nonexistent. She looked naked except for thin swaths of white fabric studded with red iridescent sparkles that crisscrossed her entire body, barely covering her ass crack in the back. The fabric climbed up one arm like a candy cane and the opposite leg in the same fashion. He curiously waited for her to turn around to see how revealing her outfit was in the front. But she continued to dance with her back turned, gliding artistically from one dance pose to another. She was talented, that was for sure, and Aariv bopped his head to the upbeat music. Then she moved her torso, fluidly sliding it side to side, and the movement struck him as familiar.

Come to think of it, her ass, so firm, like two peach halves just shy of being fully ripened, taunting the audience seemed familiar. The perfect heart shape with a strip of sparkly material down the center between her cheeks shook as her body rolled. All of a sudden, she swiveled on the ball of her foot to face the audience, just as Katy Perry sang "You just gotta ignite the light, and let it shine..."

Combined with the shot of eagerness humming through his veins, the surprise he felt at seeing her face beneath the fire engine red wig, under a layer of shimmery make-up, with a huge cat-like grin, was enough for him to slip off of his bar stool. It was Chrissy Smyth, in all of her glorious-almost-nakedness, mouthing the words cheekily to the song as she pushed the swing forward and backward with the weight of her body. The slight movement continued to gradually increase until she was fully swinging like a child free-flying high on a playground while standing on the swing.

The incredible physique of her body—the sexy curves and dips—was tauntingly on display but with the crucial parts behind the glittery slashes of white on her costume. He could make out the exact shape of her breasts, with just her nipples covered. He followed the movements of her body, along the flexing of her ab muscles, down over her belly button and slight belly, across her curvy hips, straight to the hint of lines that led to a swath of barely-there material covering the apex at her thighs.

*Jesus.* He swallowed hard, as the familiar lust for this woman came up fiercely, and he felt the crotch of his pants tighten as he continued to watch her moving sensually with fascination. Her tight, hot body was doing things a normal human body couldn't do. He was vaguely aware of the catcalls from over-enthusiastic males in the audience which made him clench his teeth in irritation. He shook off the feeling. She was up there for the sole purpose of performing and wearing a costume like that would only garner that kind of attention.

She reached for one long curtain with a foot and wrapped it snuggly around her ankle. Then she looped her opposite arm around the other curtain and wrapped it around tight. Just as the words boomed over the sound system, "Cause, baby, you're a firework, Come on show 'em what you're worth." She launched off the swing, like an explosive firework herself. Aariv's breath caught as she hovered midair for the briefest millisecond but then kicked her free leg up and caught it in the fabric around her arm, catching herself before she completely fell to the stage.

The audience gasped and clapped, as Aariv watched motionless, completely taken aback by what he was witnessing. There was no other word for it. He was entranced, his eyes following her around as she danced, binding herself up teasingly and unwrapping the material sultrily. Her allusion to sex and bondage was clear.

Part of Aariv fumed. Did she not know that everyone with an appetite for kinky sex would imagine her for days on end like this? Completely tied up and maybe at the whim of said imaginer? The other part of him let himself *be* that imaginer, letting his thoughts run wild with kinky Chrissy.

# CHAPTER 12

She loved being where she was, loved being on stage performing, acting like someone else. For four glorious minutes that night, she could forget who she was and be a person with no problems—not a care in the world. The thought made her laugh aloud before launching completely off the swing. The thrill of falling made her breath hitch as her stomach bottomed out before she sucked in her ab muscles tightly, hardening her core. She caught herself in the strategically wrapped fabric around her legs and arms.

The audience hooted and clapped in appraisal making her smile so large that it made her cheeks ache. Her heart soared with joy, and she pushed and pulled her body up, wriggling and adjusting her legs until they were widened into the full splits. The whistles and claps continued, even over the speakers and she could barely hear the music but knew the beat and the transitions of the steps by heart; dance was second nature to her.

When she pulled her grasp on the silks tighter, pulling her legs up and even above the splits, a deep, loud hoot emanated from the direction of the bar. As she swung her body forward and backward, she lowered her back leg down so that she was in a classic arabesque pose, like a prima ballerina, her energy shooting from each limb as she hung in the air.

She felt beautiful in that moment—like Princess Aurora dancing happily with her prince in Act III of Sleeping Beauty, wearing a pretty and wispy pink tutu. Not at all like the sexualized 'class act' she was at an average strip club, with jewels and scraps of fabric barely covering her privates. Whatever, she still felt beautiful.

But then someone toward the front of the audience yelled, "Take it off!" and she remembered where she was. She rolled her eyes and displayed a saccharine sweet smile before artistically giving the finger aimed in the direction of the Neanderthal in the front row. People laughed and roared with delight. This was part of her charm—sassy and classy.

Now she maneuvered through various movements and choreography until she began to winch the material around her ankles and wrists, shimmying her way up to the very top of the two curtains for her final trick. Higher and higher she went, darting flirty glances at the audience, daring them to guess what she was up to next. She saw the whites of teeth in opened mouths, and the whites of eyes widened in horror and anticipation as she paused, cinched, and wrapped up in the silky fabrics, like a bound-up butterfly in its chrysalis, waiting for the right moment to burst forth.

Right when the final lines of the song blared, "Boom boom boom, Even brighter than the moon moon moon," Chrissy let herself go like a butterfly finally emerging and flying free. She tumbled and fell along the length of the material, all the while hearing gasps and cries from those watching. She felt the material tug at the last minute on her left thigh while she landed face first, her nose mere inches from the stage floor. In this position, she bowed her body slightly, appearing like a diver caught in a photo just before hitting the water's surface.

Sweat beaded on her forehead and slid down to tiny splotches on the stage as she held that final pose, catching her breath. A laugh escaped her as the audience applauded thunderously, and her heart pounded faster and louder so that it was all she could hear now.

Finally, with as much grace as she could muster, she undid the last binding and flipped to standing, her tired arms tremoring slightly in the air as she took a bow. She quickly ran off stage as the props needed changing for the next act.

She high-fived other performers as she made her way backstage. She went to the dressing room and grabbed her silky floral pink wrap, tying it around her skimpy-covered body, and jammed her feet into her Ugg boots. She had another performance in an hour but wanted to go out to see Mariam and the others.

Her heart still beating a loud staccato to the Katy Perry song, she made her way out front. To say that she loved that song would be an understatement. Ever since she'd been a young teenager taking her first non-ballet class, she'd been obsessed with it. They'd performed a jazz and lyrical piece to the same music and she always felt like that song's lyrics spoke to her. She remembered her teacher had been impressed with her natural performance quality and her agility to take on other dance forms quickly, too. It had always stuck with her and fueled her confidence because initially, he'd insultingly labeled her a 'Betsy bun-head'—a dancer with no other skills but ballet. People tended to underestimate her, and she loved to prove them wrong.

She half skipped and half ran to the front area, eager to see her friends. The plan had been to go out that night and chill at one of their regular dive bars, but last minute, Darius added her to the performance schedule. She couldn't refuse the extra cash and begged them to come watch her instead, offering them a round of free drinks on the house.

She went to the bar to wait for them, as the next performance was about to begin with the lights dimming and Turkish-themed music blasting through the speakers. It was pretty empty where she stood, except for a few patrons on the other side of the bar closer to the stage, and a lone beer bottle sitting idly at the spot next to her. But the audience was completely packed and that's all she cared about.

She leaned into the bar and asked the bartender for a Sprite with lots of ice. She was just taking a long sip of the bubbly lemon-lime drink when someone sat next to her, grabbing the beer bottle that had been sitting there.

Her first thought was, "Damn, whoever that is smells amazeballs," and she tried to get a better look from her peripheral.

But then the person leaned in and spoke in a familiar deep, gruff voice. "Nice performance up there, Star of Xtasy. Where'd you learn to do all that?"

She whirled to see none other than Aariv Abbas, in the absolute hunky flesh, not in a suit, sitting next to her. His half grin was so sexy that she wasn't sure if it was the shock at seeing him or the fact that he looked so scorchingly hot that made the bubbles of her soda go up her nose.

The stinging in her nostrils made her eyes water and she choked, coughing.

"Whoops," he said, gently patting her on the back, then

rubbing her in small circles, the warmth of his palm penetrating through the thin material of her robe and the nude mesh of her costume. He left his hand there even after she gained some control and could breathe again. She wiped the tears from her eyes, hoping she wasn't smudging her red glitter makeup too badly.

"You ok?" he asked. She nodded and he removed his hand, leaving a big, Aariv-shaped hand print of warmth lingering on her back.

She glanced at him briefly and noticed how bright hazel his eyes were. They more than stared at her; they penetrated her; speared her, a lion on the prowl. She wasn't at all prepared for him to be here, let alone out there in the audience. Not prepared to feel so vulnerable dancing in a sleazy nightclub, despite what her fantasies had been involving him.

She shook her shoulders slightly and tossed the bright red locks of her wig over a shoulder, composing herself to face Grumpenhunk because aside from ALL the questions that whizzed through her addled brain—why was he here, did he like her performance, did he think she was disgusting because she danced at a strip club, *why* the hell was he here, was he going to be Dr. Jekyll or Mr. Hyde? She'd experienced both sides of him but could never tell which mood he was going to be in. And honestly, their last text exchange when he'd urged her to call his PI friend (she still couldn't believe he'd gone out of his way to do that) had ended with her being flirtier than she'd intended to. She couldn't help it and had no idea why she'd left it as a her-owing-him kind of scenario, but in a way, she wanted to. She didn't want their communication to end there. Because even though he ran hot and cold, she wanted to keep talking to him. But then he'd signed off so abruptly and she wasn't even surprised, just thought, "Here we go again."

She took a deep breath and faced him. She took in the long-sleeve army green waffle knit shirt he wore, the top three buttons undone showing black fuzzy chest hair. His sleeves were pushed up to his elbows with black arm hair dusting up the bronze skin of his thick forearms. She licked her lips because never had a generic article of clothing looked so good on a man. The breadth of his shoulders appeared wider, and she could make out the hard bumps and ridges of his arm muscles flexing slightly as he pushed his beer bottle back and forth between his hands. Not able to stop taking him in, her eyes glided down over his jeans and casual, rugged brown ankle boots. How was it possible for someone to be even hotter in everyday clothes versus smart slick suits?

Now she felt a little silly, realizing she was still in her uber-revealing costume and wearing her red wig. She shook it off.

"What?" she asked, forgetting already what he'd said only about twenty seconds ago.

"I said." The other side of his mouth lifted, and he wore the most beautiful smile, his white teeth flashing, his fiery eyes bright with laughter. "Nice performance." He lifted the beer bottle to his lips and asked before taking a drink, "Where did you learn to dance like that?"

His eyes were on her as he drank and waited for her to answer. She fidgeted under his stare—more like a scrutiny as he looked at her closely, his gaze taking in her hair, and moving down the length of her body. She shivered because if she wasn't mistaken, that look was appraisal.

"Thanks," she said taking a sip before answering. "I trained to be a dancer as soon as I took my first steps."

He put his beer down. "Really?" he asked, one brow arched high, skeptical.

"Basically," she said. Then she took a deep breath as she toyed with her straw and launched into a shortened version of the dance history she'd lived in the past twenty-eight years of her life, explaining her mother's dream for her daughter to become a prima ballerina. Ballet dancers were revered in Russia. The arts were, and still are, government-funded and thus once one became a dancer, one may not become rich, but was set for life. And though she'd moved to the US with her daughter, she still wanted the accolade of being the mother of a star in the coveted ballet world.

"Wow," he said, looking at her curiously, his brow furrowed. "So what happened?"

"I followed my own dreams," she said, smiling, then frowned. "Not this, of course." She waved her hand around at the club. "But events planning. It excited me because it meant going to parties all the time. And young me thought that it was going to be a lot of fun and glamorous." She laughed bashfully. "And now, the not-so-young me realizes it's way more work than getting to go to parties, but I like it, and I like who I work with." She shrugged. "This," now she gestured down her body, "is about using a talent I have to make ends meet. Can't get more New York than that!" She wasn't ashamed of having to dance for extra money—people in this town did what they had to do to get by, but she still felt disarmed and she waited to see what he would say. Would he be a Judge Judy like before?

She saw him pause thinking about her answer. She was completely aware that maybe she'd done the classic Chrissy overshare, but she got more chatty than normal when she was nervous, excited, or both. It was an actual condition called logorrhea; she'd looked it up once.

Aariv finally nodded. "That's pretty cool. You know, that you had enough gumption to follow your dreams." But then he looked around the club, his thick lips quirked in thought.

"I know what you're going to ask—why am I here in a sleazy club like this?"

His eyes darted back to hers. "I'd hardly call what you did up there sleazy." He nodded as she squinted her eyes, not believing him. "Seriously. What you did up there—that requires major skill, and the audience was into it."

She swallowed, daring not to look at him before asking, "Were you … into it, too?"

When he didn't answer, she side-eyed him and caught his nod, while he licked his lips, his eyes raking over her again. Her nipples pebbled up in reaction and pushed painfully against her clothes. That was utter and raw hunger … and it was for her? And now it felt like she left her stomach up on stage, as it flipped and dipped in continuous circles.

"So you're doing this to supplement your income because of the financial drain of the rug store."

She nodded. "I originally came in for a bartending gig but saw the sign for performers wanted." She shrugged. "I already knew I could perform, and had been taking aerial yoga classes, recently. I thought, what the hell and came up with a piece and auditioned." She looked around the club at the peeling black paint on the ceilings, and the tired velvet on the walls. "It's not ideal, but at least I don't have to strip in the VIP room." She shook her head. "My boss wants me in there, but that's a hard pass for me, no matter how great the money is."

He was silent for a while, and she wondered if she'd said too much. She switched gears by asking, "So, what, are you stalking me now? I know, I'll bet you're trying to make sure I don't do any more sleuthing, even though it *is* my case."

He burst into deep chuckles and she hadn't heard something so beautiful to her ears in forever. It was low and rough, and damn if it didn't make her want to hop into his lap and snuggle into his chest. Would it feel as soothing as it sounded? She laughed, too, at ease with his far-from grumpy behavior.

He cupped his chin, rubbing his palm over his beard while she leaned against the bar comfortably. His eyes stayed a little too long on her ass, and she almost wanted to shake it to see what he would do.

Clearing his throat, he sat up straighter, grabbing his beer and chugging it. He placed it down too hard on the bar and signaled the bartender for another. She hid her smile, a part of her squealing in delight that she could make the somber and serious Aariv behave out of sorts.

Her hands gripped the edge of the bar and she pulled her arms back straight, leaning back so her breasts were on display.

"So what brings you here, Mr. Abbas?" she asked, with mock seriousness.

His eyes were glued to her chest, and she arched her back slightly to make her breasts puff out.

*W*as she doing it on purpose—trying to make him lose control? She had to know what she was doing with that hot little body of hers barely concealed in the robe over her costume. And now, her robe dipped open and he couldn't help but seek out all the cleavage on view—the top *and* bottom of her breasts. He remembered all too clearly the hint of an ass cleft, leading to the juicy round peach-like cheeks of her ass.

His pulse hammered and his hands itched to cup her curves and pull and squeeze that flesh. He wanted to run his hands through the sexy bright red of her wig and hold her in position so he could worship with his mouth everything she'd had on display and what little wasn't. If she were any other woman, he'd suggest they go somewhere alone—a closet, or a dark corridor just for ten, maybe fifteen minutes so he could put his hands all over her while his dick plunged into her. Fuck how was he supposed to fight this? Their attraction sat between them, watching their casual tete-tete in humor, waiting for the other shoe to drop.

But she wasn't just any woman and he had to tear his gaze away. He pushed his desire down and became Aariv Abbas—attorney-at-law.

"How's it going with Tag Underwood?"

"Oh my God, Aariv. He's awesome! Thank you for putting me in touch with him." She leaned in and grabbed his arm, squeezing, bouncing on the balls of her feet, and he smelled her sexy scent—the fruity and botanical one mixed with the salty mustiness of sweat. It was a fragrance he wouldn't mind inhaling all night if given the chance and he closed his eyes briefly as she chattered away happily about how great his PI friend was, how far along they were getting.

"...can you believe it?!" she asked incredulously, still standing so close to him. "The *Russian-freakin'-mafia*! I thought the NYPD cleared those fools out years ago."

He opened his eyes and pulled away slightly. He needed to pay closer attention to what she was saying.

"Right. Tag had mentioned that briefly when I described your dilemma."

Her big blue eyes were wide and there was not an ounce of fear in the shining depths, only excitement.

"Chrissy," he said sternly. "Let Tag do his job. He doesn't need a sidekick. It's for your own safety."

"But—how do you know I was even thinking that?" She pouted, her full lips turned down adorably.

At that moment Mariam arrived with her friends, interrupting them. And thank fuck they had because Chrissy was tempting as is, but pouting made him want to bend her over his knees and spank her for her irrational thoughts.

"I always know what you're thinking, Chrissy," he said before the others were in earshot. "Don't misbehave or I'll have to punish you." He hadn't meant for it to sound so bossy, but damn if she needed a little scolding.

Her eyes got even bigger if that was possible, and her mouth fell open as she stared at him dumbfounded. And holy Christ, had he just said that? He needed to stop with the beers. He pushed his half-drunken bottle away, reaching for his wallet to close his tab out.

"Leaving so soon?" Mariam asked as she approached them, her eyes darting warily between them. "Sorry for the last-minute change in plans, Aari. Our little Chris here," she put her arm around the smaller woman, "had a last-minute performance and we had to be here to cheer her on."

"Not a problem," he said, placing a wad of cash on the bar. "This was great. Best time I've had in a while."

"You're not staying?" One of the others in the group, a

woman with an afro asked. He'd been introduced to her at the wedding, but couldn't remember her name. "Shana," she offered, sticking her hand out. "Nice to see you again."

"Same," he said, shaking her hand. "Yeah, early morning at the office again. The law waits for no one, not even for much-needed sleep on the weekends."

"Boo, that sucks." The slight skinny man standing behind Shana commented. Aariv remembered him as Antoine.

He shrugged his shoulders in an I-have-no-choice-in-the-matter way as Chrissy came to his defense.

"He's a busy lawyer, Antoine. They have a shit ton to do all the time, right?" she said looking up at him. Her deep blue eyes were almost black as they bore into him boldly, but she sucked her full bottom lip into her mouth, shy all of a sudden. It was that mixture of sexy and girlish that always seemed to confound him, making him want her more. "Maybe I'll see you around here again … since you liked the performance so much," she said cheekily, her lashes fluttering slowly against her cheeks.

Aariv felt his neck heat up as all eyes landed on him expectantly.

"You liked it?" Mariam asked surprised.

Did they think he was a stick in the mud?

"What was there not to like? Great looking girl, incredible dance skills." Not to mention she essentially exuded sex up there. He'd been extremely turned on as well as impressed.

Chrissy beamed from ear to ear and he couldn't help grinning in return before he said his goodbyes.

When he got home, he let his dirty imagination run wild. He imagined peeling that costume off of her and staring at her naked body with nothing obstructing his view. He rubbed his cock in the shower as he pictured bending her over and spanking that perfect heart-shaped ass until it was as red as the bright wig she'd worn. He rubbed himself with more frenzy, using both hands as he pictured fucking her from behind, taking what he wanted, commanding her body. He bet her pussy was sweet and tight. The thought finally made him come hard in long spurts. With his breathing jagged, leaning against the wet tiles, the shower spraying over him and the evidence of his uncontrollable hunger for her washing down the drain, he wondered what this hold was she had over him, and what the fuck he could do about it.

PRESENT DAY
a hindu holi celebration
IN NEW JERSEY

১৩

Chrissy fumbled through her explanation of how she and Aariv happened to know each other to this woman with more haughtiness in her bejeweled pinky finger than she'd ever perceived in anyone else, (even Aariv that first time so long ago). Her eyes kept meeting his, with both of them looking away whenever it happened. After occurring several times, they both started to find it amusing, both attempting to hide their smiles.

But damn, how could she not smile around this man? After seeing him at the club, *her* club, where she performed in costumes that made her look naked, he seemed like a completely different person. She wasn't sure what it was but his grumpy demeanor had never made an appearance, and she'd found herself enjoying their conversation that night. It was a shame he had to leave early. She would've liked to have continued talking with him until her next performance. He knew more about her than she did about him. But, as she had even said to her friends, he was a busy, important guy.

What had stumped her was how he'd come to be there in the

first place and she'd asked Mariam outright after he left. She let her friend think she didn't care that he was there, just mildly curious. But deep down, she was beginning to wonder what was happening to her original opinion of him. All she knew was that she was more turned on than ever because of how friendly and flirty he'd been. And *dang*! The sexy darkness that presented itself briefly when he told her he would punish her if she tried to pry into the investigation again had made her more than shiver. She couldn't stop thinking about it all night and into the next week, imagining what he meant by that. Had her dreams been wet, and filled with Aariv-shaped men? Uh, yeah!

Her friend had filled her in about him needing a night out; his work and personal life were both taking a toll on him and he needed to blow off some steam.

She tried not to ruminate on the fact that if he hadn't seen her at the bar, he might have gone into the VIP room to blow off some steam and then some, which wouldn't have been a shocker. It was a club that specialized in entertainment of the sexual variety after all, from sensually harmless performances on stage earlier in the evening to half-naked lap dances in the VIP room at any given time of the night. The burning sensation in her breast at the thought was ridiculous and she shooed it away every time it decided to rear its distasteful head.

"Interesting," Ms. Acharya said coolly, bringing Chrissy back to the conversation. She folded her arms across the fine silk of the white ankle-length tunic she wore. The slits on each side went up each leg, ending at her hips, and showed off nicely shaped legs in matching tight white silk pants. She jiggled her head elegantly, giving her silver bob a swish. Her eyes squinted as she thought for a moment. "Cristina, I need you to make sure the four guests I gave you the names of are brought to Aariv at the specific times I requested." She eyed Chrissy up and down. "Do you think you can accomplish that?" she asked, somehow managing to look down her nose at her, though she was even shorter than Chrissy's five foot three inches.

"Of course, Ms. Acharya. You hired Simran, and Simran gave me the task of managing your party because she trusts me with this," she said, pushing down the need to tell this woman off. Simran *had* given her this to manage last minute because she had to go out of town for another client. But Chrissy, in her new managerial role, hadn't complained. Events popped up last minute all the time with their class of clientele. She was eager to show Simran she could handle the responsibility.

"Now," she continued, checking her clipboard. "Two things I wanted to mention when I came out here—the DJ has complaints about the patio setup. He's under the impression he's also supposed to be on the beach?"

Ms. Acharya opened her mouth to speak but Chrissy continued, holding a hand up to her. "Second, the delayed shipment of marigold garlands finally arrived. I know it's last minute and extremely important to this celebration, but I have to warn you that they're not all orange and yellow as you requested. Some are bright pink, but I think after seeing them, you'll agree with me that they're exquisite, considering the time constraint Simran had in order to get them from our floral vendor. I've already told the set-up crew to string them up where you wanted them." Which was everywhere. There were thousands of garlands and they needed to be strung from tree to tree, across the patio, and placed on the high-top tables and any other surface that ran along the perimeter of the lawn near the house. Apparently, marigolds were a tradition for any important Indian celebration. She'd been schooled further by Simran that they represented auspiciousness, purity, and the divine, helping to ward off negativity and evil spirits even.

Ms. Acharya looked at her as if bored, and remained silent assessing her from head to toe. As the seconds ticked by, her eyes narrowed until she finally nodded.

"Thank you, Kristen. Your attention to detail is … exceptional, second only to Simran, of course."

Chrissy lifted the corners of her mouth with much effort, trying not to grit her teeth. "Of course, and thank you, Ms. Acharya."

The other woman beckoned to Aariv. "Come, Aariv." She signaled him to come with her back to the house.

"Aunty, I'm good here." He stuffed his hands in his jean's pockets. "I'll catch up with you later." He nodded and dismissed her. She stood there for a beat, her mouth set in a slight frown, before turning on her heel and heading toward the manor.

"So, you *are* stalking me," Chrissy said stepping closer to him. She hugged her clipboard and iPad to her chest, grinning up at him, tingles prickling her skin. God, he was so hot, and again without his normal full suit on. Today he had on a well-fitted tan sports jacket over a light blue shirt and jeans. Classic brogues on his feet instead of the casual boots from the club.

"I can confirm that I am *not* stalking you. *You,* in fact, are stalking *me*," he teased lazily, his stance casual as he looked down at her. "What are you doing here?" He shook his head, but he didn't sound upset, quite the opposite.

Oh, to reach up and palm that strong bearded jaw; she might just die and go to heaven if she could. Her hands practically itched to do it and she gripped her clipboard harder.

"I'm working," she said, tilting her head to one side. She'd known he'd be there though, and that was her reasoning for putting on her favorite ivory wrap dress. It wasn't too revealing and hugged her in all the right places. Did she want to drive Aariv Abbas crazy with lust? Yes, maybe just a little. She wanted him to experience what she was experiencing every God damn time she saw him—an attraction she wanted to fall seamlessly into but felt like there were hurdles to jump—mainly him and his hot and cold behavior. Yes, she'd come dressed for battle. "Simran helped Ms. Acharya plan this shindig but had to go out of town last minute. She asked me to jump in. So here I am." She did a twirl and dipped in a swift curtsy.

He chuckled and nodded. "So here you are," he said softly, palming his chin as his hazel eyes blazed.

What was *that* look?

She pulled her clipboard out to review her notes, to distract her from the quakes in her belly. She glanced at the names of the four women listed in her handwriting. Each one had a specific time jotted next to them for when she was to bring them to Aariv throughout the afternoon.

"What exactly is happening today?" She looked up confused. "Are you interviewing women to marry?" she joked.

She expected him to chuckle in return, but his expression became stoic.

"Yes," he said, his eyes traveling from her windswept waves down to her black patent leather heels, the admiration was evident. "That's right."

"Wait, for real?" she asked in disbelief, chuckling a little.

"Yeah," he sighed. "They're prospective brides." Now he looked out to the ocean. "For me."

Now her belly trembled again, but not with desire.

She wasn't sure how to respond and remained quiet for a few moments.

But, what the hell?

"Seriously?" she burst out. "Like, seriously, seriously?" Did she sound like an idiot? She thought she might. Again she was dumbfounded and rendered speechless by this man. It seemed that no matter what, their stars could never align, could never fall into place.

"Seriously," he said quietly.

"Okay." She nodded pathetically. "Wow."

After seeing him at the club, after knowing that he'd been impressed by her performance and hadn't judged her for dancing in a mediocre and seedy nightclub, she thought they were getting somewhere. She wasn't sure where—they came from completely different walks of life. But it was clear, even to simple little ole' her, that there was something between them. It'd felt so natural when they were talking to each other, or flirting, just letting their attraction simmer.

Later, at the end of the night back in her dressing room, when she'd seen that he texted her earlier, asking about Tag and the investigation (obviously not knowing he would see her that night) she'd felt stupidly warmed by that. Did he care … about her?

Well, *she* was wrong. That was Aariv the attorney only worried about the investigation.

She stood there awkwardly not sure which way to go. She turned one way, then the other, staring blindly down at her clipboard. Her mind was blank and she tried to compose herself, even as the embarrassment washed over her and scorched her cheeks with heat.

"Chrissy, hey," he said gruffly, reaching for her elbow, stopping her before she headed back into the house.

She wanted to feel disgust toward him, but she couldn't. She wanted him to hold on to her elbow and more—so much more. The fact of the matter was that she still felt this burning desire for him, except maybe now it was more acute because she didn't even have the slightest chance with this man.

*Stupid, Chrissy*, she chided herself.

He'd always been off limits. If anything, she was more disgusted with herself and her behavior. She'd almost thrown herself at him after already flirting ridiculously with him last week. Oh for shame. Did she never learn her lesson? Shouldn't she have known from the get-go when he'd been such an ass at Simran's wedding? Plus he was a lawyer.

"Do you need help with anything right now?" he asked gently. And she hated that he was being so nice as if he knew what was darting through her mind.

Did she need help with anything? Uh yeah. She needed him to relieve this feeling of want. She needed his fingers in her, maybe his tongue, with his beard scratching her thighs. And for the love of God, she would love his dick inside her, rutting at her with everything that big, hard body had.

She shook her head but heard herself say, "I have to get all of those colored powders set up down by the beach for later. What are they for anyway?"

She started making her way toward the path set in the rocks at the edge of the cliff that led down to the beach. She was vaguely aware that he followed her.

"Well, let me help you," he said, his grip on her elbow tighter as he helped her down the pebbled incline down to the sand.

He idly talked about the festivities and how *Holi* was the celebration of newness and spring. Guests would throw the powders at each other and that was why everyone wore white—

so that the explosion of colors mimicked the brightness of the coming of spring and the end of dreary winter.

"How fun," she murmured, her heels sinking into the sand. She held onto him as she reached down to pull them off but lost her balance anyway, falling into his solid chest. He held onto her, and they stood that way for a few seconds, letting his pine and woody aftershave tickle her nostrils before she pulled away. Was she mistaken that he was reluctant to let her go?

A stack of brass plates shone luminously under the white of the sky along two long tables covered in white tablecloths. She moved to them and began spreading them out on the tables.

Aariv went over to the box containing the packets of powders in an array of colors and began dispersing them onto the trays, keeping them contained for now as the wind was picking up.

"I don't think I've ever seen Pinky Aunty so shocked before," he said with a laugh.

"What?" she asked, finishing up with the plates and coming to help him.

"You basically told her to suck it when you brought up the flowers and how she wouldn't be able to complain given it was last minute and that Simran no doubt got her a great deal with your florist."

How had he gotten all of that from what she'd said to the woman back there? Though, he had hit the nail on the head.

"But—how … how did you know?" She spluttered. "I didn't mean to make her feel bad." Yes, she had.

"Yes, you did," he said chuckling. "And she deserved it. She's so stuck up sometimes." He shook his head. "She forgets that she gets things done by others doing massive favors for her. Just because she's this well-known matriarch figure in our community." He snorted. "Matriarch my ass. She's no mother figure to me."

Chrissy couldn't help laughing as they worked side by side.

"Who exactly is she to you?"

He sighed, a heavy one; one that seemed to carry the weight of the world in it. "She's the community matchmaker. And I say community in name only because she charges an arm and a leg for her services. Nothing is for free with that one."

"So … are you supposed to be engaged by the end of the day?"

He shrugged. "I wouldn't say I'm finding my wife today. I'm only doing this for my parents who want me married."

"Oh, because you're *so* old."

"I'm thirty-six, Chrissy. According to them, I should be married already with a kid, and maybe another on the way," he said drily.

He was thirty-six. To her twenty-eight. It did sound older, but not old.

"Riv, Riv!" some kids shouted as they stumbled down the beach toward them.

A group of boys surrounded him. "Riv Uncle, come shoot hoops with us!" One of them had a basketball in his hands.

"Can you show me how you do a lay-up?" another asked, tugging on his jacket.

"Guys, calm yourselves. We're here to celebrate *Holi*. And I'm pretty sure the scriptures say nothing about basket tasketball." He bobbled his head in that Indian way while saying that last part in a heavy fake Indian accent.

The kids burst into laughter but continued to whine and plead. Chrissy couldn't help smiling at the interaction.

"Okay. Okay, fellas. How about a little later when this party gets underway? I'll find you. *Atcha*? You don't want me getting in trouble with Pinky Aunty, do you?"

The kids finally agreed and dashed off, hurtling themselves up the rocks with no fear, as only kids could do.

"Basketball?" she asked aghast, but deep down the entire interaction had been super cute, though she didn't want more reasons to like Aariv Abbas. "You have some explaining to do, Riv Uncle."

He gave her a deadpan stare but told her about his love of basketball and sneaking off with the kids at events like this to blow off some of the stress that he got from the adults. They expected him to always be on as the good son with family responsibility at the top of his mind.

"So, you're a Knicks fan," she said, looking over the tables to make sure everything was in place, also realizing that what he just said explained a lot about his authoritative, sometimes grumpy, demeanor. Anyone with that kind of responsibility wherever they went had to be a curmudgeon at times.

She stared at him from under her lashes, seeing him in a different light. Something within her breast squeezed tightly, and though nothing could ever happen between them, she felt sorry for him. All she wanted to do was hug him.

He caught her contemplative stare and she looked away, saying, "I'll have to come back later and open up each individual packet, but this helps. Thanks."

"No problem." He cocked his head to the side. "How did you know I was a Knicks fan?"

"Your funky socks that time in your office." She gazed at his ankles, pursing her lips, a little embarrassed that something so stupid as his socks still stuck with her from that day. "I'll bet you're wearing something funny now." She was betting on it, but there was a chance she could be wrong, but for some reason, the idea was so him—the man wasn't *all* serious, *all* the time, was he?

He smirked and pulled his jeans up to reveal emoji-faced socks. "You got me." He tipped his head back and barked with laughter. "I can't believe you remember that."

Her face heated up and she turned away. She remembered way too much about this man, more than was good for her.

They talked some more as they meandered back up the shallow cliffs. He didn't know why—maybe because she was proving to be a good listener, or that she saw things about him that no one noticed like his penchant for funny socks when he was in a serious or uncomfortable situation—but he revealed more about himself to her. He told her that his father was a businessman back in India, married to a woman who was his stepmother. As an only child, he carried the burdens of his family on his shoulders. It was his duty to be the good son, who would eventually be a good man, all the while ensuring their good name was never sullied and making sure everyone was safe and secure amongst his immediate relations.

She nodded, saying she'd noticed how close he and Mariam were. She asked how he became a lawyer. He said matter-of-factly that he'd been advised (really told) what subjects he should study, and because he grew up listening to his elders, he chose to be a lawyer.

"Do you ever wish you'd chosen something else?" she asked curiously.

"Not at all. I appreciate that the law has no room for error. Everything is black and white and that's how I like things."

She paused on the pebbly path, just as her heel got caught in a crevice. She would have tumbled backward if he hadn't been there to steady her.

With her back against his chest, he held her tightly to him, trying not to lose his balance either. Her round ass pressed into his pelvis, and it was all he could do not to press himself further into her, his shaft between her ass cheeks.

He heard her sigh as she turned her head and looked up at him. "Black and white gets boring sometimes, don't you think?"

He squeezed her soft waist, the material of her ivory dress barely a barrier to her warm skin. "Are you calling me boring?" he asked in her ear.

He felt her body tremble, and for the briefest second, she leaned further back into him. It felt good, her weight on him, but then she pushed off, continuing up the incline. "I didn't say that, but..." she glanced over her shoulder, her wide, cat-like eyes hooded, "if the suit fits..." And she disappeared over the edge to more solid ground.

When he peered over the ridge, she was brushing her skirt off and adjusting her dress before lending a hand to him to help pull him up. "Well, seems you have everything planned out for you, including your choice of women."

He grasped her hand, though he didn't need help up. It fit nicely, snuggly in the palm of his own.

Now he was standing in front of her, her hand in his, her hair starting to whip around her cheeks, and something shook loose inside him. He wasn't sure what it was, but it felt like something almost tangible was rendering away.

"I like things planned out," he answered, but he didn't sound as sure about that as he had when he'd given that answer to numerous people—and many women he'd dated—in the past.

She tugged her hand out of his grip. "What's the point of living then, if you can't experience what the world has to offer? Make the mistakes? Learn from them?" Her voice had risen, and he could tell she was trying not to lose her temper. But he didn't mind because he was kind of impressed with her words more than anything.

*When had Chrissy Smyth become a philosopher?*

He shoved his hands into his pockets, waffling between annoyance with her for not agreeing with him, and awe. The latter was starting to win over.

"Sorry." She sounded contrite, looking down at her toes. She let out a huff. "I've been there—where people pushed me to do something I wasn't into. I didn't like it. But not everyone is the same." He knew she was talking about her forced ballet training. Her slim shoulders lifted and fell in a shrug, as she toyed with the ruby and gold cross around her neck. Glancing at the house, she murmured, "I have to go work. I'll bet that woman is looking for me." She turned back to him, a bright smile pasted stiffly on her lips. "I'll see you around. Enjoy the party." She waved and walked away.

He let her go, though he wanted to call her back and tell her that it wasn't that he liked being told what to do, but that it was what was expected of him and all that he knew his entire life.

The wind flipped her skirt up and he heard her squeal as she pushed it down, holding it close over her thighs so it would behave as she darted back to the house. He chuckled, shaking his head. But as he continued to follow her with his eyes, he knew that what she'd said knocked him down more than he'd expected it to. For once, he knew for certain that he was ready to step out of the expectations set for him. Weren't the expectations more like guidelines anyway; guidelines that were beginning to feel like limitations? At the age of thirty-six, he could be sure of one thing, his curiosity was getting the best of him, and it had everything to do with Chrissy Smyth.

# CHAPTER 14

58

*A*ariv found her later, busy directing the wait staff on straightening up the patio. The party had gotten out of hand like it always did toward the end. The DJ was usually amped up by that point and playing crazy Bollywood or Indian beats requested by the guests. Indians loved a party, and they loved to dance even more.

The outdoor area was in shambles, with beer bottles and cocktail glasses lining the perimeter near the house. Plates of leftover food and used napkins were strewn on the high-top tables.

Flower garlands lay haphazardly all over the lawn like discarded carcasses, where some of the rowdier guests had ripped them down. Pinky Auntie promptly threw the culprits out as soon as she found what they'd done. Her reaction always caused a scene. Some Indians believed the adage that many people the world over still held—boys will be boys, even those these 'boys' had been young men.

"Let them have their fun," a few elderly uncles had argued.

But Pinky never tolerated that behavior, nor the wrecking of her property. As much as Aariv disliked some of Pinky Aunty's views and what she stood for, he had to agree with her on that one.

A few lingering guests continued to idly chat as the clean-up crew worked, enjoying the opportunity of calm and quietness to catch up, while a group had gone down to the beach where a bonfire had been lit. Again, their impeccable hostess was on point knowing the younger crowd would want to continue partying once the sun had set. She'd set up food and drinks down there for later.

He was one of the guests who still lingered, speaking with a few other guys around his age he hadn't seen in a while. He spotted Chrissy gesturing in different directions to the staff, speaking sternly. She was all business. He'd never seen her this way and it was extremely sexy, just like all facets of her.

He was just about to say his goodbyes to the guys when one of them asked if they'd seen the cute event planner in the white dress. He nodded his head at Chrissy's retreating figure as she slipped into the house.

Aariv stood tall, looking down at these men (he was bigger than most). He'd hung out with them growing up and knew exactly what they were thinking when they mentioned her.

"Did you see that ass? Juicy, like two perfect *laddoos*." The man cupped his hands and squeezed imaginary spheres of the round Indian sweets, groaning obscenely. The others chuckled, agreeing.

"I know her. She's a friend of mine," he said coolly, trying not to let his temper flare.

"Ho, ho, ho. Aariv wants to butter his bread on both sides."

Aariv grimaced, while the others laughed. They, along with everyone at the party, knew he was in the market for an Indian wife.

"She's here to work, you *chodna* (horny dumbass). Leave her alone," he said mildly, trying to get these guys off his case. They were joking with him, but they didn't know how close to the truth they were. If they did, they'd never let up because *he* was the horny dumbass whenever it came to Chrissy.

All day his mind had been on her and what she'd said to him. In the middle of conversations, or meeting prospective brides, he'd catch her figure darting around in a blur of strawberry blonde and ivory white, and he'd lose his train of thought. It wasn't unlike the first night he'd met her.

At one point, one of the women, Kareena something or other, the one he still couldn't believe had been put on 'The List,' the one who'd bullied his cousin when they were teenagers, had even noticed his distraction. She began to follow his stare which was openly glued to Chrissy.

Her exact words were abrupt, breaking away from her explanation of working with a leading New York medical group.

"Who is she?" And she'd cocked her head, her tone more matter-of-fact than questioning.

When he asked her what she meant, the back of his neck heating up, she nodded and said politely, "I hate having my time wasted. Don't you?" She'd smiled and walked away.

And he had to ask himself, was there someone else? Weren't the imaginings he had with Chrissy just that? Imaginings? Was what he was feeling toward her real?

Her demeanor toward him had changed when she found out he was on the lookout for an Indian bride. What had once been an open manner was now closed off. There were moments during the day when he thought he could catch her, maybe tease her, anything to get her to glance or smile at him, but she was in work mode and madly dashed about making sure everything went off without a hitch. Was she too busy to notice him, or was she ignoring him?

One thing was for certain, she was great at her job. From the 'impromptu' conga line as the DJ played the popular movie RRR's song *Naatu Naatu*, down to the beach for the color tossing, to the small but magnificent fireworks display over the water's edge that had been timed to go off right at sunset. Everything went off like clockwork. And why should he be amazed? Chrissy Smyth was proving to be full of talents.

He'd ended up staying longer than he intended, hoping at some point to have a moment with her to … do what exactly? He even found himself making his way in the conga line down to the beach for the color tossing. The kids had a field day, targeting him, and his jacket was smeared with every color of the rainbow.

But now, as he looked around the almost empty back lawn, he thought it was a good time to find her. Though, again he wasn't sure what he would say to her.

He shook his head. He'd know when he saw her, he was sure of it. He made his excuses about an early morning; that he'd be heading back to the city and left the group of guys standing there still ribbing each other. When they headed toward the path down to the beach for the bonfire, he went into the house.

It was quiet inside, and he wasn't sure where she'd gone. He slipped into the kitchen, interrupting a few of the waitstaff packing up the leftover food and cleaning.

He headed toward the back hallway where there was a powder room just off the kitchen. At first, he didn't hear anything, but he noticed the light on under the crack of the closed door. He leaned in to listen and then distinctly heard the water running. He stepped back, and waited.

As soon as the door opened and she appeared, he said her name. She looked up surprised.

But then they both heard, "Cristina, are you in there? The back still looks in shambles and—"

He pushed her back into the bathroom, following in closely and shutting the door behind them and to any of Pinky's orders. He quickly flicked off the light.

"What—" she began, but he covered her mouth with his hand, as her eyes bulged in alarm.

"Shh," he whispered, his pulse darting a mile a minute like he was in some covert operation.

Once the older woman's voice faded, he knew they were in the clear, but only for a moment. Out the window tucked in the corner, he could just see Pinky meandering around, her white outfit still pristine, and fairly glowing in the dusky evening, as she barked orders to not only the staff, but the guests still idling around.

He slowly lifted his hand from her mouth, aware that they were standing very close to each other in semidarkness.

Her hair tickled his lips, and he inhaled her sweet scent. He was losing it—the fighting battle to stay away from her. And in this situation, he was kind of ok with being the loser.

"Aariv, what the fuck are we doing in here?" she asked, affronted, her hands balled into fists on his chest.

He couldn't help but grin at her temper. She was still upset from … well he wasn't exactly sure about what, but it had to do with him and his list of prospective brides.

He let his hands settle gently on her waist, the smooth material of her dress warmed by her skin. "How did it go today?"

She eyed him skeptically, then looked over his shoulder.

"I don't know. You tell me. Any engagements today?" she asked bitingly.

"Why are you so pissed?"

She stuttered. "I'm not pissed." She pushed him away, which was impossible given how much bigger he was and the confines of the powder room. "I'm just … tired. It's been a long and grueling day. That Pinky lady is a slave driver."

He chuckled, pushing a strand of hair behind her ear. "Slave driver Aunty."

She pursed her lips trying not to smile. "Stop it."

"General—no, Dictator Aunty."

"That's not very nice," she said, but she started laughing and he took his shot. He leaned down and covered her lips with his, a sense of utter completeness overtaking him. She tasted sweet and citrusy, and her lips were plump and pliable underneath his as he moved over her mouth.

She inhaled sharply, then shuddered under him, softening for the briefest of moments. But then, she pulled away, turning her head, a hand covering her mouth, and he found himself inhaling the fruitiness of her hair.

"What are you doing?" she asked quickly and breathlessly.

He smirked, nudging her ear with his nose. "Isn't it obvious?"

"It's not," she said, folding her arms over her breasts. He tried to keep his gaze on her face, her angry sapphire eyes as they sparkled with something akin to hate … or was it passion? But he couldn't help dropping his eyes down to her breasts, smooshed up with cleavage for days in the deep V-neck of her dress. "Oh my God, Aariv. Are you serious right now? You're practically engaged, and you're in here with me doing, I don't know…" She raised her hands in the air.

"I'm far from being engaged, Chrissy. And you know what I—correction, we're doing." He pulled at her wrists and circled her arms around his neck. "I don't want to fight this anymore."

Her face transformed into shock, her eyes big blue pools. "You've felt this, too?" she whispered.

He closed the space between them, pressing his hardening cock into her soft pelvis. "You tell me," he said softly.

Her breath caught as she closed her eyes, letting out a throaty moan and he waited. He'd let her choose how to proceed, he decided. If she refused him again, he'd back off.

But after a few moments, she pulled his head down to hers, kissing him with a force that could only be described as pent-up desire. He should know; he felt it, too.

"Chrissy," he groaned, pulling at her lips again, licking the smooth berry-like fullness. He sipped her bottom lip into his mouth and sucked tenderly.

"Aariv." She moaned again, her mouth opening under his, and he slid his tongue in looking for hers, tasting her, exploring. She kissed him with enthusiastic unsteadiness, trying to follow his lead. But she finally found their rhythm.

She tangled her tongue with his while crushing her body into him, rubbing her belly into his hardness. He grunted, sliding his hands down to her hips and grabbing her tightly, cupping her ass like he'd been imagining for months now. He squeezed the firmness, rubbed the softness, and she cried out against him.

He wanted more of her, needed to feel all of her and he quickly lifted her and stepped to the counter, sitting her up there. His hands roamed the top of her thighs and slowly pushed them open so he could stand in between them.

The heat he felt emanating from her, just as they were, fully clothed but openly touching and experiencing one another, made him drop his forehead onto hers, breathing double time.

Her hands glided inside his coat, up his abs, her fingers exploring his muscles over his shirt. She sighed each time she fingered a ridge, as she moved deftly up his chest, tickling him. He grabbed her hand and put it on his shoulder as he crushed her lips with his again, eager to taste her once more.

Her skirt was now around her thighs and his fingers caressed the velvety softness of her skin, running his hands up to grasp her hips again. She arched into him, her eyes hooded as he kissed over to an ear, biting and teasing her lobe.

She gasped and giggled but her breath caught as his hand made its way slowly up her waist, inching higher until he cupped one of her perfect breasts. The weight was heavy in his hand, and warm in the smooth material of her dress, her nipple already a hardened peak. He rubbed his palm against the stiff nub, making her moan breathily. Fuck, she was sexy as hell. He'd known it the first time he'd danced with her but had kept himself from her all these months. Why? For what!?

She whimpered breathily in his ear as he squeezed that ripe flesh, his mouth inching toward her shoulder, where he tugged the sleeve of her dress aside, along with her bra strap to kiss her bare tawny skin.

"Aariv," she sighed in what sounded like a surrender, letting him do what he wanted. Letting him explore her here in this cramped space, and he couldn't get enough of her. She leaned back on her hands on the counter, her thighs spread, as he slowly pulled at the ties to her wrap dress.

"Is this ok?" he asked, pausing, itching to rip the material off and show what he'd been wanting to see for ages.

as he really stopping to ask her if it was ok that he undressed her … now when her panties were practically soaked through?

More importantly, she had to ask herself, was this happening? Was she really getting it on with the man who'd been the main character in her dreams lately?

It had taken every ounce of self-preservation and many pep talks throughout the afternoon to not give him any attention. First, she needed to focus on work, and second, she needed to focus on the fact that the man was not only unavailable but that he was following a path in life she couldn't understand. She could get behind his choice of law—it seemed to be his personality to need things straight and orderly. But how did that pertain to marriage, and possibly love? It didn't. That was the fact of the matter. Only a robot would go through life with someone on the terms his family set and which he was willing to follow. Her brain was muddled because she wanted to dislike him after that conversation by the beach, but she couldn't. She felt bad for him and wanted to help him. But in a very un-Chrissy-like manner, she pushed it (with a ton of effort) to the back burner, needing to keep her concentration on her tasks at hand. Was she trying to ignore him? Absolutely. Was she trying to make him feel bad? Maybe just a little. But she hadn't expected him to react by practically attacking her in the bathroom. She'd just given herself another pep-talk and felt regained strength about her decision regarding him when he found her.

*What in the crap was going on?*

His look was almost pained now, as he paused, to make sure she was all right, and she wondered if she should push him away, still angry at herself, and him for letting her flirt with him. But the desire in his eyes, no doubt mirroring her own, won over. This was what she'd been fantasizing, and now it was real.

She let herself cup his bearded chin with her hands, almost closing her eyes in ecstasy at the sensation of rough hairs against her palms.

He was half bent over her, his wide shoulders blocking out the door, blocking out pretty much everything but him, and his scent filled her nostrils, the musky smell of man and the pine and woody warmth of his cologne. She reveled in it—reveled in this man commanding her body.

As an answer to his question, she grasped the ties to her dress and tugged them so that the two sides fell open. Her nude lace bra and nude thong were all that she had on underneath (along with the black heels still on her feet). When she looked up at him, she didn't need to wonder if he approved or not, if he was hesitant or not anymore.

His eyes practically set her on fire with the passion in them, and his nostrils flared as his breathing became harsher.

"Chrissy, you are so sexy," he said gruffly, his large palms cupping her breasts in the flimsy lace of her bra. He grunted as he squeezed them and pinched her nipples, making her cry out and arch her back as a streak of heat shot into her core. He lowered himself to take one into his mouth and he sucked her sensitive nub through her bra, biting down finally and she moaned in pleasure. "Yes, Little Girl, you like that."

Oh, God, Aariv's bossy side. Oh, God, it was making her dizzy—the pleasure, the eroticism … all of it.

He stepped between her legs again, and one hand grasped the back of her neck, kissing her, forcing her mouth open with his own, as his other hand brushed between her thighs, making her jump. He chuckled, slowly palming her and she automatically wanted to open her legs wider, and let this man do anything and everything to her.

"Fuck," he hissed into her mouth. "You're so wet."

She nodded, rubbing herself against his hand. "Make it better, Riv." She moaned. She was in such a state of frenzy and needed him to release the tension built in her core, or she might do something crazy like injure someone.

He chuckled. "Like that nickname, do you?"

She would have said yes if he'd let her but as soon as she nodded, his middle finger dragged down the lips of her pussy. He was outside her underwear but had deftly maneuvered within the center folds of her sensitive skin, lighting up nerve endings she didn't know she had.

"Ah," she cried, gripping his shoulders, his sports coat in her fists, as she threw her head back.

"That's it, Little Girl. Show me what you can do." He did it again and again, finally putting enough pressure on her while the heel of his palm pressed down onto her clit that her hips started undulating, bucking against his hand. "Yes. Fuck you're so hot," he grunted.

She felt hot. She felt like the sexiest woman alive as this man handled her and watched what happened. She completely lost it. She couldn't control the frenzy that possessed her hips as he unrelentingly massaged and caressed her. She needed more. She needed to be filled.

"*Riv,*" she whined, so close to … what? Was this what an impending orgasm felt like? When your body felt like it was live-wired and about to explode like fireworks?

"I know, baby," he groaned. "You have no idea how much I know." His heavy-lidded eyes watched her every movement entranced. "I want to get in there so badly," he said gruffly, watching his hand work between her legs.

And before she could whine again, he maneuvered a finger behind the crotch of her underwear and slid deeply into her wetness. Pulsing in and out slowly.

"So tight," he groaned. He slid another finger into her, and she felt herself stretch deliciously.

Her head fell back as her eyes closed. The pleasure like nothing she'd ever experienced before as his fingers started pumping her, his pace quickening. Her body fell into ecstasy, the feeling too good, as his hand worked her, touching her in a way that she'd never been touched before. It was like he was the pussy whisperer.

And she was convinced he was for sure when his fingers reached up further inside her, hitting a sensitive spot that she'd never felt before. All the colors of the rainbow erupted and danced behind her closed lids, like at a hypnotic disco club or inside a kids' kaleidoscope. She started to cry out loudly before he covered her mouth quickly with his, taking her cries for his own.

She couldn't control what was happening to her body. Wave

after wave of pleasure washed over her, and her hips continued to buck his hand, even after the waves abated.

She'd died. She must have died and gone to heaven. Nothing had ever felt so good in her life.

But, a sharp rapping on the other side of the door was enough to bring her back down to earth.

TEN DAYS LATER
new york, new york

## CHAPTER 15

ンロ

*H*er phone dinged again, and she embarrassingly turned it to silent, but not before she read the text that had just come in.

**"Tell me how you would make yourself come with your fingers at work..."**

She flipped the phone quickly, hoping no one else had seen it. She audibly exhaled and tried to hide her smile. She squirmed in the conference room chair, her body coming alive even as she tried to tamp down the lust that was churning deep within her.

She realized it was unusually quiet in the *Lavish Your Events* conference room and she looked up. Three pairs of eyes studied her across the white expanse of the conference room table, and she felt the heat bleed into her cheeks.

"Sorry, what was that?" she uttered.

"I asked if everything was ok. Your phone is blowing up today," her boss, Simran said, tapping her pen in question against her notepad, then pointing it at her phone. "Do you need to get that?"

Chrissy glanced at her phone wanting to clutch it to her and dart out of the room. The way her body reacted to each and every dirty text message from Aariv since last week's super-hot encounter at the party was forming an all-consuming need. But she was pretty sure it would be a bad idea to excuse herself from their weekly team status meeting so she could continue with their increasingly erotic sexting foreplay. It was making her more than distracted, and her body a walking live-wire of lust.

"Nope, everything's ok. It can wait." She gestured for Simran to continue updating them on their new client briefing.

She did her best to listen closely, but she left the meeting with a vague idea of a fancy Bat-mitzvah party that would circle Manhattan on a yacht. Usually, these things engrossed her, but she was not into it lately.

Nope. She was into figuring out the perfect time to meet with Aariv and continue what they'd started. But between her day job and her increasing hours at the club, it was proving impossible. Already a week and three days had gone by (ten tortuous days!), and she was in a state of constant arousal combined with her growing apprehension that he would lose interest in her. He might very well decide that pursuing anything with her, though not long-term, was a bad idea.

She shook that thought off and decided tonight had to be the night and she quickly texted him. It was Wednesday, the middle of the work week, sure … but it was hump day after all. She added that bit about hump day to her text and giggled as she hit send.

"And why have you been so secretive lately, Miss Thang?" Antoine asked from behind her as she sat at her desk.

She clutched the phone to her chest and swiveled around in her chair. Both Antoine and Shana were standing over her. She glanced at the time and realized it was their lunch break. All three of them usually walked out together.

"Nothing," she answered quickly. "Why don't you two go on without me—"

"Nuh-uh, girl. What's going on?" Shana asked. "You've been distracted all day. It doesn't have to do with your legal stuff and the rug shop, does it?"

Chrissy shook her head. That stuff was great—everything was going according to Tag Underwood's plan. He'd decided to go undercover and do a little more digging. She hadn't heard from him in a while except for sporadic handwritten notes delivered to her by messenger. And he'd asked her to stay away from the shop on weekends, in case she ran into any more scary, dangerous-looking folks who seemed completely out of place.

Antoine stepped forward. "No way. Look at her, Shay." They both inspected her closely and Chrissy did her best to keep her expression neutral. "She's talking to a boy!" Antoine said with glee.

Chrissy rolled her eyes. How did Antoine always guess it right?

"You, minx!" he said, slapping her lightly on the shoulder. "Who the F is it!?"

She'd have to dish it all out to them at some point; they could be relentless. And truthfully, she was acting weird, even for her. Was she holding in something at a top-secret-mission-impossible level? One that was about to babble out from her at any given moment? Uh … yeah. But part of her wanted to keep her secret close, though she was a terrible secret keeper. Things hadn't even gotten to real sex territory yet with Aariv and she worried that if she told her friends anything, they'd talk her out of a no-strings-attached scenario, warning that she would get overzealous and find feelings for him.

But oh no, no, no. She was a changed woman. She was going into this thing with a clear head, a closed heart, and wide-open legs … and maybe mouth, too.

"Seriously, guys—"

"Chrissy, are you still here?" Simran called from her office. "Could you come in here for a sec?"

Whew! Saved by the boss!

"Yep! I'm coming. See you guys later." She stood up and scurried into Simran's office while the other two gave her inquisitive stares and shook their heads. They would get it out of her eventually, but not yet.

She was a little smug about this new development, but also in wonder. In the biggest plot twist in the history of her life, Chrissy was about to embark on a wild ride with a real man. She wouldn't call it a true relationship—not in the traditional sense. But it was something bigger than she'd ever known in her little world; one that felt more concrete than any of her past experiences with what she would now refer to as just 'boys' in light of her new understanding.

And, Lord knew she wasn't going in naïve enough to think that Aariv Abbas would throw everything he'd built in his life into the wind and turn a new leaf (i.e. take on dating someone non-Indian) because he was horny. The man was too far gone in his beliefs of responsibilities and family duty. She was being realistic here; she was attracted to him just as much as he was to her and they were exploring that attraction further, because why the hell not? They were both grown-ups and responsible. She might be a romantic, but she knew when someone didn't have that kind of bone in their body—*aka Grumpenhunk*. No, the kind of bone he had in his ultra-hot body was completely different, one she couldn't refuse even if she tried.

Part of the fun came from the secretive way they were behaving. She still burst into nervous giggles thinking about the disapproving horror on the high and mighty face of Ms. Acharya after she'd found them together in the half-bathroom.

### Ten Days Ago – That Holi Party In New Jersey

*T*he knocking continued and became increasingly rapid as if the person on the other side had finally run out of what little patience they had to begin with.

"Chrissy?! I know you are in there, young lady. Come out this instant and explain to me why I am the one giving the waitstaff orders."

Chrissy's heart beat so fast she thought she was going to faint. And she couldn't move if she wanted to because Aariv's hard body was pressed into her, leaning over her with his forehead against hers as she came down from her orgasm high.

*Holy shit—that orgasm!*

She had never (never!) experienced something that good. She'd be willing to risk anything to get back to that out-of-body experience again.

"I knew she knew your name," Aariv murmured sardonically. She smelled the beer on his breath and wanted to connect her lips to his again. He was a fucking good kisser, and it'd surprised her beyond belief. But God, he was so good at a lot of things, she thought as she watched him slowly pull his fingers out of her and felt the emptiness that ensued.

Even in the dim waning light from outside, she saw that those two long fingers glistened with her wetness. She watched as he, too, looked at them carefully, then lifted them to his mouth, licking them gently. He sucked delicately as if he were tasting the most exquisitely flavored phenomenon.

Her body flexed, feeling hollow, wanting those fingers back inside her. Her eyes stayed glued to his face as utter pleasure replaced the usual stoic expanse. Heat slithered into her core and her body felt like it was preparing to come again. How was that possible, she wondered with fascination. And she realized how little she knew about physical pleasure. This man though, seemed to be a professional.

"What are you doing?" she asked faintly.

His eyes opened and the fire in them blazed heatedly on her like an inferno gone wild.

"Just getting a taste of what I'm going to devour next time," he said gruffly.

*Next time?*

He closed his eyes, his face looking pained. "Fuck, it'll be good." He blindly grabbed one of her hands and placed it on the large bulge at the front of his pants. "Feel what you do to me, Little Girl," he whispered in her ear, making her quiver involuntarily. He acted as if they had all the time in the world, though the knocking outside became more urgent.

Her fingers curled around him, making him shudder as he let out a raspy breath. His cock was huge and as hard as granite.

She felt him almost throbbing against her palm, even with the rough weave of his jeans as a barrier.

She'd done this to him? It was difficult to wrap her head around the fact that she could make a man like him come undone like this.

"I will have this door broken down if you two don't come out of there this instant!" Pinky's voice shrilled. Now the doorknob rattled.

"Fuck," Aariv muttered. "I swear that woman is a witch. How does she know everything around here?"

"Informants," Chrissy whispered, absolutely certain that was the truth.

Aariv chuckled. "You're probably right about that." He pulled Chrissy's hand away from him. "We'll continue this another time."

"We will?" she murmured, still a little dazed, but completely thrilled about his decisive attitude.

His eyes scanned down her almost naked form as if to memorize her like this.

"Let's get you fixed up," he finally said, but not before he kissed the top of her hand that he was still holding, the pressure of his lips gentle but firm, thrilling her even more with that chivalrous gesture.

*Not so fast, missy,* she thought. This man had a way of abruptly changing his mind.

He tried to help her fix her dress but she pushed his hands away, tying the dress closed herself. She bounded off the counter just as Aariv switched the lights on.

The current in the bulb above clicked and twitched almost imperceptibly, blinking briefly. The brightness shed them in the realization of what they'd just done. Chrissy was pretty sure that in the light of the real world, Aariv would change his mind, thinking they'd made a mistake.

She looked at herself in the mirror and found her reflection almost delirious. Her cheeks were scarlet pink and her eyes looked glassy. Her hair was more than disheveled, and her dress was stained with the colors that streaked down the front of Aariv's jacket. Anyone could take less than three guesses to figure out what they'd been up to.

Their eyes met in the mirror and she waited. She took a deep breath and steeled herself for the rejection because that was what she was used to with him.

*A*ariv was dumbfounded. He was at a loss for words—something that didn't happen often with him.

*What had they just done?*

The question kept circling the insides of his mind, but was dimmed, and finally over-ruled by the urgent request from his body—when were they going to do *that*, and much, much more, again?

He had a raging boner, no doubt about it and he wanted more than anything to finish what they'd started. His body was running on overdrive. He took a few deep inhalations to calm himself, not looking at her. If he did, he didn't think he'd be able to stop himself from grabbing her again and fucking her right then and there with the shrill complaints of Pinky Aunty as their soundtrack.

He cleared his throat, adjusted his jacket, and ran a hand

through his hair before his glance finally met hers in the mirror. She looked beautiful—sensual, and her perfect outfit mussed. Her eyes shone deep blue, almost black like the Bay of Bengal on a stormy night. Her cheeks were reddened as though she'd exerted her body physically, which she had … exquisitely—a performance he would never forget with her near-naked body writhing in front of him. He'd wanted to strip her completely, rip off her underwear, and see it all—the dusky haze of those hardened nipples which he could just make out behind the thin material of her bra; the mound of soft flesh he'd handled and the sensation of no pubic hair. The thought of her naked pussy with nothing to obstruct his view or touch excited him beyond anything he'd experienced before. God, he was a pervert, but she did things to him.

The look of utter shock that had passed across her face, and then acceptance of the pleasure he'd induced in her was something burned into his memory. And how her warm body shuddered over and over again, how her hot pussy sucked at his fingers, milking him, trying to get more. How she'd whined his name, finally screaming, forcing him to kiss her so people outside wouldn't hear. It had felt good—too good. And when her body had calmed down, but she continued to clutch him and tremble, Aariv had the inkling that for all her sexual and bold flirting, it was apparent that she'd never had a real erotic experience.

Even now she confirmed this as she stared at him in awe, her berry-like lips swollen and pink from his beard, open in confusion as she combed through her wild waves. Her once pristine ivory dress was ruined with wayward stripes of color from his own jacket, and he wasn't sorry one bit. He felt a constriction in him, one that made his breath catch. It was the feeling you get when you want something badly, and he wanted her. He wanted to tame her and teach her what her body could do and do for him.

What did that mean for him and his future? Fuck it, he had no clue. His future could continue to go on its course while he and Chrissy explored each other, surely? Or would she be opposed to such an idea?

The doorknob rattled again. Bringing him back to where they were.

"Okay," he muttered under his breath, running his palm along his beard, thinking. Then he said louder, with more resolution, "Okay." His decision made.

He reached for the door handle, but not before maneuvering Chrissy in front of him. Pinky didn't need to bear witness to the hard-on he sported, thus only confirming what they had been up to. Oh, she would guess, there was no question, but he'd made a career out of being able to talk out of certain sticky scenarios and could handle this.

He reached around Chrissy and unlocked the door, flinging it open to the angry, red face of Pinky, as her hand was poised in a fist to bang on the door again.

"Aunty," he said calmly. "Did you need something?" He kept his tone mild, even as his pulse raced with that same secret-mission feeling from before.

"What were you two doing in here?" she demanded, looking Chrissy up and down carefully, her eyes missing nothing.

He heard Chrissy inhale sharply. Before she could say a thing, he uttered, "Chrissy's dress got soiled from the colored powders earlier. I was trying to assist her with removing the stains."

The look on the older woman's face was enough to deflate

his boner partially. She eyed them both, her sharp glare becoming two slits—the better to hunt the truth out with.

"My dear, you could have come to me," she said cooly to Chrissy. "My housekeeper would have helped. I didn't bring her all the way back from India for nothing. She's quite talented with the laundry," she tutted. "And what does a man know about getting stains out of clothes?"

Aariv grunted. He'd been doing his laundry since moving to the States. Only recently in the past few years had he finally succumbed to a good laundry service when he landed his first job out of Law School.

She grasped the hem of Chrissy's skirt and looked at the fabric closely, fingering it between her thumb and forefinger.

"Did you even try water to treat it—" Her tone was accusatory.

Chrissy tugged the material, her dress hem slipping from the other woman's bejeweled fingers. "It's all right, Ms. Acharya. I have a pretty great way of getting stains out myself."

Pinky again stared from Chrissy's face up to Aariv's, then back to Chrissy. "I'm sure you do," she murmured, arching a shaped eyebrow.

What she thought she saw—Aariv had a pretty good idea. It looked damning because it was exactly what had happened. But even if he couldn't fix it, he could act as though nothing happened, thus throwing her off their scent.

"Pinky Aunty. I was just leaving. Thank you for the party. It was great. And I think I made some headway." He couldn't help but lay his hand on the small of Chrissy's back as he said this. She jumped at his touch.

Pinky's smile at the compliment of the great hostess turned into a scowl as she noticed Chrissy bounce on her toes. "I'm sure you did," she said coldly. "Kristen, I need you to finish clearing things out. It's getting late—"

"Aunty, just a minute," Aariv interjected. "Chrissy, would you mind walking me out? I'd like to see how my detective colleague has progressed with your case." He turned to Pinky with a bored expression. "Is it ok if I steal her for a minute? I promise she'll come back to finish the job."

Pinky threw up her hands and rolled her eyes. "Fine. What's ten more minutes? Always work, work, work with you young people. But I expect you to finish up soon, Kristen. I'm not paying overtime."

He heard Chrissy exhale loudly. "I would never dream of asking for overtime," she said politely, though her shoulders had stiffened. If he could see her face he was sure she'd be struggling to keep her composure. He rolled his lips inward and hid his smile.

He walked with Chrissy through the kitchen, careful to keep his distance as they turned into the wide hallway and finally out the door into the brisk ocean air.

"Jesus, that woman," she burst out on an exhale as soon as the heavy front door closed behind them.

Aariv couldn't agree more. And he shook his head.

"This way." He motioned down the flagstones of the long front walkway and out onto the sidewalk. He'd parked his car a few blocks away, thankfully. There wasn't the risk of probing eyes peering at them from behind the window curtains.

She walked silently behind him until they got to his car, and let out a loud gasp. "This is your car!?"

She stepped to the curb and ran her hands lightly over the side of his vintage burgundy '85 Porche 922 Carrera—his pride and joy. He'd saved and scrimped for this car after he got his first attorney job. His father had poo-pooed it saying he could buy it for him right then and there, and a brand new one at that. But Aariv didn't want any more gifts from his father and wanted to purchase it himself. And he'd always loved the vintage Porsche look, the feel of the motor under him, the control he had with the manual stick-shift. This particular model was a timeless classic, though not the fastest. But he'd always wanted one since seeing them in some of his favorite older movies from the 80's and 90's.

"This car is so *Risky Business*," Chrissy said still in awe. "You're full of surprises."

"You know that movie?" he asked amazed.

"Who doesn't? It's an 80's classic. And don't get me started on a hot young Tom Cruise in tighty-whities," she said cheekily, looking over her shoulder at him and winking.

He chuckled, stepping closer to her, his chest up against her back. She immediately straightened up, her hands still on the car. He placed his own on the car's hood, boxing her in.

He leaned in. "Are you a fan of tighty-whities?" he asked low in her ear. Where the fuck had that come from? His attempt at flirting was horrible—worse than horrible.

Her shoulders shook and she turned in her caged-in space looking up at him with a toothy grin; that cute misaligned tooth on display. She fiddled with the collar of his shirt as she murmured, "I'm not opposed to any hunk in his underwear." A hand dragged down his chest boldly and rested on his abs making him flex involuntarily. She audibly sighed.

"Chrissy?

"Yes, Aariv?" she answered, staring up at him with big dark eyes, her lids slowly fluttering open and close.

"We should…" What was he trying to offer here? He didn't

want to sound like a horny frat boy, but damn if she didn't do that to him. What he wanted to say was that he was ready to fuck her boneless, she just had to name the day and time. He decided on, "Explore each other more," and nodded. "I have a feeling you might not know what your body is capable of. I'd like to show you if you'll let me."

"Mm," she said but didn't deny that she might not be as experienced as she may have let on before. "I'd like that, Aariv," she said huskily. "And then I can find out what kind of underwear you *do* wear."

He grinned, laying his forehead on hers. "Hint one—I don't do tighty-whities." She licked her lips staring at his chin. "Hint two, I can guarantee we won't wear *anything*."

Her entire body flexed, her back arching momentarily before she relaxed and sighed. "Okay."

Good. She knew this was happening. There was just no way around the sexual tension between them except to meet it head-on. It would be both practical and enjoyable for both of them.

He leaned in to kiss her but before his lips touched hers, she asked, "And what about your wife quest?"

He paused, thinking for the briefest moment. "Does it matter?" he finally said.

"I'd like to know where we stand in terms of that … since we're exploring each other and all."

He sighed, running his palm across his beard. "The fact of the matter is the wheels are already in motion. And what we're going to embark on has nothing to do with that."

This was a pivotal moment. She could completely deny their sexual attraction because she wanted a storybook ending. But he wasn't in any position to give anyone that, not even to the wife who was eventually arranged for him.

"I understand," she said slowly, but she didn't look sad about that answer. "I can live with that. But I can't promise you that you won't like spending time with me," she joked, her smile so big, her dimples perfectly framing her mouth before she tossed her head back and laughed. "I've been told I can be loveable when I want to be."

He smirked. "Little Girl," he said low and a little dangerously while leaning into her again. Her breath quickened as his face came near hers. The shallow warm puffs heated his skin. "Only bloodthirsty lust is what's going to happen between us." His hands slid down her back slowly, pulling her into him, molding her warm curves into his hardness. "And I *will* promise you something." He leaned down further and nudged her chin up with his forehead, while his hands comfortably grabbed a handful of her ass. He squeezed with enough pressure to make her squeak, as he kissed the length of her neck, leaning down to suck on her collarbone.

"And—and what's that?" There was a tremor in her voice as her palms flattened against his chest. She tossed her head back further giving him a better angle to explore the expanse of skin exposed by the V of her dress.

He dipped his face into her cleavage, breathing in her fragrance. The sweetness went straight to his dick and he growled, making her jump. He inserted his tongue into the warm moist cleft and heard her gasp before he gently nipped the velvety skin on the curves of her breasts, thoroughly enjoying the soft flesh feel between his teeth. Then he inhaled up the length of her neck, finally answering, "I promise it'll be like nothing you've ever experienced before, and you won't be able to get enough of it."

She lifted her hands to cup his face.

"If that's your promise, when do we begin?" she asked before pulling him down to her, licking him before pulling his bottom lip with her teeth and sucking it into her mouth with fervor.

*Fuck.* She was going to make a more than willing partner.

Pepsi-Cola
PRESENT DAY
new york, new york

# CHAPTER 16

Aariv's body couldn't settle. He felt like his blood bubbled under his skin, along his vessels, and within his veins. It sounded like a loud, churning hiss in his ears.

He couldn't remember the last time he'd felt this way. Usually, he pushed forward with all of his life choices with calm and clarity, as if he were an instrument enacting the story that was written and expected of him. Never mind his past and Leila Majid, and that this jittery feeling reminded him of that more innocent time when regret had been the outcome. Because regret was something he didn't do anymore. He'd learned long ago that if he played by the rules, he wouldn't have to deal with being in the wrong ever again.

So this feeling he experienced, how his body felt alive, how he felt an almost nervous energy as he sat behind the wheel of his car, shifting gears harder than was necessary as he practically flew over the Queensboro bridge was newish, but invigorating. Was it excitement? Lust? Want?

All of those things, he mused, maneuvering the gears again, changing lanes, and roaring past a slower-than-normal yellow cab. And the best part was that it came with no repercussions because he wasn't breaking any rules. This thing with Chrissy had nothing to do with his life rules and society's expectations. Neither of them expected anything—no relationship—no future. And thus he could pursue this without guilt whatsoever. It felt fucking freeing.

Hell, the idea of not having to worry about consequences, along with knowing what kind of journey they'd be embarking on had him sporting a boner all week. The fact that she'd finally decided that tonight—hump day as she called it—would be the night for them, after over a week of sexual foreplay via text, had made him almost laugh out loud when he read her message. Something that wouldn't have been prudent as he was sitting with the partners and a few other of the firm's top lawyers regarding the Turner & Turner case.

In reaction, he did something he never did—he left at six on the dot, but not before assuring the partners he'd be back to review the new case notes later as he had a prior obligation he couldn't get out of. Was he lying? No. He damn well had an obligation—to get this burning desire for Chrissy Smyth out of his system once and for all.

When he'd arrived back at his place to freshen up before meeting her at her apartment, he'd found himself pulling his clothes off and hurrying to the shower—a jack-off session was in order. The eagerness of finally getting to be with her, combined with his lust-driven thoughts these past few days would make him come embarrassingly fast if he didn't take the edge off first.

He planned to keep it together tonight and show her what their bodies were capable of—what pleasures he was sure they could have together. Even now, the exhilaration filled his limbs at the thought, and he rolled down his window to feel the spring air whip across his face.

He arrived at her condo building, a nondescript concrete square painted white like all the others on the street. The area was an older development of Long Island City in the borough of Queens, near the famed neon Pepsi-Cola sign that lit up the water's edge along the East River. It was now recognized as a NYC landmark and considered a memento from bygone days when industry and commercial businesses dominated the area. Now the place was filled with green space and beautified for residential living. Chrissy's street looked like old warehouses that had been converted to more modern living spaces.

He circled the block a few times, trying to find parking. The neighborhood had prospered and changed, even from when he'd been there a few years ago, visiting family friends who'd moved from India. They didn't live there anymore, so he had no real reason to step foot in Queens. But taking it in now, the place was different—alive and electric. Trendy boutiques and eateries, as well as eclectic art galleries lined the streets. He could see why Chrissy would love living here. It felt cozy but cosmopolitan, homey, but artsy.

He finally decided to park in a parking garage as he couldn't find a space on the crowded streets and he hated double parking. Especially since he didn't know how long he was planning on being there; at least a few hours surely before he headed back to the office.

He'd barely pressed her call button in the small lobby when she buzzed him up quickly. He arrived at her door, on the 6th floor, a bottle of wine in hand, along with a long strip of condoms tucked neatly in his back pocket. He couldn't arrive with only protection now, could he, he mused, and he'd always been taught that coming empty-handed when visiting guests was bad manners.

The door flung open, and she stood there wild-eyed and excited. He had a feeling he appeared the same way and not for the first time wondered what this attraction was. She was hot, that was a given. But she was so different from other women he chose to spend his time with—and that was his error. Trying to compare her to others in his past didn't make sense because she wouldn't be someone he intended to date. Maybe it was the fact that she was so unlike the more sophisticated, put-together women he'd been with before, and was looking for in an arranged marriage, that made this—and her—appealing. There were no airs to worry about, and he could relax.

She stood in the doorway giving him a once-over as he did the same. She held one shoe in her hand, the other already on her foot—velvet dusky burgundy heels that perfectly matched the material and shade of the dress she wore. The length was long, hitting her at midcalf, but the fit was like a second skin, molding to her curves. Fuck was she even wearing underwear? he thought, eyeing her chest in the low neckline, the top curves puffing out tauntingly. It was held up by two skinny straps of the same material. Her nipples were hardened like they always were, and he let himself openly stare at them pushing against the velvet fabric, eager to do something about it.

She licked her lips while her stare moved slowly from the top of his head, down his casual grey Henley, over his jeans, to his boots. She didn't say anything but from the way her eyelids slowly fluttered, he knew she liked what she saw.

He pushed through the doorway and shut the door behind him, while she took the bottle of red from him and moved over to the kitchen area.

"This is nice," she murmured, barely glancing at the label before setting it down.

She came back to the entryway and sat on the bench near the door to put her other shoe on. "You got here quickly!" she remarked.

She didn't know how he'd practically flown across the bridge to get here, and he wouldn't tell her. Something about that feeling was strange to him—good, but strange. He'd need to unpack that later, but right now he had other more pressing matters.

He took two quick steps toward her and hauled her to standing before she got anywhere with her footwear. She tumbled into him, and they stood there for a beat, bodies pressed closely, her plush softness molding into him.

"Not fast enough," he uttered, his pulse hammering as he covered her mouth with his own, possessing her lips as if it were the first time he'd ever kissed her. In a way it was. The last time at the party hadn't been nearly enough time to kiss her thoroughly like he wanted to.

She yelped in surprise, but he heard her other shoe drop (literally on the hardwood floor) as she wound her hands up and around his neck. Her fingers tangled in his hair, tickling him as she crushed herself to him.

He pushed through her plush lips with his tongue, exploring her warmth and seeking out her tongue. He sucked at her, licked her, tasted her sweetness before finally coming up for air.

On an exhale, she asked, "Did you want to grab a bite—"

"No." His hands slid up and down her back and up through her copper-hued waves.

"Oh," she sighed happily, as his mouth dropped to her neck, moving quickly to her breasts. "What … about … the

… wine—Oh!" She gasped as his mouth wrapped around a nipple over the velvet material of her dress and he bit down lightly.

"It can wait," he said gruffly, his hands already on her hips, feeling the minuscule, taught string of her underwear under the thin layer of her dress. His fingers reached around to her ass cheeks and he squeezed the perfect peach curves of flesh and grunted in pleasure. His dick was hardening by the second and his lust was swelling up to a breaking point.

"Aariv—" she whimpered.

"Little Girl, where's your bedroom?"

"Over there." She pointed to a wall next to the living area that didn't quite make it to the ceiling. It acted like a divider and he realized her place was a studio apartment. Black and white photographs of a female body contorted into different poses hung on the partition. His first thought was he wanted to take a closer look, and his second was what the hell was he doing? He had her all to himself. Art could wait.

He hoisted her over his shoulder and she squealed, giggling, one shoe still on as he carried her behind the wall. He briefly registered large picture windows that gave a pretty great view of the city before dumping her on the bed, chuckling as she bounced and giggled on the mattress.

"Aariv!" she cried in mock horror. "No gentle lover, I see." She leaned back on her elbows, her body laid out ripely before him.

He grinned, pulling out the condoms from his back pocket and tossing them on the bed next to her. She looked at the foil packets in fascination, her cheeks burning red.

"Gentle might come later … we'll see." He toed his shoes off and pulled his shirt over his head.

Her eyes became huge orbs as she stared at his chest. He involuntarily flexed his abs; he couldn't help it.

"OMG. You're *so* hunky." She sat up and leaned forward, dragging her palm over his chest, her fingers curling in his chest hair. Her hand continued down to his abs where she fingered his muscles, exploring, sighing each time she traced a ridge, then through his happy trail. And he was flattered. He knew she found him attractive, but it was nice to hear her accolades and witness what he did to her without even touching her.

"Thank you." He rubbed the back of his neck. Then he grinned lazily, and asked, "How many times did you make yourself come at work with your fingers?"

Shit. Their texting the past few days had driven him crazy. They teased each other to such a tipping point that he even locked his office door and closed the blinds to jack off, not able to wait until he got home. She turned him on so fucking much.

She licked her lips and batted her eyes slowly. "None. I saved it all for you."

Jesus Christ. He swore under his breath. Now he was even more turned on than ever. So much for getting it out of his system before getting here so he wouldn't be an actual fucking maniac.

He reached for her hands and placed them on the front of his jeans.

"Take my pants off, Little Girl," he commanded, watching her chest rise and fall, his palms itching to rip her dress down. But he waited, and her chest quickened, her nerves apparent. "You're mine tonight." She looked up at him with a mixture of apprehension and desire, the same mixture of innocent and womanly that he found so mesmerizing. "Do as I say," he urged.

She nodded, licking her lips as her fingers worked his belt

undone, and then his button and zipper. He clenched his jaw, willing himself to continue to hold still as she pulled his jeans down, leaving him in his grey boxer briefs. There was no way for her not to stare at his cock, which was bulging in his underwear like a raging bull ready to be let out and ridden.

Her breath was shaky as she stared at the evidence of his lust for her.

"Everything all right?" he asked lightly, trying to take the edge off her apparent nervousness as he stepped out of his pants. "You can tell me to stop whenever you feel uncomfortable, but I doubt you will." Was he a little too confident about his sexual prowess? Not in the least. He'd been making women come hard and then some since his teenage years.

She nodded wordlessly giving him a once-over. A giggle escaped her as she eyed his feet.

"Excuse me? What's so funny?" he asked as seriously as possible, but pretty sure she'd just noticed his light blue funky socks with white flowers printed all over them.

"How did you know that daisies are my favorite?" she asked, raising a brow, her mouth twitching as he pulled them off and tossed them on the pile.

"What's that now?"

"Those are daisies on your socks. I love daisies," she said, pointing to them.

He reached for her and paused. A familiar feeling was at his periphery, the same he remembered when she came to his office soaking wet, walking into his life for the second time. It was strange—that feeling—because they were talking about something as mundane as socks. He pushed the thought back because, nope, he was not going to see this as some weird sign. Just because he grabbed the last clean pair from his drawer, and they happened to be printed with her favorite flowers.

Instead, he lifted her one-shoed foot. "Your turn, Sunshine," he said gruffly.

"Sunshine?" she asked with surprise, her brows shooting up and under her bangs.

He pulled her shoe off and tossed it over his shoulder.

"You're always smiling and laughing at something."

"Or someone," she said cheekily. She grinned, proving his point. "Is that such a bad thing?"

"Not when you shouldn't be." He slipped his fingers underneath the straps of her dress and tugged it down to her waist.

Her smile disappeared and their breaths hitched collectively. Her breasts bobbed slightly after escaping the snug material of her dress. They were perfect round globes, with small, dusty pink nipples.

"Damn, these titties. Driving me to fucking insanity, all day, every day," he growled, an animalistic want barreling through him. He palmed her breasts, squeezing the weighted warmth in his hands. She moaned, arching back, and letting him. "Perfection," he groaned, before roughly dragging his beard across their softness, leaving tiny red marks that marred her smooth sun-kissed flesh. His tongue licked her hardened nubs making them shine, then sucked each one tenderly, biting down briefly.

"*Riv*," she whimpered, now leaning back on her elbows, her body bowed in want—in need.

He pushed her dress further down to her hips, revealing her stomach. Her abs muscles jumped every time she whimpered and moaned.

"Do you like it when I take what I want?" he asked, his mouth moving down over her stomach, reaching the point where her dress hid what he knew would be utter succulence. "Tell me, Little Girl."

He wanted to hear her say she wanted him. He watched her with his eyes as his mouth tickled her belly, nipping and licking, tasting her skin. Fuck, she was gorgeous, her body splayed out before him. He wanted to command it, bend her to his will.

"*Yes,*" she gasped. Her eyes were open and on him, her lids hooded with desire over her cat-like eyes. "Do what you want with me," she said breathlessly.

He nodded and pulled her dress down her hips and over her legs. She shimmied, helping him until she was left completely naked except for the tiny black G-string she wore.

"What a hot little body this is," he said, climbing over her, his thighs around her. His hands cupped each breast again and he tugged at her nipples making her arch and cry out. Then he stroked his palms down her heated skin, so soft, yet cut with muscle definition, indicating her dancer's physique. Down he went, feeling her abs constrict under the smoothness of her belly until he met the tight elastic of her underwear. He slid his hand underneath the slip of material to cup her nakedness between her thighs, feeling the heated wetness he knew would be there.

She moaned, her body flexing. His lust boiled like a geyser. God, he wanted to plunge into her hot tightness and rut at her with abandon. Fuck. Everything about her was making his usual libido more heightened. From her wild eyes to her wild copper hair, her plush bottom lip tucked into her mouth, her beautiful body writhing sensually below him. And the fact that they both wanted him to do whatever he wanted with her.

But he wouldn't, not just yet. He wanted to take his time.

"So hot, and wet," he murmured, using his palm to rub her with her juices.

His thumb caressed the naked skin where a woman's pubic hair should be. "No hair?"

She nodded. "What's the point when my costumes are so revealing?" She sighed and closed her eyes as he continued to stroke her.

"Lucky me." He scooted himself down and hooked his fingers into the elastic of her underwear, tugging it off.

Lucky him, indeed. She lay before him, completely naked, and his eyes couldn't take in everything at once as they darted around her perfect, luscious form and hairless pussy.

He took a few shuddering breaths as he closed his eyes, his dick pushing so hard against his underwear, that pre-cum was no doubt smeared on the front, soaking through.

"What's wrong?" she asked, her tone devoid of any flirtation.

He opened his eyes to see her concern, the frown marred between her brows.

"Holy fuck, Chrissy. Nothing. Absolutely nothing. You're perfect."

He pulled his underwear down and her eyes went from large orbs to practically bulging.

The breath got stuck in her throat as she stared at him. *Breathe.* She told herself.

He was—for lack of a better word—ginormous. She'd never

seen a man so big before aside from the pornos she and her friends had watched curiously and jokingly together. His dick practically throbbed at her, protruding from a nest of short black hair. He was long, sure, but had girth, too.

She shook, and she wasn't sure if it was from anticipation or fear. She had never (never!) experienced a hot man like him or his ginormous dick.

Her excitement at finally getting to be with him this way had teetered between ecstatic and over-blown horniness all day. She'd come home in a daze, barely registering the rest of her afternoon and her train ride home.

When she got to her apartment, she'd showered and carefully gotten ready, as much as her excitement would let her. She'd picked out her sultry dress and styled her hair into big loose curls, wanting to appear like a sexy bombshell with more experience than she had. And she'd achieved it, she'd thought, giving herself one last look in the mirror. It was a person with more confidence than she felt staring back at her. Faking it came naturally—that's what performers did for a living. But then her buzzer rang loudly, shaking any calm she may have attained in the last half hour.

But faking it wasn't necessarily needed with this man. His expression as soon as she'd opened the door said it all. He was a man starving, his eyes wild, roaming over her body, coaxing it back into the low hum of sexual energy she'd felt the last few days. And she felt beautiful and desired, assured that she was what he wanted and that she could give him what he needed.

*But now ...*

"Now I have to ask you—what's wrong?" His hands were on his hips, his muscular legs splayed wide, his cock standing up straight with wetness glistening at the tight tip. He grinned and for the love of God how was one man so stacked in every department? Good looks, hard body, big cock. She should thank her lucky stars, but even she knew she couldn't be so cavalier about this. Yep, she was a little frightened if she was being honest with herself.

"You're … you're huge!" she squeaked out.

That only made his grin more devilish.

*Hot and arrogant son-of-a-bitch.*

"And from what I remember, your pussy is oh so tight," he said gruffly, stepping forward and placing a hand between her legs. He palmed her, massaging her with the heel of his hand. "Relax," he said gently, surprising her, his cut arm muscles tensing as his hand lightly manipulated her delicate flesh. He continued massaging her as he lay down next to her.

"Relax," he whispered in her ear. She shuddered, the scent of him pushing her fear aside. His nakedness felt more like a protector with her at this moment. And she did relax. Her leg muscles softened, and her thighs widened, wanting more of the magic his hand was weaving. "You have a sexy, tight little body that will enjoy everything I give you," he said firmly, and with authority.

Those words alone made her back arch off the bed with need. The heat in her body seemed to liquefy, slithering to her core, straight down to her pussy. She had no idea until meeting this man that she liked to be bossed around, that she was so turned on by it.

"You're a bad little girl." He slipped a finger into her, groaning and closing his eyes. "So tight, so fucking wet. You've been a cock tease the entire time I've known you." He grunted through gritted teeth in an accusatory tone. "Watching you dance in that skimpy costume—such a sexy body just asking for it. And from me. Only me. Tell me."

She stared at him as he spoke. His closed eyes, at the pleasure written across his handsome face as he finger-fucked her with eloquence. As a lawyer, she should've known the man liked to listen to the sound of his own voice, but hot damn she liked to listen to it, too. The grittiness took over his usual deep smooth tone when the dirty words spilled from his thick lips. The look of almost pain that the pent-up pleasure wrought on his face made her speechless and in awe of him.

When she didn't say anything, he stopped moving his hand.

"Tell me or I won't continue."

"Tell you what?" she asked breathlessly, confused.

"Tell me how bad you've been. How you've been teasing me," he said, his hand hovering over her ignited flesh. She bucked her hips looking for his touch, but he remained elusive.

*Okay.* Aariv really liked his dirty talk. She could do this.

She placed her hands on his shoulders and caressed his arms, over his steel-like muscles.

"You're all I think about." She wasn't even lying. She closed her eyes and thought about the state of frenzy he put her into every time she saw him, spoke to him … shit, just texting him.

His hand found her again and he slipped two fingers in this time as if to reward her. She didn't feel the stretch from last time. She was too wet. She lifted her hips to gain some traction and it felt incredible. But she continued speaking because she wanted to tell him.

"When I'm dancing up on stage, I imagine it's just you watching me." She opened her eyes and the intensity and heat in his gaze scorched her. She went on. "And I imagine I'm completely naked, nothing hiding me from your view. I'm there only for you."

He nodded licking his lips and he slid three fingers inside her, widening her, exploring every inch of her. His breathing came out thick, harsh, as if what he was doing to her gave him pleasure, too.

"Yes!" she gasped, her hips undulating back and forth, up and down. His fingers felt so good, filling her up, stretching her even more deliciously.

"That's it," he murmured. Now his hand jerked in and out of her, reaching deeper.

But she wasn't finished with her daydreams, and she spoke, through her haze of pleasure. "I want you to own my body, Riv. I want you to fuck me hard like you've never fucked anyone before. I want that huge cock so far up in me, I'll feel the burn for days."

Where the hell were these words coming from? They were true, but she'd never been so … articulate with her wants and needs.

He chuckled. "Oh, that'll happen, Little Girl. But let me see you come for me first." And he pumped her even faster, creating a friction like she'd never felt before, reaching even further inside her until he tickled that special spot like last time and her insides clenched. Her pussy tightened around him, and she felt like she couldn't breathe. "Relax," he murmured again. And she obeyed him, and when she did, her body fell, hurtling off of some unknown precipice. She distinctly heard herself screaming, but it sounded far away. Her back arched off the bed and her hips bucked, and she held onto him tight as she saw rainbows dancing behind her lids. "Jesus," he muttered in wonder, no doubt in reaction to her. Did she look crazy?

Probably. But how could she not when this man seemed to hold the key to a secret pleasure she'd never known she had in her?

She heard the ripping and rustling of foil then, the jerky movements of Aariv putting on a condom. And she was ready, even as her body still trembled and her erotic fog still surrounded her. The mattress dipped and he was on top of her, his hard muscular body pressed into hers and she opened her thighs, welcoming him. He kissed her hungrily, sucking at her lips, moaning as his dick, that huge, enormous thing, pressed into her heated, sensitive flesh.

He started grinding into her, and she wrapped her legs around his torso, her arms around his back, tracing his taut skin.

"Chrissy," he groaned, rearing up. "Are you ready?"

She smiled nodding, still dazed that this was all happening, her body already wild with need again, her base instinct wanting to engulf his cock inside her.

He guided himself to her entrance, and it didn't take long, though huge he was. She was so wet down there that he slid easily in, stretching her deliciously, minuscule nerves tensing around him, making her moan, and he groaned. When he was in all the way, he paused, letting her adjust. But the feeling of being filled up by him wasn't enough and she bucked her hips, wordlessly urging him to move.

He reacted by pulling out and plunging back into her, grunting in pleasure. "Fuck," he hissed under his breath. He did it again, moving slowly, their bodies suctioning as he plunged back in. "Fuck," he spit out again, his eyes closed tight. Beads of sweat glistened along his hairline, and she realized this was hard work—easing an inexperienced person into eroticism.

That thought, along with how incredible he felt filling her up while slowly fucking her made her shudder. She flexed her hips up, taking him in even deeper. She gasped. She'd never had anything or anyone so deep inside her. If this wasn't pure paradise, she didn't know what was.

"Fuck, Little Girl. I'm trying not to be too rough here," he grunted, his head in her neck breathing heavily, his breath fanning her hair.

Something warm spread inside her chest and her pulse beat loudly in her ears, even as she flexed her hips up urging him to move again. He lifted his head to look at her, his gaze questioning.

"Aariv, remember, no gentle lover?" She pushed his damp hair from his forehead.

Something changed in him at those words. His face contorted into determination. He pulled out and rose to his knees. His large hands palmed her thighs, pulling her flush into him as he sunk back into her. He groaned loudly closing his eyes.

She didn't know where to put her hands, so she gripped his thigh muscles as he plunged in and out of her with a speed and roughness she'd not been expecting. But watching him fall apart, as she had just done only moments ago, not only fascinated her but pushed her desire over.

She started bucking her hips in reaction to his movements.

"Yes," he encouraged. "Yes, move like that, Chrissy," he said through gritted teeth. He opened his eyes and his fiery gaze roved over her face, down her body watching every move she made. "Yes. Come with me."

He lay on top of her, and though most of his weight was on his elbows, she knew from the first moment she'd met him that him lying on top of her like this would be the best feeling in the world. He grasped one of her thighs, angling it up so that he hit a different spot inside her as he moved with a piston speed.

It was insanely good, making her moan over and over again. She couldn't move her hips fast enough but moved in a wildness she (even as a dancer) didn't know she possessed, clutching onto him.

"Oh my, God, Aariv. It's *so* good!" She tossed her head side to side on the pillow. "You have to feel this, it's *so* good!" she cried, her eyes out of focus from the force of it all.

He chuckled and grunted. "Oh, I'm feeling it, Baby. It's so —yes!" His growl echoed throughout the room as his body tensed, the sweat on his forehead now dripping down the sides of his face and onto her breasts. "Fuck, *yes!*" He kept grunting on his exhales.

She closed her eyes, though she wanted to observe that look of freedom on his face; that she could do that to him still stunned her. But the pleasure he ignited was too great. Her fingers dug into his arms as she exploded from her core to the tips of her fingers and toes, feeling like a wayward firework crashing and bursting into fiery sparks. Her body felt alive and tired all at the same time. Every nerve lit up ready to party, but her muscles were heavy. It was such a juxtaposition that she just let go, letting the experience disarm her, moaning over and over again, pulling Aariv down to her. His body collapsed, squishing her, but she didn't care as he bellowed a final "Fuck yeah!" in her ear; his release such a force inside her she wondered if the condom would pop.

She felt like she was floating as he jerked over and over again. His groans dissipated, followed by heavy breathing.

When she finally felt like she'd grounded, like a wayward leaf fluttering in the wind and landing, she was more than satiated. The tiny thought crept into her—just for the briefest second before she dashed it way—that she wished beyond wishes that this feeling with him would never end. Not just the ecstasy, but this warmth and closeness. It was temporary though, and she'd take what he gave her while it lasted. Happiness didn't always need to be in the arms of someone you cared about. And then she chided herself while she threaded his thick damp locks with her fingers at the base of his neck. She didn't care about him, did she?

*Oh, shit. What a cliché ...*

Falling for a guy after having sex with him. She knew better than that, and yet ... unwittingly, but not, that small seed had already implanted itself in her chest.

# CHAPTER 17

"*Beta*, tell me exactly what was wrong with this batch. I need to hear this straight from your mouth because Pinky couldn't understand it either. She told me you'd sixty-nine-ed them—*all of them!*"

Late the next morning in his office, Aariv paused mid-scribble; he was buried in the large stack of discovery documents he was supposed to have reviewed the previous evening. Along with a multitude of meetings as well as trying to juggle his work, he was addressing Huma's concerns about the *Holi* party which felt like ages ago. He'd tried ignoring her calls, but his phone buzzed incessantly until finally, she tried another tactic—calling his work line. His assistant, Terri, had patched her through. He couldn't blame her; Huma's tone made it sound like a real emergency.

"I think you mean eighty-six-ed them," he said, pushing one file closed and placing it on top of the large pile on his desk. Everything would go to his assistant to organize, and he'd do it all over again tomorrow if new evidence came up. In all honesty, he'd probably have to go back through everything with a fine-toothed comb. He wasn't doing the client any favors by multi-tasking the review of new witness interrogations along with his personal life. He grabbed the next file anyway and flipped it open, glancing over it.

"Are you sure?" she asked, querulously. "You Americans and your funny sayings. I can't keep them straight."

"Yes. I'm pretty sure you mean I rejected all of them, not performed a famous sex position with them."

He didn't mean to sound curt, but he had a lot of work to get through. Though, last night had been worth it with Chrissy.

*Jesus.* Just the mere thought of her and how incredible the sex was had his eyes blurring on the fine print before him while his brain turned into complete mush. He put his pen down and pushed the paperwork aside, attempting to concentrate on the conversation at hand and think about Chrissy later.

"*Eeesh*! What nasty talk is this?" Huma asked outraged.

He leaned back in his chair and swiveled to face the windows. After the morning torrential downpour, the sky had cleared to a pretty powder blue. But, big fluffy clouds appeared suspended in the distance, indicating that April wasn't done with raining its showers down on them just yet.

"You said it, Aunty, not me," he teased.

She sighed loudly. "Anyway, *Beta*, what was wrong with these girls?"

"Women."

"*Ki* (what)?"

"These are women we're talking about. Grown adults. Not girls," he said testily, taking his glasses off and rubbing his eyes. He'd be lying to himself if he didn't admit he'd rather be back in bed with Chrissy; a grown woman whom, ironically, his dirty mind liked to think of as a little girl when they were together.

He'd taken her again last night and now his mind couldn't help jumping excitedly back to that memory, no matter how hard he tried to listen to Huma's lecture. The pleasure of watching Chrissy, straddling him on top, lost at first and then figuring out how to reap her pleasure had been fascinating. He couldn't believe that a woman like her, one who was both a scintillating combination of cute and hot, independent, and headstrong, hadn't been given the chance to experience good sex. Who were these a-holes she'd been dating? Well, no harm no foul, he was here to pleasure her, and teach her. And honestly, something about her orgasmic innocence turned him on. His dick thickened right at that moment just thinking about it.

## LAST NIGHT

"*I*'m not sure I can do this," she said, her eyes squeezed tightly shut; as tight as her pussy clutched his dick while she sat naked on top, straddling him.

His arms were behind his head, as he watched her, a lazy smile playing across his lips. He was enjoying the view of her curvy tight body open on him, her tan skin flushed, her pink-tipped tits bouncing with every movement she made.

"We got time, Sunshine. You can do this." He encouraged her, pleasantly disarmed by the way she became flustered, her face burning bright red, her hair a shiny mess around her shoulders. She was usually so certain—a performer always on.

Did he have time? Probably not. He'd told the partners he'd be back at the office later. But for some reason, time slowed down when he was with Chrissy. He wanted to relax and explore her; enjoy her.

"I thought you said you had to get back to the office," she said, echoing his thoughts. She crossed her arms over her chest, making her breasts balloon up, as she blew her bangs out of her now open and wide eyes. "How will you ever make partner if you ditch paperwork to instruct lil' ole' me?"

He chuckled, reaching up to pull her warm body flush onto his as he lay back down. Her breasts flattened against his chest, and he sighed, enjoying the sensation, his dick still inside her—still hard as granite—but after fucking her like an animal the first time, he was ready to make this time last longer.

"I'll risk it." He ground his pelvis up into her softness, his cock pushing further, and her heated muscles practically sucked him up. She gasped into his neck, feeling the sensation, too. He did it again, but she lay listless on top of him, so he continued moving languidly, the tension starting to build from the base of his balls up to his tip. "*Fuck!*" He'd groaned. "You're even tighter like this, Little Girl."

He reached a hand up behind her neck, while the other gripped her hip, his fingers digging into the flesh. He wanted to own this body. She was his tonight.

It didn't take long for her to react to his movements. She started shifting herself so that her hips undulated on him, her wetness seeping between both of their thighs.

She paused then. "I—I think I ... squirted?" she said faintly, burying her head into his neck, embarrassed.

Her back trembled, then her shoulders quivered. Was she upset?

"That's a good girl," he responded, stroking her back. "That's what I like. You squirting all over me; getting us messy while we fuck."

She giggled, her warm breath fanning his neck. He smiled; glad she wasn't upset at all. But he smacked her perfect peach-shaped ass anyway and she squeaked.

"As a learning experience, Little Girl, I expect you to take this seriously," he admonished sternly, a little dangerously.

Rearing up to sit on him again, she retorted with mock seriousness, "Oh, I do, *Uncle Riv.*"

She rolled her hips on him, and he wasn't sure if it was how good that felt, or the fact that she was calling him "Uncle," as if he was some kind of father figure to her that had him so turned on.

God, he really was perverted. Fuck it. He was going to lean into it with her and get it all out of his system, no matter how long it took to 'teach her.'

And he should've known better—she was a quick learner, rocking on him, rolling her hips with him, figuring out what felt good to her. The sound of her wetness squelched between them as they groaned and moaned their way to a release. And she looked like a glorious other-worldly being riding him, her eyes darkened blue-black in determination, her mouth open and wild as she screamed, punctuating her cries with his name, finally coming so hard that her entire body shook from it. Merely watching her like that made him fall over the edge. He closed his eyes, while he careened toward a release that lit up the darkness behind his lids. Her insides convulsed around him, her muscles pulling at him and he bucked up into her, shooting his cum into her with such force that she almost toppled over. He held her in place, grunting and groaning as he finished.

"*A*re you listening to me, Aari?" Huma Aunty asked, forcing him back to their less-than-enjoyable conversation.

He shifted his crotch, trying to ease the tightening. He swiveled back around to his desk, but that didn't help because all he saw was the expanse of a wide flat surface, and the couch in the corner; two perfect places for Chrissy and him to explore each other more.

"Aari?" she asked again.

"I'm here," he said irritably. "I don't know, Aunty. I can't put my finger on it. The chemistry felt off with this bunch."

"With *every* candidate? That's what you said last time." Her impatience was growing, making her voice higher.

But he wasn't ready to placate her. "And Kareena Sharma? Really?"

"What's wrong with Kareena Sharma? She's perfectly lovely. Very attractive, though with a darker complexion than the others. She might be a widow, and have a child, but these are modern times. It shouldn't matter."

God, the irony. Aariv shook his head in disbelief.

"It's not—"

But Huma continued as if he hadn't said anything. "She, out of all of the gir—women on the list, is the best match for you. Your birth charts alone are a high factor. And her sign is very compatible with yours. Remember, *Beta*, you are a *Khumba*—an Aquarius. As a *Simha* (Leo), she compliments you perfectly—"

"Mumbo jumbo," he said under his breath. But Huma heard it.

"*Abishwashyo* (unbelievable)," Huma muttered, something Aariv used to hear all the time when he lived at home. But it was usually directed at his father's obnoxious behavior. "Isn't this what you asked for? We are trying to find your perfect match."

He was silent. Is this what he wanted? Did a perfect match rely solely on cosmos and birth charts alone? Shouldn't there be more to it than that? Did he even want a perfect match? Hell, did he want a match at all? His head was spinning.

"Kareena is the furthest match from me," he uttered, grasping at what he did know. "Don't you remember how she treated Mimi when we were younger?" He scoffed. "Does that count for nothing?"

"People change, Aariv," Huma scoffed right back. "She's a successful physician now. Think what a great match that would be for our family. You an attorney, she a doctor."

"You sound like *Abba,*" Aariv retorted, almost snarling at Huma's gleeful attitude. But it did sound like something his father would say. Oh, everyone might think it, but his father would say the words out loud, boasting about it very loudly.

Huma spluttered on the other end and then became quiet. He'd hurt her feelings, but something was making a tide of angst well up slowly within him. It wasn't an unfamiliar feeling —actually what was unfamiliar was that it'd disappeared for the past few days, making him feel so much lighter than he normally felt.

"*Beta,* is something else keeping you from focusing on this?"

"What do you mean?" he asked, surprised at her change of tactics.

"Pinky mentioned *ekti sada may*—a white woman. Someone you might be friendly with…"

*"Who?"* he asked, confused, his mind already jumping back to the paperwork in front of him, his meetings, and finding the next opportunity to see Chrissy again. He felt wound up all of a sudden and wanted that free feeling back from last night with her.

"At the *Holi* party at her house," Huma said quietly. "She said there was a woman there who kept you busy. Someone, *not* marriage material."

That grabbed his attention and he sat dumbfounded for a moment. So, they knew about Chrissy. Shit. But it wasn't as if he'd hidden his interest in her that day so well, and the meddling woman *had* found them in the bathroom together afterall.

Huma sighed. "Aariv, if you need to sew your wild oats, I understand. Get it out of your system. Men usually need to before they can be serious about marriage commitments." She chuckled and continued with steel lacing her usual gentle voice. "And some men still cannot control themselves, even when married."

His father. Aariv knew that was who she referred to. It was no secret that his father had affairs, both with the household staff and prostitutes in brothels.

"Here's the thing," he said, "Considering what I've seen between you and *Abba,* I'm not so sure I want to continue pursuing an arranged marriage."

Huma sucked her teeth loudly in irritation. "Your marriage will be nothing like ours. You are a much better man."

"I appreciate you saying that, Aunty. But can I ask you something? And please, answer honestly."

"*Atcha.*" He heard the hesitation in her tone. "I am ready."

He cleared his throat. "Are you happy?"

This was a hard question to ask. Her generation of South Asians and Indians didn't usually discuss mental health and happiness. To them, depression and anxiety could easily be fixed with sleep, or drinking more water.

Her laughter was girlish, tinkling like Christmas bells. "*Heh, Beta.* I am. Why? What is there not to be happy about?"

"Don't you wish you and he got along better?"

She sighed, but not in sadness, more like a parent realizing they should have explained something of importance long ago to their child.

"Honestly, Aari, your *abba* and I—we are fine. He doesn't beat me and I live very comfortably. Let me tell you something you might not know. Your *amma*, may she be in peace wherever she is, left you motherless, and that is the main fact. You, an honest, innocent little boy, needed a mother. I was arranged with your father and I couldn't have been happier. His family was successful, had an old and respectful lineage, and had money and power—but you know this," she said hastily because the fact of the matter was that his father had begun to mismanage the family wealth.

Jute fiber—the crop used for twine, rope, rice bags, and even mattresses—was still doing pretty decently considering the price hikes, but his father was beginning to cut corners with the number of laborers. A major upheaval was brewing, and the whispers were everywhere concerning mismanagement and the quality of the product. They were slowly losing business. His father had taken up gambling, too, more voraciously than before as a way to forget his troubles. But he wasn't great at that either. Aariv would inherit this mess when the older man died, debts and all. And he couldn't wait to get rid of it all, despite the family legacy ingrained with the jute company. Times were changing.

"So," she continued, "what more could I ask for as an uneducated girl from a family down on their luck? I didn't have a college degree which is what all the families had started looking for in a woman by then. And things were different between us in the beginning. You probably cannot remember those days. You were too little. But I found out I could not have children, and well, that was when your father became the way he is now. Some of it is my fault because rather than divorce me, he decided to let me stay and step in as a mother for you. And I am *fine* because of this—because I have you. You've always been a good boy. And you've turned into a good man. I'm so proud of you, making sure all of us are fine, all the time. You put others first. Let us help you find a good partner in life; someone who will put you first and care for *you*."

Aariv leaned back in his chair thinking. He'd had no inkling that this was part of the narrative—that she couldn't have children and felt like she was dealt a good hand nonetheless, though he shouldn't be surprised. Things were still so backward in the Indian culture. The abuse she received at the hands of his father—nothing physical, thankfully—didn't seem to wear her down, though no one deserved that kind of treatment. And she felt like she was living the life that was planned out for her—to be his stand-in mother, even though her husband was a total dick.

And, here was the thing—was he any better than his father? He'd never given any thought to why they hadn't had more children; just that he was the apple of both of their eyes and he'd basked in that attention.

He grunted under his breath. He was selfish—absolutely his father's son. And when it came down to it, he did want to make Huma happy. Now that he knew her sacrifices, he didn't want to let her down.

"Listen, I'll look over the biodatas again—the ones you've already sent me. But I will not consider Kareena. That's where I draw the line."

"*Atcha, Beta*," she said, placating him. "Don't think too hard about it. They're all very good matches. Pinky and I have assured this. Now this … *may* (girl), this involvement—do what you need to do, and then focus."

She said it so easily as if he could separate duty from physical want. He should be able to, shouldn't he? He'd done it before. But something felt different this time. It wasn't that Chrissy was easy to be with (she was, though she wasn't normally his type). But it was that he liked it—liked her forthright manner, her simplicity in life though she had a complex past. It was fascinating to him. He was in no hurry to get back to his own world.

Somehow he'd found himself lying in bed with her, talking of all things, after she'd ridden him with more than successful outcomes. That was the real reason he hadn't made it back to the office later last night—because he was also enjoying their non-sexual time together.

# CHAPTER 18

১৮

**LAST NIGHT**

She bounded out of bed naked and threw his shirt on, the length reaching her mid-thighs. She skipped out of the bedroom, and he heard her rummaging around in the kitchen.

The black and white prints he'd noticed earlier on the other side of the dividing wall, continued on this side as well. They were arty photos of the same body, face hidden, contorted into artistic poses. Originally he thought the body was nude, but after getting up to discard the used condom, and putting his boxer briefs back on, he saw the slight shadow of a skin-colored bodysuit along the woman's skin.

Aariv looked at each one carefully, a series of nine 11x17 prints framed in simple black frames. They were beautifully taken. The photographer created an aura of mystery but captured the elements of finesse and agility with the poses that the person (clearly a dancer as she wore the kind of ballet shoes with ribbons wrapped around her ankles) held. Along with the natural shadows and angles of the form's feminine and muscular physique, the entire series was bold but wispy, powerful, and sensual.

When Chrissy returned, she had the bottle of wine he'd brought in one hand, now uncorked. In her other, she clutched two wine glasses. She watched him as he examined the pictures.

"This is you," he stated.

She cocked a head and an impish grin lit up her face. "Yeah, how can you tell?"

"Are you kidding?" He smiled, lifting one corner of his mouth. "I'd never mistake that body."

He took the bottle and a glass from her and filled it, and then filled the one she still held as his eyes raked over her in his shirt, her curves hidden. He had to admit he liked seeing her in his clothes.

"Do you want to listen to some music?" She asked, just as he told her he thought the photos were incredible.

She laughed and thanked him.

Music filtered into the room, and her eyes sparkled, her grin easy. It was a jazzy, French number; sexy and relaxing. He lifted a brow. She'd already presumed what he might like, and she wasn't wrong. "Nice choice."

She tucked some hair behind her ear. "I figured I'd pass on Tay-Tay for now."

He quirked his brows in response—as in who?

She giggled, that husky throaty sound. "Taylor Swift?" She climbed onto the bed, balancing her full glass as she snuggled up against the padded headboard.

"Ah, yes. That phenomenon." He shook his head, realizing how much younger she was from him. But if he remembered correctly, when Mariam had told him about her months ago, it wasn't as if she was *that* young; more like late twenties.

She took in his smirk and nodded. "I was right. You aren't ready for her."

He followed her into bed and leaned back next to her, chuckling. "Yeah, pop music isn't my thing. I'm more of a rock and reggae guy. I like some jazz, too."

She nodded, smiling to herself. Then asked curiously, "Rock and reggae? I could be into that." She sipped her wine and said primly, "Don't knock pop stars until you try them, though. 'Swifties' come in all forms, shapes, and sizes, you know."

He grunted, his answer conveying that in no way would he deign to listen to that kind of music. She giggled and they sipped and stared at the wall of photos.

"These are seriously cool." He nodded. "But your hair is different now than in those photos. And at the wedding, wasn't it blonde?"

She side-eyed him from under her lashes. "Do you prefer blondes?"

"I prefer any color. But red suits you," he said chuckling. It did. The red illuminated her tawny skin and somehow her eyes appeared even deeper blue.

"Well, thank you." She flipped her hair dramatically over a shoulder. "The blonde was a thing my mom and I used to do together. But with my financial woes, I can't afford it anymore. And I like my natural hair, now. It's grown on me." She winked at him and he leaned back further into the squabs of the cushion, feeling extremely relaxed with her.

Her fingers skimmed along his jaw, leaving a warming sensation. "What about you? What's with this? You didn't have it at the wedding."

He cupped his chin, rubbing at the bristly hairs. "I was trying something new. But I like my beard." He wasn't going to explain his convoluted reasonings regarding his attempts to erase any similarity to his father. They seemed extremely childish in hindsight.

She nodded. "It's damn sexy," she said shyly, looking away.

It didn't escape him that this idle chit-chat part was out of character for him. He typically didn't say much of anything when it was just about the sexual attraction. Usually, he left quickly, not leaving any chance for small talk. But the conversation was easy, and it wasn't so bad. It was light, not serious.

"So your mom, how did she die?" And he wondered what the hell had made him ask that. He tried to backtrack "You don't have to tell me if it's too personal. I lost my mom, too."

"You did?" She looked up quickly, searching his eyes. "I'm so sorry." Her voice was soft. Then she took a deep breath. "It's ok. It happened about six years ago, right after I got those pictures taken actually. I was just about to graduate from community college." She leaned back against the ivory-padded headboard, her eyes squinting as she thought.

He couldn't help himself from asking, "How?"

She shifted and the ruby and gold cross around her neck dipped and caught the street light outside which lit through her bedroom window. She tugged at the thin gold chain, adjusting it.

"She gave this to me when I was a teenager, by the way. She wanted me to be more religious like her. Religion—ha, not my thing, Mama," she said tenderly, as though remembering a fond memory. "Anyway, she was a smoker. I tried to get her to quit so many times." She shook her head and snuggled down further into the cozy, fluffy white duvet, the glass still in her hand.

Taking a long sip, she looked up, watching the shadows dart across the ceiling.

He suddenly felt sad for her. She'd had to wade through adulthood without the one person she'd known her entire life.

"Lung cancer is a bitch," he said somberly. "I'm so sorry. That must have been tough, watching her go like that." He'd watched his grandmother die of Alzheimer's and it hadn't been pleasant.

The husky laughter that escaped her surprised him. She covered her mouth with a small hand, mortified.

"Oh, God. I shouldn't laugh." Her blue eyes shone big and bright as she turned to him, but she became more serious. "Lung cancer *is* a bitch. But she didn't die from that. She was a strapping, healthy Russian who came from farming stock—even with the chain-smoking. No, she was crossing 19th Street and 6th Avenue, on her way to the rug shop when she dropped her cigarettes in the middle of the crosswalk." Chrissy's expression was flat now. "She tried to pick them up and a bike messenger flew right into her. Ironically, none of the cigarettes were crushed in the process. It was *the*—" She sighed. "Would you be completely grossed out with me if I said 'It was the stupidest way to die'?"

Aariv wasn't sure if she was being serious or not and a chuckle exploded from him. But she was so earnest he could tell she spoke the truth and he immediately apologized for chuckling. Her mother had died and that wasn't a laughing matter. But he understood her perspective.

Bemused he finally said, "I wouldn't be grossed out. It was kind of silly. Still sad though. But at least you know what happened to your mother."

She turned to him curiously. "What do you mean?"

And he told her, with little difficulty, what he never shared with anyone outside of his family, about his real mother. That she'd walked out on him as a small boy; that he barely had any memories of her except her long hair braided thickly, and how he liked to clutch it when they cuddled. That her sweet, fruity perfume (which he realized right then and there, was what seemed so familiar about Chrissy's scent, but he didn't say anything about that) surrounded them comfortingly. He did recall shouting matches when he was little, between his mother and father. His nanny would take him to his room and shut the door, keeping him occupied with songs, games, and puzzles. And then one day, his mother wasn't there. He looked for her everywhere, even the little closet he'd find her hiding in at times. No one would tell him anything. But that day turned into a week. That week turned into a month until he almost forgot about her. But when his stepmother came into the picture, he remembered his mother and cried and cried, inconsolable. Huma, his stepmother was his saving grace, becoming more of an aunt than anything else, and playful like a friend. She refused to fill in for his mother but persisted in becoming someone else for him whom he could rely on.

Later, when he had the means, he was able to hire a detective he'd met at work—Tag—to search for her in India because no one knew what became of her. And no one, not even his father seemed to care about what happened to her.

"Look, forward, *Beta*, not backward." His father would rebuke whenever he asked about her. The servants had even turned over, his nanny was gone—no one knew anything, not even Huma.

"So you never found out what happened to her?" she asked outraged, her blue eyes bright in anger. "That's bullshit!"

"Tag got so far as a lead to—" He choked never telling anyone this part, not even his cousin Mariam. "A brothel in the countryside, in a tiny village where women have absolutely no rights." He burrowed down into the duvet, closer to her, comforted by her anger for him. "That's where the search ended because she wasn't there. Just a few of her random belongings remained. Some people think she … killed herself because she wasn't right in the head."

"Oh, Riv." Her hand grasped his, her rough fingers caressing his palm. "I'm so very sorry."

He nodded and murmured, "Thank you."

He drained the last of the wine from his glass and reached for his phone which he'd left on her nightstand.

"Shit!" He sat up in bed.

"What?" she asked startled, as he kicked the blankets off them. She sat up too, juggling her half-full wine glass, trying not to spill it onto her white duvet.

He rubbed his chin. "I was supposed to get back to the office and review some things."

Her eyes widened, and she stuttered, "Oh—well—sorry—"

He glanced at her sharply and the words died on her lips. Whatever look he was giving her made her look away, and her cheeks reddened as she finished her wine.

He immediately felt bad and rubbed the back of his neck. Did she think that he was just fucking and dumping her? That was kind of what he'd thought they'd be doing, but now a part of him didn't want to leave.

"Don't be sorry, Chrissy. This was … fun." And he meant it. He hadn't felt this open and disarmed in a long time and it didn't feel awkward.

She smiled, cocking her head to the side before she said,

"Are you saying that *you*, Mr. Serious Lawyerman, are having fun with *me*?"

He felt himself relax at her teasing, and he pulled her to him so that both of them knelt on the bed. He kissed her slowly, less urgently than he'd ever done, and it was exhilarating, more than he wanted to admit. He could get lost in the tangy, wine flavor of her soft lips.

He pulled himself away and as she came to, her lids fluttering slowly open, her eyes in a daze, he studied her, not hating at all that he'd lingered there longer than he intended. His hands slid from her waist down to her hips, squeezing the soft flesh, and finally letting her go, his brain trying to focus on the fact that he needed to get home.

"Do you want to—"

"I should go," he said abruptly. The sooner he got out of there the better, so as not to muddy up what they were doing together.

He rubbed the back of his neck and climbed out of bed looking around for his clothes.

He was busy putting his jeans on as he muttered, "I have an early day tomorrow. This Turner & Turner case is a real bitch. I'll sleep better in my bed. I'm sure you will in your bed, too. Plus I don't have my melatonin pills…"

Was he …. babbling? He took a deep breath to calm himself. Why was he so nervous? Because he'd said too much—told her too much about himself, though it had felt more than natural doing so.

"Here," she said behind him, and he turned around just as his shirt hit him in the chest. He caught and held it, staring at her naked form, her hands on her hips.

"You have trouble sleeping, too?" She asked.

He heard the words, but he couldn't answer because a part of him was saying, 'Stay,' and for sure his dick was pleading, 'Fuck her again,' as he stared at her luscious, naked form. He shoved his shirt over his head and his arms through the sleeves, willing his limbs to at least comply.

"What kind of melatonin pills do you take?" She prodded.

His glance darted to her face, confused. "What?"

She grabbed her silk and pink floral robe off the back of her vanity chair. "Melatonin? I have trouble sleeping, too." She shrugged it on, tying the ties, finally covering her lush form.

He rubbed his chin, finally dragging his gaze from her as he sought out his socks and shoes.

"You do?" He sat on her bed to pull them on. He wanted to ask her why, but he pushed that question away. "Well, I prefer the chewy ones. I can send you the name later if you want."

"Okay. I'd like that," she said before she left the bedroom area.

He hurriedly tied his shoes, stood up, and shook himself. This was all just physical, he reminded himself, and he needed to keep clear boundaries with her. No sleepovers.

He rounded the corner out of her bedroom and saw that she waited in the entryway. She gave him a bashful smile as she opened the door and said softly, "Thanks for coming over … and for all the orgasms."

Her face flushed and she looked down at her toes. Oh, Jesus. Could she be any more sexy-adorable?

He stopped in front of her and lifted her chin. Her eyes were sparkling, and her lips parted in a soft gasp.

"You are so welcome. Thank you for letting me," he teased. He leaned in and left a quick kiss on her lips, trying not to linger, and then he was out the door. Just as she was about to shut it he said over his shoulder, "I'll call you."

She smiled and said she was looking forward to it before she closed the door. And he whistled—actually whistled on his way to get his car.

By the time he got home, he was exhausted, but in the best possible way. He pulled his clothes off as he made his way to his bedroom and collapsed into bed. His eyes shut immediately and he fell into a deep sleep.

When he woke up the next morning, he was bright-eyed and refreshed, and it was odd because he hadn't felt that way in months. He stretched languidly, feeling calmer than he normally did. The anxiety about work (a usual fixture in his morning routine which only mounted throughout the day as his mental note of what needed to get done got bigger) was surprisingly absent. He suddenly realized that he hadn't taken his sleeping aid, as he stared at the melatonin pill bottle on his nightstand. And yet, he'd slept like a fucking rock.

# CHAPTER 19

ও

"Again, Chrissy," she barked loudly to her reflection, red-faced and puffy, her dance clothes sticking to her. She restarted the music on her device and took her beginning pose.

"And one, two, three, four—*shit*!" she exclaimed, stumbling out of a triple pirouette.

She was working on some new choreography for her next routine at the club. She'd begin on the stage, going through lyrical dance moves, gliding, and sashaying sensually across the wide expanse before climbing up the aerial silks for her acrobatic tricks. Her big finish was an uber-sexy pose cradled by the curtains high up in the air.

She tugged up her light blue sports bra which was splotchy with perspiration, and hiked up her black, stretchy dance shorts. The material stuck to her ass cheeks before releasing in a slap, and she wiggled in discomfort, adjusting to the immediate cooling of the sweat-wicking material on her heated flesh.

She put her hands on her hips and stared at herself in the long mirror. She was completely off her leg. What was wrong with her today? She looked at herself more closely. Did she appear any different? No. But, did she feel any different?

*Hell, yes.*

Alone in the small dance studio that she'd rented for practice (in exchange for volunteering to teach classes and answer the phone at the off-off-Broadway dance studio she'd frequented in the past, because why not add more to her already packed schedule?), she let her hand glide down her chest, over her belly and pelvis, palming her crotch. Her chest rose and fell, glossy and damp under the fluorescent lights that notoriously showed every angle, and adjustment, good or bad in the wall-to-wall mirrors.

She stood there, holding her flesh. It burned but in the most delicious way. She felt her inner muscles tensing up in anticipation for the next time, and she shivered just thinking about being with him like *that* again.

She let out a loud, breathy sigh that bounced off the walls, pulling her hair from its mottled ponytail. The strands fell limply around her shoulders, as limply as her body felt. Her muscles whined in dismay every time she danced through her choreography. She hadn't even attempted to practice with the curtains today, needing to feel the new steps without the props.

But damn, despite the tiredness, she felt amazing. Last night with Aariv had been spectacular, better than any sex she'd ever experienced, pushing her muscles in a different way than she was used to. Dear God, she'd missed out on a lot, hadn't she?

Thankfully she knew a guy who was more than happy to show her the way, she thought with a rueful smile. That smile grew bigger as she thought about their conversation afterward. She liked trading stories about their past. She knew they were just sexually involved, but it made her happy that he trusted her enough to share these tidbits about him.

She made her way over to her dance bag in the corner of the room and grabbed her water bottle, drinking thirstily from it. She checked her phone. There was an unknown number with a voicemail, but it didn't make her as nervous as before. Thanks to Aariv, she had Tag Underwood working for her and she wasn't so freaked out when she got calls like this. Which reminded her that she needed to follow up with him soon. The PI had recently left her a message at work needing to speak to her urgently about something but to not get into contact with Boris, the store manager, at all.

Her first reaction was to ignore that piece of advice. Boris had been like a pseudo-father figure to her when she was little. Lately, he felt more useless than tits on a bull as she was constantly reminding him to pay the bills with the extra income she regularly deposited into the business account. She still loved the guy like family, but his mind was elsewhere, and worry for him was instinctive. She wanted to return his messages, which seemed fewer and far between, she realized. Or try to check up on him again. That last time she'd surprised him at the store when that delivery had arrived on a Sunday—that was some strange shit.

*What the fuck had he gotten himself into?!*

But Aariv's words from their conversation at the club, which seemed so long ago, crept into her mind whenever she felt the urge to check in on Boris. She needed to trust the process, let Tag do his job, and not interfere, no matter how much she was itching to. But, God, the concern was hard to ignore. What would her mother say?

"Don't worry, Mama. I'll find a way to make sure he's ok,"

she said aloud. She'd find a way to ensure the little man was still alive and breathing, though he was acting like a *spustya rukava* (sloppy worker), a Russian saying her mother had used frequently and with gusto for anyone (including her daughter) who wasn't living up to their potential. Plus, Chrissy had a feeling they were in danger. They needed to seriously talk about getting rid of that place. She needed it off her shoulders like yesterday.

Now, staring at the unknown number on her screen, she curiously plopped down, spreading her legs wide and stretching into the middle splits. She leaned forward letting her torso glide along the Marley floor, the vinyl cool and tacky on her skin as she lengthened her back. Resting her chin in her hands, she put her phone on speaker and played the message.

"Hello, Kristen. This is Ms. Acharya." The hoity-toity voice ping-ponged around the small studio. "Simran gave me your number. Please give me a call back at your earliest convenience."

And now that familiar nervous feeling prickled at the back of her neck because, what the fuck? The message seemed harmless, but what could this woman have to say to her?

She quickly texted Simran.

**"Why does Ms. Acharya want to speak with me? Did I mess something up?"**

As she typed, her pulse quickened while her irritation bubbled. She knew she'd done a fantastic job. What could that woman have to complain about? Maybe she was too high-handed with her about the floral decorations? Aariv had pointed it out that day but had said the older woman deserved it. Prickles continued up her scalp in uneasiness, nonetheless. The lady might have deserved it, but she was also a client.

Her phone pinged back with Simran's response.

**"No! You did fantastic. She just wanted to thank you personally for your hard work, which is saying something because that woman is f'ing hard to please about anything! Good work, Chris!"**

**"Okay, good! I'll call her back right now."** Whew!

She dialed the woman's number. It barely rang twice before she picked up.

"Kristen, hello. How are you?" she asked smoothly over the phone. "I've been expecting your call."

"Oh. You have? Sorry, I just saw your missed call from only an hour ago." She didn't even bother trying to correct her name with the woman, it was useless.

"Yes, but what I have to say is extremely important and my time is very precious."

Of course, it is, Chrissy mused, rolling her eyes.

When the older woman didn't go on, Chrissy spoke, "The party was a success, wasn't it? I hope you were happy with how everything turned out."

"It was lovely, yes. Thank you for your work."

When nothing further came from her, Chrissy said, "Well, okay. If that's all … you're very welcome. I was happy to help out—"

"There is one thing I should mention, though," the older woman said sharply.

Here it comes. Chrissy was dying to hear what this judgy woman had to say. It wasn't lost on her that after she'd found her and Aariv together later in the evening, her demeanor had gone from frigid to practically Antarctic toward Chrissy. But maybe it had to do with the way she spoke to the staff. No. Ms. Acharya was beyond rude to them, including her own housekeeper—a very lovely older woman from India who wordlessly took the sharp-tongued comments from her employer. Perhaps she didn't like how Chrissy yelled (along with her) at the crowd of unruly young guests who were tearing up the place and who they eventually kicked out of the party. Or maybe she just didn't like Chrissy … period. It wasn't the first time she'd rubbed people the wrong way. The first moment she'd ever spoken to Aariv darted through her mind—but that was different because that man was a walking, talking conundrum.

"Okay," Chrissy said carefully. "How can I help you?"

The older woman paused—whether she needed to prepare herself for what she was going to say, or for the theatrics, Chrissy wasn't sure, but she was quickly losing her patience. But she knew she had to hold onto it because as one of Simran's … what was she to Simran? Probably similar to what she was to Aariv—a matriarch of their community—so she deserved some respect. She waited for the woman to go on, though she drummed her fingers irritably on the floor.

"Do you know what the term BMW refers to?"

Chrissy circled her ankles, popping them as she thought. Was this some sort of trick question?

"Are we talking about the luxury car brand?"

Why the hell would this woman be talking about cars with her? She hadn't been in charge of parking for the party. Come to think of it, no one had. There hadn't been a valet staff present. Any damage to anyone's car was not her responsibility. Did this woman have the balls to place blame on her because she was an outsider at the party?

"Did a guest's car get damaged? I honestly know nothing—"

"It means," the older woman cut in, "Blacks, Muslims, and Whites."

Say what now?

"Excuse me?" Chrissy asked. "What does that have to do with the party?"

Chrissy sat up and crossed her legs. An ugly, uncomfortable feeling churned in her belly as she stared at the giant sweaty mark she'd left on the floor—but it had nothing to do with that.

"You don't meet the requirements needed to make him a good wife."

Huh?

"Who are we talking about here?" But she had an inkling. It pecked at her brain incessantly like a woodpecker gone mad.

"Why, Aariv Abbas, of course. Did you think I hadn't noticed the way you practically threw yourself at him?" She laughed, but there was no humor in it. "My dear, I see everything." And that Chrissy knew though she'd barely spent time in her presence. As Aariv had mentioned a few times, the woman was aware of everything.

But was she being for real right now? She'd done absolutely no throwing. It'd been the other way around.

Chrissy's pulse thrummed loudly in her ears as she struggled to keep calm. How dare this woman fling accusations at her.

"I'm sorry, but I don't think that's any of your business. And for the record—" Don't say it, don't say it, don't … say … it, one part of her brain pleaded. But her mouth didn't comply. "Aariv Abbas isn't as innocent as you think. *He* was the one who threw himself at *me*." Did she like the guy? Yes. Did she care for him maybe a little? Probably. But damn it felt good to toss the goody-two-shoes Uncle Riv persona under the bus.

Ms. Acharya scoffed. "Young lady, men only act that way if they are encouraged."

What in the-nonprogressive-bullshit was this?

"Pardon my French, Ms. Acharya, but what the hell? How can you not support a woman in this? What if I had complained that he attacked me and it was unwanted?"

"So, it was mutual?"

Good God, the woman only wanted to hear what she wanted to hear.

"So what if it was? We're two consenting adults, free to make our own decisions."

"That's where you are wrong. He is not free to make his own decisions. He is shopping for a wife, and I am the one facilitating it. His parents are my clients hence he is my client. Do not go messing this up for him, or me."

"What if he and I like each other? What if we want to pursue a relationship?" she asked boldly. These weren't questions that had just popped into her head. They'd been trolling the back of her mind attempting to make themselves known, because of course her thoughts would go there. She was an and-they-all-lived-happily-ever-after kind of person. She'd been doing her best to ignore them, given their initial agreement, but that was already becoming an issue. Opening up about personal angst, like dead mothers, would do that. There'd been a connection there and—

*Nope!* She needed to remember what they were doing. Aariv would never consider her like that; he'd said as much himself.

The other woman snorted. "That's not possible. Are you an Indian Hindu?"

Yikes. Now it made more sense. As in, no BMWs for Prince Aariv. Gross.

"Well," Chrissy said, her anger manifesting into a heavy rock that sunk to the bottom of her chest. She shook her head. She'd known from the get-go that he was off-limits. Why was she feeling any sort of melancholy about this? "It's a good thing I'm not trying to marry him then."

The older woman was silent. She finally uttered, "You aren't?"

"Nope, not in the least."

"May I ask why not? What is wrong with Aariv?"

"No, actually you may not." Chrissy chuckled. The gall of this lady!

"So, what are your intentions with him now?"

"And that, my *dear* Ms. Acharya, is where I draw the line on this conversation. It's none of your business. Now, it *was* a beautiful event. Let's not muddle it up with this ugliness. It was so great speaking with you. Bye!" She couldn't help the glee that lifted her voice at that last part as she pressed the End Call button. There was just no way she would continue to take that kind of abuse from a woman she barely knew, and whom she had no obligations to.

But man, she couldn't wait to tell Aariv about this. How again this woman—this villain—kept trying to thwart them. They'd laugh their asses off and then go have incredible sex. She giggled and sighed at the thought.

CHAPTER 20

२०

*O*kay, so maybe she'd been wrong.

It'd been three days since she'd spoken to that vile woman. Three days of those awful words ricocheting inside her head until she finally came to a depressing conclusion—she could not let things roll off her back as easily as she thought she could.

Chrissy truly believed she was a changed woman and had agreed to this thing with Aariv as a no-strings-attached pleasure adventure, with not a hint of feeling involved. But that brief conversation with Ms. Acharya—the one she thought she would laugh about with him—started to fester, like a barely-there blister on her right baby toe that cropped up hours after dancing on point. One that ended up a juicy painful mess within days that needed constant tending to. This idea of 'no BMWs' bugged her, and deep down, it was hurtful, too.

But why? She was used to this kind of bias, albeit from the other end. Russians flocked to Brighton Beach, Brooklyn as a home away from home. She and her mother had spent countless days there, too. The thing was, Russians weren't very welcoming to immigrants from other countries moving into their neighborhood. Many of the older generation were disheartened by the younger ones dating from outside the community (non-Russians). Though she vowed never to be like that (she'd date, fall in love, and marry whomever the hell she wanted to), she saw where they were coming from—they were scared of something different after living in and leaving a country fraught with political and social turmoil. They were scared of change.

So what she was feeling was completely familiar, but she was on the unfamiliar side. All the horrible things she could ever muster about people who exhibited racial bias hurtled through her. She felt angry, disgusted, and even confused about those feelings. What was worse was that she couldn't believe she found someone so attractive and even admirable who held the same views. She'd had sex with and wanted more sex from this same someone, too. He was after an Indian wife after all.

It was a conundrum she wasn't sure how to fix within herself. So, unlike how she behaved in the past when faced with a challenge, she decided to ignore it instead of facing it head-on. She disregarded the physical pull to Aariv and thereby ignored him altogether. Maybe it would all just go away and she wouldn't have to face this confusing hurt.

His texts about meeting up again went unanswered. It was hard. So many times she reached for her phone and hovered over the keyboard to respond.

She had to busy herself with work, taking on any little errand or task, and by the weekend, was thankful for her dance gig. She had no time to think because her body was on autopilot, performing two back-to-back shifts both Friday and

Saturday nights, and getting as much rest and TLC as she could during the day.

Come Sunday morning, she felt dead. She lay in a dazed stupor, trying to get her mind off of the fifteen (fifteen!) texts Aariv had sent her since the day after their incredible, for real hump day. The messages started sexy and even adorable.

The first one read, **"Hey, Sunshine. Last night was good. I hope I gave you what you wanted, but you can still use your legs ☺. I need to see you again sooner rather than later. This time I think we should focus on your oral skills. :P"**

Unlucky for Aariv, she didn't read that text until *after* her conversation with that despicable woman, otherwise she would have giggled and thought the hunky lawyer's use of emojis was swoon-worthy. But that's not what happened. While she tried to maintain focus on rehearsing, the fact that she couldn't regain her balance and continued to be off the music's beat told her she was bothered by that talk.

Frustrated, she packed up her things and went home, and that's when she saw his message. She snarled in frustration as she stomped out of the dance studio and into the subway. Though her body warmed up even further at his sexy words, her mind fired up with annoyance.

Even as she stood on the train, jostling side to side along with other commuters as they sped through underground tunnels, she continued to fume.

The offensive phrase, "No BMWs," was on repeat in her head and she realized she was making this personal. She wasn't supposed to make this personal because personal equated feelings. She was starting to see Aariv in a different light. Her initial impression had been grumpy, asshole lawyer—which he was—but he had another side to him when his guard was down.

He was funny, and even sweet, if not a little downhearted when it came to his family, and enormously sexy. But, admittedly he was sexy even when he was a crank, and she liked him then, too. So, what was it that was making this so twisted?

*Damn it, Christikka! You're starting to more than like him. Rein in that shit, stat!*

His texts had become more concerned and persistent as her silence wore on. She felt terrible, but she didn't know what to say. At one point he asked her to give him anything, a sign that she was still alive and not murdered by the US-Russian mob syndicate who might be involved in her family's rug business. To which she answered with a thumbs-up emoji, but that was it.

That was Saturday evening before her show. Then it was radio silence from him.

That Sunday morning, she languished in bed, rolling around, trying to get comfortable. It was only eight am, why was she up? But she knew why. Whenever something bothered her, she woke up a bazillion times during the night, usually from crazy dreams she couldn't remember, and then her internal clock got her up between seven and eight, anyway, despite her exhaustion.

Gone was her surprisingly peaceful sleep, like the night after Aariv had come over last week.

She rolled over huffing into her pillow just as her phone pinged. She groaned, picking it up from the nightstand.

The text read, **"I'm here. I've buzzed you twice but you won't answer."**

Her heartbeat picked up and her face flamed. It was Aariv. What was he doing here?!

**"My buzzer is broken."** She typed back, which was the truth. Her landlord promised to fix it within the week.

Another text came in. **"Will you please let me up?"**

She sat up, thinking. **"Why?"** She finally texted back.

**"Don't you want to continue with what we started?"**

**"I'm not sure."** She typed hesitantly, staring at her screen. She finally hit 'send.'

His answer came back immediately. **"Can we at least talk about it, so I know what happened?"**

Why did he have to care about this? Couldn't they just go on their merry way with one night of passion in their history? It wasn't like it could become anything more, could it?

**"I'm letting you up, but just so you know I'm in my pj's and I'm also rolling my eyes."**

**"I wouldn't expect anything less from you, Sunshine."**

*Harumph. Sunshine, my ass*, she thought.

*A*riv went through the front door as soon as it buzzed and headed to the small elevator. He rode the rickety contraption (no doubt a major selling feature for the old building) up to Chrissy's floor.

He'd barely knocked on her door when she flung it open. She stood there in that same pretty floral robe. It was open and underneath she wore tiny white shorts with an all-over strawberry print and a matching tank top. Her hair was in two messy buns on her head, reminiscent of his favorite Street Fighter video game character, and she wore tattered puppy slippers on her feet.

"Hey," he said, trying not to stare at how cute she looked, even sleepy and in simple sleepwear. Wisps of light red strands framed her face, and her rounded cheeks were puckered in as if she were trying to give him a serious glare. But unfortunately, she looked adorable when she was annoyed. Just like that time at the party when she learned he was in the market for an Indian wife.

"Well, don't just stand there. Come in," she said, after giving him a once over in his grey Knicks jersey and black sports shorts. She headed inside and left the door open. He went in.

"I brought coffee and pastries." He lifted the to-go coffee tray with two cups of coffee, and a bag of pastries, both from the local shop on the corner.

"*The Mill's* famous coffee and sweets. The best in Long Island City. You shouldn't have," she said, a bite in her tone.

He sighed, unsure what had gotten into her, and moved to her kitchen area to set everything on the counter.

Something told him he needed to tread lightly, though. A hard feat for him considering how much he'd craved to be with her these last few days, and his usual tactic of fixing a problem was to get right to the heart of the matter.

He'd been daring with his text, telling her that he needed to see her again sooner rather than later. And he hadn't been lying either. Sex with her had been better than anything he'd experienced in a long time. He'd even be so bold as to say ever. And he believed a woman like her, one who probably appreciated romanticism and whirlwind theatrics when it came to dating (even though this wasn't dating by any means), would appreciate his choice of words. But he got nothing. No response ever came, not even a single yes, no, or maybe.

Had he been the only one who'd enjoyed the fuck out of fucking her? Apparently so. Or maybe he'd offended her somehow—maybe she wasn't into the teacher/student role-play. But that couldn't be it. He'd witnessed her expressions and cries of pleasure and had felt her body shudder hard with orgasm after orgasm. So what in the hell had happened? Had she really just changed her mind? He needed to find the answer because, after months of lusting after her and finally having a taste of her, he wasn't going to be silenced out so easily, even after getting more personal than he normally would. No. The sex was way too good, and him being like a horse to water in a stark desert wasn't the only reason he needed to see her again (though it played a huge factor along with the huge boner he wore every time he thought about being inside her again). He needed to get to the bottom of this. He was a lawyer after all.

He proceeded to unload things, removing the lids from coffees, and releasing their steam.

"I wasn't sure how you liked your coffee…" He pulled a variety of sweetener packets and creamers from his shorts' pockets.

She moved next to him and surveyed everything. She peered into his cup and then watched him line up three packets of sugar in his hands, rip off their tops, and dump them into the piping-hot liquid. Then he opened a creamer packet and poured it in as well. He gave it a stir with one of the wooden stirrers he'd also brought from the shop.

"Wow," she said surprised.

"What?" he asked, taking a sip of the milky, sweet brew, closing his eyes to the complex flavors that the coffee pushed through, even after he'd doctored it up the way he liked it. "This is great coffee," he said pleasantly.

He opened his eyes to see her watching him lick and smack his lips.

"I thought you'd take your coffee black, like a stern lawyer with a dark soul."

He chuckled. "So many things you don't know about me, Little Girl. Like my insatiable sweet tooth." He couldn't help looking her up and down in her little pjs and her hair up in that girlish hair-do. She was so sexy.

She fumbled for the sashes of her robe and tied them up with gusto. But he could still make out the luscious round outlines of her breasts and the nubs of her constantly hardened nipples through the silky material.

"Well, here's a secret for you—I *do* take my coffee black, though tea is my preferred morning beverage." She smiled as she grabbed her cup. "We Russians *love* our tea."

"That is a shocker," he said smiling, relieved that her cranky mood had subsided for now. Maybe she just needed caffeine. Tea. He'd need to remember that next time. He loved tea, too.

She took a long sip and murmured, "Seriously the best coffee in Queens, probably all of New York."

He leaned back on the counter next to her and they drank in silence.

"So … tell me. Why did you change your mind? Was the sex that terrible for you?" he asked nonchalantly. She practically choked on her coffee, and he patted her back as he turned halfway to grab a raspberry danish from behind him. When he knew she was ok, he took an enormous bite of the confection, and he couldn't help smacking his lips in delight at the tart, gooey sweetness.

After she'd cleared her throat and sufficiently coughed out the sip that had gone down the wrong pipe, she pursed her lips, as though lost in thought. Her cheeks were now the same color as the bright pink flowers on her robe. She finally took a deep breath.

"Do we have to do this?" Her voice was small. She looked vulnerable standing there, more child-like than he'd ever seen her, as she stared blindly into her cup.

A wave of protectiveness hit him, and he almost stepped back with the force of it. It didn't deter him though. He needed answers.

"Uh, I think we do." He put his danish and coffee down and faced her profile. "Chrissy, what happened? Did I do something to offend you?"

She shook her head quickly. "No. Nothing like that. I'm just not sure we should continue this."

"Why?" he asked, not able to conceal his bafflement. When it was that good between two people, with no strings attached, why the hell not continue?

"I've been warned to stay away from you."

"What?" What was she talking about? When she didn't say anything immediately, he tipped his head back and started laughing because it was absurd.

"Aariv, I'm not joking here. I'm a 'W.' I shouldn't be anywhere near you."

He remained silent, staring at her, confused.

"I mean, technically I'm not a 'W,' at least fully. My mom was Russian, but my dad was a Romani gypsy. Did you know Romani gypsies came from the Indian sub-continent? That's why my skin tans so easily in any sunlight. Sometimes even grey skies!"

What in the hell was she going on about?

"That's because the sun's rays are more concentrated behind

the clouds and—wait a minute, back up. You're a … what?" he asked, still lost.

"A 'W,' as in BMW—as in Black, Muslim, or White," she said simply as if he should know this information, too.

"What the fuck—" And he stopped talking as it dawned on him what she was referring to. He hadn't heard that acronym since he was a kid back in India. He rubbed his hand down his chin. "Who in the hell—wait—" He put a hand up. "Don't tell me, it was Pinky Aunty," he said in disgust just as she uttered, "that Acharya woman."

"But that's only in regards to finding me a wife." He couldn't help cringing as he spoke because it was just so ugly— the basic rules of finding a spouse within the Indian culture, even in a progressive Western society.

"Your face says it all, Riv," she said with disbelief, her eyes large in alarm. "How can you go along with this—" She stopped herself and sighed, throwing her hands up. "No," she said under her breath. "I'm not here to change his mind." She took a deep breath and faced him. "I don't know if I can be involved—even if it is the most amazing sex in the world—with someone who's got … you know…" she waved her hand around him, "a lot going on."

She looked extremely uncomfortable as she spoke, and he wanted more than anything to rip that barrier down. He wanted to get back eager and fun Chrissy from a few days ago; the one who wanted all the sex pointers, but was a great, sympathetic listener, too. Someone he liked and might call more than a hook-up.

"So what you're saying is that because you don't agree with all that's happening in one part of my life, you don't think you can be with me on the other side—the physical side?"

"Well, yeah. I would start to dislike you. And I don't know if I can be with someone like that whom I dislike."

"Chrissy, come on. Didn't we have an agreement?"

"We did." She hesitated. "But people can change their minds. And I don't want that woman calling me and warning me all the time."

People could change their minds; this was true. But he was determined to have her change her mind back and he wasn't sure why. Maybe it was the connection, more than just the physical that was making him dismayed about not getting to be with her again. In truth, she was becoming like a friend to him, too, one whom he enjoyed great sex with, and frankly, he wasn't ready to give that up yet.

He took her coffee cup and set it down on the counter next to his. He pushed the bag of pastries aside before putting his hands around her waist and lifting her so that she was sitting on the countertop. She was in front of him now, and he could see her eye to eye. He stepped between her legs before she could close them, making her gasp.

Her hands were on his chest, but she didn't push him away.

"Riv, this isn't fair," she whispered, staring at his chest, her own rising and falling quickly.

He leaned down, face to face with her.

"What's not fair, Sunshine, is you giving me the best fuck I've had, probably ever, and then just taking it away. How fucking unfair is that?" he asked softly. His hands were beside her thighs, but he made no move to touch her. Being this close was sheer torture, though, and knowing she could firmly say 'no' and he'd have to walk away would be way worse.

Her eyes turned up to him in bewilderment, and the deep blue entranced him. Honestly, he could stare at them all day—

"I'm the best you've ever had?" Her lids fluttered up and down slowly. "How is that even possible? You're a … a sex master. And I know nothing about good sex."

He smirked. "You're a natural."

Her fingers toyed with his shirt, grasping, and crushing the material. "Or maybe you bring it out in me."

"I'd like to think that, too," he said softly, nudging her nose with his. "So, what do we do about it?"

CHAPTER 21

W hat did they do about it? Was he honestly asking *her*? Wasn't he the decision-making professional here?

She pushed him away and folded her arms across her chest, staring at him in his grey Knicks jersey and black sports shorts. It was Sunday, so she had some recollection of him having mentioned a standing basketball meet-up when they'd been trying to find time together previously. He looked good though. He ALWAYS looked good.

"Don't you make educated decisions for a living? Mr. Lawyer?" she asked archly.

"I do," he said, backing up and standing a few feet away from her now, but his presence seemed to spark her body up no matter what. She swung a leg over the other, crossing them to tamp down her stupid base needs for this man, while she bounced a sad-looking puppy slipper on her toes.

"So, tell me what you're thinking," she urged.

"I'm not playing around here, Chrissy. I want a fix so we can continue with what we started."

He cupped his chin, rubbing it as he gazed at her thoughtfully but remained silent.

"That woman—" She began but stopped as he blew out air in a loud whoosh and his face contorted into a hardness she hadn't seen on him in forever. His eyes became cool, and greener as he scratched his chin.

"I'll talk to her."

"What will you say to her?" She was curious to know what could ever get that woman off her high horse.

"Do you want me to tell her the truth? That we're just having fun right now?"

She shrugged, looking past his shoulder out the window. "I'd like it if she didn't harass me whenever she felt like it, and that what we're doing is a decision we *both* made." But what she wanted to ask him was, 'Is that all we're doing right now—having fun?' She couldn't though because that was what they had agreed on—unattached (and erotic) fun; despite the kernels of personal truths they were finding out about one another and could commiserate with. Despite how she was starting to see a fuller picture of a complex man that any woman might give their right tit to be with, including herself.

He nodded curtly, his arms crossed in front of him, his muscular biceps flexing at her. "Fine," he said.

"And if this is only fun between us, then you have to also be ok with me dating if the opportunity comes around."

Not sure where that came from, but it was valid. If he was going to continue with wife hunting, then she wasn't going to deny a guy who might be interested in getting to know her beyond the physical. Plus, he probably wouldn't even care, but she had to make sure to put that stipulation on the table. She was dealing with a lawyer after all.

With thick brows raised, he took a step closer. "Is there someone waiting in the wings?"

*No.*

"Maybe." She didn't look at his face as she said it. Instead studied her nails.

He took another step closer.

"So, what? Am I priming that sexy little body for another man to enjoy later?"

Oh, shit. He sounded rather angry now, and she peeked up to catch his eyes burning hazel golden again, his cheeks hardened with a muscle twitching right below his left cheekbone.

She looked away from his angry handsomeness that beckoned to her and nodded. Because why the hell shouldn't she? This wasn't a double-standard scenario like what she was beginning to witness more of in the culture he was raised. She was independent and sexually free. She could do what she wanted given their no-strings-attached commitment.

He took another step toward her and now he was right in front of her again. The bright orange Knicks emblem on his grey shirt screamed at her in her peripheral. His smell—a concoction of woody and pine that had underlying tones of pure man—made her lids close, tipsy on his scent. His palms lay on the counter, one on each side of her thighs once more, his breathing heavy against her cheek.

"Little Girl, I'm not sure I like that," he said dangerously gritty and low, and it was such a turn-on. Her pulse danced inside her chest with anticipation. Tremors instinctively fluttered up and down her body, and damn it, she couldn't control them. Nor could she control the liquid sliding inside her pelvis to the area she was trying to squeeze tight by crossing her legs that were now smashed up against Aariv's hard, immovable thighs.

*Dear Lord, please stop this man from being so fucking hot so that I can have some form of control around him. Amen.*

Maybe she was more religious than she thought; her mother would be proud, she considered with humor, though her musings were dashed away as Aariv leaned in closer.

"Do I need to remind you who you belong to right now?"

She scoffed, but this game always shot a thrill right through her—when he acted like her teacher, parental figure, lover, and master of her body all rolled into one grumpenhunk of a man.

"You don't own me, Aariv," she said with more attitude than was necessary. She tossed her head for good measure.

"No, that's true, Little Girl. But I own the pleasure I give this hot little body, and you'd do well to remember that. Now lie down. I think you need a reminder of who's boss."

She rolled her lips in, trying to contain her smile and she had to ask herself if she'd lost her goddamn mind. This man had somehow gotten her to agree to be with him sexually … again … even after her misgivings about everything—which were totally legit! And yet, she wanted to grin like a loon because His Hotness still wanted her.

"Do as I say, and I'll try not to be rough … much." He took a step away from her.

She went to pull her hair out of her messy buns when he barked, "Leave it."

She jumped but complied. Then she scooted back and lay down on the expanse of her kitchen counter, the white granite frigid on her back.

His hands roamed up her thighs to her robe sash, tugging the material apart and spreading it so she lay exposed in just her tiny pajama shorts and tank top. He pushed her thighs apart and stepped between them staring down at her with a look of absolute ownership written across his face.

He licked his thick lips and picked up his coffee, taking a long sip, his eyes fixated on the rise and fall of her chest. Was she nervous as hell? Yes, but she was also extremely eager for what he had planned.

"Now what should I do with you, Little Girl?" he asked. "The options are endless."

He set his coffee down and put his index finger in. He brought it to his lips and licked off the sweet mixture.

"This will taste so much better on you, don't you think?"

Huh?

She watched as he dipped his finger into his coffee again and brought it to her lips, spreading the liquid across her mouth.

She flicked her tongue out to taste it. Sugary sweet, such a contrast to the man.

He leaned down and licked her lips and her tongue. "Mm. That's more like it."

He dipped his fingers in his drink again and dragged a line of milky coffee down her neck. He licked and traced the drink with his thick lips, moaning as he went, eliciting sighs from her.

When he'd reached her breasts, he dripped coffee in her cleavage and lapped it up with his tongue. She arched her back at the sensation of him licking warm liquid off of her.

"You like that, Little Girl?"

She nodded and gasped a yes.

"I like it, too. I can't wait to taste all of you."

His large hand cupped a breast as he nuzzled the other over her tank top, circling her sensitive nipple with his tongue, wetting her tank top before covering it completely with his mouth to suck with a force that rocked her hips into him.

She moaned as he pulled the material down, exposing her breasts to his gaze. He nodded, licking his thick lips and his approval made her reach for him, wanting to feel his body against hers, his chest against her hardened and sensitive nipples.

"Not so fast. I've still got more tasting to do."

He reached over and dipped his fingers in a cup.

"I've never been a fan of black coffee, but this might make it go down easier."

A warm, wet finger circled one nipple, and she inhaled sharply at the sensation of almost hot liquid on her breast.

He leaned down and lapped it off hungrily. When he lifted his head, he blew on her already wet nipple, making goosebumps pucker up tightly around it.

"Mm." He smacked his lips. "More palatable this way."

He dipped his finger in her cup again and covered her other nipple, doing the same.

He did this for some time, playing with her breasts, driving her crazy with his mouth and tongue, making her back arch completely off the counter, while her hips flexed into him. She whimpered in pleasure, the smell of coffee all around her. She felt his dick hardening by the second between her legs, as his nylon shorts and her thin cotton pajama bottoms were barely a barrier. It only drove her mindless with want.

"Riv—" she gasped.

"Not done yet, my tasty, Little Girl."

He fingeried her belly button with the warm liquid. He dipped his head and slurped it out. Then he licked up and down the sides of her where it had spilled. She would be a hot mess of coffee very soon and she didn't give a crap.

She tugged on his hair as he licked down her belly, nipping and kissing her delicate flesh, grinding it ever so gently between his teeth.

He hooked his fingers under the elastic of her shorts and underwear simultaneously, tugging them both down. She lifted her ass to help him. He pulled everything completely off, taking her tired slippers as well.

"There now," he said, looking for all the world like the big bad wolf about to eat Little Red Riding Hood as he gazed at her naked pussy. He dipped his face between her legs and inhaled deeply. "I don't think I want coffee covering this tasty delicacy."

His large hands splayed her thighs, squeezing as he spread them. She was completely open to him, but she didn't feel any shame. She felt glorious and beautiful as she watched him look at her.

"Fuck, this pussy is so pretty." He dipped his head, his face now hidden from her view, and licked her, from bottom to top, making her pelvis lurch off the counter.

"*Oh!*" she cried, as the sensation was soothing, tickling, and arousing.

"Not so fast, Little Girl," he said harshly. "Hold still while I taste you."

Hold still!? Was the man insane?

She lifted her head to tell him to fuck off, just as his fingers spread her folds, exposing her clit to the cool air. He immediately thumbed her gently before sucking that tiny bud between his lips that must have held billions of nerve endings.

She wouldn't know, she'd never paid attention in Biology 101, but dear God, it reacted as though he'd lit a billion fuses in it.

She thumped her head back down, dazed, as his mouth lavished her clit, licking, sucking, even cooing at it. Whatever he was doing, it felt so damn good.

But she needed more.

"*Riv,*" she whined, trying to move her hips but to no avail. His large hands held her in place. All she could do was clench and unclench the insides of her pussy for any relief. "More," she moaned.

"More, my dirty Little Girl?" He lifted his head and his eyes looked at her quizzically.

Was the man made of stone?

"Yes!" she shrilled back.

He laughed—fucking laughed, the asshole, but slipped two fingers into her clenching muscles.

"Oh, yeah, baby. Tight and sucking my fingers up. Imagine my big dick in this hot, slippery hole—*Fuck*!" He cut himself off, no doubt extremely turned on.

He pulled her legs over his shoulders and pulled her further down the counter to him as he lowered himself to a better position. His hot mouth replaced his fingers then, his tongue entered her and he let the tight hold on her thighs go so she could wriggle her hips and find her groove, finally allowing her to fuck his face.

He pulled back briefly with a gruff, "Good girl," before diving back in.

And it was the final encouragement she needed to spin her out of control—like a Roman Candle firework gone berserk, wildly whipping around uncontrollably, flames and sparks dangerously close to creating an even bigger inferno.

"*Riv!*" she moaned, her blood dancing insanely under her skin, the pressure building in her belly. Her hands clenched at her sides as her body bucked up and down, feeling the rough prickles of his beard along the most tender place on her body.

He pulled away then, and she was momentarily lost as her body and brain tried to grasp what was happening. The sound of a condom packet ripping got her attention along with the grunts and expletives of a man who couldn't put it on fast enough.

Her brain understood she was going to get fucked out of this world, but her body struggled, still in a haze of wound-up desire. He pulled her down, her feet touching the ground and he held her for a moment.

"Are you ok?" he whispered in her hair.

She nodded and before she knew it, he'd whipped her around and pulled her ass to him, his dick an enormous weight up against her ass cheeks.

"Hold on tight, baby," he murmured before she felt him maneuver the head of his cock so it pressed into her pussy from behind.

He rammed himself in fast, and her hip bones pressed into the counter. She barely registered it though because the pleasure of his giant length widening her, filling her, had her mind and body reeling into an abyss of delirium.

He pulled her hips away from the counter and gripped tight as he pumped hard. Groans and grunts interspersed each thrust as his hands squeezed her flesh.

"*Damn it,* Little Girl!" He growled heatedly in her ear. "This tight little pussy is mine. You … understand … me?" He punctuated each word with a thrust.

She nodded, unable to speak as a moan erupted from her chest because the force of him behind her, inside her, lighting up everything she had within her, was a novel experience. It'd never felt this good being taken from behind. She'd never been on the verge of coming like this, feeling the intensity building up, overheating her.

She clutched the edge of the counter, registering briefly that they'd spilled both coffees. The milky liquid mingled with the black, spreading into a dysmorphic yin-and-yang sort of pattern, dripping over the opposite edge.

On a thrust, she closed her eyes to the feeling of her body tightening, her chest closing up, and making breathing almost impossible. She felt light-headed.

Somehow, he knew and growled out, "Breath!"

She pushed air out of her mouth and that did something to her. She reared back and pushed her hips onto him, squeezing him inside at a different angle and he let her take the lead now. Their tempo was all her as she bucked backward on him, feeling him push even deeper within.

"Yes! Holy Shit!" She squealed, panting. It was so good, almost too much pleasure for her body to handle. Before she could get a reign in on losing control, she lost it, letting herself go into a rainbow-filled, ecstasy-driven chasm. She moaned like her life depended on it, her body convulsing, her grip on the counter loosening and she might have collapsed and knocked her head on the counter's edge if Aariv hadn't pulled her against him, his breath heavy and coffee-laced in her hair.

"Just a little longer, Baby," he whispered, almost tenderly, and now her chest expanded with something sweet and warm, and that combined with her orgasm pushed her hips back on him again, telling him to keep going.

It didn't take him long. He pushed her gently back down and

she gripped the counter again as he rode her fast making her entire body jiggle.

And … she came again. *What in the almighty hell is going on!?* This man just coaxed them out of her!

"Ahh," she sighed, this one with less force than the last one, her body suspended in a gentle wave of ecstasy, with her muscles pulsing in waves around his girth.

"Chrissy … yes!" He grunted, stiffening behind her. She felt him swell inside her as he jerked, coming forcefully, his pelvis gyrating behind her, up against her ass. He collapsed heavily on her, moaning deeply, gasping. And this again, she realized, was more enjoyable than the act of him screwing her. Oh, that was insanely, out of her mind good, but the closeness, their breath mingling afterward was an intimacy she craved.

She stood there, his weight on her, letting himself catch his breath. Her hips now ground down into the hard surface of the counter and she wiggled trying to get more comfortable.

"Fuck, Chrissy. I mean it when I say this belongs to me." He reached around her hips and palmed her pussy, his fingers reaching back to where he was still inside her.

She couldn't deny it. Her body wanted only him and when it got him, it behaved as if it bent only to his will. She'd be telling herself the biggest, fattest lie in the world if she denied it.

What in the hell was she going to do with herself when he found a wife?

# CHAPTER 22

२२

"**F**uck you, Cuz. What happened to you?"

The text from Zayn was left unanswered until he'd safely parked his car at the garage he used on the same block as his apartment in Manhattan.

"**Sorry, Z. Had some things to take care of.**" He responded while getting out of his car. Mainly ensuring that Chrissy was still participating in their fuck-tastic fling. Considering their morning coffee and screw, he could be confident she was in again.

"**Wife bullshit?**" Came his friend's response.

"**Yeah.**" He lied.

"**Who did you meet with this time?**"

"**You wouldn't know her.**"

"**Is she it? The ONE deserving of *sindoor*?**"

If Aariv could see his friend's face while he texted, he was sure the guy was smirking. It'd been his mission from day one to rib Aariv about agreeing to an arranged marriage and ALL the BS that went with it. Now he was mocking the *sindoor* tradition, too, where the new husband applied a red-orange powder to his bride's hairline to indicate she was now married at the end of the wedding ceremony.

A vision popped into his head right then. One that included a completely naked Chrissy as she lay spread out on his bed, red-orange powder lining the middle part of her copper hair, tousled around her shoulders as she waited for him.

He dashed that image away as he threw his keys to the parking attendant and left the garage.

Why in the sick fuck was he imagining that? And why was he always thinking about her?

He couldn't deny that hearing her admit she was keeping her dating options open had affected him. To be exact, he'd felt a burn of jealousy streak through him. There was no way he couldn't dominate her body then, showing her who was the master of her pleasure. Her tight little body had come so hard that morning, he worried he'd injured her. He should know better—that girl was made of stronger stuff.

Anyone else might have thought that what he did with the hot coffee constituted legal action, but she'd taken it without complaint, thoroughly enjoying herself, and then he'd given her more. Because he followed that up by screwing the daylights out of her. He would've stayed longer but he realized how late it was. He'd missed his late morning pick-up game with Zayn.

He changed the subject as he entered his building. **"What's up with you, Z?"**

**"Lots of restaurant BS. I need a break. Thankfully an opportunity came up to be a private chef for some Greek shipping tycoon."**

Aariv entered the elevator.

**"Nepotism will get you everywhere."** Aariv shook his head grinning, his turn to rib his friend.

Zayn was half Indian and half Greek. The Greek side was wealthy and had more filthy rich connections than one could count on both hands. But Zayn wasn't the type of guy to take advantage. He'd worked hard to get where he was.

**"A man needs to eat."**

Whether he was talking about the Greek shipping tycoon he'd be working for, or himself as his father had cut him off financially when Zayn decided to enter the food business, Aariv couldn't be sure. Considering how much his friend busted his ass to make it, he was hoping he was referring to the Greek guy.

**"Let's catch up later this week if you're around."** He texted, entering his apartment.

He went over to the fridge and grabbed a beer. He looked at the clock. Seeing it was just past eleven that morning, he decided it was a little too early for alcohol. He put it back and grabbed a bottle of water instead. Maybe he'd work out later—anything to get some focus on what he was starting to feel for Chrissy Smyth.

Fuck, he thought, opening the bottle and downing half of it. Feelings. Was that what was happening? If it had been a month ago, he would've been pissed at himself. But at the moment, he was pretty calm about it. He sank into his deep leather couch in the living room, reliving what had happened after she came exquisitely a second time; her body so responsive to him.

When he'd pulled out of her, he couldn't help twisting her around to face him. He wanted to make sure she was ok after everything he'd done to her. The enormous grin she wore on her pretty face, the extreme, almost feverish flush to her cheeks, and her delirious gaze before her lids closed completely relieved him.

She hummed a 'Mm,' low and languid. And he couldn't stop

himself; that hum was like a radio wave signaling him—a ship out to sea—into a haven and he leaned in and kissed her, consuming her lips slowly, and just as languidly. He pulled her close again, rubbing her back, and finally threaded his fingers through her hair, into her twin buns, pulling them out so that they were a mess around her shoulders.

She sighed and let out little sweet moans as she went onto her tippy toes and wrapped her arms around his neck, holding him tightly as she met his lips with hers. It was a slow and consuming kiss … one that he didn't want to end. It made him dizzy with desire again for her, and something buzzy and warm unfolded within him.

When he did release her, her eyes were still closed, and her mouth was open in that small smile. Her hair was a rat's nest now and she was still so sexy he could have taken her again if he wanted to. But he needed to pull the reins on this want for her. It was a lust-driven craze that he was falling under—or was it?

She'd grinned goofily and stepped away from him, her clothes still askew, shorts and underwear-less. And he was just as much of a mess with his shorts and boxer briefs around his ankles, his dick still encased in the used condom.

"Thank you. I needed my medicine," she said huskily in that mixture of sexy and shy. "Now I can sleep better tonight." She wiggled her brows, and he couldn't help but grin because he could commiserate. He'd slept like the dead the night after being with her.

Not sure he wanted to unpack that with himself just yet, he focused on the spilled coffee spreading on the kitchen counter and dripping onto the floor. He hastily jumped into action, removing the condom, and tying it up. He pulled his shorts up and found her kitchen garbage on the other side, throwing away the rubber.

She came out of her haze, too, knotted up her robe, and grabbed some paper towels. She handed some to him, too.

"Sorry about the mess," he'd said, bumping her shoulder teasingly. He wasn't sorry at all. It'd been worth it. He hadn't had that much fun since … well … the last time he'd fucked her.

She laughed that husky, sexy giggle that was completely her own. "You're joking, right?"

She was kneeling on all fours, wiping up what had dripped onto the hardwood floor, and she shot him a mischievous look over her shoulder with dancing brows. That's when he noticed the bottom half of her naked ass cheeks and the swollen lips of her pink pussy staring back at him tauntingly under the short hem of her robe.

He gulped, his pulse hammering. He had to drag his eyes away or the day would be completely lost to giving and receiving orgasms with this woman.

They finished cleaning up and he'd brought up her case.

"I called Tag back," she'd murmured. "It's been a while since I heard from him, but he said he had news to share." She cleared her throat. "I don't know, Aariv … how long have you known him?"

She stood with her arms folded across her chest. Her face was scrunched up in thought.

"I've known him for almost a decade. Remember? He was the in-house PI at the first firm I worked for. He left there after I did and opened his own business, consulting with other law firms. He's got a great reputation, or I'd never put you two in touch."

Finished with cleaning up the last of the mess, he crumpled up the wad of coffee-soaked paper towels. He aimed and chucked it into the trash that was a few feet away.

"Yes! Three points for Abbas!" he cheered.

Her look changed from thoughtful to humored wonder, a smile dancing on her lips. "Shut up, you did not just do that."

"Do what?" he asked innocently, but the back of his neck heated in embarrassment, and he rubbed at it looking away. He wasn't sure why, but it was so easy to be less rigid around Chrissy, and he wasn't completely sure he liked that.

"Aw!" She walked over to him and put her arms around his waist, hugging him. See. Even that gesture made him relax and feel less embarrassed. "It's ok, Uncle Riv. You can play basket tasket-ball whenever you're here, whenever you want."

He reached under her robe and pinched her bare ass, making her hop and squeak. But he wrapped his arms around her, too, and he wondered what they were doing right now as they held each other in silence. It felt really good.

He rolled their conversation back, though, wondering what she was getting at with the PI. "Chrissy, about Tag—yeah, I completely 100 percent trust the guy. Why?"

She pulled away and moved to sit on her couch in the living area, tucking her legs underneath her.

"He said I needed to stop any communication with Boris." She looked up at him, her eyes widened in disbelief. "He said Boris might be fully involved. I knew he had to be in on it, but," she gulped. "It's hard to hear."

Aariv sighed. This was never easy when investigations opened dark secrets possibly leading to family being the crux of the problem. The thing was, Aariv could have told her that from the get-go. How could the store manager *not* be aware of the shady ongoings of the business during off-hours? Chances are he facilitated them himself.

Aariv sat down next to her on the couch. Despite how blind she may have been, he felt bad for her. He put an arm around her shoulders, trying to think of what to say to make her feel better. She immediately scooted into his side.

"Chrissy, you need to listen to Tag. The man knows what he's doing. If he thinks Boris is fully involved, then he probably is."

She frowned and wrinkled her forehead. He saw her visibly swallow as she blinked her eyes quickly. He realized she was trying to hold back tears, and it was a sight he didn't like.

"Hey, now. It'll be ok."

When she didn't say anything, he pulled her onto his lap without even hesitating, engulfing her in a bear hug. She went willingly, snuggling her face into his shoulder. He didn't like seeing her like this. She was usually all sunshine and optimism, with more than a dash of sassy thrown in. No one, nor nothing should ever cramp her usual positive attitude.

She sniffled against his shoulder. "I need to talk to him."

"Who? Tag? I'm sure he'll lay out all the details for you—"

"No." She shook her head vehemently. "Boris."

Aariv was sure he hadn't heard correctly, because why the hell would she want to willingly step into an unknown den of deceit and put herself in danger?

He tightened his hold on her as if to keep her from harm's way.

"You're not thinking clearly, Sunshine. That could be extremely dangerous."

She struggled in his arms, pulling back, and now her face was a mask of fury. "Aariv, I need to talk to Boris and knock some sense into him. The man is a legit idiot if he's completely tangled up in this shit, but he's been like a father to me, ever since I was little." She huffed out. "He could go to jail or something."

'Or something' was more like it if the Russian mob was involved. And if they found out Chrissy knew and was investigating…

"Chrissy." His patience was wearing thin. He admired her gumption—had from the beginning—and her forthright attitude about life, but this was downright ludicrous. "You're not thinking clearly." This seemed to be the advice he always shared with her when it came to her troubles. "You're too close to it. Please don't do anything stupid like go to the store to talk to Boris."

She didn't answer but fiddled with his red-roped bracelet. "I never asked you where you got this." She traced each stone.

"Chrissy," he warned, staring at her hard. "Promise me." He didn't know why he was pressing this. Of course, he didn't want her to get hurt, though she should be able to make her own decisions about this. But sometimes, when one's emotions are clouded, they can't see the obvious, which was obviously happening with her right now.

She threw her hands up. "Okay!" she said a little petulantly. "I promise not to do anything stupid."

"Like?" he prodded. She remained silent and he couldn't help reaching under her robe to pinch her delicious ass again. She squirmed.

"Ugh! *Okay*! Like going to the store to talk to Boris."

He stared at her for a beat, trying to ascertain if she meant it or not. She seemed to, as she smiled reassuringly at him.

"Good." He nodded his head, appeased. "Now, did you

really want to know about my bracelet or were you trying to distract me?"

She laughed. "Okay, tell me."

"Mariam gave me this bracelet last summer…"

He'd told her about the annual summer Hindu festival of *Raksha Bandhan*, the significance of celebrating the bond between siblings in the Indian culture, and how the bracelet and charm were meant to protect him. He'd given a similar one to Mariam as well, but she only wore it for the parties and then probably threw it in a drawer somewhere.

"Well, that's a nice tradition. But, protect you? From what?" she'd asked curiously. "I hardly think *you* of all people need protecting." She reached over and her fingertips smoothed out the wrinkle between his brows. "Aren't you a big badass lawyer?" She teasingly squeezed his biceps and he flexed involuntarily.

In all honesty, he didn't know anymore when it came to the protection part. He'd been more than a touch superstitious at the time thinking about his future marriage and the cosmos aligning. It was as though he couldn't wait to get that part of his life decided, started, and over with and he'd needed any talisman to help him along.

"Not sure." He shrugged. "I guess I'm a little superstitious."

"Well, you seem to have your shit together already." Her lips quirked as she thought. "Maybe it's meant to protect you … from you." She picked up his wrist to study it closer. "Like, choose the path that makes you happiest, even if it might not be what you thought it would be, or even what's expected of you."

He looked at the top of her copper head, bent as she studied the lotus flower detail. She'd remembered. At the *Holi* party weeks ago, he'd lamented about always being 'on' as the good

Indian son. It felt gratifying that someone heard his complaints. He didn't usually unload, but he was feeling the pressure lately.

Like Mariam, she alluded to him possibly making a mistake with his view of an arranged marriage. She was bold with her opinion, and though he usually felt more than irritation toward unwanted advice, he didn't mind it coming from her.

Funnily, the exact words Mariam had spoken as she'd tied the bracelet on him last August were, "Now, this is so you don't go doing anything I wouldn't do." They'd both chuckled because she was joking of course. As close as they were, her path had led to a very different one from his; in her personal life where she'd fallen in love, and in her home life which was a broken home with divorced parents.

Now, he did pay attention to her words and this woman sitting in his lap. Was he making a mistake? So far, the process of looking for a wife had been nothing but tedious, even close to bringing him misery. The only thing joyful was Chrissy. She was an escape and he had to remind himself it was just that—a physical escape.

But hang on, was that all it was with her?

He ruminated this now, as he got up from his couch and decided he did need that beer. He cracked it open and took a swig as he walked into his study, switching on his computer, and setting the beer on a coaster.

As his computer booted up, he thought about what she'd mentioned before, about her Romani gypsy father. Genuinely curious about that side of her, he brought up a search engine and typed in 'Romani gypsy.'

A flood of information popped up on the screen before him and he took a deep dive into the culture. Chrissy was right— they did come from the Indian subcontinent thousands of years ago, which probably explained her tawny skin color and wide-set eyes.

They still lived in migrating groups, but unlike the days of old with covered wagons, they lived in campers, some extremely luxurious even. Similarly to the Indian culture, the Romani were patriarchal, with women having less power within the extended family structure. He wondered if any of that was changing as the times were modernizing, similar to some more progressive Indian societies and families.

He pondered if she knew her father at all. Or even met him. If she hadn't, how did she reconcile with that fact? She was such a strong, multi-faceted person, and no one would ever guess that she was parentless or didn't have a sense of her identity. She was strong because of what she didn't have, he thought, and confident as hell. He genuinely admired her for that.

He switched over to a website he'd pursued recently—*A Guide to Vedic Astrology*. He scrolled down over the sun signs, past the section on perfect matches, and found the calculator tool. He clicked on it.

He typed in his birthday and then when he came to the part for entering a prospective marriage partner's birthdate, he paused. He didn't know what he was doing, and the cursor blinked back at him.

*When was Chrissy's birthday?*

The thought was so sudden, he sat back in his chair, staring at the screen, his pulse a loud thud in his ears. Was he really doing this? He pulled out his phone to ask her, but as soon as he typed it, he deleted it.

*What the hell are you doing?*

He shook his head and then he did something he hadn't done

in years—he opened another search tab and typed in 'Leila Majid.' Would he be lucky after so many years and find out what happened to his high school sweetheart, even if it was only a hint?

The screen flickered as a list of many Leila Majids appeared, along with people named Leila with similar last names to Majid, or people with Majid as their last name with first names similar to Leila. A quick scan gave him nothing. His old high school sweetheart wouldn't be going by her maiden name anymore anyway, he was pretty certain about that.

He leaned back again and chugged his beer, again unclear of what he was doing, the usual tidy set of his rules and actions becoming untethered strands. He'd put Leila aside years ago, vowing to ignore the unknown, but the itch to know what happened to her was clawing at him again. Was she happy? Was she miserable? Was he the cause of that misery for what he'd done when they were eighteen? And if he was, why did he dare to think he deserved even an iota of happiness?

# CHAPTER 23

২৩

"I think he's a nice guy, *but...*" Shana murmured, frowning.

Everyone around the table groaned.

"Oh no, here we go." Mariam threw her chopsticks at her, and the other woman ducked just in time.

Chrissy was with her friends. They were at their favorite sushi spot after work, sitting outside on the patio, taking advantage of the incredible Monday happy hour maki roll specials and half-off yuzu martinis.

"Guys, you *have* to hear me out on this." Shana pushed her long braids over her shoulder. She took a deep breath as everyone waited on the edge of their seats to listen to her excuse about sending her current unsuspecting victim to the curb. "He told me he wants to get plastic surgery on his nipples … his *nipples!* And all of this on the first date." Shana was disgruntled. She pulled at an edamame shell and dragged the little green beans into her mouth, tossing the empty shell in a bowl on the table.

"What the hell?! His nipples?" Mariam asked, aghast. Then

she started laughing. "I'm sorry, Shana. But that's the most ridiculous thing I've ever heard."

"Ridiculous or not, shit's the truth. I just can't with these boneheads," Shana said, shaking her head.

"Why his nipples?" Antoine asked, cocking his head. "What's wrong with his current ones?"

All this talk about nipples had Chrissy thinking about her own nipples, which were still sensitive after what Aariv had done to them yesterday with his mouth and hot coffee. God, the man was insane, super creative, and oh-so-good with his mouth. She wriggled in her seat and hid her smile, remembering how he'd gone down on her after that with that eloquent mouth of his, making her feel like she'd gone to another realm.

Shana became even more disgusted as she sipped her sake. "Oh, I asked, believe me," she said, snorting. "Get this—David Beckham has beautiful oval-shaped nipples and that's what he's in the market for. Apparently, *all* the men are these days." She waved her hand and rolled her eyes.

"Okay wait. I have so many questions," Mariam interjected. "*All* the men? Am I on another planet? And David Beckham the soccer guy? Isn't he old?"

Antoine's eyes protruded behind his round wire glasses. "Mar, you *must* be in another universe, honey. Beckam never ages and the man is divine. I can't believe you even said that. You're engaged to a Brit. Ask him!"

Mariam scoffed and her upper lip hiked up in irritation. "Bruce might not look at him the same way you do, Antoine."

"Girl, everyone looks at Beckham the same. You don't have to be gay or sporting a hoo-ha to notice the man is fiercely hot!" He took a huge bite of sushi and chewed thoughtfully. He swallowed then said, "And being taken doesn't mean you can't look. I know I'm with Callum, but I have eyes!" He rolled them manically making everyone crack up. "Anyway, Shay, to your point about nipplage mods, I've heard that these Wall Street types are trending on this. And why not? If you want to fix yourself, and you have deep ass pockets, why not?"

"Because it's stupid, that's why," Shana said dead-panned. "Personally, I think they look fine. Regular, normal, round man nipples."

"You've already seen his nipples?" Antoine asked chuckling.

"Well yeah. I didn't say I wouldn't sleep with the guy, just that I didn't want to date him. We don't see eye to eye, and that nipple thing is one of those factors." She looked around at her friends, crossing her arms over her chest. "Tell me I'm wrong."

"Is it just me, or is the word 'nipple' starting to sound weird?" Antoine teased.

Chrissy giggled but didn't agree one bit. She was still lost in her daydream concerning Aariv, his wicked tongue, and her nipples.

"What about you, Chris? You've been quiet about all of this. Do you think I should give this guy another chance?"

Chrissy looked up at her and shrugged. "Oh, I don't know."

"Not going to joke around about me always dating 'himbos'?"

"A guy on Wall Street is hardly a male bimbo," Chrissy said, chuckling. "But into their looks, they certainly are."

She pushed her plate away and took a deep breath. "Guys, I have a confession to make."

They all looked at her and she continued. "I'm seeing someone—well not really seeing, more like … 'sexing' … someone?"

"Sexing or sexting? There's a huge difference." Mariam said, pushing her empty plate away.

"Both," Chrissy said, aware that she was not supposed to tell anyone about this. Not that Aariv had explicitly said that, but she got the feeling that what they were doing, no matter how good it felt to both of them, was something to keep under wraps, especially since the man was technically engaged to an unknown woman.

Here was the thing, per usual, Chrissy *had* caught feelings for the man. But it wasn't her fault! He was so amazing at listening to her issues with Boris. And his worry for her safety made her heart melt. She wasn't sure if he was aware of it or not, but he was sending out all sorts of I-like-you-more-than-just-a-casual-hook-up vibes. So, though she was trying to keep her head clear, it was proving to be hard and she needed some advice.

"Chris? Both?" Antoine asked, a huge grin on his face. "See, Shay. I told you it was a man making her act weird. Wait, it's a man, right? Or, were you serious when you said you might go all 'muff-in' next time?"

Oh, Jesus. They remembered that, did they? It'd been a night when they'd had a few too many, and it was about that time when verbal diarrhea took over with her woe-is-me moment, lamenting the New York dating scene. She'd proclaimed that lesbianism might be in her foreseeable future because men were such immature weenies. Little did she know back then that she'd very soon meet the man of her sexual fantasies, both real and nonreal.

"It's a man," she said, rolling her eyes. "Big dick and all."

"Oh! You have got to spill!" Antoine almost shouted, bouncing in his chair, as the others agreed, excited for her, too.

She shook her head. "That's all I'm going to say. He's not really dating material." She shrugged going for casual, but her heart was racing whenever she thought about this non-dating-material man.

"What's wrong with him? Does he want to get some kind of plastic surgery, Botox, or some other kind of shit?" Shana asked, hooting.

"No, nothing like that." She was doing her best to avoid Mariam's gaze, though. The woman had no idea she was referring to her cousin … right? But Mariam was looking at her closely with her honey-colored eyes—so similar to Aariv's, as she continued. "He's just not into dating right now. But I do like him."

"And you're ok with that?" Mariam asked in disbelief. "I thought you were looking for 'the one.' Enough of the hookup bullshit and the shitty way boys have treated you…"

Chrissy looked at her thoughtfully. She *had* said that. Again she was both grateful and annoyed that her friends had paid attention when she'd spilled her guts out months ago.

"Hey, your words not mine," Mariam said. "And because of that, I may have found 'the one' for you."

Curious, Chrissy asked, "Who?"

"Well, I met him in California—you know, when I went to get Bruce back," she said, looking down, her face and neck pinkening, as they always did when she spoke about her fiancé. "He worked as a barista and he was so sweet to me. A true friend—"

"Wait, that Taylor guy? The one who works in the coffee shop?" Antoine stared at Mariam with bug eyes.

"Used to. He used to work in a coffee shop. He was taking a break from the corporate world and Silicon Valley. The dude is some kind of computer nerd, but you wouldn't know it by looking at him."

This was true because, of course, Chrissy and the others had deep-dived into this guy's social media profile once Mar had told them about him last fall. What kind of good friends would they be if they hadn't? And his looks hardly resembled what one would think of as a computer geek. He was more of the uber-sexy-surfer-dude-type with shaggy blonde hair and a lazy smile.

"Didn't you say he had a little crush on you?" Shana asked impatiently.

Mariam grunted. "Okay, yeah, it's the same guy. But he's over me. And he's moving to New York for some big computer tech job."

She looked around the table stopping at Chrissy. "He'll be in town scoping out neighborhoods next week. What do you think? You've been here practically your whole life. Would you want to help him out and show him a few good areas to check out?"

Now all eyes were on her as she pondered this. Why was she feeling slightly nauseous right now, as if she was betraying someone? Wasn't this just the most fortunate thing? Any single woman in New York would tell her that this guy was a rarity, and she should be jumping at the chance. He was unattached, good-looking, and didn't know the area. He needed a cute available insider (like her) to show him around. And she—aka the cute available insider (also technically single)—had first dibs and could snap him up in well ... a snap! And she should. Lord knew some other single woman wouldn't even hesitate. New York was a rat race in every facet of life including relationships. Plus, she needed to remind herself that the current man she was sleeping with wasn't emotionally available. As if he would care if she started dating, which she'd already warned him about.

So why was she hesitating?!

She squared her shoulders and made up her mind. "Yes," she said. "I'm in."

Though, she was maybe only about fifty percent in at this point, she was being smart here by keeping her options open.

# CHAPTER 24

२8

"I don't understand, Aariv. Why do you need this information? It is water under the bridge. *Bas*! Why can't you forget about it? I'm sure she has." Viraj grunted deeply over the phone; his usual on-edge tone edgier than normal.

Aariv had noticed early on that his father usually took this tone with anyone when he'd had a particularly bad night. No doubt an all-night bender of poker or some other form of gambling, with maybe a prostitute by his side.

"Rough night?" Aariv asked coolly.

He heard his father breathing loudly on the other end.

"I'm fine," the older man said distantly.

"How much did you lose this time?"

The sound of his father sucking his teeth in aggravation was a loud clicking hiss; a rattlesnake ready to pounce. He hated to be questioned about his decisions no matter how misguided they were.

"Is that how you speak to your father after months of ignoring me?"

Aariv balked and started chuckling. "*Abba*, is that what you call never being available to talk whenever I call?" Aariv was past the point of feeling hurt by his father's unavailability. But it seemed that his father was still pining for some kind of relationship with him, though he'd never put an ounce of work toward that endeavor in Aariv's entire life.

Silence and heavy breathing again answered Aariv.

"Well, here we are, finally talking." He turned the subject back to his original question. "I would like to find out if Leila Majid is all right. I have no idea what happened to her. You know people, have connections back there. You must know someone who knows something."

He couldn't understand the need to keep things so hush-hush. Especially since the entire thing had been fixed and her, and her family's honor had been saved.

"Aariv, understand this—that family wants nothing to do with us."

"And I want nothing to do with them. But I need to know."

"*Kenno* (Why)?"

He sighed. "Abba, have you ever felt like some things in your life have never been tied up? That you can't move forward unless you know the answer?" He was trying here. Maybe his father would identify with this, considering they never knew what became of his birth mother. He must have *some* feelings about the matter. If not sadness, at least curiosity.

Viraj snorted and started chortling.

And maybe not.

"Aariv, your generation has had so much more opportunity than mine, or those of your grandfathers before you. You are a successful lawyer in America, educated by American standards.

You live in one of the best cities in the world. The future is wide open for you. Why are you determined to dig up the past?"

Why *was* he determined to dig up the past? There was a fifty percent chance that what he found out could be so terrible that he wouldn't be able to move on with his life. That this feeling of not deserving happiness was valid.

It was all Chrissy Smyth's fault. The woman was on his mind constantly lately. He'd be lying to himself if he didn't admit that he was starting to like her more than just for sex. That she pulled a more easy-going side out of him that made him like himself more. It was a feeling he hadn't experienced in years—decades—and it was like an old friend finally coming home from a long journey whom he hadn't known he'd missed in earnest.

"Abba, unlike your generation, and that before yours, mine is more aware of finding the crux of emotional problems so that we are happy all around, not just because we have material things and money." He knew his father wouldn't care for that statement.

"*Atcha, Beta.* If that is how you think then you should call up that investigator of yours." To say his tone was condescending was an understatement. "Maybe he can find out what you seek. Nothing stopped you from learning what happened to your mother and where did that leave you? Do you feel better knowing that she was *pagal* (crazy)?"

Aariv was stunned. So his father knew about his digging around, and more importantly, was aware of his mother's mental instability. Yet, he hadn't done a damn thing about it. His anger rose like a monsoon and he wanted to shout foul language at the older man. But he took a few deep breaths, trying to contemplate the situation, concluding what he always did when it came to his father—railing at Viraj would do absolutely nothing. It would only be a waste of his energy. His father was set in his ways. The family came first, but even before that, the notion of 'what will people say' lived at the top of his way of life. He didn't want anyone to think their family was crazy. He'd let his mother run away—disappear— though she was incapable. He took no blame and didn't care that she was the mother of his only child because reputation was everything. He was heartless, cruel, and would never change.

"Fine, *Abba*. I *will* do that."

His father grumbled in response. "Before you go off to your busy schedule, tell me, have you picked a wife, yet?" He didn't let Aariv answer. "What is taking so long? I've reviewed the biodatas and it's a good assortment of girls."

"I'm caught up with something at work here and haven't had that much time to look closely."

"Are you sure it's not this *sada meh?*"

Jesus, he couldn't keep a lid on things with Chrissy though he'd not mentioned her once. The rumor mill was whirling out of control.

"I don't know what you're talking about," Aariv deflected. Chrissy didn't need to be dragged into this. Gossip was vital in the culture, and more often than not it got ugly.

"Is she ripe and juicy?" Viraj jeered, laughing. "Ah, my boy. You are more like me than you think. Your appetite for women is big like mine." He boasted. "There's nothing wrong with this. Nothing wrong with keeping her on the side while you marry someone suitable. You can even discard her and find someone new when you get tired of her. It's a man's way and healthy."

It sounded about as unhealthy and toxic as ever, and Aariv

felt nauseous. He could never do that to Chrissy, no matter what their relationship was.

Part of him was starting to wonder what would happen if he and Chrissy were in a real relationship—one where he could shirk off this old-fashioned way of finding a partner. The thought wasn't so terrible. He felt less weighed down thinking about it. What if, he thought? What if he could pursue her for real?

But his father's continued litany of the positives in cheating on one's wife persisted, dragging him back to the conversation at hand

"You are a real piece of work, aren't you, *Abba*." It wasn't a question. "How can you treat Huma like that?"

His father laughed loudly again, ending with a hacking cough. When he could speak, he said, "Life is about living, Aariv."

He spoke briefly to someone in the background, chastising them about his tea being too hot. Aariv heard him threaten the servant that he'd throw the tea in his face if he did it again. The man was a real shit.

He went on, "Huma has known from day one what I was like. And I did her family a favor by taking their eldest unmarried daughter off their hands. Not the brightest, but the sweetest, and she has known about my behavior and had the decency to not complain. The key is honesty."

That Aariv could agree on. But he sighed, getting tired of this conversation. "I have to go, *Abba*. Work meeting. Tell Aunty I was sorry to miss speaking with her." And he hung up, not able to stomach his father's 'words of wisdom.' Plus, he'd learned long ago that there was no point in unsticking something that was stuck in its ways.

He buzzed his assistant.

"Yes, Mr. Abbas."

"Terri, can you get Tag Underwood on the phone?"

"Yes. Give me a minute." He waited until she said, "He's on line one."

He picked up the receiver. "Hey, Tag. Long time."

"Long time, my ass," the craggy voice barked back, his southern accent drawing out his syllables. "You never let me take you out for that beer to thank you for all the business you're throwing my way."

"I thought that's why I gave you Chrissy's case," he joked. The man was as much a workaholic as he was and jumped into new cases with enthusiasm. He'd been more than excited to take on Chrissy's case as a favor to Aariv due to the high probability of involving any one of New York's underbelly crime syndicates. He couldn't wait to get his hands dirty.

"Ha! You got me there. I'm havin' a ball of a time with that one. And that girl is a spark plug!"

Aariv smiled. Spark plug sounded about right when it came to Chrissy.

"Yeah. She's something."

"I'm not sure if she filled you in but I told her to stay away from the shop. But then she comes to me with new evidence. She's really smart, Abbas, but she's also taking some risky chances. I'm pretty sure she went there and…"

Aariv stopped listening because his fury soared. Chrissy had done more digging?! She'd put herself in danger when he'd asked her not to—and she'd agreed (promised even) not to. What the fuck?!

"…and that manager…" Tag continued, having no idea that

Aariv hadn't been paying attention. He let out a whistle. "Aariv, the shit I'm digging up here goes way back."

"What do you mean?" Aariv asked, trying to focus on what the other man was relaying.

"I think not only is this Boris guy running the show right now, but the mother, Natasha, was involved, too. She may have been the one who set it all up to begin with! I mean think about it, why would a Russian immigrant take on a long-standing business she knew nothing about? And why did the previous owners turn it over to her so quickly?"

Aariv considered this. He didn't see the problem. Immigrants took over all sorts of businesses they knew nothing about to live the American dream. He knew Indians who'd taken over smoke shops, or even taco chains in the burbs, though they'd never smoked a day in their lives, or knew nothing about Mexican food. It was an opportunity they couldn't turn down. Becoming a business owner, and having something tangible of their own was much easier in the American system than back in India.

"It doesn't sound that sordid to me—"

"The old owners may have got the ball rolling—most likely coerced into it—and then enlisted a more hungry, younger, poorer immigrant from the motherland to take over. Washed their hands clean of the entire kit and caboodle."

Now that did make more sense.

"What have you told Chrissy?"

"Nothing about that until I'm completely sure. She was already torn apart finding out about that Boris guy's involvement. But I'm almost there. I think I'll have something by the weekend."

Aariv recalled her frustration, tears even, about the store

manager a few days ago. Honestly, he could relate. He'd felt that kind of emotional turmoil with his father keeping things from him on and off through the years. He now knew how to handle it. But this was all new to Chrissy—the lies, the misinformation.

And, it'd surprised him, the force of anger and empathy he felt at seeing her tears. He'd been able to calm her down, thinking he'd had her fine with sitting back and watching the drama unfold. But he should've known she couldn't resist poking around. She was headstrong and stubborn. What would happen in this instance, when she found out her mother might've been involved—maybe even the ringleader in all this? Would she try to confront the Russian mob themselves? He felt ill thinking about it. And the sense of wanting to protect her came to him again. He had to find a way to keep her from putting herself in harm's way.

"Listen, tell me everything she discovered. And I'll talk to her about keeping herself safe." Oh, he'd do more than talk, he thought. "First I want to ask you another favor."

"Shoot."

Aariv told him about Leila Majid and the basic facts of her life before she disappeared from Kolkata, the town they'd lived in, and when she'd disappeared.

"Another disappearance, case?" Tag asked, his voice soft. "Abbas, are you sure you want to go digging? I can't promise a more positive outcome from the last time."

He was referring to what he'd found out about his mother. The dead end and talks of suicide had been a hard pill for Aariv to swallow, let alone finding out she'd been mentally unstable.

"I'm sure. I need to know her whereabouts, no matter what the outcome."

Tag sighed heavily. "Ok, Captain. You're the boss. May take me some time since I'm working Chrissy's case, and a few others, but I'll send out some feelers—wait a minute, the name sounds familiar. Didn't we go down this road a while back?"

Aariv was hoping he wouldn't bring that up. "Yeah, but I told you to stop." It was around that time that he'd decided to let his parents choose his fate and his future partner, removing the happiness factor from his life once and for all. But now he wasn't so sure about that anymore.

"All right. I don't judge, you know that. And like I said, it'll take some time."

Tag then filled him in on what Chrissy had discovered. It was enough physical evidence to bring her justice, but they still needed facts and names.

When Aariv finally hung up, he grabbed his cell phone and swiped over to his text messages. He found the exchange between himself and Chrissy and thought a moment before he started typing.

**"Hey, Sunshine. Before I forget, here's the link to the Melatonin pills I take."**

He forwarded a link from a local drugstore website.

Her response came back quickly. **"That's candy, Riv, not medicine."**

He chuckled. True, they were in gummy form, and were pretty tasty, satisfying his sweet tooth craving while helping him sleep at the same time.

**"Besides,"** she continued typing. **"I'm fine, as long as I get a good, big dose of my medicine."**

"Dirty girl," he chuckled under his breath.

**"What are you doing right now?"** He texted, unable to keep the grin off his face, despite the fury he still felt for her putting herself in danger. It was the middle of a workday but he hadn't seen her since Sunday. He could use a good dose of that medicine, too.

Her text came back immediately. **"Thinking about when you'll be inside me again."**

He sat up straighter in his office chair. Fuck. She got right to the point, didn't she?

**"Are you wet right now, Little Girl, just thinking about me?"**

**"You have no idea."**

**"Then tell me."**

He swiveled to face the windows and the overcast skies. Drizzle pinged softly against the window as he imagined her wriggling her tight ass in her chair, uncomfortable at how wet she was.

**"I'll do better than that."** She texted back. And quickly an image followed. It was of two of her fingers, glossy with a sheen.

He groaned, closing his eyes, imagining what she'd tasted like, what she'd felt like suctioning him snuggly. He was quickly turning into a horny maniac. Shit. This part of him was like his father. But what did he expect when it came to her? She had a way of driving his level of crazy from zero to one hundred in a matter of seconds.

**"I just painted my nails. What do you think?"**

Fucking tease, he thought, chuckling as he noticed her bright red nails. God, he wanted those nails clutching his dick.

**"I think I need to see them in person to appreciate them."** He texted back, his groin starting to tighten in his pants.

**"Do you? I never thought you'd be a man who was into a woman's manicure."** He could picture her giggling on the other end, and it turned him on even more.

**"I need to inspect them, make sure your hands can still handle my big cock."** He was shit when it came to flirting dirty with this girl, but she seemed to like it as her response was a kiss emoji.

**"What are you doing for lunch?"** She texted.

**"You, Little Girl. I expect you here at noon, sharp."**

**"What if I have a meeting or a lunch date?"**

Oh, she wanted to play this game, did she? He couldn't help smiling a little madly as he responded, **"You come when I say come."**

*H*er breath caught and she giggled again, lust snaking its way throughout her body, and down into her already soaking panties. This man ... she closed her eyes and clenched her pussy. She could come right there, right now in her little cubicle, if she wanted to just thinking about him and how much he wanted her right this minute.

She opened her eyes to the wonderful thought of being wanted. If felt great, more than great. Her heart cinched inside her chest, and she squeezed her eyes shut again.

*It's just sex, Chrissy. He just wants your body, not you.*

Well, she wanted him like that, too. But, wait, did she have lunch plans? She'd get out of them, she had to, her body couldn't wait. It was practically vibrating with need.

"Let's go, Team!" Simran called as she came out of her office, her trench coat already on as she zipped up her oversized work bag. "The yacht—and the Bittermans—wait for no one, not even this crappy weather!"

Oh shit. Chrissy scrolled through her work calendar. That new client lunch meeting was today!? There was no way she could get out of this one. They were taking the yacht cruise around the island that the Bittermans wanted for their daughter's bar mitzvah. And they were doing a menu tasting, too.

As much as Chrissy had been looking forward to this client lunch, getting the chance to see Aariv and what they were going to do in his office had climbed its way to the top of her mind. There was room for nothing else.

"Let's go, Chris! I bet we get to try all sorts of caviar, not to mention top-shelf bubbly!" Antoine tittered excitedly, throwing his scarf around his throat, and zipping up his black leather jacket.

"This is for a kid's party, you dope," Shana said buttoning her coat.

"Um, yeah, but that's never stopped the hoity-toities from providing top-shelf booze for the adults and those teens that they know sneak it into their soda."

"Truth," Shana said.

Chrissy quickly texted Aariv that she did indeed have an important client lunch meeting. Could she meet him later? Shit, she wanted to meet him later—needed it. She hoped he got back to her.

He didn't text back, and her friends were hovering.

"Let's go," she muttered as she threw her phone in her bag and grabbed her jacket so as not to keep everyone waiting.

CHAPTER 25

ૠ૯

*H*ad she checked her phone rudely throughout lunch with the Bittermans on their private yacht while Manhattan's skyline glided by lazily? Yes, yes she had, and in between luxurious bites as they planned an over-the-top-twelve-year-old's party with over-the-top entertainment, too.

Why wasn't he getting back to her?

She realized halfway through dessert that she wasn't getting any cell service. Well, really, when Barbara Bitterman—Babs as she wanted to be called—noted that cell service was spotty on their yacht, no doubt also noticing Chrissy darting glances at her phone.

"My dear, I've always found cell service terrible when we're on The Bitterman (yes, they'd named their yacht after themselves), and I've always chalked it up to the universe telling me something—relax and enjoy." She smiled indulgently at Chrissy. "And look, the sun has made an appearance. Thank goodness." She put a hand to her angora-covered chest, flashing the enormous diamond on her hand as well as the stack of tennis bracelets on her wrist.

"You're right, Mrs.—Babs." Chrissy corrected herself. "It's not every day I get to experience a beautiful yacht, with exquisite food, and company." She threw in that last part to completely kiss her ass and make up for being rude. She got a very white-toothed smile from Babs in return.

As she put her phone in her purse, she caught Simran nodding at her in relief. It seemed that everyone noticed her checking her phone too much. And all for naught because whether Aariv had gotten back to her or not, she wouldn't know until they got back to dry land.

She tried to enjoy the afternoon. But when a person is craving something so vitally that their brain is nothing but a bowl of mush, and their body feels like a live wire, it's nigh near impossible. Chrissy found herself answering questions in monosyllables, and unable to expound on details that she usually did with enthusiasm.

It was official—she was an addict when it came to sex with Aariv.

Much later, once they docked at the west side landing, she pulled her phone out of her bag. A response from him waited for her and she danced a little jig right there on the spot.

As she was about to read it, Antoine said behind her, "Look at you already excited about making plans with that Taylor guy."

She hid her phone and turned to her friend smiling as innocently as possible. "Uh-huh," she responded. But her stupid cheeks bled with heat in embarrassment.

Antoine noticed that and the way she clutched her phone. Never one to miss a beat with his friends, whether they liked it or not—the guy was some kind of emotional guru or something —his eyes squinted in consternation.

"Wait a minute," he said slyly. "You're not texting coffee man. You're texting hot sex man."

She lifted her chin. "So?"

He wiggled his eyebrows but turned to walk off the gangplank following the others.

Chrissy hurried after him.

"What?" she asked him.

"Nothing, girl. Go get it."

Chrissy wasn't convinced this was all he had to say and waited.

He took a deep breath. "But—"

"Uh-huh," she said blandly waiting for his unsolicited—but actually solicited—advice.

"You might need to wrap it up before computer guy gets here."

"I know. I know." She did know. She'd been talking herself in circles about this and had concluded that she wasn't ready to give up the best sex of her life yet. She had so much left to learn and was having an amazing time. And didn't she have a few weeks to figure this out before Taylor came into town?

"Just watch that little romantic heart of yours," he said. "Now, do you want to share an Uber or a cab home?"

"Um…" She glanced at her phone.

"Oh, Lord. Check out what the big dick man has to say. And I better get more details soon. A best friend can only be patient for so long." He crossed his arms and waited.

She hadn't told him much but had revealed the incredible coffee sex because it had been such a juicy tidbit she couldn't keep in. Now he was salivating for more specifics.

She nodded, grinning, and clicked on Aariv's last response to her.

**"I'm very disappointed in you, Litte Girl. You know I'm a very busy man, with very important needs. Don't expect me to be nice next time. How about 5 pm sharp, today at my office? Don't be late."**

Her grin turned into simpering giggles as her nipples hardened under her white button-down dress shirt—the same she'd worn that first time in his office.

"Well, okay then. I guess I'm flying home solo to *my* man. Have fun, girl!" Antoine said, blowing her a kiss as he turned and headed down the block.

Chrissy barely noticed him. She saw she had twenty minutes to get to Aariv's office and pleasure beyond her wildest dreams. She practically danced her way to the corner searching for a cab, tripping in, and almost yelling the address to the driver.

"And step on it!" she said. She'd always wanted to say that and never was a time more appropriate. The driver looked at her in the review mirror and rolled his eyes. He proceeded to go east one block before getting stuck in traffic.

Chrissy realized she was going to be late, but didn't care, as the clouds rolled in again and started dumping rain on the city. What would he do to her if she was late, she wondered, shivering deliciously.

*S*he was late. But instead of impatience with her, he had the hardest hard-on thinking about what he was going to do to her. It was pure madness how turned on she made him; how crazy with lust she filled him.

He loosened his tie and stood looking out his window as rain washed over the city again that day. It was déjà vu, waiting for her, but he anticipated this more than he did the last time. He shifted the crotch of his pants as his boner pulsed against the fine wool blend material.

He glanced at his watch again just as his intercom buzzed.

Leaning over his desk and pressing the button he answered. "Yes, Terri." His heartbeat thudded loudly in his ears just as the city lit up with lightning followed quickly by a loud boom of thunder cracking the air outside. Was she here?

"Mr. Abbas, I have the copies you wanted. I can leave them for you on my desk if you're otherwise preoccupied."

"Yes. Yes, do that," he said impatiently. "And go home. It looks like a nasty storm is on its way."

It wouldn't do to have his assistant lingering outside while he had his way with Chrissy, though the thought of someone hearing her cries and moans was titillating. But he was also getting no more work done tonight so there was no point in her sticking around.

"Mr. Abbas, are you sure?" She sounded flabbergasted. Sheesh, did he never give her a break? True that when he worked long hours—which was often—she did, too, but he wasn't that stingy of a boss, was he?

"Absolutely sure. Go home, have a nice glass of wine, and relax."

"Mr. Abbas, I have three kids and a husband to go home to. As nice as that sounds, it would be impossible. But if you're absolutely sure…?"

He grunted. Five years he'd been working at this firm—two of them with the same assistant, and he had no idea who she was.

"I am." He pulled his tie off, tossing it on his desk in irritation. Why was he so annoyed about this? And the answer came as soon as he posed it to himself. It was very much like his father and the way he treated his staff and laborers both in his home and at the jute mill.

He rubbed his hand down his beard, vowing to change that, just as a knock came at his door.

"Terri," he barked. "I said go home."

He turned to find a wet and bedraggled Chrissy standing in his doorway. A sexy smile curved her lips and as soaked as she was, she was the most gorgeous, brightest thing he'd seen all day. He grinned back at her, but remembered the game they were playing and wiped it off, putting a stern mask on.

"No sign of Terri out there. It's just lil' ole' me," she said tauntingly, a hand on her hip.

"You're late, Ms. Smyth."

She sighed her hands in the air. "I'm sorry, Mr. Abbas. It couldn't be helped. What with the weather and all." She shrugged nonchalantly as she removed her soggy trench coat, hanging it up on the coat rack in the corner. She was wearing that same blouse from last time, the filmy white one, but the buttons were buttoned up to her neck. His hand itched to rip it open, but he stayed where he was, taking in her slim red pants that molded to her hips and legs and those sexy shiny black heels he remembered from the *Holi* party.

He lay his hands flat on his desk, leaning toward her. "And what have we discussed regarding checking the weather?" He scanned her from her wet hair, over her breasts (fuck her nipples needed attention) down to her feet again, and back up, giving her a severe look. "Where is your umbrella?"

She shrugged her slim shoulders, with her hands up again. "Oops. I left it in the cab," she said sassily, her juicy lips twitching, her blue eyes big and round.

"This is bad, Ms. Smyth." He shook his head, tsking. "Please shut the door."

She nodded and went to comply. But looked over her shoulder licking her lips when he added, "And lock it."

He took his glasses off and came from around his desk and to the corner of his office with the slate gray couch. He sat down, keeping his eyes locked on her, and leaned back.

When she turned back around, he crooked a finger at her. "Come here," he said harshly.

She sauntered, taking her time, her hands folded demurely in front of her. When she was in front of him, she paused waiting for his next order.

"Take off your clothes, and tell me exactly what the hell you think you were doing by going back to the rug shop when you promised you wouldn't."

He rubbed his chin with his palm watching her expression go from docile to surprise. Her mouth rounded in a perfect 'O'—the perfect shape to stretch around his cock.

"Well, I—" And she glanced over her shoulders at the windows. He'd already pulled the shades half down, anticipating fucking her all over this office.

"Is there a problem, Ms. Smyth?" he asked, keeping his tone dangerously low.

"No," she squeaked out, shaking her damp copper waves. She visibly swallowed, her chest rising and falling quickly. "No," she said again with more confidence.

"Then proceed." He leaned back spreading his legs on either

side of her, while lengthening his arms along the back of the couch, getting comfortable.

Her eyes darted to his crotch, and she licked her lips before tucking the bottom one's fullness in her mouth. She was eyeing his raging hard-on and couldn't hide her excitement, but the wrinkle between her brow told him she was wondering about his knowledge of her recent escapade.

"Yes, Ms. Smyth. All in good time. But first, naked and explanations, now!" he barked, just as lightning and thunder cracked, illuminating the room briefly.

She jumped and began unbuttoning her blouse, pulling the tails out where they were tucked into her pants. Her lacy bra was baby pink today and pushed her breasts up to swelling over the cups. And her nipples—

"Your tits are gorgeous, Ms. Smyth. But we need to do something about those naughty nipples of yours." He reached forward and pinched a hardened one, making her eyes close as she moaned, while her hands paused on the side zipper of her pants.

"Did I say you could stop?" he asked, masking his lust for her with that dangerously low tone as he fondled and pinched her other nipple.

"No," she said breathlessly.

"And talk, now."

He watched her unzip her pants and slide them down.

"Aariv," she said, as she stepped out of her shoes and slid her pants completely off. Now she stood in just her pink bra and matching tiny pink lacy underwear. "Why—How—"

"Shoes back on, Ms. Smyth. And I spoke with Tag."

She bit her lip and slipped them back on. Now she stood

proudly in front of him in just her black heels and skimpy, sexy underwear.

"What!? Isn't there something about client confidentiality?" She was outraged, now. Making her even more erotic to him.

"Turn around," he said, almost growling. She was so supple, so sexy, so gorgeous. He wanted to throw her on the couch and fuck her until they both died of pleasure. His cock was straining in his pants, revving to be let out. He swallowed harshly as she complied, giving him an incredible view of her perfect peach-shaped ass in the lacy thong, her flank muscles flexing.

He couldn't help it, he unzipped his pants and pulled his cock out, giving it a few long strokes as he watched her hands grip into fists at her sides. Oh, she was irate for sure at this new development.

"There is client confidentiality, sure," he said. "But when you put your life in danger, I need to know."

He heard her sigh in irritation. "Aariv—"

"Mr. Abbas to you. And take your bra off. If I don't hear an explanation soon, I will bend you over my knees and spank you."

She gasped, looking over her shoulder in shock, but he didn't miss the slight shudder of her body. She was excited at the prospect, too.

He tamped down his groans as she reached up and unclasped her bra, letting it fall to the floor.

"I went to the shop super early last Friday morning. I was really careful. I wore all black so no one would see me—"

"You think pretending at some kind of stealth mode would have protected you?" he scoffed. "I want to know why you didn't keep your promise. You said you wouldn't go."

"I did keep my promise! I didn't go to the store to meet

Boris. I went to check out the inventory. Boris was nowhere in sight."

Aariv paused from stroking himself as what she said sunk in. He burst into chuckles. She was right. She might have made a damn good lawyer in another life.

She glanced over her shoulder again, her eyes sparkling. "Are you still mad at me, Mr. Abbas?"

"I am, Ms. Smyth," he said harshly, still thinking about what could have happened to her if she'd been caught. "I don't like you putting yourself in danger." This, he said softly, gently. She tugged something in him, a protectiveness and he wasn't sure what he would do if something had happened to her.

"I'm safe, Riv," she said, equally gentle. "I mean, Mr. Abbas." She straightened up.

"For now, Ms. Smyth. Don't do anything like that again. Or—"

"Or what, Mr. Abbas." She sounded breathy now and her hands fondled her breasts as she arched her back.

"That's it. Tease me, Little Girl," he said through gritted teeth, clutching himself again. "And was the discovery of cocaine worth your safety?"

He hissed as she slid her fingers under the tight elastic of her thong and slid it down her legs, bending over as she pushed the flimsy piece of fabric to her ankles, and then artfully stepped out of it while still wearing her heels.

Her pussy lips were shiny and swollen, and all too quickly she stood up, hiding her lushness from his view.

"Yes, Mr. Abbas."

"Wrong answer." He growled, aware that his breathing sounded heavy and uneven. His irritation was at the forefront again, fighting with his lust for her. He wanted his dick inside her so badly, but he needed to make sure she wouldn't do that kind of stupid thing again. "Turn around," he ordered.

She swiveled on the ball of one foot and came around. He nodded his head in approval as his stare roved over her nakedness. Her breasts were incredible. High and perky, and her pink nipples were tight and hard, puffy little berries that needed his mouth's attention. He licked his lips as he slowly gazed down her stomach, her ab muscles apparent by the slight lines running on each side of her midsection. Her flat belly with a slight curve and down to her pussy, hairless and naked, the fleshy mound of skin on display. Every inch of her skin was tawny with a slight flush along the surface hinting at anticipation.

Her chest rose and fell quickly as she said, "I can't stand by and watch from afar. I needed to see for myself. I was there for maybe fifteen minutes tops. I saw the most recent delivery sitting there in the stock room. All I did was inspect it. But there was a slight rip in the plastic. All I did was make it a tiny bit bigger, and white powder spilled out. Now, I'm not stupid enough to think it's sugar. Why would they be smuggling sugar? I snapped a few pictures and sent them to Tag. Then I deleted them from my phone." She rushed out the rest of her story and stood there proudly, almost daring him to call her activities senseless. "*And* from my storage cloud as soon as I got home."

She was pretty brave, and intelligent, thinking of completely deleting any signs of those incriminating pictures.

"You're sexy, you know that?" he asked severely, staring at her body, unsure of the heat that crept into his chest. But the way she held herself so proudly with her shoulders back was definitely something. It was defiant and sensual.

"You tell me that and I still find it hard to believe."

He glanced up at her in surprise. Why would she find that hard to believe? She was hot—hotter than hot—beautiful in fact. Every time he was around her, he found it hard to keep his hands to himself.

Her face said it all—she was confused, her forehead wrinkled between her brows.

"You don't believe me?" he asked.

She shifted on her feet and shook her head, her strands tumbling around her face and rounded cheeks.

"I'm very disappointed that you don't," he said quietly and with gentleness. He took one of her hands and pulled her closer to him. He stood up and put his face in her neck, inhaling her sweetness, and rubbing his lips up the column of her soft skin. She sighed and he pulled her up against him as his lips found hers, kissing her softly, nibbling her lips, teasing her.

"Why?" he murmured against her mouth as he continued to kiss her slowly. He lifted his head slightly, waiting for her answer.

"I just find it so hard to believe that you—this uber attractive, big successful lawyer—finds me, a nothing, so sexy. Like, what are you even doing with me? You could have anyone you wanted—"

"You're not a nothing," he said firmly. "Maybe a little more careless than you should be, given the criminal activity going on around you. But I trust that after today, you won't do it again. And it's obvious I want you." He took her hand and placed it on his exposed dick. He moved it up and down, stroking. He looked down at her hand on him, barely able to enclose his girth. "Your manicure works," he choked out, as she squeezed him. He leaned his head onto hers. "Fuck, Chrissy. I want your mouth on me."

She continued squeezing and stroking him unhurriedly, her palm circling his tight tip, spreading the precum oozing out.

"What do you want me to do?" she asked breathlessly.

He pulled back and looked down at her. She was all curiosity and wonder as she stared up at him with lids heavy over her eyes.

He sat back down. "On your knees, Ms. Smyth."

# CHAPTER 26

२७

hrill shot straight threw her, zinging her like a spark. This man, in all his arrogant, asshole glory was the key to her every sexual desire. She would do anything for him, she thought as she stared at him in his fine denim-colored suit pants and white button-down oxford with the top three buttons undone. He looked so relaxed with his long legs splayed out, his enormous dick in his hand. He was enjoying bossing her around, and she was relishing in taking it because it had his concern for her wrapped up with it. She'd had no idea he would find out—did Tag and him gossip together like two old biddies? But what surprised her more was his depth of anger for going there and putting herself in danger. He cared about her. She hid her smile. In some small way, he was coming to care for her.

She nodded and went down on her knees, not even caring that the carpet was rubbing her knees in discomfort.

"Promise that you won't go back to the store."

"I promise not to go to the store again." She nodded and his chin jerked in response, satisfied with that statement.

Here was the thing, she didn't need to go back to the store.

Her rush of excitement at sneaking in during the early morning had been tinged with terror. But she couldn't help it. She wanted to find out for herself what Boris was up to. No matter how many times she asked, he wouldn't tell her. It was pissing her off. Everyone was treating her like a little girl, even Aariv, outside of their sexual role-play. So she'd done what she had to. Her excitement at discovering the cocaine wrapped tightly in the rugs had her almost squealing. But when she noticed the security camera in the office staring down at her from the corner, she almost had a stroke. Upon inspecting it, though, she realized it wasn't working. Good ole' Boris and his sloppy ways, she'd thought. He hadn't replaced the batteries, and come to think of it, she hadn't seen a bill paid to the security company they used. He must have canceled that service.

What she hadn't relayed to Aariv was that she'd been snapping photos when she heard a commotion in the alley. The prickles on her neck were almost painful as her fear kicked it up a notch and her teeth chattered.

She'd immediately ducked and crawled her way back through the showroom and out the front door, locking up as her hands shook, and finally able to run away. Once she was far enough away from the shop, she briefly paused to catch her breath and sent Tag the images before deleting them from her phone. Once she got home, she'd need to figure out how to remove any evidence from her cloud storage, which she did by asking Shana the next day who was great with technology. But she had real hard evidence and wouldn't need to go back.

No, he didn't need to know that portion, given his reaction that she'd gone in the first place, she thought staring at his engorged dick as it threatened to attack her. Her palm was still sticky with his precum and she salivated, wondering what he would taste like.

"Have you ever sucked cock before?" he asked, rubbing himself languidly, his hazel eyes fiery and fixed on her.

"Not one your size, Mr. Abbas." She breathed out because the man was huge. She was trying to figure out how she could dislocate her jaw to pleasure him this way.

He chuckled. "Don't look so scared, Ms. Smyth. I assure you we'll get past your hesitation, given how brave you've shown you can be in light of danger. Now, begin by licking me." Now his voice sounded tight, and she noticed his facial muscles were taut. And wait a minute … he thought she was brave?

Oh, he was so turned on by the idea of her mouth on him, but maybe also by the fact that she'd succeeded in a mission that he'd thought was risky and senseless to begin with. She tried to hide her smile as she leaned down and licked his tight crown and the juice that oozed from him.

"Is something funny, Ms. Smyth?" he said, his voice still tight.

"No. You taste good, Mr. Abbas," she said, feigning a demure attitude.

He jerked his head in approval.

But she wasn't faking the fact that he tasted good. She practically suckled the tip of his dick, trying to taste more of his musty saltiness. He groaned in pleasure.

"Mm," she moaned.

She felt him shift and his hands were on her breasts, cupping and squeezing them as she sucked on him. Her own grasped the sides of his muscular thighs for anchor.

"Yes, Chrissy. Very good," he said gruffly with another groan as his pelvis lifted off the couch cushions and his dick pushed further into her mouth. She slid a hand up and down the bottom half of his shaft as her mouth worked the top half. She slid her other hand further down between his hard thighs and into his pants and underwear, boldly cupping his balls in her palm. She squeezed them gently and he moaned in pure pleasure.

Contrary to her lack of experience with good fucking, she'd given head plenty of times. She knew what to do. But she'd never given it to a man this sexy, whom she wanted utterly to please, in every way possible. She'd also never experienced his size before. It was a challenge she happily accepted. She squeezed again and licked him from his base, up his veiny rigid length, to his tip, making him growl deeply.

Oh God, he was so hot, and she was getting him off, which in turn was getting her off.

"Fuck, Chrissy. Tell me."

She knew by now what he wanted.

"Riv, your cock tastes so good," she said breathlessly. She blew on him, making him shudder. "You're so big and hard, I can barely get my mouth around you," she pouted. "But I want you down my throat, fucking my mouth." She took as much of him into her mouth as she could and started moving up and down, trying not to choke.

He pulled her off him and looked at her in wonder, the muscles of his face still clenched.

"Not my first rodeo, Cowboy," she said, leaning back on her heels and swiping at the film of saliva and precum on her lips.

He chuckled. "Chrissy," he sighed. "You're full of surprises."

He brushed the hair from her face and tucked it gently behind her ear. He stared at her for a beat, his eyes spearing her.

She wondered what he was thinking. Finally, he asked, "Would you like to continue, or do you want me to come inside you?"

She stared at his cock, long and big. Both options sounded appealing to her and she deliberated, putting an arm across her belly and the other to her gold cross, fingering the rubies.

"You're cute," he said, his voice deep and gruff, his cock bobbing up and down in agreement. "And so sexy sitting like that, thinking."

"Shh!" she said, lost in thought. It might require some gymnastics, but she could do it.

He chuckled again, the rumbles emanating from the depths of his belly it seemed. "I'm not a mountain to scale, Ms. Smyth."

"Could've fooled me," she murmured, blowing her bang out of her eyes. She wanted to make him come with her mouth—but it was like facing Mount Everest.

"Come here," he commanded, leaning back on the couch, a hand extended with palm up to her. His stern voice was back. "I'm losing my patience."

She grunted but scrambled to stand. He pulled her onto the couch and quickly maneuvered her body so that she was on her knees kneeling beside him. He positioned her hands so that they were between his thighs, but resting on the couch cushion so that now she was on all fours.

"There now," he said with admiration. He spanked her ass sharply and then clutched it. "That's for defying me and breaking your promise." Cripes, he couldn't let it go, but she took it. "So erotic and dirty." He hissed, rubbing his hand down her ass cheeks, and cupping her pussy.

She arched her back in pleasure.

"*Riv!*" she cried, as he pushed two fingers into her. She

immediately clenched around him and pushed her ass in the air, forcing his fingers in further. "Oh." She moaned, bucking back and forth on his fingers.

"Yes, Little Girl." He twisted his fingers inside her, giving her a taste of his magical touch. Her wetness squelched. "Such a wet cunt." But he pulled his fingers out all too quickly leaving her empty. "Now, you're in the perfect position to suck my cock. So, do it." He ordered severely, rubbing her ass cheeks, his touch soft, belying his tone.

She shuddered though, needing the asshole boss to come out to push her further to the edge. His palm glided up her rump, along her back, and came to rest on her neck. He gently pushed her down and she let him as she widened her lips and took him into her mouth. She went down as he continued caressing the back of her neck, but he wasn't pushing, now. Gravity was taking her, and he filled her mouth until his cock hit the back of her throat and then some.

"Breathe," he murmured, and she realized she'd been holding her breath. She inhaled and exhaled through her nose, adjusting herself to the fullness in her mouth that knocked the back of her throat and down.

"Good girl," he said soothingly. "You look incredible like this." He breathed in deeply and let it out, the whoosh of air warm on her. And that was enough encouragement. She began dipping up and down, moving slowly at first as her mouth fucked him. "*Yes*, that's it," he groaned, his hand sliding up and into her hair.

She swirled her tongue in the downward motion and sucked with gusto in the upward motion making him shudder and his breath hitch. She smiled (as much as she could with the mouthful she had) aware that it was driving him crazy, especially when he now clutched her hair tightly in his hand. His pelvis started to lift off the couch again and she picked up her pace.

"Fuck, yeah, Chrissy. God, you're good. So fucking good!" he shouted, just as another crack of lightning lit up the room followed by deep thunderous booms, echoing off the tall buildings and skyscrapers.

She felt him lose it, his body undulating under her in a nonrhythmic rhythm while his breathing became harsher and faster.

"Chrissy, I'm coming!" He groaned, his pelvis jerking, his swollen cock making her head bob like a rag doll. Thick, salty liquid spurted into her mouth, like a hot geyser, flowing down the back of her throat. And she let it, as she swallowed his cum up, letting it slide warmly into her belly mixing with the lust that was already swirling.

"Holy Christ," he murmured, heaving as he continued to pump her mouth until he was empty. He finally leaned back on the couch. His arms splayed wide along the back, his head leaning back as he stared at the ceiling.

She sat up, wiping her mouth with the back of her hand, and moving her stiff lips and jaw around. She felt proud of herself, and when she saw how spent he was from what she'd done to him, a giggle gurgled up and escaped from her.

He lifted his head to stare at her. His eyes crinkled and he chuckled. "What's so funny, Sunshine?"

She felt fuzzy inside at that nickname. She loved *all* the names he called her. She shook her head. "You."

She had the sudden urge to climb onto his lap. So, she did and straddled him. She paused to see if he was ok with it and when his hands glided up her back to pull her close, she lay her head on his shoulder and moved up and down with his chest as he breathed deeply.

Ok, this was nice. Did he think this was nice, too? She dared not say anything to break the spell and they sat like that for a while as he caught his breath, enjoying his strong arms around her.

"I'm thinking you need some water. I could use some before we get to you," he murmured in her hair. But he didn't move. His hands grazed her. The office was darker now, and the rain was coming down heavily.

Suddenly, a knock came at the door and the handle jiggled. There was a jingle of keys and the sound of the lock on the door clicking.

"What the fuck—" Aariv said sitting up. Chrissy scrambled off his lap and nestled into the furthest corner of the couch just before the door opened and an older man poked his head in.

"Mr. Abbas? Is it ok if I come in to clean?" the janitor asked.

He peered into the dim office, searching. His eyes landed all too quickly on her pile of clothes in the middle of the room then darted to the couch. Chrissy was folded into the smallest ball she could muster behind Aariv's wide back as he tried to hide her as well.

"Oh … Oh! I'm so sorry—" The older man put his hand over his eyes. "Goodness, I'm sorry, Mr. Abbas. I'll come back later," he said hastily, shutting the door. They heard him quickly shuffle away with his cleaning cart.

She giggled first into the silence. Mortified, yes, but it was pretty funny that they kept getting caught.

Aariv turned an amazed gaze to her, and a smile broke his serious face before he started chuckling, too.

"So much for locking the door," Aariv said shaking his head. "I think we gave Clarence a heart attack. I'm not sure what he saw, but it's going to be interesting talking that man off a ledge. He aims to please and this might kill him."

"I think he saw enough," Chrissy said trying to hide her indignity. "But, you're not mad, or embarrassed?" she asked, surprised.

"Mad, no. Embarrassed?" He cupped his jaw to consider this. "No, I'm not. This was too good to feel embarrassed about." He grinned thoughtfully at her. "Though, I will have to ensure he doesn't say anything to the partners or any other person who works around here. What about you? I'm sorry about that—" He waved his hand at the door. "We can't seem to not get caught…"

She nodded in agreement. "My thoughts exactly. But I'm fine. As long as I never have to see that man again."

"No more office sex, Chrissy? You wound me." Aariv put his heart over his chest and feigned a painful expression.

She laughed, suddenly realizing how naked she was to his fully clothed. She sat up, folded her arms over her chest, and crossed one leg over the other.

His piercing gaze traveled down her body and his nostrils flared, making her wiggle on the couch. Then he looked away and stood up, reaching for her clothes. He handed them to her, and said, "We may have to take our party elsewhere—if you're available that is, and ok with it." He cocked his head to the side in question, as he buttoned and zipped up his pants.

"We're doing more tonight?" She tried not to sound so incredulous as she put her bra back on and then her shirt, buttoning it. She slid her underwear on, shimmying into them while still seated.

Usually when she gave a man a blow job or a hand job, they were done with her. Granted those men were one-offs or shitty dates. Aariv was—

"Are you trying to get rid of me?" He leaned over her, putting his hands on either side of her naked thighs on the couch. His eyes were slit, and his cheek muscles were tense. Goosebumps rippled along her flesh at his nearness and his penetrating stare. "Have you already found someone to … date?"

"No!" she said immediately. It was the truth … technically. She'd never met Taylor, and an actual time for when he was available was still up in the air. "I'm just not used to doing more after I go down on a guy." She lifted her shoulders and let them fall, trying to hide her embarrassment. She realized that it appeared like she let men take advantage of her, though in those moments she went along with it and believed she was in control.

"Those men are all idiots. What's the fun in it if I can't get you off, too?" He was so close that his breath tickled her cheeks. He leaned in and brushed her nose with his and she turned her face up to receive that seemingly tender gesture.

Oh, this man was going to be the death of her. Not with his wicked and dirty sex ways. That was a close call, sure. But how generous he was with his partners. It just showed that there was more to him under that stern exterior—someone who resembled an all-around great guy.

Her heart pitter-pattered inside her breast, matching the tempo of the rain outside, as she reciprocated brushing his nose with hers. Then her heart turned tightly in her chest as she remembered he wasn't hers to feel this way about. For not the first time since knowing him, she envied the woman he'd end up with.

"So, what do you think? My place is only a few blocks from here. We can grab a bite on the way, and continue with my … tutelage." He stood up and walked to his desk. He shuffled files together and put those in a glossy brown leather briefcase, along with his laptop. When he turned back to her, he'd put his glasses back on and he had a relaxed grin on his face.

"I like … that idea," she said, instead of the "you" that was on the tip of her tongue.

"Good." He reached for his suit jacket that rested on the back of his chair and shrugged it on, stuffing his tie into one of the pockets.

He glanced outside at the rain still coming down. "We can make a run for it."

She looked up at him in shock, reaching for her pants and pulling them on. "Don't tell me you don't have your umbrella! Did you not check the weather app this morning?" she teased.

"Alas, my brain has been on other things." He put his hands in his pantsuit pockets as he stared at her while she slid into her shoes again. She darted over to the coat rack and put her now-dry jacket back on. She could feel his eyes on her back as she busied herself with tying the belt and grabbing her purse.

"Are you a fan of Indian?" he suddenly asked. "There's a really good street food place on the way to my apartment."

"I think I'm more than a fan of Indian," she said meaningfully, meeting his bright intense gaze with her own. "Let's go!"

THE FOLLOWING SUNDAY
FIVE DAYS LATER
new york, new york

# CHAPTER 27

२९

The Metropolitan Opera House stood in the famed Lincoln Square on the upper west side. It was the crown jewel of the Lincoln Square Performing Arts Center in Manhattan and one that Chrissy didn't frequent enough.

It looked different in the light of day, she thought as she entered the grand building and looked up. Tall, white, double columns were flanked between two elegant curved staircases. They were bathed in the natural sunlight that filtered in through the five notable high-arched windows that went across the front of the famous building. Everything was cast in a fuzzier glow than she remembered—but brighter and whiter that afternoon.

Even the thick, deep red carpet under her feet seemed more subdued than when she'd been there last with her mother years ago. They'd seen the Nutcracker Ballet, having splurged on orchestra seats. The place had felt alive then with holiday gaiety, and sparkled under the well-known Sputnik-like chandelier that hung in the lobby. She remembered that there were more hanging high above in the theater's rafters as well and she couldn't wait to look up and stare at them in awe—

cosmos in a make-believe world—before the performance began, like she'd done so long ago with her mother. Truly, everything about the ballet was magical, from the performers to the costumes, the sets, and even the opulence of the theater.

Though not glittering today, the Met held an ethereal quality, with beams of sunlight slashing across the open lobby. It matched the ballet they were here to see. *Giselle* was one of her favorites. The story centered around a village girl (Giselle) who has a love for dance, but also a weak heart. She falls in love with an aristocrat who notices her while passing through her village while out hunting. He tricks her into thinking he too is a villager and the two are happy until she finds out the man's true identity and that he's already engaged to another woman of noble birth. The village girl dies, going crazy with heartbreak. She becomes a ghost—a *Willy*—doomed to dance at night with other unmarried women who also died from heartbreak. When her lover comes to visit her grave at night, the *Willy* queen orders Giselle to dance with him and kill him. Giselle cannot bring herself to do this. Though she's most certainly the victim in this story, her heart still loves him and she wants to save him. She encourages him to keep his strength up as they dance, and come sunrise, he is saved.

Now if that wasn't the most romantic story Chrissy had ever heard, she didn't know what was. It was eerie, sure, but it told the story of the strength of love, and how it went beyond the grave. It was beautiful to her.

"Miss, would you like a playbill?" an usher asked, beginning to set up a stack next to his post. She took one happily and went outside to sit on the fountain's ledge at the center of the square.

Flipping through the program, she read the bios of those

playing the main characters. The ballerina was a well-known soloist, who in a matter of a few years had already risen to the coveted position. No doubt she would take a principal role within the company in another year or two. The male dancer was an established principle, and Chrissy knew his strengths to be elegantly acrobatic. She couldn't wait to see the two paired on stage together, playing off each other's attributes.

She lifted her face to the sun's warmth, welcoming its appearance today. The morning had started grey and overcast with drizzle spitting on everyone and everything. But when Chrissy had left her apartment to catch the train, carefully dressed in a simple, off-white, cap-sleeved, and off-shouldered maxi dress with a beautiful large graphic rose printed on the front paired with pretty black pointed-toe, kitten-heeled mules, she noticed the sun fighting with the damp grey and the rain stopped. A rainbow appeared in a hazy watercolor, right behind the Manhattan skyline. She'd smiled and stopped to enjoy the view with others who'd done the same.

It was going to be a good day, she thought, looking around as more people went into the building.

First of all, she'd never seen her favorite ballet live. And here she was, finally doing that, with one of her favorite well-known New York-based ballet companies. Second, she couldn't ignore that rainbow. It felt like a positive sign of change and good vibes. Third, the man who'd purchased the tickets (plural because he was joining her) was none other than Aariv.

She checked her watch again. There were still thirty minutes before the performance began. Considering his rule for punctuality, she thought he'd be here by now, and she looked up glancing around as more ticket holders went inside.

A giggle bubbled forth from her at the thought of him. She

was tickled pink with the strange turn of events in just a short period since last Wednesday. Unbidden, her mind rolled back to that evening, when Aariv invited her to come over to his apartment. She didn't know what to expect, but in that moment, she felt like she was starring in her own Rom-Com movie. It was classic, the way they huddled together in the rain, him having taken his suit jacket off and letting her use it as a pseudo umbrella as they darted through the rain. Both of them laughed as they skipped over puddles and then went into fits of giggles as a cab splashed what looked like a small lake all over them as they stood on the curb across from the little snack shop he recommended. When they dashed into the cramped restaurant, they over-ordered, as Aariv excitedly recommended one thing, and the next … and then the next!

She'd looked at him, his thick hair wet and dripping over his forehead, his glasses fogging up as he spoke to the cook behind the counter in a language that sounded familiar—she'd heard Simran speak it before. She'd learned later that it was Bangla and it sounded similar to Hindi. She'd had no idea what they were saying but he was so animated that she couldn't not stare if she wanted to.

A crazy notion passed through her mind at that moment. Was he Harry and she Sally? Were they friends (with benefits unlike the famed Rom-Com *When Harry Met Sally*), destined to be together?

LAST WEDNESDAY
new york, new york

CHAPTER 28

২৮

They tumbled through the front doors of his apartment building with a plastic bag of steaming Indian food.

"You're completely soaked through!" Chrissy exclaimed, attempting to wipe the water off his already-drenched button-down shirt with his undershirt showing through. She wasn't exactly dry, as he watched her squeeze water out of her hair. As they shook themselves off wet dog-like style, his doorman, Ed, hurried over.

"Mr. Abbas, do you need some dry towels? It's raining buckets out there!" Ed looked past him and Chrissy, staring up and out to the ominous sky. "No global warming, my ass," he muttered. "This rain is the worst I've ever seen."

"Right?" Chrissy said. "I keep saying that, too."

Aariv chuckled. "Ed, I think we're ok. We'll just get out of your hair and dry off upstairs. Have a good night."

He led Chrissy back to the elevator bank.

"Glad to see all-weather rugs down," she commented, walking over the line of black heavy-duty mats that covered the white marble floor, shaking his suit jacket as she went.

He pressed the button and turned to her in humor. "What's that?"

She shook her head and her wet strands stuck to her face. He put his briefcase down and reached over to push them gingerly behind her ears. Their eyes met and the look they shared was like nothing he'd ever experienced. Desire-filled, yes, but interspersed with a belly-flopping feeling that made him want to stare into her eyes all day while being this close to her.

He stepped back as she said, "I slipped on the marble floors in your office's lobby that first day I was late," she said. "I had a humongous bruise on my butt for days afterward. I had to use stage make-up on my ass to cover it during performances."

The elevator dinged and the doors slid open. He gestured for her to go in, and picked his briefcase up, following her. His hands were full, so he told her to hit the button for the fifteenth floor.

"Why didn't you tell me this before? Was it really bad?" he asked, concerned, his eyes darting to her ass.

She shrugged, her cheeks almost the color of her red pants. "It ached, but I dealt with it. Your building needs to be more responsible," she said primly. "They could have had a lawsuit on their hands."

"I completely agree." He nodded with seriousness, fuming a little. "I'll bring it to their attention. They need to be accountable. I wouldn't want you slipping again."

Again. Did he expect she'd agree to come to his office and do more of what they'd just done that day? The thought was more than stimulating.

They arrived at his floor, just as she shook her head and said not to bother. The attendant already felt terrible. But he insisted and she smiled shrugging.

He led her to his apartment, setting everything down, and pulled his keys out of his pocket. He opened the door and let her in first.

"If it's any consolation, your ass is perfection," he said, staring at the perfectly round pert curves as she took off her jacket.

"I know," she said mischievously, glancing at him over her shoulders, her brow wiggling comically.

"You do do you?" he said archly, setting everything on the bench by the front door. He took her jacket and his and hung them up on the rack above the bench. He pointed to the shoe rack underneath lined with his shoes and she nodded, slipping her shoes off and placing them next to his basketball sneakers.

"I've seen the way you stare," she said knowingly making him guffaw. Had he been that obvious? "You can deny it, but I won't believe you."

He kicked his shoes off and shoved them under the bench. "I wouldn't dream of it. When I like something, I like something."

The silence that ensued was deafening. He noticed her lick her lips and open her mouth to say something, but then shook her head as if she thought better of it.

"So, show me your place, Riv. I can't wait to see how the big bossy lawyer lives." Her grin was wide, her deep dimples in place, and he was pretty sure that was not what she'd been about to say before.

He took the bag of food, and they walked through his front hallway into his living area. It was an open-concept plan that included a sleek kitchen and dining area. It was a pretty standard two-bedroom with a two-bathroom design like all of the newer condos in the city.

He put the bag on the counter. "Well, it's not anything to

write home about." That was a lie. His parents had wanted to know *everything* about his place when he first purchased it. He was living the American dream. "And sorry it's a bit of a mess." He hurried to the leather couch and grabbed his basketball and a handful of law journals spread open on it. He dumped them in the hall closet, returning.

Chrissy snorted. "This is the furthest thing from a mess," she said, turning first one way to examine the ceiling-to-floor wall of windows that gave a view of more neighboring condos. Then she looked around with curious eyes from his simply decorated living space with a black leather couch and matching chair, steel coffee table, to his steel and glass dining table. Then she turned to glance at his kitchen with black granite countertops, warm wooden cabinets, and steel appliances. It was sharp and no fuss he'd thought when he'd decorated, but he wondered what she thought.

"I'm going to go change. I'll grab some towels to dry off with." He looked her over, at her somewhat soaked shirt and wet pants. "And maybe a change of clothes for you, too. Wouldn't want you to catch a cold or anything."

"*T*hanks," she said as he disappeared down the second hall off the dining area.

She looked around, surveying the home of this man who was becoming more and more interesting to her by the minute. On the one hand, his arrogance and stern attitude turned her on beyond anything she'd ever experienced. On the other hand, his concern for her safety, his gentleness when she was frustrated with Boris's asinine behavior, and then finding out about his complicated relationship with his parents—well, all of those things made her head confused and her heart melt. She already had a soft heart; if he kept up this behavior, she'd be confused even more about what they were doing, and fall hopelessly head over heels. She needed to keep her head on straight and remember their original agreement … right?

When he came back, barefooted, having changed into grey jeans and a blue Knicks t-shirt, and with towel-dried, combed-back hair, she couldn't help it when her heart pitter-pattered. She took the fluffy grey towel that he held out to her and turned away from His Hotness to dry her hair.

"Here. I'm sorry, they're going to be big on you … but you need to get out of your wet clothes."

She took the folded shirt and what looked like plaid pajama shorts.

"You can change in the bathroom." He started to walk in that direction but she stopped him, beginning to unbutton her shirt. "Chrissy, the blinds are completely up. Anyone can see—"

"So. Let them stare," she said impishly, as she unbuttoned her damp shirt. "And you've already seen everything." She pulled off her sticky shirt and threw it on the leather chair. It landed with a loud smack. He watched her with a hunger that seemed like he hadn't already seen everything she had to offer. She pulled the t-shirt on which was white with the University of Connecticut Law School logo printed in dark blue on the front, and a huskie on the back. She fairly swam in it and chuckled looking down at herself. The hem came to her mid-thighs. "I'll skip the shorts," she said, undoing her pants and slipping them off. "Where can I hang these to dry?"

After a beat, he moved, taking her things, and disappeared into the hall again, but he went into the first door on the right—the aforementioned bathroom—and came back empty-handed.

"I hung your things to dry over the tub."

"Oh, thanks." Then she turned to the windows on the far wall. "It's nice," she said looking around. It was, if not a little stark, with only a few mementos here and there. She walked to the windows and stared out at the city view. She looked closely at the glass. It was so crystal clear, it almost looked like there was no glass. There was; she could see her reflection, but man, he must have to clean them religiously—or have them cleaned because he seemed like a guy with a cleaning service—to get that kind of sheen.

She didn't know why, but she glanced over her shoulder and caught him watching her. She smiled mischievously and raised her hand to the glass.

"What—" he began.

She pressed her hand onto the cool pane, then pulled back, leaving a print on the pristine surface.

"Chrissy," he said, a warning in his tone.

She rolled her lips in, holding in her smile as she turned and waltzed past him to the kitchen counter. Her hunch had been correct. The man liked his windows like that! He was very particular about things, wasn't he?

Before he could comment further, she clapped her hands together and looked at the bag of food as if it was the most interesting thing she'd seen all day (for the record, it kind of was at the moment, she was more than famished).

"I'm starving!" she exclaimed, feeling her stomach rumble.

He slit his eyes, clearly not sure what her game was, but he seemed to let it go as she moved to the cabinets and began looking for cutlery.

"Plates?" she asked just as she opened a fixture in the corner. "Oh!" she exclaimed as it was unexpectedly crammed with bags and boxes wrapped in colorful cellophane packaging. One of the bags was open and tipped over, spilling its contents. She watched as tiny bright candy-colored balls rained down all over the black countertop. She stepped back, watching the little balls roll across the surface for a moment before glancing up quickly to examine the packages in the cabinet. It was an assortment of candy. Mango, guava, orange, coffee flavored—she could only make the flavors out by the pictures on the wrappers. The writing wasn't in English.

"What in the Willy Wonka's freaky factory do we have here?" she asked, trying not to laugh. This man constantly surprised her but not in a bad way. It was so adorable she had to hold herself back from tackling him with a bearhug.

He huffed in frustration (or embarrassment, she wasn't sure) as he came over.

"Aariv, you told me you had a sweet tooth, but, gee-whiz, this is enough to keep your dentist in business for life." She teased, as they scooped the tiny balls into their palms and dumped them back into the bag they'd spilled from.

He huffed again. "My dental health is just fine. And these are fennel seeds coated in candy, so not technically a complete sugary treat." Did he sound a bit miffed? Yes, he did.

Chrissy giggled. "Okay, Aariv." His expression was stoic, but his brow was wrinkled. She had the sudden urge to kiss that look off his face and make him feel better. "We all have secrets we keep. I won't tell." She was as serious as she possibly could be given the situation, and he shook his head rolling his eyes, as her grin broke free. Then she asked, "Can I try some?"

He offered her the ones he just swept into his palm. "Be my guest."

He watched carefully as she placed the few she took in her mouth and sucked. Sweet, pure sugar melted on her tongue, and she bit down, crunching on the hard center. A pungent, root-like, liquorish flavor filled her mouth. It was more bitter than she expected and her mouth puckered.

He laughed at her expression. "What do you think, Sunshine? It may not be for everyone."

She choked out, "Water, please."

He continued chuckling as he pulled water bottles out of the fridge.

"It's a digestive. Fennel is good for that. Also, a great mouth refresher." He opened a bottle and handed it to her.

She chugged the refreshing liquid, still thirsty from earlier when they'd left his office in excitement and haste after she'd gone down on him so enthusiastically.

"So, you have tummy troubles?" she asked innocently.

The sting of her ass from his hand made her welp, but she started laughing. He was smiling as he went to grab plates and cutlery, and she marveled at how different he was from the first time she met him. He was relaxed and easy. He'd been like that at her place, too.

"I don't. But it's always good to start preventative care early."

"Okay," she said rolling her eyes. "Spoken like a true adult adulting."

He grunted and went to open up the food, releasing insanely

delicious aromas into the air. Her stomach rumbled in hunger and she stepped closer to take a look at everything.

As he opened containers, he explained everything and she nodded in enthusiasm, smelling and examining, before asking what she should try first.

He placed what looked like a burrito on her place, calling it a *kathi* roll, and proclaiming it was his favorite. It was filled with marinated meat, eggs, spices, peppers, and onions. He opened it up and poured a dark red sauce over it and a watery green sauce. He explained as he went—ever the good teacher—that the red one was a tangy tamarind sauce and the green one mint and cilantro. Then like a pro, he wrapped everything back up tightly and pushed the plate to her.

She picked it up and took a bite. She couldn't help closing her eyes in delight because the flavors burst in her mouth in a choreography of savory, sweet, spicy, salty, and tangy. "Mm!" she said around her mouthful.

"I like seeing your mouth full like that."

Her eyes popped open as he grinned lazily watching her, taking a bite of his roll, and now it was her turn to shake her head and roll her eyes.

"I can see why you like these," she commented, taking another bite.

"There was this stall that my friends and I used to stop at every afternoon on my way home from school back in Kolkata. These taste almost exactly like the ones they made there."

She loved hearing these little tidbits about him, and she nodded, hoping he'd go on. He didn't so she asked, "What was it like living there your entire childhood, and then having to leave as a teenager?"

She knew this about him from Mariam.

He thoughtfully chewed and took a long drink of water.

"It was difficult, no question. What kid wants to leave all their friends they'd grown up with? Luckily Zayn moved to the US around the same time. You met him, he was at the wedding."

"Right. The funny one. So, he's not your real cousin?" She took another bite trying to keep her eyes from rolling to the back of her head with how good the food was. It was almost as good as sex with the man standing in front of her.

"No. But we're tight. I play basketball with him almost every Sunday and we catch up."

She nodded. "So, why did you leave?"

"Well." He fiddled with the bread, tearing pieces off in long strands and fishing them into his mouth. "My grandmother needed medical care; the kind she could only get in America. My dad, her son, couldn't leave his business unattended, so he sent me. I wanted to go to college here, too, so it worked out." He put his food down and went to the fridge opening it. "I'm going to have a beer. You want one?"

"It's a school night, Riv." When he didn't respond, she could tell something was on his mind. "Sure," she said.

He pulled two bottles out and cracked them open with a bottle opener magnet—the only thing on his fridge except for a picture of himself and Mariam, a middle-aged Indian woman, and an even older Indian woman in a wheelchair.

She pointed to the picture. "Is that your grandmother?"

His gaze turned to where she was pointing. "Yeah. And that's Mariam, you know that. And the other woman is her mom. She's my dad's sister. I'm pretty tight with those two. They were the only family I had here and were a huge support with my grandmother's care."

He gave her the open beer as he practically drank the entire bottle of his own. Something was weighing on him and she had a feeling that his saying previously that things 'worked out' may not be accurate.

"It must've been tough to come here, practically still a kid, and be responsible for the care of your grandma."

He shrugged. "It wasn't that bad. I was close to her. Plus, my dad is a real dickhead, so it was nice to not be around him. I felt bad leaving my stepmother though. She's a real sweetheart." He turned his back to the counter and leaned on it. "And look at what came out of everything." He waved his beer bottle at the apartment. "I'm living the American dream."

She put her beer down and turned to him. "For someone living the dream, you don't sound so thrilled about it."

"Can I tell you something?" he asked, staring into his bottle.

He looked so humbled at that moment. So far from the arrogant asshole lawyer who always knew what to say. His thick black hair flopped over his forehead, and she tentatively reached over to push it back. She wanted to know what was bothering him. Maybe just speaking about it would make him feel better.

"I'm all ears," she said as gently as she could.

"I'm only here because I fucked up someone else's life."

She blinked rapidly, the statement coming from left field. And … that was it. He didn't go on but continued to stare into his bottle. Until he didn't. His gaze met hers and it was the wildest, most vulnerable she'd ever seen him. Her heart felt like it was tearing in two for him.

"Riv, whatever happened can't be that bad." How could this guy, this rule follower, 'Mr. Good Son,' have messed up someone's life *that* badly?

He barked out a bitter laugh. "Oh, but it is. It really is."

"Tell me, then. Tell me what could possibly be worse than … than that giant stash of candy hidden in your cabinet." She cringed. Now was not the time for a sassy joke.

But he tipped his head back and laughed, and it didn't sound bitter at all. It rumbled from the bottom of his belly and up through his chest.

"Ah, Chrissy. I can always count on you to be a ray of sunshine." He finished his beer and picked at the softened label, tearing it off. "I was in love with a girl from a strict Muslim household. Me, a guy from a Hindu family. Being Hindu alone made me the wrong match for her, and we dated secretly. We wanted to get married and made all these big plans to leave India. Then her family found out and they shipped her off to God knows where, marrying her to some distant cousin. I've held this guilt inside me since then. I can't shake it. I have no idea what happened to her. Is she happy, is she angry, is she sad? Whatever it is, it's because of me. And I have a feeling it's not happy. I forced her parents' hands into doing this to her."

Chrissy considered this for a moment. Then she took his beer bottle and put it on the counter. She wrapped her arms around him and held him tight.

"Riv," she said softly into his chest. "You were a teenager. You couldn't have known what would happen. You just wanted to live and love. That's what most teenagers want to do."

He sighed heavily into her hair. "I know. But I need to know. This responsibility—"

She put her hand to his mouth silencing him. "What happened, happened. You can't change the past. You couldn't have foreseen how her parents would react. But if she lived in that house, she probably did."

He was silent, his jaw working, and she felt it against her

hair. He finally said, "Her happiness depended on me. Then it was forcefully taken away. Now, I feel like I don't deserve anything remotely close to joy in my life." He exhaled again. "I have to live my life in a sort of repentance."

"Well, that's silly. It wasn't your fault," she said, her voice rising. For some reason, she was getting all worked up about this. And she realized it was because there was more than his need to marry an Indian woman that stood between them—it was an old flame that had ended worse than badly. His obligations seemed to have no bounds and she couldn't help but think that it must be mentally exhausting.

"Riv—" she began but didn't know what to say. She wasn't sure how to comfort him but did know what would comfort her. She reached up on her tippy toes and kissed him. "It wasn't your fault," she whispered against his lips. He'd been carrying this guilt for a long time. She wished she could take that pain away from him. She wanted to try, at least she could do that for him now.

CHAPTER 29

২৯

"Chrissy," he murmured against her plush lips, his hands now on her waist, pulling her up against his hard frame.

She was all light and bright, sunshine, and fresh air, and he held on to her tight as his mouth now devoured hers. He kissed her wanting to get lost in her—forgetting his responsibilities and duties. He didn't know why he'd told her all of that, but he felt some of the heaviness of Leila lift from him as soon as the words left him. When she said it wasn't his fault, he believed her, if only momentarily.

His mouth sucked at her lips, his tongue dove in to find hers, and her slight murmurs and sighs gave way to moans as they got lost in one another. Her hands were now at the back of his neck, holding her to him, pressing herself to him.

His dick was hardening. There was no way for it not to with her warm curvy body crushed into him. And this is what they were here for, wasn't it? She'd agreed to come back to his place to continue with their incredible fucking. But he didn't want to just fuck her right then. He wanted something else; he wasn't quite sure what though.

She broke away first, panting. "Now it's my turn to ask— where's your bedroom, Riv?"

He smiled, rubbing his nose in her strands. "I'll show you." He scooped her up in his arms, bridal-style, as she exhaled surprised, but then she wrapped her arms around his neck and held on as he strode through the hallway off the living area.

"Office," he said, passing the first bedroom. "Bathroom one, but you know that." He nodded to the same bathroom from earlier. "Master bedroom complete with master bath," he said as they approached the door at the end of the hall that was slightly ajar.

He kicked it open and took her to his bed, sliding her down his length to standing and he kissed her again, sipping her lips, suckling gently.

Her hands pushed the hem of his t-shirt up, caressing his stomach and his chest. He tugged at the material, pulling it over his head, and reached for her again. His hands glided up her ass, taking his shirt that she wore along with them until he tugged it over her and off. He needed her naked, needed to feel her skin on his. He reached for her bra unclasping it as her hands dove to his jeans and unbuttoned and unzipped them. She dragged them, along with his boxer briefs down around his pelvis, and he stepped back, pulling them off completely as she quickly slid her panties off.

Completely naked, he pulled her with him until they tumbled on the bed together, landing on their sides facing one another. Her warm body instinctively curled into him, her thighs widening around one of his. He pressed his thigh into her heat, feeling her wetness already seeping out. She moaned and whispered his name, and he rolled her onto her back, his mouth finding hers.

He moved down her neck, landing kisses along the path that fluttered with her pulse. She sighed, combing her fingers through his hair.

When he reached her breasts and sucked at her velvety skin, teasing her, biting her lightly, she pulled at his hair in impatience, her back arching off the mattress. He obliged by cupping a breast and squeezing the softness gently, angling it so he could lavish her pink nipple. He licked and teased that tightened bud, until he sucked it and the dusty skin around it into his mouth, grinding it gently between his teeth.

"Ah," she moaned, her voice husky. "Riv," she cried breathlessly.

He smiled around her tit. He loved hearing her use that nickname—her special name for him. No one had ever used that (except for the kids in the community), only using the typical 'Aari' to shorten his name.

"Yes, Baby. You're so beautiful." He coaxed, encouraging her to continue letting go as he worshipped her.

He moved to her other breast and did the same, marveling at how responsive she was to him. Her hips were now bucking under him as if she couldn't get enough. His dick was so hard, he could take her immediately, knowing by now how wet and ready she was. But he didn't. Not yet. He wanted to pleasure her, take his time.

His hand glided down her belly until he cupped her heat, and he groaned around her other tit as he felt her hot juices.

"Baby, always so wet for me. That's my girl." No arrogant bossiness in his tone, but gentle praise.

"Yes." She gasped. "Always for you." He glanced up to see

her eyes shining blue black watching him with a passion that might've made him back off only weeks ago. It reminded him of the first time he met her at the wedding when she was just trying to be friendly and he'd rebuffed her. But now, he was experiencing something completely on the other end of the spectrum from that and he wanted nothing but to bask in her.

He pulled his gaze away and continued pleasuring her by slipping two fingers inside her wet heat. Her muscles pulled him in, and her hips lifted as she moaned in pleasure, arching her back off the bed again.

He couldn't get enough of her body. Even watching her writhe in pleasure was something he would never get tired of. Her body was so supple, so lithe—her muscles were carved in all the right places but gave way to curvy softness in a perfect combination of strength and femininity.

"You're so sexy," he murmured, watching her move as he worked her with his fingers. He pushed another finger inside her, stretching her further and she became more frenzied.

"Yes!" She gasped. "Oh yes!" Her tits bounced deliciously, her abs flexed exquisitely, and as he reached up further inside her, she paused, her body bowed, her eyes closed tightly before she exhaled on a long and husky moan as her body shuddered over and over again, her pussy trying to swallow his fingers. "Riv!" She squealed, her body trembling, her mind lost to some pleasure world and he wanted to be there with her.

He quickly grabbed a condom from the nightstand and tore open the packet. His dick was thrumming and bobbing in anticipation and he couldn't get it on fast enough.

When he did he moved quickly between her legs, spreading her thighs, and slid right into her heat, the fit so perfect it was as if this was where he always belonged. He grunted as her inside muscles gripped him tightly, while she wrapped her legs around him and her arms around his torso, holding him close.

He kept his weight on his hands, not wanting to crush her, as he began sliding in and out of her, groaning out his pleasure as he went.

"Chrissy." His pleasure building, pressure swelling his balls. "Fuck, Chrissy, you're so incredible."

"Mm." She moaned into his neck, licking and biting, teasing him as he moved inside her. "You make me incredible," she whispered huskily.

And those words, combined with her luscious sexy body, and well … just her, pushed him to ecstasy.

"Chrissy," he called, moving quickly, feeling her muscles tighten around him as he started to come, trying to be gentle as he rutted into her, releasing himself.

"It's okay, Baby. Let go," she said, caressing his back. And it felt like freedom coming from her. He reared up and grasped one of her thighs and pounded into her with force. "Yes, that's it —oh!" she exclaimed in surprise and her eyes closed as he felt waves of pleasure ripple her inside muscles along his length. He chuckled which turned into a deep moan as he finally fell into the abyss with her, his dick exploding inside her as he completely released this time, emptying himself, his pelvis like a jackhammer gone rogue.

He collapsed on her, rolled to his side, and held her close. She was a ray of sunshine he didn't want to let go. He had a feeling it wasn't going to be as easy as he thought it would be when it finally came time for him to release her.

PRESENT DAY
new york, new york

# CHAPTER 30

ๆ๐

Chrissy checked her watch again. Now it was fifteen minutes before show time. She'd been daydreaming about Aariv and that last night they spent together. It was more intimate than anything she'd ever experienced with him. And it had felt belly quaveringly good … and so right. It seemed like he felt it, too.

But now, her heart beat uncomfortably fast inside her breast and she tried to calm it down with deep breaths. He wasn't late, she reassured herself. The show hadn't started yet. And wasn't it his idea to see the ballet this weekend?

It was the truth. They'd lain together in the dark on his enormous bed afterward. She'd cuddled into him with his arms wrapped around her in the center of the mattress, and of course, she couldn't help teasing him about the size of the enormous bed when they were only taking up a small percentage.

His laugh was deep, and her cheek vibrated with the sensation, and he'd said something about having plans for another time to show her what exactly could be accomplished in such a big bed. Then he hinted at her dance performance as his inspiration.

Immediately her mind raced to the performance he'd seen at the club. Did he intend to use a swing? Was he going to instill bondage? Was he going for sex on a swing *with* bondage?! Her mind whirled like a tornado, trying to come up with ideas and he knew what she was thinking, or rather that her thoughts were a whirlwind of possible eroticism.

"Leave it, Sunshine. It'll be a surprise," he'd urged, his expression filled with humor. Then he'd asked her about her time in Russia. He was curious to know if she missed it or not.

"To tell you the truth, I hardly remember it," she'd answered. "And Brighton Beach over in Brooklyn is enough of a pseudo-Russia for me to handle when I want to, minus the bad politics." She toyed with his chest hair. "But if you're ever interested, there's this amazing cabaret club with really good Russian food. Their borscht is amazing. I could show you—you know, if you want." She nervously wound the longer coils gently around her finger.

"I'd like that," he'd responded simply and squeezed her waist. "Is the performance as good as yours at the club?"

She'd guffawed at that. "Oh, I don't know—" She playfully hit his chest then, embarrassed.

*He thought she was that good?*

"Chrissy, you're a really good dancer. I'm serious when I say you have talent." He'd stroked her back, making her sigh, and she'd felt comfortable enough to snuggle deeper into his embrace.

"If you want to see really good dancing, go see the American Ballet Theater. They're doing a preview of some of the ballets from their summer repertoire this weekend," she'd said offhandedly.

His hand paused before he responded with, "I'm game."

"Wait—no. I wasn't—you'd want to go see the ballet?" she'd asked, tripping over her words.

"Sure. If it was with you."

Her face had contorted into confusion and her lack of answer made him pull back and lift her chin. He'd grinned at her scrunched-up expression.

"I'm serious, Sunshine. Could be fun."

"What exactly are we doing?" she'd had to ask, though she may not like the answer.

His answer was immediate, though. "We're enjoying each other. No rules are being broken here." He'd started to get out of bed. "Why don't you go grab my laptop from my office while I clean up."

He waved down to his penis still covered in the used condom. She'd just stared at him as he got up, distracted by his incredible body padding to the bathroom attached to the bedroom. His back muscles flexed slightly as he switched on the lights, rippling down to his solid ass. The light illuminated him like some kind of otherworldly god. Then he'd looked over his shoulder, at her non-action and caught her staring. He smiled slowly, saying something like "Chop Chop," and then he disappeared into the bathroom.

## HIS APARTMENT– LAST WEDNESDAY NIGHT

She jumped out of bed, still confused by what was happening. Now they were spending non-sex time together? Huh? And to see the ballet?!

He was right, though; they were just enjoying each other. There was no harm in this. She decided not to question it further. Wasn't 'go with the flow' something she was trying to master?

She scooped up his shirt, threw it on, and went into the hallway illuminated by the lights still on in the living room and kitchen. She went to the door that he'd pointed out as his office and went in, switching the light on.

It was less stark in here, she thought, glancing around. A worn twill navy blue futon sat in the corner, and a beautiful round rug covered the floor in deep hues of blues, maroons, and reds, on white, that swirled together into a paisley-like pattern. Woven Indian pictures hung on the walls, with scenes of laborers working in some field made up of tall lively, grass-green stalks, and another larger one that depicted waves flowing along a beach in threads hued from deep blue-black to vibrant turquoise. She wondered where that beach was. Even in textile form, it looked gorgeous, making her want to jump right in, Mary Poppins chalk-drawing-style.

His large steel and glass desk stood in the middle of the room, facing the windows on the far wall. There was a single picture frame on it. She went around to the other side of the desk to take a closer look. It was of a stern-looking man, very similar in countenance to Aariv, and a short, chubby woman who was all smiles standing next to him. Immediately she knew them to be his parents. So, this was the man even a grump like Aariv thought was an asshole.

She shook her head at her dawdling and grabbed his laptop, which was already open. As soon as she unplugged the charger, the screen became active and the printer next to his desk started printing. Paper after paper came out, at least twenty pages, and she couldn't help but glance at the contents. They all had the title 'Biodata' and then a woman's name underneath.

She suddenly felt ill as the printer finished and quieted down. But then, it revved up again, and she almost told it to shush and keep it down so Aariv wouldn't catch her snooping. But it was only one page this time. Curious again, she glanced at the contents. The top read 'Vedic Cosmic Calculator.' This was too interesting to not take a closer look, she thought, glancing over her shoulder to make sure she hadn't already been caught.

She twisted her body sideways to scan the paper, not wanting to disturb its positioning. It looked as though it was a short calculation on whether two people were a good fit based on some of their birth facts. There were fields to be answered by each partner to figure out their matchability. Aariv had filled in one portion and her jaw dropped when she saw when his birthday was—it was February 14th. The man was literally born on the day of love—he was a Valentine's Day baby! She covered her mouth and stifled a giggle, absolutely delighted to learn this fact. She had a feeling he was disgruntled every year that he had to share his birthday with hearts, roses, and cupid-shaped balloons celebrating love. But then she remembered his high school sweetheart and the giggles subsided. He probably felt less disgruntled and more heavy-hearted than anything. Her chest physically hurt from it, knowing how pained he was—how responsible he still felt decades later for a girl he blamed himself for letting down.

She shook her head and continued scanning the page, seeing the other fields he'd put answers in for. One of them was what time of day he was born. He'd typed in 'who cares.' She smiled at that because honestly what *did* that have to do with how much of a connection one had to a person? Maybe in some cultures, it mattered, but it meant very little to her, and it looked like to him, too.

Her heart was in her mouth when she let her eyes drag down to the second portion of the page. Who had he put in, wanting to know if they were matchable?

Legit she thought she was seeing things and blinked her eyes several times. In the next portion for the birth date, he'd posed the question, 'When is C's birthday?'

Her heart was about to pop out of her mouth as she murmured, "Shut the fuck up," out loud. Was C her?

"Chrissy?" Aariv called from the other room, making her jump.

What was she doing? He'd hate that she was poking around, she was sure of it. And now she had all these questions that wouldn't stop churning a mile a minute in her head.

She hastily grabbed his computer, shutting the light and the door, her pulse beating so fast she thought it might explode inside her. What if the C was her?

But, whoa, whoa, whoa, she thought, slowing her train of thought from high-speed train back to normal and sometimes sluggish, Amtrak. What the hell did this all mean?

As much as she wanted to say something to him, she dared not. Past experiences still made her skittish because of his caution when it came to them. And clearly, he hadn't shared any of what that Vedic Calculator meant with her. Did he intend to?

She came into the bedroom with his computer and handed it to him, snuggling down next to him. He was sitting up in bed, having donned grey boxer briefs. He looked hunky-yummy and she burrowed closer to his side as he put an arm around her.

"What's that grin for, Sunshine," he asked, grabbing glasses from his nightstand with his free hand and putting them on.

She felt her face and sure enough, her grin went from one ear to the next. Crap. It probably would've gone 360 degrees around if that was possible.

"The ballet." She fibbed, but not really because that *did* make her happy. "I can't believe you want to go with me."

He'd grunted but kissed the top of her head sweetly as he opened the screen. His expression turned irate as he muttered, "Don't need this open," and closed the open tabs. She looked away, pretending to stare out the window, not wanting to see evidence of his marriage planning … which also might include her! Her smiled spread again and she had to keep herself from asking questions.

He finally loaded the ballet company's website and perused the page for performance times. In a matter of minutes, he'd purchased two tickets for the matinee on Sunday.

"All right. We're off to the ballet! We're seeing—" He looked at the screen again. "*Giselle*?" He glanced up at her, the screen reflected luminously in his lenses. "I hope that's okay. You've probably seen them all, given your dance background—"

She bounced on the bed squealing in excitement as she

clapped. "Shut the fuck up! I haven't ever seen that one live and it's my absolute favorite," she said dreamily, collapsing on her back onto the bed, her arm covering her eyes dramatically.

She heard him close the laptop and put it aside as he climbed over her.

Her eyes popped open to him looming over her as he leaned on his hands and knees. He'd taken his glasses off again and his gaze seared her right down to her toes and the tips of her hair.

"I'll only shut up if I get to fuck you again, right now."

And dirty, asshole lawyer was back. She smiled demurely as her body reacted wantonly, arching her body up to him, her legs spreading.

He climbed off the bed and extended a hand to her.

"Come." He commanded sternly. She noticed a condom packet in his other hand.

Her chest flipped, adrenaline coursing through her as she put her hand in his palm, and he pulled her off the bed to follow him.

When they entered the living room, he flicked the lights off, leaving them in the glow of the city from outside. He continued walking, leading her to the windows.

They stopped right where her handprint was. He leaned in and whispered grittily in her ear, "This is grounds for punishment."

Her breath hitched, and she gave herself a mental pat on the back for putting that print there earlier.

"What did you have in mind?" she murmured, staring at her handprint and the sparkling city beyond.

From the back his hands moved up her sides, over her waist, and to the front, gliding underneath the t-shirt. He tugged it up and over her head so she was naked to anyone who happened to look up or across from the condos on the other side of the street. Thank goodness he'd shut the lights off.

She felt the coolness from the window emanating onto her heated skin as his hands roamed all over; up her to her breasts to fondle them, pulling at her sensitive nipples making her mewl in pleasure. Down her belly, gliding until he reached her hips and squeezed.

"Spread your legs, Little Girl."

She shifted and did so.

"Wider," he barked.

She immediately stepped her legs further apart and then she felt one of his hands handling her pussy from behind, massaging, his fingers gliding from the front to the back over and over again as her wetness oozed and became stickier.

She pushed her ass back but had nothing to grab onto in front to stabilize her.

"Hands on the window," he said harshly. "If you want to dirty it up, do it properly."

She instantly placed her palms on the window and being in that position felt so good. She arched her back and pushed her ass even further in the air, letting her breasts sway pleasantly.

"Fuck, so hot," he muttered, ripping his boxer briefs down and opening the condom packet, rolling it on.

He lined his hardness up to her opening and dragged himself along her wetness, his breathing harsher now.

"Tell me." He ordered.

She shuddered, rubbing her sensitive skin along him, easing his tip into her. He gripped her hips tighter, making movement impossible.

"Not so fast, Little Girl. You tell me first."

Oh, Lord. What should she say? Stupid Chrissy. She

should've thought of something when she'd made that print in the first place. Then an idea came to her. Honesty was always the best, wasn't it?

"I did it on purpose, Uncle Riv," she pouted, looking over her shoulder at him and biting her bottom lip. "I was bad, but I did it on purpose because I wanted you to punish me with that big cock of yours."

She waited, batting her eyes slowly, excited beyond belief at what his reaction would be.

His expression turned from stern, to almost demonic as he grinned, the whites of his teeth glowing in the semi-darkness. And holy shit it only made her want him more.

"Is that so? Then you'll take your punishment and love it, Little Girl." And he thrust into her forcefully, making her take a few steps toward the glass. But it was so good she hissed in reaction; the stretch burned but she adjusted quickly.

He fucked her like that, slowly, sensually, and with a force that tore her release out of her, her hands getting slippery with sweat on the glass as her body convulsed almost immediately in front of him.

"Yes, that's it. You take it so good."

"Yes, Uncle Riv! Give it to me. I deserve it—*Ah!*" she cried, bucking her hips as he pounded into her from behind, her entire body shaking with the force of him, her feet on tiptoes trying to contain all of him inside her.

He hissed and leaned over her, one hand gripping her hip, the other now creating a larger, splotchy hand print in between hers on the window. He grunted loudly and on one last "Fuck!" he came, fast and hard inside her, bucking against her ass, pushing her so that her elbows bent, and her body was almost flush against the glass.

They stood like that, for how long, she wasn't sure. She watched hazy circles form and disappear as she panted, her form now pressing into the smooth pane.

Finally, she said, "Riv?"

He exhaled; a loud cool whoosh that sounded exhilarated. "Yeah, Sunshine?"

"Your punishments aren't really punishments; you know that, right?"

He barked out a laugh, and she felt so silly even stating that obvious fact.

"Fuck, I'm glad to hear that." He pulled out of her and stood her up, pulling her back to lean against his chest. "You love the idea of it, though. Just as much as I do." It was a statement, not a question and she nodded, relieved he didn't think she was some naïve ninny.

They both stared at the window—at the splotchy hand prints and the large smudge that faintly looked like breasts and a torso.

"My cleaning lady is going to have a field day when she sees this," he murmured into her hair.

PRESENT DAY
new york, new york

# CHAPTER 31

৩১

The quiver in her belly was unrelenting now. It had spread up to her chest, tremoring uncontrollably behind her ribcage in a bitter concoction of disappointment and anger.

*Where the fuck was he?!*

She now waited in the empty lobby as last-minute ticket holders hurried into the theater to find their seats. The curtain was going to rise any minute now, and then no one was allowed in until intermission before the second act, so as not to disturb the dancers on stage.

She checked her phone once again. Nothing from him. No text, no missed call, no voicemail. She'd already texted him twice. The first one was to tell him how excited she was, and the second was to find out his ETA. Her fingers moved to send him another message, but she stopped herself. She didn't want to keep texting and seem like a nag—a word that a previous guy had called her when she wanted to find out why he was tardy and it had stuck with her.

She stared at her screen, willing it to light up with some

form of communication from him, and it blurred in front of her as wetness filled her eyes. She sniffed hard, swallowing the ball in her throat, persuading herself not to cry. But as soon as she heard the symphony playing the opening swell of the ballet's introduction—the string section soaring out a melody that was jubilant but hinted at the tragedy to come—she let the tears fall in giant drops on her screen.

*Oh, Chrissy, why do you always do this to yourself?*

She had a romantic heart. She'd always been told that, and she believed it, too. It was too soft for any sort of manhandling. The sudden thought occurred as she continued listening to the beautiful music—would she die from this heartbreak, the way Giselle had? If only. Now she'd have to deal with working through her feelings and the rejection from a man she'd fallen hard for; one she wasn't supposed to have, and yet had inescapably fallen harder for than any guy in her past. As much as she wanted to ignore that slip of paper in his office, and the possibility that it was her, she couldn't. All evening after discovering it, her body trembled sporadically in excitement, her pulse dancing in delight.

He'd driven her home late that night, in his sexy vintage Porsche. They both had to be up early for work and it made sense. Sitting in the tan leather bucket seat had made her feel like the main character from one of her favorite movies, *Pretty Woman*, while her lawyer hunk flew them through the now-empty streets of Manhattan to Queens.

She'd even quipped saucily, "This thing corners like it's on rails," as he shifted gears. But unlike Edward, the main character in that movie, Aariv's large hand and long fingers knew what to do with the stick shift.

Aariv had grinned, that same lazy grin she was getting used

to and beginning to adore, and proclaimed that was one of his favorite films, too, even going so far as to mention a classic movie night in their near future.

*Near future.*

He'd laid it on thick, hadn't he, she thought in disgust. And in hindsight, he probably did view her like a hooker. In return for having sex with him, he was treating her and placating her, knowing some of her favorite things. It wasn't hard not to, she was an open book. She would never be one of those mysterious women who could hold their cards close.

Simple lil' ol' Chrissy Smyth. That's what she was in a tiny little nutshell. One that was easy to crack open if you even smiled her way.

As she dashed her tears away and left the theater, she gave herself a talking-to. Hadn't she been the one to assume they had something? She didn't ask him about the Cosmic Calculator thing. Fuck. She should have. Why was she tip-toeing around his feelings all the fucking time? He wasn't some delicate Faberge egg. What about her goddamn feelings!?

*And those printouts weren't for you to see, now were they?*

She wished she'd never seen those pages. She berated her too-curious self. Didn't curiosity kill the cat or some crap?

And she should've known when he dropped her off at her front door that night, after giving her a sweet, lingering kiss, and thanking her for a great evening. He'd insisted he'd be buried in work all the rest of the week and into the weekend as they were closing a huge case. He needed to focus so wouldn't be in touch until Sunday at the ballet.

She'd nodded and grinned like an idiot. She hadn't even really thought about it as him ignoring her until she'd sent him a quick text to say she was thinking about him a few days later.

She didn't get a response then, having been told not to expect one. But why did that twinge of disappointment pinch her heart?

No. She wouldn't die of a broken heart. She needed to stay alive so she could give him a piece of her mind. He deserved that with his pulling and pushing her around like his sex rag doll.

Now, she huffed her way back to the subway, almost damning the sunshine that kissed her skin happily.

She wanted it to rain. She wanted it to rain buckets and help her celebrate her misery—one she'd surely helped to create. Why had she agreed to go back to his place? None of this would have happened if she hadn't.

All she had to do was give the arrogant ass his office blow-job, and she could have gone home and watched the latest episode of one of those ridiculous reality dating shows (that she not so secretly loved) and called it a night.

But she was addicted to the guy. Like a coin, he had two sides to him. The good and the bad. Both personalities called to her, and she couldn't deny either of them.

Ugh! She was hopeless!

When she got back to her neighborhood, she immediately sent Antoine a message. She needed a friend, someone who understood her.

**"Have time for a busted-up friend?"** She texted him.

He didn't respond immediately, and her eyes welled up again as she walked back to her apartment building. The feeling of being alone was so severe at that moment and she had to shake off the desolation. She was a tough cookie, no matter how much of a softy her heart was.

Her phone dinged with a message as she entered her elevator and part of her dared to hope it was Aariv apologizing for missing her. He'd misplaced his phone, or the subway had given him issues. Maybe he'd been a good Samaritan and had stopped to help a woman give birth on the sidewalk. Perhaps he'd gotten stuck in an elevator, or even gotten sick, that was why he'd missed the ballet with her.

She laughed bitterly at the last thought. The man never got sick. His cousin, Mariam had told her that in conversation in what seemed like ages ago. No. It was more likely that the guy had stood her up.

She left the elevator and went to her apartment, unlocking it and going in, not letting herself look at her phone just yet. If it was Aariv, she wasn't sure how she would respond. He'd think she was a lunatic for getting so upset, especially since they were just 'enjoying each other.'

She kicked her shoes off and went to the fridge, opening it. There was old leftover Thai and a browning banana. She sighed. She needed some kind of sustenance, mainly of the sugary variety.

She took a deep breath and checked her phone. The message was from Antoine, making her tear up once again, and she dashed those silly tears away.

It read, **"Oh, honey. I'll be over in thirty. Which one do you want, Moose Tracks, or Double Chocolate Fudge?"**

She didn't even hesitate. **"It's a both flavors kind of situation."**

**"You got it. Big hugs. See you soon."**

*A*n hour later, Chrissy and Antoine were sitting on the floor of her living room. She'd changed into pajamas, and thrown her perfectly coifed big sexy curls into a bun.

Tubs of open, half-eaten, ice-cream melted on the coffee table. Antoine, ever the good friend, had also brought over wine, cheese, a really good baguette, and an assortment of charcuterie, knowing Chrissy needed real food aside from sugar. Those sat, having been nibbled at on her coffee table as well. This wasn't his first time getting her through a break-up scenario and knowing her and her busy schedule, her fridge was a wasteland. Because of that, he'd also brought some prepared food and fruit, stocking her fridge.

When he'd arrived at her door, at exactly the time he said he would, Chrissy opened it dressed in her comfy clothes and saw the bags of food he'd brought. She promptly burst into tears, hugging him.

"Why do you have to only like guys, Tone-tone?" she'd lamented.

He'd rolled his eyes and said, "All right, girl, let's go inside before your neighbors come out to watch the drama."

He ignored her lamentation because she said it every time her heart broke. And there was no way he would date Chrissy if he was straight. She'd heard it from him before. She wouldn't be able to keep up with his high maintenance. And Callum … well his current boyfriend was proving to be his soulmate, high maintenance, and all.

"*O*kay, so let me get this straight because the tea you're spilling is completely straight-up crack. Your big dick man is Mariam's lawyer cousin!? And this has been going on for a few weeks? Get the fuck out of town!"

Chrissy was on her back, her legs resting on her couch. She nodded her waterworks on pause for now. If she wasn't so emotionally wrecked, she might have laughed at Antoine's expression which was a mixture of astonishment and horror. The man literally clutched the necklace around his neck.

But then his eyes slit behind his round gold-wire framed glasses. And she saw his lips working, as though he wanted to spit something out, but wasn't sure if he should.

She sighed. "Go ahead, Tone-tone. Ask away."

He batted his hand at her. "No, girl. You're in crisis. I can find out another time."

She let it go. He probably wanted to find out how big Aariv's dick really was. When she was ready to tell him, he wouldn't be disappointed.

"I think I have feelings for him," she blurted out.

Antoine sighed and picked up his wine glass sipping. "You think or you know?'

"I know," she said without a doubt.

"I'm not going to sugar-coat it, Honey. But it sounds like you got used and abused."

Chrissy sat up. "Don't say that!" She grabbed her wine glass, drained it, and poured more. "I thought I had my head on straight this time. I was going in for the incredible sex, and then we just started getting more comfortable with each other and sharing stories about ourselves. Then this ballet date … what did it all mean then?"

Antoine bit his lip and said, "I don't know, Chris. But you need to try to forget about him. He's a total ass."

"But that's one of the reasons I liked him so much," she whispered, dropping her head. Tears streamed down her puffy red face silently and spilled into her wine glass.

He sighed again, grabbing more tissues from the almost empty box, and handing them to her. She took them and did nothing with them, letting her tears fall and her snot run.

"Something's different this time," Antoine murmured, hugging his wine glass to his chest.

She nodded. She felt it, too. Usually, she railed and screamed bloody murder at the injustice of men. This time though, she was angry all right, but also downright sad.

He hugged her and then sat back. "He's a jerk, Chrissy. One who doesn't deserve you—the kindest, sweetest, peppiest woman I know. Just remember that."

She nodded. "I know," she whispered. She looked up and gave him a watery smile. "You're a really good friend, Antoine. Thank you for coming to my rescue … every time."

"How about we talk about the Russian mafia that's after you now," he said lightly, trying to change the subject if only for a minute. She laughed at his attempt to get her mind off of what a lousy day she'd had. And talking about the rug store always fired her up in a different way.

"I'm secretly meeting with Boris—"

"Girl, *no*! Didn't Inspector Gadget say *not* to do that?"

"Taggett—Tag!" Chrissy corrected, rolling her eyes. Then

she huffed. "And Aariv, too. But Boris is like family, Antoine. I need to make sure he's ok."

"You're going to rip him a new one, aren't you?" Antoine asked knowingly.

"That and maybe more. I have this feeling that he's known about this shit for some time now."

"Do you think—" Antoine started. "Never mind." He waved his hand shooing away the idea.

"What? Tell me."

Antoine suddenly looked uncomfortable, shifting from his seated position on the ground up to her couch.

"Well, and don't get mad, I'm just putting it all out there—but do you think your mom was involved?"

Chrissy looked up from staring into her wineglass.

"I think so," she said tightly. "I didn't want to believe it at first. But I saw this scary dude a few weeks ago with Boris, at the shop. And he was familiar to me; like I'd seen him before. It took me a while to place him, if I even could or if I was making up memories in my head—but I *had* seen him before. When I was little. He used to come to the shop, and he was the only person that ever scared my mom shitless."

"Whoa, girl. That's crazy! I'm sorry."

She nodded, but her anger was fired up about this now. "I have to take care of this first. Then I can worry about Aariv and how to deal with him."

"Chris, why can't you just let that whole thing with lawyer-hunk go? Why do you have to kick at it? Just cut him off."

"I can't." She shook her head. "I want him to know that I have feelings for him. He made me care about him. And I genuinely thought he cared about me. Just, the way he looked at me at times. His concern for me and my safety. Opening up about his past. And his sensitivity … I can't have been making it all up." That last part had her blinking back tears, and she was frustrated with herself. Making up romantic storylines in her head was what she tended to do when she met a guy. The cart before the horse thing kind of defined her.

"I don't think you were this time, Chris. I mean, it sounds like there was way more going on between the two of you than down-and-dirty sex."

She didn't say anything, but she knew she hadn't made this all up. "Why are men such fickle fucks?"

She poured them both more wine.

Antoine shook his head slowly. "Beats the hell out of me. As if I would know." He guffawed, making her giggle. She already felt better, but she knew she had to talk to Aariv and end whatever it was they were doing. Until she did so, she'd be a waffling mess of sadness, irritation, and anger. And there was already so much going on inside her messy head and her equally messy life, that she needed to get rid of the unnecessary angst, no matter how hard it would be.

# CHAPTER 32

৩২

"**You** **don't happen to know the recipe for that old Russian remedy off the top of your head, do you? You know, the one your mom forced down you when you were sick?**"

Mariam had sent her that text early the following Tuesday morning. But Chrissy was in a flurry of throwing herself into work so she wouldn't have to think about a certain person who'd ruined her weekend, and possibly her hopes forever in the straight male species.

She'd barely read it as she dashed into work that morning and didn't have a chance to address it until she was shutting her computer down that evening because she was trying not to be attached to her goddamn phone. It only disappointed her when the damn thing remained message-less from that certain disappointing person. So she'd tossed it in her bag and kept herself from constantly checking it by shutting it off.

Monday had been rough, but she'd resolved to keep a brave face. The man was an asshole, and nothing could change her mind. She'd already had Sunday to feel desolate and now she had to get on with things, at least during the day when she had responsibilities and had to be around other people.

She'd arrived at the office, hiding her emotions behind a wide smile, vowing to get through the week without falling into misery at work. She'd remain a busy bee and not wonder what she did wrong because she did nothing wrong. Everything with Aariv had felt right, so how could she have overstepped anywhere? She realized that she was not only saddened that Aariv had stood her up Sunday afternoon without any word of why, but that she was embarrassed by how much emotion she'd unwittingly put into the moments they'd spent together. She was the only one with those feelings apparently. And that stupid piece of paper in his office with the initial C? Well, it was just a mere coincidence, wasn't it?

By late Monday night, she was tossing and turning, that familiar hurt feeling festering. She imagined every possible thing she could say to his face if she ever saw him again. By one in the morning, she couldn't hold in her frustration at him any longer and left him a voice message—yes, an actual message using her voice. She wanted him to hear how she felt, not sure if he would listen to it or ignore it, but it gave her a little bit of satisfaction getting it out there.

Admittedly, the message took a detour, which was completely unplanned. She started it cordially by telling him more than anything she was left wondering what happened to him and wondering if he was all right. But then it quickly morphed into not-so-nice, calling him the arrogant asshole he was when she'd first met him, with not a hint of feeling toward the people he used. Yes, she'd utilized *that* word because that's what it felt like. Never mind that it had begun as her using him, too. She told him she would never have ended it the way he had

—so abruptly like a coward—if she felt like it was the right time. She wouldn't have given mixed signals of heading toward something real and then stood him up like that. He was cruel and she told him so as her voice shook almost uncontrollably. She wished him luck in his wife search and hoped he'd find someone who would make him more than miserable.

After ending her voicemail, her moment of satisfaction wavered, as she realized she may have acted brash and childish. But she was determined not to blame herself. Because if he was any decent kind of person, he would've told her what was going on with him instead of leaving her in a silent void.

So, Tuesday evening as she powered down her computer, she pulled her phone out, turned it on, and finally read her friend's text more clearly.

Did she have that recipe off the top of her head? No. Because it was so disgusting that she promised herself that when she got older, she would never touch the stuff again. She'd rely on modern medicine and her local Duane Reade to get her through illnesses. Heck, she'd diagnose herself via the internet, on her deathbed, before she drank even a drop of that putrid tonic again.

**"I don't,"** she texted back. **"But I can look it up for you when I get home. My mom wrote it down on a recipe card and I have it somewhere. Are you super sick or something?"**

She shut her lamp off and pulled her jacket on. Then she added, **"Honestly have you tried drugstore meds first? The tonic is some real nasty shit going down."**

Mariam answered immediately. **"It's not for me. It's for my cousin. He's been on death's door since the weekend. I wouldn't have known if I hadn't checked on him this morning. The guy's phone was ignoring calls and messages because of**

**his crazy work schedule. Get this, he was trying to sweat it out because the guy *never* gets sick. He thought it was some weird fluke.  I think he was delirious, too, because he didn't even know what day it was this morning! Idiot. Anyway, I thought, along with OTC drugs, he could use a healthy dose of something nourishing, and I remembered the one you said your mom made you take when you were little. Personally, if it's disgusting, I say all the more better. Ha!"**

Chrissy had to re-read that message several times before it sunk in. The 'oh shit' that reverberated through her mind started as a murmur but very quickly became deafening. It echoed and bounced around, rattling inside her head until she uttered it clearly with agitation to an empty office.

$\mathcal{A}$ariv was certain that this was what dying felt like. His body, usually an impenetrable fortitude of strength and natural defenses was reduced to such a weakened state, crawling to the bathroom to piss wasn't out of the question. His legs wobbled, and his balance was off. The room spun and he felt the need to collapse back into bed after every long journey to relieve himself.

It'd had been like this since Friday. While at the office, he experienced light-headedness but attributed that to burning the midnight oil the previous evening, only showing up back to work at the crack ass of dawn after showering and finding a change of clothes. He shut himself behind closed doors with copious amounts of coffee at hand. The only interruptions allowed were from partners or others also working on the Turner & Turner case. A resolution was in sight, and they were approaching a point where they could settle out of court, but he needed to focus. So he'd put his phone on silent and then thought better of it, switching his setting to Airplane Mode. He knew that if a certain person texted him even a mundane line about the weather, there was a chance he'd get side-tracked because Chrissy Smyth was his compulsion. Not that she persuaded him to do things outright, but that the idea of her made him throw all good judgment into the wind to find any moment to spend with her.

He'd already told her he was in work mode and to not reach out to him. He'd see her Sunday for the ballet, and he was looking forward to it. And after the ballet? Well, he had to keep his head down and concentrate on the negotiations at hand or he'd fantasize about what they could do together, in his big bed, the one she'd teased him about wondering why he needed such a large one.

And now he wheezed, alone in that big bed, rolling over in the sweaty sheets, though he wore sweats and socks, feeling frigid, not able to get warm enough. He'd been wearing the same clothes since he'd come home Friday evening, grabbing a handful of water bottles from the fridge before hastily changing and diving into bed, where he stayed.

He fell in and out of sleep, twisting and turning trying to get comfortable as his muscles ached almost unbearably.

At one point he dragged himself, wrapped in his thick comforter, to the kitchen to grab a few crackers and swallow down pain relief medication. The crackers went down like sandpaper. But he needed something for his body pain, and he knew enough from doctor friends to not take pills on an empty stomach.

Then he dragged himself back to his room, and settled back in, needing to rest. His eyelids closed immediately, and he went into a deep dreamless stupor.

He woke up delirious at odd times to make the long trip to the bathroom again. Then the long trip back. He sipped his water as diligently as he could and then fell back asleep. He just needed rest, then he'd be better. This would all go away in a day.

*H*is eyelids lifted groggily as he heard the sound of someone calling his name. His room was dark with the blinds drawn, and he wondered what time it was.

The voice was approaching his room, becoming louder as the door flew open.

"Aariv?" a woman asked with hesitation into the darkness.

The flick of the light switch made him cram his eyes closed tightly to the harshness that felt like it burned his eyeballs.

"No lights!" he croaked, hiding his face in the sheets to block it out.

"Aari!" His cousin gasped. "What the hell? I thought you died or something." She practically screamed in concern at him.

"Shit!" he said hoarsely, barely a whisper. "Shh. Why are you shouting?"

"I'm not shouting."

Wasn't she? It sounded like she was using a megaphone and he buried his head into his pillow.

She came a little closer and leaned down. She spoke more quietly. "You're barely whispering. Can you speak? What happened to your voice?" She put a hand to his forehead. "You have a fever, *Biya*."

What?! He did *not* have a fever. Fevers were for sick people, and he never got sick. He tried batting her hand away but failed miserably. His arms felt like noodles.

"And you're as weak as a kitten." She stood up brushing her hands on her slacks. She took a look at his empty water bottles and picked one up. "Is this all you've been doing for the past few days?"

Her tone was incredulous, and he couldn't figure out why. It had only been a day. And he croaked that out to her, as well as admonishing her for using her spare key to his place in a non-emergency.

"Aari, this *is* an emergency. It's Tuesday morning. I've been trying to get a hold of you since Sunday. How long have you been like this!?" Her shock was laden with concern. "You could've been way worse!" Now her voice was getting shrill, and he groaned for her to stop.

There was no way he'd been out since Friday and it was now Tuesday, of all days, the day they were so supposed to meet with their client and the opposing parties.

"Where's your phone?" Her gaze darted around. "You don't have it on you?"

His phone. He hadn't even realized that it wasn't with him. It must still be in his briefcase, or his suit jacket, or—

"Wait, it's Tuesday?" he wheezed. That thought finally

registered. "How can that be?" He'd been in and out of sleep that long? Impossible.

"Yeah. Oh shit, you're probably worried about work. I can call them for you. Wait. I don't have your office number." She laughed. "God, how dumb. As soon as I find your phone I'm putting my gallery number in, and I'll put your office number in mine. Now, where would it be?"

He waved toward the living room, and she headed in that direction, but he wasn't even thinking about that, nor the big case. He was thinking about how he'd completely missed Sunday at the ballet with Chrissy. He'd stood her up.

Mortification and anger duked it out within him as he thought about her waiting for him with no word or communication. She'd been ecstatic about going to the ballet and more than anything, her excitement stemmed from him wanting to go with her. After kissing her goodbye, he couldn't wait for Sunday to come—he just needed to get through work before he could enjoy their time together.

And he knew that what they were doing had just evolved—snuck up on him—from wanting only sex with her to exploring new experiences with her. He wasn't a ballet kind of guy. Theater, maybe; the opera, once. But ballet—he'd never shown an interest, until her. And he was going to enjoy himself because he was with her—light and bright, funny, and sassy; someone who cared about his well-being. Her concern for him and all that had happened in his life and what he held himself responsible for were new to him. Not because no one had ever shared that kind of worry, but because her outlook on things, coming from a person who'd experienced so much hardship so young, was calming. He respected her opinions. He listened to what she had to say, and wanted to drink it all up, asking for another round immediately afterward.

But it wasn't lost on him that she was vulnerable when it came to men. Hearing her inexperience with sex, her trusting nature and of the dicks she dated, and how they took advantage of her made his head swell. He would never treat her like that. And now, though it wasn't his fault entirely, he had. She must be worried or mad, or worse, upset with him.

It was ok, he thought, she would understand when she heard why he'd missed their ballet date, and he'd see how he could make it up to her.

"Found it!" Mariam called from the other room. "It was in your work bag." She came back in, handing it to him to unlock.

As he did so, he noticed no alerts but then recalled that he'd set his phone to Airplane Mode. He disabled it and found he had messages galore. Texts and voicemails from Chrissy, Mariam, Zayn, Huma, Terri (his assistant), and even one from one of the partners.

Before he tackled the personal stuff, he scrolled through his contacts and found his office number. He swallowed a few times as he dialed, trying to get his voice back. Once it picked up, he attempted to speak before Mariam took the phone from him and explained to the receptionist what had happened and to notify his team that he'd been deliriously ill. He would be out for at least another few days. He shook his head vehemently as she spoke, but she ignored him.

When done, she held onto his phone, sliding it into her pocket.

His stare was as livid as he could muster with what little energy he had as she started clearing empty water bottles from his nightstand.

"What?" she finally asked.

"I needed to speak to my assistant and have her forward any updates to me via email. Then have any important documents messengered to me. This case will make or break us, and my career—" He tried to croak out.

"No." She headed to the door. "You need to rest. I'd say when everyone finds out how sick you were—are—they'll all conclude that you're pretty useless to them right now." She shook her head. "You don't take enough downtime, Aari. You've been go, go, go since that partner position came up. Well, guess what? You might be the best lawyer out there, but what's the point in that if your body fails you?"

He spluttered. His body failing? He went to the gym, and ate right, what the hell was she talking about?

"This is your body's way of telling you that you're working too hard. We're not in our twenties anymore where we bounced back quickly."

He huffed heavily. "Can I at least have my phone back?"

She shook her head and juggled the bottles.

"It'll be in the living room. If you're strong enough to get it, then you're getting better. But don't go thinking that's happening anytime soon," she said drily. She looked at the clock on his nightstand. "Listen, I have a half hour before the gallery opens. I'm running to the corner bodega to grab you some things." He started to protest, but she put her hand up to stop him from interrupting. "I know you don't do R and R, but you need it. Aside from more fever and pain reducer medication, how about some crackers and 7up? And more water." She was making a mental checklist. "Now, do you want me to dip the saltines in 7up the way my mom and Huma Aunty used to do for us when we were little and sick?" She chuckled and made a gagging sound "Shit was gross, but it worked." She paused at the door.

"No 7up soup," he whispered, the thought revolting to him at the moment.

"Oh, soup. I'll bring you some chicken noodle soup, and anything else I can think of." She tapped her chin thinking. "I think one of my friends has an old family recipe for a tonic that works wonders. Considering you want to get back to work sooner rather than later, maybe I'll see if she has the recipe handy."

What could he do but huff back into the pillows, completely in her care. He was helpless and he hated it.

"I'll check in with Zayn." Her upper lip hitched up in irritation when she said his friend's name. "Doesn't he have that doctor friend of his who could give you free medical advice? Or do you want me to get in touch with your doctor's office?"

"*Kenno*?" All he could muster was the one word for 'why' in Bangla. He was starting to get groggy again, his lids heavy.

"Why? Look at you. You can't even get out of bed, and you have a fever. We need to make sure you're doing what's needed to get better."

"Z," he mumbled. He didn't have the energy to help her find his doctor's information, and she had Z's number anyway. He'd take the doctor friend's advice for now, though he was the one who supplied Z with his on-and-off pill-popping habit.

"Okay. I'll be back with supplies and maybe a hazmat suit for myself because, Aari, believe it or not, you *are* sick."

# CHAPTER 33

৩৩

ater that evening, Chrissy held on to her canvas grocery bags tightly as a gust of wind rushed at her again. Wind and skyscrapers were a lethal combination, she thought, as hair whipped her cheeks, and she clutched her bags close. They created funneled airstreams between the behemoth glass and concrete buildings. The result at ground level was so strong it could carry away tiny dogs and small children. Chrissy wondered why such wind tunnels didn't do more for the city, like carrying away the overrun rat population.

She reached Aariv's door and pulled at the heavy glass just as the doorman rushed over to help her.

"Thanks … Ed, right?

He tilted his hat. "At your service, Ms.—?" He looked at her curiously. "You were here with Mr. Abbas a few days ago." But he didn't let on what he was probably thinking—that she'd been there for a booty call. Instead, his tone was polite as was his gaze.

"Oh, just Chrissy. No formalities with me."

He nodded and headed back to his desk. "Should I let Mr. Abbas know you're here to visit, Chrissy?"

She moved the canvas bags to one hand and dug out a key from her pocket. She lifted it for him to see.

"I don't want to disturb him. He's been ill. I'll just let myself in."

"Ah, go on up. Have a good evening."

She smiled and went back toward the elevators and pressed the button for up.

As she waited, she thought about how she'd gotten that key and how she'd had to come clean with Mariam. Any other person might not have done what she'd done, but Chrissy was so horrified by the new knowledge of what really happened to Aariv (Superhunk got sick!?) that she needed to see him and make sure he was all right. Selfishly, she wanted to know if he'd already listened to that voice message she sent. Cripes, she'd sounded like a fucking shrew. And that message would no doubt be the nail in the coffin for the beginning of the end of them, which deflated her all over again, except this time *she* was the asshole. It was probably for the best, though. She had feelings for him and wouldn't be able to continue just the physical, with the grey areas of also hanging out with him. It was too confusing.

## EARLIER THAT EVENING

"Hey Chrissy," Mariam answered. "What's up?"

"Hey. You wanted that recipe?"

Chrissy stared at it blindly, now back in her apartment that evening after work. Her mother's elegant cursive writing looked like foreign squiggles as she tried to figure out what she wanted to say to her friend.

"Yeah. Do you have it? You could have just texted it."

"Here's the thing, Mariam. Do you mind if I bring it over to Aariv?"

"What? You don't have to do that. Don't you not like him anyway?" Mariam chuckled.

"No, I mean yes." She huffed. "I mean … I *do* like him," she stumbled.

*More than like him.*

She took a deep breath and rushed on. "We've been seeing each other—me and your cousin. And I said some things to him, and I would like to face him to clear things up—apologize."

A long pause ensued before Mariam laughed. "Hold on, rewind, please. You've been seeing each other? As in dating? Since when?"

Why did she have to sound so disbelieving, as if a guy like him wouldn't be interested in a girl like her?

*Can you blame her?*

It was only recently that Chrissy had believed a guy like him found her attractive and wanted to spend more time with her.

"Not exactly dating but—"

"Wait … is he your hot sex guy?! Eww, gross." There was an awkward silence and then she continued. "Sorry, Chris. It's just he's my cousin, and I saw the look on your face when you described the fun you were having with your secret lover, and I just can't believe it's Aariv."

"One and the same," she responded guiltily. This was more embarrassing than she'd imagined. Her scalp prickled with anxiety as her cheeks flooded with heat.

"Okay," Mariam said carefully. "Well, I'm completely shocked. Usually, he tells me everything." She sighed. "Look, I'm not going to act like it's a good idea. You may not know this about him, but the man has baggage—"

"I know."

"You do? You know about his past and how it's affected him?"

"Yes."

"*You* know about Leila!?" Now Mariam sounded shocked to the core.

"I just said I did, didn't I?" she snapped. She took a deep breath trying to calm her irritation. "I'm sorry, Mariam. I'm just having trouble wrapping my head around what was going on between us. Anyway, I know about his birth mom and his shitty-ass dad. But I get him. Yes, we were having sex, that was how it started, but there was something more to it than that."

"*Was*? Why do you keep saying that?"

Chrissy exhaled loudly. She'd need to explain everything, and it was mortifying.

"We were supposed to go to the ballet on Sunday. And when he didn't show up, and I never heard from him, I thought he'd taken the chicken's way out and stood me up." She blew her bangs out of her eyes and sighed. "It wouldn't be the first time a guy has done that to me."

"Aariv would never treat anyone like that!" Mariam sounded affronted and Chrissy had to remember how close they were, more like brother and sister than cousins. "I know he can be an ass sometimes, but he's not a jerk."

"I know. And I should've known then that something spectacularly wrong had happened for him to not show up. Because I know he's a good guy. But, I was hurt, and mad, and I left him this horrible message and—"

"Okay, okay. I get it." Mariam hesitated and then continued. "This is a lot to process … Um, so, you and he had a date on Sunday—"

"I wouldn't call it that."

"Oh, come on, Chrissy. What would you call it then? Have a little confidence here. He obviously really likes you."

"Yeah, for my body. I think the ballet was his way of saying thanks for all the orgasms."

"Um, no," Mariam choked out. "First of all, Aariv doesn't just go to the ballet on a whim. I have never, in my entire thirty-three years of life, ever heard his name spoken in the same sentence as the word 'ballet.' Now basketball and the Knicks, eh, you probably already know how obsessed he can get. Second, you know about his birth mom—and Leila! Chris, I swear, he never shares that stuff with anyone other than family, or his best friend. Every woman he's dated in the past never got past the 'so what do you do for a living' conversation. And look at you, knee-deep into his complex history."

Chrissy didn't know what to say. It felt like he'd shared those things because she'd told him about her complex past first and how her mom had died. He'd only been reciprocating to make her feel better. But that hadn't stopped Chrisy from liking the guy and developing feelings for him, now had it? And those conversations *had* made her feel better.

"I like this for you two," Mariam suddenly burst out. "He needs a loose cannon in his life. And people don't believe opposites attract," she muttered wryly.

"Um, thanks?" Was she a loose cannon? Yeah, she probably was considered one. She jumped before she thought in many instances. But in this one, she was going to think first because experiencing the littlest hint of pain from Aariv had turned her into an emotional whack-a-do. "I don't know if I want to see him like that anymore—"

"Wait, what?"

"Mariam, I have feelings for him."

"But that's awesome, Chris! Maybe he won't go through with this stupid arranged marriage crap if he feels the same way."

Chrissy sighed. "I wish. I'm pretty sure he can't return them, and it's too hard for me to do this with him. I'm not made for this wishy-washy non-committal stuff. I need it clear-cut. And considering he has this huge guilt he's carrying around I don't think he can. He won't ever let himself find happiness."

"Chrissy, I'm shocked."

"I know. He's a catch—I should do whatever I can to 'catch him.'"

"No. Not at all. You're right about him. You see him inside and out. But if he wants to hold onto the past, that's on him. You have no responsibility to stick with him if he can't give you everything you want."

"Thank you for saying that. It makes me feel better for what

I need to say to him. And I'd rather do it sooner rather than later, so *I* don't change my mind."

"I hear you loud and clear. Come to my place when you're ready and I'll give you the key to his place. Also, tell me how much I owe you for the ingredients—"

"Don't worry about that. It'll be like a parting gift from me." She smiled wanly at that.

"Okay. But heads up, go easy on him. He looks and feels like shit."

Great. And what she had to say would only contribute to that, if her voice message hadn't already.

## CHAPTER 34

৩8

"...So, good luck in your wife search, and I hope you find her. I hope you find the one who makes you more than miserable!"

The voice message ended and all Aariv could do was stare up at the ceiling and take it. Mainly because he'd mustered enough energy to stumble slowly (very slowly) from his bedroom to the living room in search of his phone later that evening. But couldn't get the energy to go back to his bedroom, yet, let alone pick himself up where he'd tripped on the floor.

He'd only been able to take the phone mission on because Mariam had come back as she'd promised that morning before she went to work. She set up a 'wellness' station that he could reach by putting a tray on the bed next to him filled with water, crackers, soda, and medication. She'd also left a thermos of chicken soup, encouraging him to take a few sips of the nourishing broth.

She'd confirmed that Zayn's doctor friend agreed with him remaining in bed for now and taking his medication at regular intervals so his fever would go down. He should get up only if he had to use the restroom and felt strong enough to take a few steps to keep the blood circulation in his limbs. And for certain the intake of fluids, fluids, and more fluids was a must. If he didn't get better by the next morning, he should head to the ER or the nearest urgent care center. He most likely had the flu, but since he was up to date on his vaccines, proper care would make the symptoms go away.

So, the day had been spent sleeping and making sure he kept up with his medication schedule. It wasn't hard, he was used to schedules and routines. He almost sneered at Mariam when she'd offered to check in on him every four hours to make sure he was taking his pills.

"Man, being sick makes you crankier than usual," she'd commented before she left. That wasn't the only thing making him cranky, he thought with frustration. But he *was* as weak as a kitten and didn't even attempt to leave his bed unless his bladder called. Falling asleep didn't take much either, so he did what he was supposed to do and slept throughout the day.

By evening, he'd awoken with the urgent need to pee, and he felt a slight hunger pain. He was getting better, he thought and tried hoisting himself out of bed. But he ended up needing to move slower than anticipated to the bathroom, and then back to the bed where he sat on the edge and thirstily drank the thermos of now tepid soup Mariam had left earlier.

He knew she would be back to check on him later after work, so he decided to attempt his mission before she caught him. A mission that was vital and needed his attention. And it would be a piece of cake. It was just the living room. A mere twenty feet away.

He'd pulled off the rust-colored throw blanket from the foot of his bed and wrapped it around his shoulders. He paused, taking a few deep breaths.

*Now why the hell was he winded from just that?!*

But he'd been determined, and he hefted himself to standing, wobbling on what now felt like al dente noodle legs. He'd shuffled, taking his time, looking at the doorway of his bedroom as his goal. If he could make it there, he could make it further, he'd been sure of it.

It felt like eons before he was able to grab the door jam and lean on the wall, huffing and puffing like his life depended on it. Sweat beaded his forehead and he cursed himself for not putting a water bottle in his sweatpants pocket for this expedition.

"Too late to turn back now, you *boka*," he'd muttered tiredly.

After catching his breath, he continued on his journey, making a pit stop to rest in his office doorway.

"Halfway there. You got this, buddy."

When he'd finally made it down the hall and to the living room, he peered into the darkness looking for where his cousin had left his phone. He shuffled and reached as far as his arm would let him, flipping on the overhead lights, and he immediately spotted it on the TV stand … across the room.

"Fucking hell. She's worse than anyone's mother," he said through gritted teeth.

Taking a deep breath, and invigorated by keeping his eye on the prize, he'd continued his shuffling, eager to grasp the device in his hands. But hadn't counted on the edge of the thick jute and wool rug underneath the couch being so difficult to get over.

"Left foot," he grumbled, barely clearing the edge. "Right foot," he said, but that damn right foot didn't cooperate, and he went down, tripping over the thick lip, momentum landing him close to the TV stand and thus his phone.

He reached for it and held the item close to his chest as he "Woot-wooted" himself. "Victory is mine!" he'd growled hoarsely, feeling a shit ton happier than he had that morning.

But taking one look at his battery supply told him he had a short time to get through his messages. His decision had already been made though and he looked for any messages from 'Tiny Dancer'—his name for Chrissy in his phone. He saw a text from her last week saying she'd been thinking about him. Then two from Sunday relaying how much she was looking forward to the ballet, and asking when he was arriving.

Then he saw her voice message. He hit play, nervous to listen to it, but eager to hear her voice. Yeah, he missed her and had been thinking about her, too.

But what had started as concern for his whereabouts transformed rapidly into hurt and anger. His stomach twisted at the knowledge that he'd made her feel that way—that she could think he would ever stand her up like that; that he would *ever* give her up, because Aariv was certain now that he had feelings for Chrissy Smyth. As arrogant as he knew it sounded, he wasn't one to give up his standing Sunday basketball games two weeks in a row for a woman, let alone for a snoozefest like the ballet. Okay, admittedly he needed to give the ballet a chance, but seeing the look of joy cross her pretty face when he thought he'd stupidly uttered that he would see it if she was with him, was more than enough to convince him to give it a chance. And he could read between the lines—he was giving them, whatever it was they were evolving into, a chance, though he didn't say it, continuing to keep it casual with the "exploring each other" bit.

Her message continued saying he was cruel and that he'd

used her. Shame washed over him as he thought about the over-dominant act he played with her, demanding she come when he said, making her perform things she may not have been originally comfortable with. But he'd thought she enjoyed it as much as he had—that it excited her as it did him. He'd gone too far with her—using his sick and twisted games of punishment on her. Where had those disgusting games come from? He was a brute.

And now, as an ambulance and then a fire truck blared in the distance, coming increasingly closer until it passed his building in a whir of ear-ringing sirens, he realized the only brute he knew in his life was his father. And he wanted to vomit because the only thing he wanted more than anything in life was to be the opposite of him—the antithesis of his evil father's ways. But it was inside him. It ran in his blood. He'd never be able to get away from it.

Just then he heard the lock turn in his front door. His cousin was back to check on him and would find him lying flat on his back like a moron in the living room.

He couldn't get any lower, so he stayed put, making no move to get up. He felt dejected.

She came in, shutting the front door quietly behind her, and then paused in the front hall. He heard the slight rustle of her taking her jacket off and putting her shoes on the rack below the bench.

Then he heard her pad into the living room. She paused as she passed the kitchen counter, and he listened to her unpacking items.

She began walking toward the hallway and he heard her breath hitch, no doubt finally noticing him splayed on the floor.

Her quick steps came in his direction, and he braced himself for his cousin to berate and tease him for leaving his bed. But instead of a tall form with dark hair and similar eyes to his own staring dead-panned down at him like she always did when she was annoyed, a shorter form appeared above him. Copper hair fell around her curved pink cheeks, and her blue eyes were enormous in shock, her mouth a perfect 'O' as she continued to stare down at him.

"Riv, what the hell are you doing down there!?" Chrissy finally gasped. And he wanted to simultaneously embrace her jean-clad legs and kick her out of his home.

"**I** could ask you the same thing, but obviously up there, not down here," he grunted hoarsely, and he closed his eyes in frustration.

She couldn't help but notice that he did indeed look and sound like shit. Her heart dipped lower than it already was.

Handsome still—and she'd missed that arrogant hot face and to-die-for muscular man—but his beard was longer and stragglier, in need of a trim, and his hair stood up around his head in all directions. His skin was pale, more of an ashen pallor compared to his usual bronze skin.

She pushed her hair behind her ears, suddenly nervous and she licked her lips before she spoke again.

"Do you need help up?"

He grunted something she couldn't make out in response and turned his face away from her.

She leaned down closer, so close that her cross escaped her

shirt and dangled over his face on its thin chain. From this vicinity, she smelled him—a musty, sweaty, somewhat sweet smell—the odor of sickness.

"Huh?" she asked again.

He turned his face back to her and stared at her gold and ruby pendant, hanging right in front of his nose, making his hazel eyes cross humorously. She smiled; she couldn't help it. He was so cute, though vulnerable. His head shook, and he lifted a hand to bat her and her necklace away. She immediately stepped back.

Right now she felt like she needed to not poke him. But she wanted to know if he was grumpy because of his illness, her voice message, or worse, both.

*All in good time, Chrissy. He appears to be unable to go anywhere.*

Truly it was mystifying witnessing him like this. Her grumpenhunk of a man; her bronzed Superman was reduced to this weak state, with not enough strength to get up off the floor.

She made a quick decision and plopped down on the floor next to him, crossing her legs.

"So—" she began.

"What are you doing?" he angrily whispered. Had he lost his voice, too? Jesus, the man couldn't catch a break, could he?

"I'm here to take care of you," she said simply, shrugging her shoulders. She couldn't help it, she reached over and smoothed down some of his hair sticking up. He closed his eyes and she visibly saw his Adam's apple bob as he swallowed.

"Water," was all he responded with.

She quickly got up and dashed to his fridge, grabbing a bottle of water. She hastily went back to him, twisting the cap open.

He'd managed to heave himself to a sitting position with his back resting against the couch and she sat back down on the floor. He took the bottle from her and drank it slowly, methodically, until he'd finished the last drop. He sighed in pleasure, putting the bottle on the floor next to him.

"Thank you," he said softly but cordially.

"You're welcome. Do you feel strong enough to stand? Do you want to go back to the bedroom?"

His gaze turned to her, and even in his sickened state, his eyes were intense on her. Fiery gold burned bright making her shiver under his stare, which scrutinized her messy windblown hair, her long-sleeved pink shirt with 'C'est la vie' printed on the front, and her relaxed faded jeans.

"I'm staying right here for the moment," he answered.

"Okay. Good. I have this tonic I can make for you." She scrambled to stand. "My mom used to make it for me when I was little—"

"Ah. Now it makes sense." He lifted a finger shaking it slowly, but he seemed to be talking to himself. "You're the friend Mariam was talking about who had some concoction that tastes like crap but is supposed to make you better."

"Well, yeah. Sorry if I surprised you. I didn't mean to. But I —" She took a step toward him and stopped. She turned to the kitchen, then swiveled back around, taking a huge lungful of air. She wanted to get this all out of her system. "I wanted to also apologize in person for my voice message," she said, staring directly into his eyes. She needed to quit being a sniveling little girl who couldn't speak her mind when it came to him. He deserved to hear it, and she deserved to get it off her chest.

She gripped her hands in front of her. "I didn't know what happened to you. I was feeling things that maybe I shouldn't have been feeling, and I made it bigger than it was. I—" she blushed, her cheeks turning hot. "I don't know if you know this about me, but I tend to do that—get carried away with my emotions." God, now she couldn't look at him and averted her gaze to the window and the splotches from their shared passion last week. She swallowed a few times, her mouth suddenly salivating uncontrollably seeing that evidence still there, and familiar desire swirled low in her belly.

*Holy shit, was she getting horny off of window smudges?! And in front of a sick man? What was wrong with her?*

"Believe it or not, I saw that in you from the very beginning," he said, his voice a little stronger now that he'd had some water.

"Oh, back in your office when I first came to you for legal advice? Yeah. I was pretty headstrong and emotional then, wasn't I?"

He smiled faintly. "Yes, you were. But I meant back at the wedding last fall. It was hard to forget."

"I know." She put a hand to her cheek, willing the heat to dissipate. "My emotions can get the best of me. They usually do." She walked to the kitchen counter and to the items she'd lain out and started busying herself with preparing her mom's tonic.

"I meant that you were—are—hard to forget."

She stopped what she was doing, letting that sink in, contemplating. Then she continued with what she was doing, her hands shaking as she opened the plastic containers and dug out measuring spoons. She wasn't exactly sure how to feel about that statement.

She rounded the counter and headed toward the cabinets. "Glasses or mugs?" she asked over her shoulder.

"Third cabinet from the left."

She pulled out a glass and brought it back to the counter.

"What have you got there?" he asked curiously, eyeing what he could from where he still sat on the floor, his back up against the couch.

"Okay." She turned business-like, glad for this distraction. "So, this is a classic immunity-boosting remedy. Every Russian family seems to have their own recipe, and my mom's is a little extra funky."

She began measuring the plain yogurt with the container of milk she brought with her. "It calls for kefir, but I couldn't find it at my local corner store. I mean, you'd think they would carry the fermented milk product since so many different cultures live in my neighborhood and probably consume it on the regular." She was babbling, she was quite aware of it. "So, I'm mixing milk and plain yogurt to get a similar product." She searched her bag for her whisk and realized she'd forgotten it. "Oh, crap. I need a whisk."

"First drawer by the stove."

She scurried to get it and came back, giving the milky liquid a good whisk.

"Now," she continued, opening up a container with bright orange mush in it. "I didn't have fresh pumpkin so I grabbed the canned stuff." She measured out the right amount and dumped it in. "Honey next." She took her honey bear bottle and squeezed out an eyeballed measurement of one tablespoon. Then she gave the mixture another hearty whisk.

"Doesn't seem so bad," Aariv said right behind her, and she jumped a bit on the balls of her feet. How had he snuck up so quietly? "Kind of like a mango *lassi,* only this yogurt drink is flavored with pumpkin.

"Ah, but you see, that's where you're wrong. My mom added some stuff that she was sure made all the difference. They were ingredients that the older women in her village proclaimed to be what worked."

She pulled out a small jar of brown gelatinous stuff and a jar of deep purple liquid.

"A heaping tablespoon of liquified beef liver and a slurry of beet juice."

She stirred everything together creating the most horrid color of brown. It almost resembled—

"That looks like diarrhea," Aariv said, alarmed, his nose wrinkled up at the glass.

She turned with the glass in hand. "Your pumpkin and beef liver *lassi,* my good sir." She waved her hand with a flourish at the tonic. He didn't make a move to take it. And she realized she had forgotten the most important part. She dug around in one of her bags, coming up with a red and white striped paper straw. "Ha! This will make it go down easier. I always needed a straw when I was little."

His facial expression never wavered from disgust. "How do you drink it now?"

"Now? Oh, I don't touch the stuff. I might make it with just the pumpkin and honey for an immunity boost, but that's about it." She could tell she was losing him as he rolled his eyes. "But Mariam said you were really into getting better fast, and this liver-yogurt mixture always did the trick for me when I was little."

Now he looked skeptical and less disgusted. "Just take a few sips," she cajoled, handing him the glass. "You might like it."

"Sure," he said sarcastically. He sniffed at it a few times, finally taking a few slurps from the straw and nodded in contemplation.

"Well?"

"Probably the worst thing I've ever put in my mouth." He put the glass down. "Hard pass."

She sighed. At least she tried. He sidled up next to her, leaning heavily on the countertop, his breathing heavy. She pulled a barstool out from under, and he thanked her and sat down, leaning his elbows on the black granite surface.

"Do you have enough to make another minus, the stuff that makes it look like diarrhea?" He peered into one of her bags, then the other.

She laughed and said she did. He smiled lazily—that warm grin that hit her smack dab in the middle of her chest.

She went and grabbed another empty glass and pulled more stuff out to make a pumpkin *lassi*-like tonic for him, and he said, "I meant it when I said you're unforgettable, Chrissy."

She paused what she was doing and gave him her full attention.

"Don't you have anything to say in response?" he asked, his eyebrows low on his forehead.

"Um, you're unforgettable, too?"

"Chrissy…"

She threw her hands up in the air. "What!? You are. You're so stinking hot it's hard to look at you sometimes. You're a complete asshole most of the time but it only makes me want to get underneath that grumpy shell. And when I do get under that shell, I find a man who is so good, funny, nice, and smart that I can't believe he would even want to be with me. I *know* I'm unforgettable. It's nothing new. Let's see, I've been called annoying, a nag, too sensitive, not sensitive enough (that one was a real shocker), too loud ... the list goes on. Oh, Mariam called me a loose cannon today." She shook her head, her eyes closed. "You don't have to be nice about it. You can tell me what you really think. I'm not *that* weak-hearted." She went back to mixing his drink.

It was the loudest silence she'd ever experienced. She waited for what he had to say if he had anything to say at all.

"Can we backtrack here?" he asked slowly, and she chuckled, remembering his cousin's similar statement earlier.

"Sure," she said carefully.

He sighed heavily. "I'm sorry I got sick—"

"Oh my God, how is that possibly your fault?"

"Please, let me finish," he said, his expression pale and stoic, and she waited again.

"I'm sorry I got sick and was too stupid to remember that my phone was set to Airplane Mode. I saw your text about being excited for the matinee. Believe it or not, I was too. And then the other one, asking me about my ETA. You know I would have answered those in a heartbeat if I had seen them."

"And what about the one from Friday, telling you I was thinking about you?" she asked softly, feeling childish.

"That was really nice. And I was thinking about you, too. But trying not to. You distract me."

She swallowed hard, her emotions choking her up.

He continued. "Chrissy, you *are* too sensitive." She nodded confirming what she already knew. "Too loud. Brash at times, and a complete emotional whirlwind—"

"You forgot annoying." She chuckled.

"No, I didn't."

"Yes, you did."

"And I'll add argumentative in there, which is a complete turn-on."

Her breath caught in her throat, and she stirred the mixture so vigorously that milky orange liquid sloshed onto the counter.

"This entire weekend ended up being a cluster-fuck. Can we both agree on that?"

Did he mean missing the ballet with her, or her voice message to him?

"What part of the fuck was clustered?" she asked, sliding his drink over to him, this time with a paper orange and white striped straw.

He smiled quirkily at her choice of words. But she needed clarification and waited. "The missing *you* part."

Okay, that didn't answer her question, but it was also a way better answer, summed up in an Aariv-shaped bow. He'd missed her like she'd missed him. But hold up, wasn't she there to tell him she couldn't do this anymore?

"I can't do this anymore, Riv," she said, blurting it out so that she wouldn't chicken out.

He swiped his lips with the back of his hand. "Can't do what anymore?"

"This." She gestured back and forth between them. "I have feelings for you, but before they get completely unmanageable, I need to end this. You aren't available—"

"Chrissy—"

"No. Now you let me finish." Her hand shook as she held it up. Her heart was beating quickly, and she was sure he could hear it as it was deafening in her ears. "I can't separate you and sex with you. It's impossible for me, and I need to stop being so passive. I was so hurt by this past weekend. And now that I know the reason, I feel terrible for my message. But that doesn't change the fact that I need to protect myself."

She crossed her arms over her chest, keeping a shield between him and her body, which was a complete traitor right now. Even in his sick and weakened state, her nipples thought it would be a good idea to tease him by hardening up.

"Chrissy, what are you saying?" His eyes penetrated her, and she felt naked in front of him. She tightened her arms across her chest and lifted her chin.

Did he need her to spell it out for him? Wasn't *he* the brilliant lawyer? "We're done. No more of this."

He tipped his head back and chuckled. "You're young, Chrissy. How can you even know what you want in your life right now?"

Oh, they were going to play this game, were they?

"I might be younger than you by more than a few years, but I know what I want and don't want. I want full commitment and love. Love so strong that it makes you feel carefree and weightless."

He scoffed. "We were exploring something together; can't we go back to that?"

"Aariv. You're looking for an Indian wife—" He shook his head. Confused now, she asked, "You *aren't* looking for an Indian wife?"

"That's on hold. I don't think I want that anymore."

"Okay. Well good for you. You almost know what you want." She had to stop herself from rolling her eyes. "But," she had to be gentle here, this was a touchy subject for him, "but you can't give yourself fully and freely to anyone. You're hung up on this guilt about Leila and possibly ruining her life."

There she'd said it.

He growled, a low dangerous sound, not sexy at all, but frustrated and a little frightening. "You made it seem like you understood that."

"I do understand that. But I'm not going to be second to any of your hang-ups, Aariv. I know myself. I would lose myself trying to please you, trying to be everything to you, and in the end, I wouldn't be everything to you, would I?"

His gaze met hers, and the hurt there almost made her take a step back. But his expression changed so quickly to hard determination that she almost dared to hope that he would say something to prove her wrong.

"I'm sorry, Chrissy, I can't change that part of me. It's there to stay until I find out otherwise about her."

Her shoulders sagged and she nodded. He was steadfast in his beliefs; she'd known that from the beginning. "Then find out about her. Relieve this burden you've carried with you for so long. And move on to happier people and places."

She started packing her things up.

"Are you going?" he asked, his tone suddenly urgent.

"I have to go," she said listlessly.

"Stay. Please, Chrissy." He sounded so tired all of a sudden. She glanced at him, and he was gripping the edge of the counter, his back slumped, his eyes fighting to stay open.

"Aariv," she gasped, moving to him, and holding him. His weight settled heavily on her as his head leaned on her shoulder. "Let's get you to bed."

She helped him up and let him continue leaning on her as she led him back to his bedroom. She helped him get under the covers and tucked the blankets around him.

"I'm going to go," she said, standing back from the bed, watching him.

"Don't," he said sleepily.

"You need to get more rest, Aariv."

"Riv," he mumbled.

"What?"

"I like it when you call me Riv." His eyelids flickered and shut.

Her heart did more than flutter as it beat wildly.

His eyes were closed now, and his chest rose and fell in rhythmic breathing. He'd fallen asleep. She'd stay, she decided, but only until the sun came up. Just to make sure he didn't need anything.

She went to his linen closet in the hall, finding extra sheets and blankets. She decided to set up the futon in his office. She lay awake staring at the pretty woven art on the wall, not even remembering when she fell asleep. Unsurprisingly, given her angst about him, she slept fitfully.

It was the incessant knocking that made her open her eyes just as the alarm on her phone went off at six a.m. She'd left the office door open so she could listen for any movements at night. In her sleep-filled stupor that morning, she thought it was him knocking at his bedroom door from the other side. But when she opened his door and peeked in, she saw his form still and asleep in his bed. That's when she realized the knocking came from his front door, and it was loud.

She stumbled into the hall, and went into the living room that was awash in early morning shadows and hazy orange rays, rushing into the front hallway. As she put her hand to the door, something all too familiar hit her about this scenario but she went ahead and opened the door anyway.

"I knew it. I just knew it!" Ms. Acharya said, standing in the door frame in a slim beige power suit. Her Birkin bag swung casually on her wrist as she waved her hand around. "I just knew you'd found a way to wheedle yourself into his life and keep him from his family duty."

## CHAPTER 35

৩৫

Aariv awoke completely rested, almost feeling like a new person. He sat up and then realized how easy it was to sit up and he stretched loudly. Then he remembered that Chrissy had come over last night to care for him in his sickness, and to apologize. She'd tried to end things with them, and he'd not wanted that at all. He'd asked her to stay. Had she?

Swinging his legs over the side of the bed, he was amazed at the strength back in his limbs. He stood up and stretched again, groaning as his back cracked.

He heard movement outside in the living room and he smiled in relief. She was still there. Of course, she was. She wouldn't leave without saying goodbye after last night, would she? And she must know that he cared about her, too. He hadn't said as much yesterday because he was so shocked by her decisiveness, her will to end this connection they had—both mentally and physically.

He went to the bathroom and relieved his bladder, his legs strong as tree trunks and he vowed never to take his body for granted again. He would need to schedule in some regular R and R, but hey, at least he was thinking about it. Maybe Chrissy had some ideas.

He washed his hands and splashed water on his face. He looked like complete shit, he thought as he looked at his haggard self in the mirror. But a shower could wait. He wanted to see her and plead his case.

He practically bounded on his almost back-to-normal sturdy legs as he made his way out into the living room and kitchen.

"Chrissy?" he called.

His nose met a barrage of unexpected smells. It was a combination of fried bread, eggs, and curry—all of which made his eyes water with nausea. He wasn't ready for those flavors just yet.

"What the hell?" he murmured as he saw a spread of paratha, scrambled eggs, and *bhaji* (an Indian vegetable stir fry) on his dining room table.

"Aariv, *Beta.* So good to see you up," a familiar snooty voice said. "*Esho* (come), have some breakfast."

He had to rub his eyes to make sure he wasn't hallucinating. What was Pinky doing here?! And where was Chrissy?

"Uh, hi. How did you get in here?"

She laughed self-consciously. "You think I can't work the system like your *gore*?" She smiled secretly, and Aariv was taken aback. She was calling Chrissy an outsider when they all collectively lived in America as outsiders still trying to make their voices heard and feel like they belonged. It was so absurd that he laughed, too.

"No, seriously, how did you get in and what are you doing here?" he asked again, all humor erased now. This was too much. The nerve of this nosy woman.

"Oh, don't be mad. Huma was worried about you. She hadn't heard from you and asked me to come over. Seeing as how that girl was here this morning when I arrived, I now fully understand the picture." She waved her hand and bobbed her head from side to side. "But you can't just drop your duties, Aariv. We have work to do to find you the proper wife—an Indian wife in case you forgot. You're making this so difficult for everyone involved, *Beta*."

Bitch. He thought. He almost said it out loud and caught himself.

"Pinky Aunty, I was sick. That's why I wasn't answering her calls. It had nothing to do with Chrissy and why she was here." He was doing his best to keep his voice even, but his temper was rising. "Now please tell me how the *hell* you got in here. It's an invasion of my privacy."

"Oh!" Her brows arched high. "If that girl wasn't here for what I think she was here for, then *why* was she here?"

"Are you joking? Do you have the gall to ask me this in my home? I need you to leave right now. I'll question the doorman downstairs about how you snuck your way in, and then I will make sure they know to never let you in."

"*Atcha, Beta. Atcha.*" She waved her hand and bobbled her head again. "No need to get so upset. I can see that you were sick." She looked him up and down, eyeing his scruffy and tired appearance. "And it was that girl who let me in. Your doorman thought I was your mother." She shrugged as if the occurrence of mistaken identity was a norm for her. It probably was. Non-brownies thought all brown people knew each other or must be related somehow. Not all the non-brownies, but it was still prevalent.

He needed to talk to the condo board about this. But first,

she needed to leave, and he needed to find Chrissy. It made sense she'd left as soon as this unpleasant woman showed up.

"Aariv, you really should be more discreet about your relations. What will people say?"

His jaw dropped. "What people are you talking about? The maintenance workers who are Mexican? The doormen who are both Polish? Or maybe you mean Dr. Gupta in 8E who is a third-generation American and a Buddhist. He most certainly knows all the same people we know," he sneered.

Christ, the nerve of this woman. Their society here was nothing like the strict and old-school rules of back home.

"Aariv," she said, slipping off her stool aghast. "How can you speak to me this way—"

"*Bas!* How can *you* speak to *me* this way? You're in my home, serving—" He glanced at the food on the dining room table. The flatbread looked thick and doughy, and the vegetable stir fry had a soggy quality to it. She was serving him Huma's food from his freezer. "This is my food, isn't it?

"*Heh.* But—"

"Get out," he said pointing to the door.

"What have I done? I'm only doing what Huma asked me to do," she said, though she began to gather her things. "And this place was a mess when I got here. You let that girl do what she wants and make a pigsty all over your counter—"

"Enough!" He barked, scaring the older woman silent. "Get out. I'm done with you."

"But your match—"

"Is none of your business. You're fired."

She tittered nervously. "You can't fire me. Your parents hired me."

"And I will continue to make this job difficult for you. I will make your life a living hell," he seethed. "No amount of money will make it worth your while."

She grabbed her things and practically ran to the front hall, slipping her shoes on.

"I'll make sure your father hears about this," she warned as she opened the door.

"Great. Tell him I said 'hi.'"

She slammed the door behind her at that.

Aariv exhaled loudly, and slid to the floor, exhausted.

"Enough of this shit, Aariv. What the fuck do *you* want?" he asked himself.

"The answer is so obvious it's living rent-free up your ass," Zayn said about an hour later.

His friend had found him, similarly as Chrissy had the night before, but this time he was sitting on the floor lost in thought. Zayn too, had a spare key and he'd used it to come in and check on him, as Mariam had done the previous morning—making Z the fourth person in twenty-four hours to enter his apartment without notifying him first, surprising the shit out him. If Aariv was sure of anything out of all of this, it was that he needed to have his locks changed—and Pinky Aunty banned from the building.

"I have *got* to get my spare keys back," he grumbled, shaking his head after Zayn had startled him.

Aariv had startled his friend in return, after relaying everything that happened with Chrissy, and why he had been sitting on the floor, lost in thought. Zayn had promptly spat his iced coffee out dramatically when Aariv said Chrissy was the woman from the wedding months ago. The hot one that Zayn had encouraged him to hook up with.

Now his friend came out of his bedroom a few moments later, buttoning up one of Aariv's shirts freshly returned from the dry cleaners.

"Fits like a glove, Cuz."

Aariv grunted, picking at the now cold, reheated frozen food that was probably months old by this point. The chewy bread certainly had a freezer-burn quality to it.

"Anyway, how can you not see that this woman—Chrissy—cares about you?"

"I know."

"And that you obviously care about her."

Aariv grunted again.

"I assume that answer is a 'yes,'? Zayn asked. "Because I haven't seen you like this since—"

"Don't fucking say it, Z," he said harshly around a particularly tough bite of the hockey puck like *paratha.*

"Leila," his friend said anyway, ignoring the warning, and took a bite of the food. He made a choking noise and promptly found Aariv's trashcan to spit it out, shivering in disgust.

"Sorry, bro. Had to be said." He shrugged, grabbing the dishes of food from the dining table and promptly clearing them into the trash. "Stuff is shit. Let's go get some real food."

Aariv ignored him, sitting back in a hardbacked dining room chair. "Because you are the quintessential relationship guru with your different piece of ass every week?"

"What do you want me to say? Sex and the culinary arts go hand in hand," his friend said with conviction. "And listen, I know you. This woman is different from your other relationships."

"How would you know? I've barely seen you."

"Bingo Bango! You've missed our basketball games. Bro, you're the one who has a fucking fit when I'm even ten minutes late!"

Aariv scratched his chin in thought. Zayn was right. Aariv was anal about time management and keeping appointments but lately hadn't given much thought to it.

"Admit it, she's good for you."

"How so?"

"You're less rigid. Not as tense all the time." Zayn wiggled his brows. "How's the sex?"

"Not up for discussion," he said curtly crossing his arms over his chest.

"That good, huh?" his friend asked knowingly.

Aariv rolled his eyes. "Well, I don't know what to do now. Chrissy is set about not wanting to continue things with me because I'm … hung up on the whole Leila thing."

"Bro, seriously, you need to sort that shit out. Are you going to go through life like this? Throwing away anything good and fun for you? Completely depressing."

"Chrissy said as much, too."

Zayn nodded. "She's smart."

"She is. No question." Aariv agreed. "I have feelers out through my PI friend about Leila. I'm supposed to get an update soon." Tag had messaged him a short but sweet text saying that they may have found her.

"That's awesome! Finally!" Zayn sounded relieved and

Aariv realized how much his friend had worried about him over this. "So, go tell her that. Make sure she knows you're trying to —I don't know—fix your shit so you can be with her."

Aariv didn't say anything, remembering the unyielding expression Chrissy wore when she said she wanted to end things between them.

"What if things turned out badly with Leila?"

Zayn thought a moment. "Then you know, and you move the hell on. Why should that factor into your decision?"

Aariv scoffed. "Have you met me? The duties in my life—"

"Hate to say it but fuck 'em all."

"Wow. What?" He scratched at his scraggly beard again.

"You heard me. Fuck. Them. All. As in your life rules, your parents; everything you think you need to do to be the 'good son.' You're already a good guy—the best out there. I hear it from my dad constantly. But sadly we can't all be brilliant lawyers." He shook his shaggy head.

Aariv smiled wryly, aware that Zayn's dad compared him to Aariv daily, encouraging Z to be more like him—responsible with his two feet firmly on the ground. He wondered what the older man would say once he found out Aariv rejected the whole matchmaking bullshit. He was over it and pretty sure no match could make him feel as free and light as he did when he was with Chrissy.

"Fine."

He pushed his chair back and stood up.

Zayn did a double-take. "Wait, that's it? Damn, I'm good."

"No. Don't go thinking it's all you. Meeting a woman who makes me question everything I thought I stood for was a huge part of it."

"Awesome. Whatever. I'm just glad to see you leaving the

dark side. Now, go shower, you fucking smell. And trim that beard. You look like someone's *nana* (grandfather) for Christ's sake."

"I can always count on you to have my back. Thanks, Z." He engulfed his friend in a bear hug, while the other man grimaced at his stench.

# CHAPTER 36

৩৬

It was all going according to plan. Chrissy had switched her schedule at the club, asking for a mid-week slot instead of the big-money Saturday night spot. She told her boss, Darius, it was because she wanted to give some of the newer acts the opportunity for exposure, when in actuality she didn't want to draw attention to herself or her special guest.

"Sure. Whatever, Star," Darius had said. He couldn't complain. She'd helped bring in so much new business in the last month that her randomly taking a big show night off wasn't a big deal.

She'd just finished her act, the newer routine she'd been working on, and had perfected, and felt good enough to perform in front of an audience. Now, all she had to do was get into the VIP room at the agreed-upon time, and they could talk. She could get the facts straight once and for all, shut down whatever illegal shit was happening in the rug shop, and then get out of the rug and smuggle business for damn good.

She'd been sitting in the VIP room now, for about ten minutes, fending off the attention from patrons when she realized he might not show. Had he been found out? Worse yet, was he in danger?

She took a nervous sip of her lemon-lime soda when she saw him enter the room surreptitiously. His beady eyes darted around, landing on half-naked women gyrating on laps, before finding her sitting in the corner.

He nodded discreetly and headed in her direction, finally slipping into the seat next to her.

"*Malyshka,* it is good to see you," Boris said, his eyes softening as he looked her over. Not in a slimy way, but in a concerned way. "You are ok?" He looked around the VIP room, at the neon blue lights lining the ceiling of the dim room. "This is not what Natasha had in mind for you."

Was that reproach in his voice, Chrissy thought? How dare he, when he'd been part of putting her in this predicament in the first place.

"Yeah, well, I don't think Natasha knew she'd die so suddenly, leaving her daughter fucking high and dry," Chrissy said scathingly.

"Language, Chrisstika," Boris said, using the same rote command that both her mother and he'd taken with her from as far back as she could remember. No wonder she had a potty mouth, she mused. They'd tried to tamp it down, and in true Chrissy form, she'd fought to maintain it.

"Star, Boris," she reminded him. She wanted to remain under her stage name in case he'd been followed or something. "I'm trying to make ends meet, worried beyond fuck-all about you. So, please, have the decency to fuck off about my language usage."

He sighed, a sharp whine that whistled in and out of his

nose. He eyed a particularly buxom blonde, watching her closely as she peeled her top off.

Chrissy waved her hand in front of his face. "Hello? Hi? This isn't a social call."

"I need a drink first. I am parched." He watched the blonde straddle the man she was entertaining and gyrate sensually on him.

Chrissy twirled her finger in the air, signaling for the server to swing by their table.

"Vodka double for him. Whatever we have that's Russian."

The server left.

Chrissy turned back to Boris whose attention was still elsewhere. She pulled her robe tighter around herself and snapped a finger sharply in front of his face. He jerked his beady eyes back to her.

"Refreshments are on their way. Now spill." She kept her voice from wobbling and held her bitchy like attitude. That seemed to be the only thing Boris answered to.

"What's the rush? Can I not enjoy a little? At least before my drink comes?" he asked with his hands together in supplication.

For fuck's sake. Boris was making her want to gouge her eyes out. Thankfully his double vodka arrived right then.

She pushed it to him and said, "Talk."

And talk he did. Chrissy learned what she suspected all along—her mother had been involved. She'd walked into a situation that had already been percolating. She'd had the opportunity to get out before she knew too much—but the money was too good to be true, and it was with a crime syndicate that had been running illegal goods across the borders for a while. They were good at what they did and hadn't gotten caught once in the years they'd been in business.

Her mother jumped into trouble like a fish into water. She had a talent for it—the negotiating, the secret keeping, the stashing of illegal goods, and the movement of those goods. And she made bank. The money rolled in, a portion of it keeping her and her daughter living comfortably. Chrissy wondered if that was how her mother paid for her dance camps and rigorous ballet training. Outside of her scholarships, they still cost a pretty penny for her to attend, along with ballet point shoes that weren't cheap and which Chrissy went through quickly with her demanding training.

The Russian underworld had hands in everything, Boris explained to her. They mostly did business in Brighton Beach, sure, but they wanted a location that could throw anyone off their scent. So, they picked the antique rug shop run by an elderly Russian couple in Mid-town Manhattan. That couple saw it coming as they kept their ear to the ground like so many business owners in precarious positions.

"Natasha was the one to approach them, having heard the gossip from a niece of theirs who ran a salon in Brooklyn. That's how she came to take over the business."

He looked at her over the rim of his glass as he knocked the drink back. It took her a minute to piece together what he was saying—there was just so much information already thrown her way. But finally, it clicked.

"Hold the fucking phone. Are you talking about Salon Milaya? The one we visited every other month so she could color and touch up her hair, and then made me do it, too?"

"Very good, Chris—Star."

"So, the owner, Mila, was in on it."

She remembered the big-lipped, big-haired, and big-boobed woman who treated her like her own daughter, giving her treats and trinkets. She let Chrissy twirl and practice dance steps in the back of the salon when her mother and the other women gossiped.

"Yes. She still is, but your mama never wanted you to find out," Boris said sadly. "She didn't want you involved, her prima ballerina." He finished his drink and tapped the edge of the glass, indicating another. Chrissy twirled her finger in the air again.

"Well, that was ridiculous. How would I not find out?"

"It was a messy business," he continued. "You were still little when the smugglers partnered with the *Shulaya*—the Russian mob here in the States. That's when things started going down, down, down. They demanded more pay to keep the operation safe and quiet, and the goods went from harmless items like vodka and other spirits to drugs. There's talk about ... importing talent, too."

Their server returned with another drink for Boris. He jangled the rocks in the tumbler nervously.

Chrissy nodded, already aware of the drugs sitting in the stockroom. Had they been moved already? But the idea of human trafficking made her ill. "That's so low, Boris." She shook her head in dismay. "And the big black-haired *scotina* (brute)? The one I saw a while ago when I ran into you on a Sunday?"

Boris smiled indulgently like a proud papa whenever she threw Russian words into her conversation, but quickly the smile disappeared, and he hastily looked over his shoulders.

"You're safe here, Boris," Chrissy assured him, putting her hand over his hairy one. To be truthful, Chrissy was glad to see

Boris healthy, at least on the outside. He didn't look harmed or battered, but he was acting skittish, proving that his safety was in jeopardy. "The bouncer here is in cahoots with me and is watching out for you, too."

Boris's beady eyes widened as far as they could as his head shook. "You don't know these people, what they can do … the elderly couple—the former owners—"

"Did he have them murdered!?" Chrissy asked, her pulse racing. She shuddered.

"No. But they feared so much for their lives that they left the country altogether and are in hiding back in Russia."

"Oh, thank, God." She put her hand to her chest, relieved with this at least. "So, back to that *scotina.* Who is he?"

"He runs the entire East Coast smuggling chain now. A big deal with *Shulaya.* He's known for good business decisions and negotiations, but also brutality if people don't comply." He ducked his head and looked around again. "He's called The Lawyer."

Chrissy sat back in her chair a little dumbfounded. This was the 'lawyer' she'd pegged her bias for actual lawyers on? And no wonder she thought he was an actual big scary man of the law. That's what her mother and Boris had referred to him as, and what she heard as a child.

She shook her head and wanted to laugh at the stories kids make up. But that in this instance, she'd had no other reference to correct her.

She took a deep breath, ready to ask her last question, the one she needed to clinch this thing in the bud. Then Boris could scurry out of sight. He was becoming increasingly agitated.

"What's his name, Boris?"

"Ivan Petrov," he stated under his breath.

This was proving easier than she thought. After months of begging and pleading for information, he was spilling easily. She couldn't even count the number of times she'd asked what was going on; why the books looked off; why the fuck more inventory kept piling up when they hadn't sold anything the prior month. He'd always denied her even a word of information, saying she didn't need to know, or that he was protecting her like her mother had wanted him to. But she was finally sick of the bullshit; sick of being treated like a little girl who couldn't handle the ugly truth. She was glad he finally trusted her enough to tell her now, but why?

The prickles on the back of her neck suddenly stung her with unease. He was talking too readily to her.

"Why are you telling me all of this?" she asked hesitantly, now peering over her shoulders. Did any scary mobsters get past the big burly bouncer?

"You wear a wire, *da* (yes)?

How on God's green earth had he guessed that?

Boris' eyes twitched as he waited for her answer, and she noticed a muscle ticking spastically under his right eye. The man was stressed as fuck.

She swallowed and nodded. He was more astute than she gave him credit for.

"I want out. No more of this. My life becomes more unsafe. And bringing in young women, girls is sickening." He tapped a finger on the sticky table. "I want immunity."

Ah, there was the kicker, but at least Boris was finally showing a conscience. "I'll see what I can do—"

Just then a large, warm hand landed on her shoulder, and she jumped about three feet in her seat.

"I thought you planned never to set foot in the VIP room.

What the hell are you doing, and who's your friend, Sunshine?" a deep voice said smoothly in her ear.

Oh, Christ on a bike—what was *he* doing here?!

She glanced up and found Aariv staring down at her. His expression was behind an indifferent mask, but his jaw worked so hard she could see the muscles jumping under his beard.

He looked at Boris, who physically got smaller in his seat. But, damn, he looked good—Aariv, not Boris. Had he finished the extra tonic she'd made for him and stored in his fridge, minus the liver and beets?

His hair was swept back, his beard was trimmed, and he stood tall in a light blue plaid shirt, with the sleeves rolled to his elbows. Faded jeans encased his muscularly thick thighs, and he wore black workman-type boots.

Was it just her, or were other women, both clothed and not, gawking at him the way she was, too? He commanded attention, with his good looks, and wide stance.

But hold on, why was he here? She'd ended things with him.

"Aariv Abbas," he said, extending a hand to Boris. "The … boyfriend."

Boris now looked downright confused, mimicking the expression on her face.

*Boyfriend!?*

Chrissy spluttered aghast. "What are you doing?" she asked, looking up at Aariv like he'd lost his mind. Maybe he was still sick and delirious.

"I asked you first. What are you doing here in the VIP room entertaining?"

"Oh my God—"

"Star, I leave," Boris said quietly to her.

"No! Wait—"

He shook his head and kept it down as he rose and skedaddled out of the room without a backward glance. She could do nothing but let him go because she had this new development to deal with.

Aariv slipped into the vacant seat beside her, his hard, warm thigh pressing a little too intimately into hers. She glared into her drink as he ordered a club soda from the server who pushed her tits out obscenely to him while taking his order.

"So, Star." He spread his arms comfortably along the back of the booth, studying her profile. "Tell me what's going on." His voice was pleasant, and she peered at him, finding his bright eyes practically spearing her.

# CHAPTER 37

৩৭

$\mathcal{A}$ariv was finding it extremely difficult to tamp down the discomfort that gripped him. Admittedly, he was most likely still slightly sick. But he'd dragged himself up and into the shower and got dressed. He wanted to see Chrissy and talk to her about how he felt.

Especially after talking with Zayn. It was enough of a push to step outside of his comfort zone and see if he and Chrissy were on the same page. He'd texted her about talking that evening, and her response was curt, saying she had a shift at the club.

He didn't take that as an invitation to come see her per se, but neither had she told him to back off.

He decided to meet her there. And he was glad he did. He'd caught her performance which ignited the space dramatically. She moved sensually and daringly to Pink's "Trust Fall" (now a new favorite song of his). Her performance persona was in place, the one that was larger than life, both mysterious and sexy, with just a hint of her bright, teasing personality peeking through.

Her costume was a see-through long-sleeved black mesh body suit this time, with a thick zipper running along the front center from the top of her neck down to her crotch. Black lace detailing covered the shoulders and extended down to cover just the nipple portion of her breasts, allowing the outline of the high and weighty curves to be exposed through the material, swaying with every move she made. Fuck, it was erotic as hell. The back had one center seam that started at the top, mimicking the zipper in the front. As usual, she was gorgeous up there, commanding attention with her star-like quality. And he couldn't keep his eyes off of her.

He burned with a flood of emotions as he watched her. She was incredible—her dance skills knew no bounds and he felt awe at the natural performer she was. But rage tore through that cloud of awe, while he heard a table of men next to him jeer at her, cat-call, and whistle. White hot jealousy ignited within him quickly, aware that other men looked at her body with lust, appraisal, and appreciation, the same as him. He wanted to be the only man who got to see her like that—wild, sensual, with not a care in the world.

When she performed her last trick where she landed in a seated position with the curtains cradling her high up in the air, and her back arched with her breasts jutting lusciously in the air, the words of the song blared, "What if we just fall, what if we just fall." All he could think at that moment was why the fuck couldn't he? Why couldn't they? What was stopping them from freely falling together—to being together? It was him, and he needed to get his head out of his ass, so he didn't fuck it up with her.

He needed to tell her; he needed to tell her that he was falling for her. But he had one hurdle he needed to see through before he could let himself fall freely for her. He was taking a huge chance, but he wanted—needed—to be honest with her.

Chrissy continued sipping her drink, ignoring him. He stared at her profile, how her cheeks rounded delicately, and flushed bright pink, brightening under the silver stars she'd drawn with stage makeup along her cheekbones.

She looked gorgeous. Her hair was swept up high, and she'd attached long black, glittery strands to her shorter hair somehow, gathering it at the crown of her head in a thick ponytail.

She wore that same kimono-style robe as a cover-up she'd worn last time, and thick sheep-skin lined boots on her feet.

He reached over and fiddled with a lock of her faux hair as it grazed her neck. She shifted in her seat but didn't make another move.

"You're feeling much better, I see," she commented, stabbing the ice with her straw.

"How do you know? You aren't even looking at me," he quipped.

"Oh, I saw you. I think every woman in here saw you." She squirmed; her voice flecked with annoyance.

Was that jealousy he detected in her tone? This was a good sign, he mused, hiding his smile. He knew exactly how she felt, having previously been in the audience with every other guy salivating over her sexiness.

"What are you doing here?" she asked, finally turning to him. "Did Tag tell you something? Are you checking up on me?"

He sat back and watched her closely. "Why would Tag know about you entertaining gentlemen in the VIP room?" His fury at the fact that she would even give some random guy a lap dance suddenly disappeared as it swiftly dawned on him why she was in there.

"That was Boris, wasn't it? You were meeting Boris, here."

"Way to go, Sherlock," she said, now her tone dripping with sarcasm.

"Sherlock was a detective, not a lawyer."

"Whatever." She waved her hand.

"I can't believe you keep doing this—putting your life in danger. You promised you wouldn't do this again. What would Tag—"

"I didn't promise you that I wouldn't see Boris. I promised I wouldn't go to the store again. And that's beside the point. Tag put me up to this." She turned on him, her eyes shining like sapphire jewels with anger. She slowly pulled her kimono open and unzipped her bodysuit, only going as far down as her sternum. She turned the material over to reveal a skinny silver line attached to a tiny recording device and microphone.

A wire? She was wearing a fucking wire? "Say 'hi' to Tag. He'll be listening later tonight."

He leaned back in his seat, surveying her as she smugly put the wire and costume back in place. "Well, I'll be damned," he uttered.

So Tag had put her up to this. He'd trusted her instincts and her tenacity to meet with Boris. Fuck, he felt like an ass. One who didn't have any confidence in how she could help tie up the situation that involved her family's business.

"And for the record, I don't need you checking up on me. It's not like you're my boyfriend or anything."

Her cheeks flamed the same color as her bright red lipstick, and she looked him once over before she coolly turned back to her drink to take a long slurp.

"Maybe I'd like a shot at it, Sunshine. And since we're collecting data, I didn't come to check up on you, although, you can't blame me if I wanted to."

"Wait. A shot at what?" she asked, still irate, one leg crossed over the other jiggling. But she hadn't moved away from him, and his thigh was still pressed up against hers.

"Being your boyfriend." He sipped his club soda.

Now she faced him once more, her eyelids blinking slowly as she looked at him from head to toe.

"What are you playing at, Aariv?" she asked, still incensed.

He had to tamp down his urge to haul her onto his lap and kiss her. When she got angry it fired up his desire for her more than ever.

"When have you ever known me to play games?" He arched a brow at her.

She tapped her chin to the tempo that she continued jiggling her leg with. "True. But then I've never seen you perform in the courtroom. Who knows what you're trying to get me to do."

"I'm not trying to get you to do anything but go on a date with me, for real. No sex expected, just enjoying each other's company over dinner ... at a restaurant ... with other people."

She was still skeptical, but her leg had stilled. "What about Bitchy Aunty and your wife quest?"

"Not going to happen. I pretty much told her to fuck off this morning, when you weren't there, and she was."

He saw her chest rise and fall quickly, his words affecting her.

"Why?"

"Because I don't want to search for the perfect partner when I've already met her."

She sat up straighter, and continued with her questioning.

"But what will your parents say? Won't they be disappointed? Won't they disown you or something?"

"Let them disown me. I can't keep living by their rules. Come to think of it, I'm coming up with a new list of rules. Go for what, or who you want. Something or someone who makes your heart feel lighter."

"Why?"

"If you can't guess by now, then you'd make a terrible lawyer," he teased.

Her expression softened and she laughed. "I might be able to guess, but I want to hear you say it."

"Fair enough. I like you, Sunshine. In fact," he leaned toward her and bumped her nose with his, "I more than like you. I think I might be in love with you."

That got her attention, more so than the boyfriend comment from before, and she turned large, almost bulging eyes to him.

After what felt like eons, their eyes glued on one another, she finally said, "Don't let your mouth scribble a check that your butt can't cash." Her eyes flickered to his lips.

He pondered this for a moment. "*Dazed and Confused*?" he asked. It sounded like a quote from that movie. She nodded, but — "I think you have the words wrong—"

She threw her hands up. "Can you ever not be right, or a know-it-all?"

He considered this. "Well, sure, if I'm wrong. But I think the quote actually goes—"

"Shut up, Riv, and listen to me," she demanded, and he zipped his lips, awed by this angry, sexy creature that made his stomach do twists and turns. She crossed her arms over her chest. "I *might* be in love with you, too. But that doesn't change the fact that you have a shit ton of baggage."

He couldn't stop the grin that spread across his face at the fact that she might feel the same way. Warmth seeped throughout his body, through his limbs, and pinpointed his heart.

"Let me stop you right there," he said happily. "I know I have baggage. I'm going to talk to her."

"What?"

"Tag has some information for me on Leila's whereabouts. I'm going to finally face her and find out what happened to her."

"Does that man ever sleep?" she muttered under her breath. Aariv chuckled, having thought the same thing about his PI buddy many times before. But her face contorted as if she'd sucked on a sour lemon.

"This doesn't change anything," she murmured firmly.

"Excuse me? How exactly can my addressing my past *not* change anything?"

"Because you *have* to do it, Riv. You *have* to do it no matter how you feel about me. I want you to, don't get me wrong. I think you'll feel so much better knowing. But what if it's bad? What if she's so unhappy that you feel even more regret and guilt and you imprison yourself to a life of misery forever? Then we can never have a shot, because even if we are together, you'll still feel like shit, and I will never be enough for you."

"Chrissy, pardon my language, but what the hell? I choose you, no matter what."

She nodded, quiet for a moment and Aariv wondered if he was in some kind of alternate universe. Again, he'd misjudged her for a romantic who would fall into his arms and proclaim herself his girlfriend forever as soon as he'd said the words. Fuck, it was aggravating. She wasn't just full of daydreams. She was a complex woman who had so much to offer, but only to the person who deserved her everything. He couldn't blame her, and the warmth he'd felt just moments ago turned to a cooled-out fire and he couldn't hide his disappointment.

"Riv," she said softly, reaching for his jaw and caressing. "You know I'm right."

He nodded. She *was* right. She knew him well, understanding his basic need to always make things right and to never think of himself first. But wasn't he doing just that by going after Leila and finding out her outcome? So that he could bring some kind of peace to himself?

"I'm going to prove you wrong, Chrissy." He hadn't meant to, but his voice was gritty and harsh. He leaned in. "I'm going to come back for you."

He pulled her onto his lap, assuaging his need to feel her against him—*all* of her against him. He thought he would have to find a way to persuade her to let him kiss her, but she gasped loudly and kissed him first, her need just as great as his.

"Riv," she whispered, sucking at his bottom lip, and sinking her teeth into him. She maneuvered herself so that she straddled him, and her arms snaked up and around his neck, combing through his hair, messing it up. He groaned in pleasure.

He parted her robe, letting his hands feel her barely covered warm flesh, moaning as he took a handful of each breast in each palm. She arched, pulled away from him, and moaned sexily. He pulled her back to him, covering her mouth with his again, only wanting her moans for him and him alone.

She began grinding on him, slow and low, to whatever song was playing in the background of the VIP room. The beat was base-heavy and erotic.

"No touching," a deep voice said sternly, coming from a big man standing next to them all of a sudden.

Chrissy tore her mouth from his and looked up at the big beefy bouncer. "It's ok, Domino. Just give me five minutes. I'm ok."

The bouncer, Domino, just stood there unmoving, unsure of what to do.

"Please," she pleaded.

He jerked a nod. "Five minutes, Star. That's all I can allow."

He stood in front of them, hiding them from the other patrons, his back turned to them and let them continue with what they were doing.

Chrissy dove back hungrily for him as he clasped his hand behind her neck and dragged her back. He pulled her robe completely open and let his hands skim to her fleshy hips, squeezing what should be all his. She flexed her pelvis on him, and he dared to reach a hand between her legs. She was hot and wet.

He cupped her and groaned, as she whined softly into his mouth. He couldn't believe that he was doing this with her, here, in the strip room, but fuck if he wasn't more than turned on. If he had condoms in his pocket he'd take her right here, with Domino's big form standing guard.

Instead, he slipped his finger under the crotch of the black mesh and entered her heat.

"Fuck!" she whimpered, starting to grind against his hand. "Oh God," she whispered into his neck, her hands fumbling for the zipper of his pants.

"Not here, Baby." He stopped her shaking hands. "But let me make you feel good."

She shook her head, pushing herself away from him, and slid off his lap, closing her legs and her robe.

"Go, Riv," she ordered, panting, but looking away from him.

"What?" he asked, breathing heavily, his hard-on about to explode from his jeans.

"Get the hell out of here. Go find Leila. Take as long as you need to and get your answers."

He saw wetness shining on her cheeks as tears rolled down slowly. She angrily dashed them away as his chest caved in.

"I'll be here," she continued, her voice trembling. "But I'm not going to promise you I'll wait."

TWO WEEKS LATER
new york, new york

৩৮

"**I**'m thinking about you."

She stared at the text from him from last week. It sat untouched; she hadn't responded to it and didn't intend to. She needed space from Aariv and how he'd affected her. Her mind was still reeling from seeing him at the club two weeks ago when he'd caught her meeting with Boris. The arrogance of him believing she would do something stupid and endanger herself had made her seethe and it took everything in her not to slap him.

But the look of awe and respect that followed closely, as he realized she was working alongside the investigator, not hiding things and acting brashly, had made her warm and tingly inside. She'd wanted to tell herself to cut it out and kick him out of the club, but then he went and explained that he was giving up his wife hunt, that she was his ideal partner, that he might be in love with her, and all those things tore down what little strength she had against him.

She touched her lips, as she sat in Tag Underwood's nondescript office in midtown, that very early Monday morning.

She still felt the scorching kiss and the raw hunger between them as if it had happened yesterday.

But it wasn't only unadulterated passion that swelled whenever they were near each other, but a visceral, emotional tug that compelled her to answer. She needed him and if she was right about him and their connection, he needed her too. More than anything, she wanted him. But he wasn't fully hers to keep right now, if ever.

She knew without a doubt that she was in love with him. And she was mad at herself for letting her feelings run away like that. The problem was, her feelings had already begun percolating the moment she met him again, in his office that first time. The push and pull of his attitude that followed only made her fall harder because we always want what we can't have, right?

She shook her head and tried to focus on what was happening in her life—which was a shit ton. Aariv needed to do what he needed to do, and she needed to do what she needed to do.

But no matter how hard she tried, she wanted to glance at her phone and just see the words, though his text had arrived last week. At the time she'd had no idea where he was and what he was doing and didn't want to know. Except that Mariam had called her soon afterward and told her he was on a plane to Dubai.

"I thought you'd want to know," Mariam had said, always straight-forward, not an ounce of bull-shit in sight.

"And why would I want to know?" she'd asked tersely, fighting down the ramping up of her pulse whenever Aariv came into the conversation or someone mentioned him, or she even thought about him (which was most hours of the day).

"So you know that he's safe, alive, and maybe not as well as he could be—emotionally that is. But he's doing what he said he was going to do."

And then Mariam had changed the subject, thankfully, asking Chrissy to be one of the few she and her fiancé, Bruce, invited to the courthouse. They were scheduling a time to exchange marriage vows.

That got Chrissy's attention, as she gleefully responded that she'd love to, though inwardly she wondered if she'd ever be a bride. She asked if Mariam wanted any kind of bride-to-be hoopla, like a bachelorette party. Mariam explained they were keeping it simple with no bridesmaids or best men, but that those present at the exchange of their vows were the best people in their lives.

Chrissy agreed to whatever she wanted, just happy for her friend and her man, considering the struggles they'd gone through to be with each other. She'd drop anything and everything to help them celebrate.

"Everyone good? Are we ready to start?" Tag Underwood asked, shaking Chrissy out of her meandering thoughts, and calling everyone around the table to attention. They were in the office's one tiny conference space for interviews just like this.

Her cup of generic office coffee sat steaming in front of her and she raised it to her lips to erase the idea of kissing Aariv again. She was there to support Boris that morning. He had come in willingly to speak with Tag and tell him everything he knew about Ivan Petrov. Petrov, Tag had confirmed after listening to her recorded wiretap of the conversation at the club with Boris, was a huge presence in the East Coast *Shulaya*, specifically the smuggling and extortion crime rings.

Tag needed Boris to come in and answer a few more

questions so that he could assist him with immunity, and get the bad guys once and for all. When they were through there, he would contact law enforcement, specifically, the NYPD detectives he knew were working on this case.

An hour later, Tag had everything he needed and pressed the stop button on his recording device. Most of what Boris had relayed was what he'd said to Chrissy a few weeks ago, but he had more intricate details to share like dates and other specifics.

"Boris, thank you for coming in. Your testimony will be more than helpful in bringing down this crime ring."

"I have immunity, though, yes? I do not need to testify," the smaller man asked, clutching his hands nervously in front of him.

Tag scratched his chin. "That depends on the prosecution. But I'm going to discuss transactional immunity. Your testimony is imperative to bring down the bad guys, but in return, you'll get full immunity and protection. You may have to leave New York, though, and everyone you know here."

Boris glanced at Chrissy. His tired eyes filled with tears, making hers well up, too.

"Chrisstika, I cannot leave you."

"You have to Boris." She hugged him. "I'll be ok. They don't know that I know anything. What can they do to me, especially if I sell the place?" She was hoping beyond hope that she was right. It sounded like there was an intricate web of these types of small businesses that fronted big crimes in plain sight. Why would they care about a tiny rug store like hers?

While Chrissy and Boris talked, Tag's assistant rushed in and whispered something urgently to him.

"What!?" He stood up, the metal chair scraping noisily on

the parquet floor. "I'm sorry to interrupt you two, but your store is on fire, Chrissy!"

"What?" She wasn't sure she'd heard correctly. "My store? Natasha's Rug Emporium? On fire?" She stood up, too. What was going on?

"The fire department just got there and are putting out the flames. Damn!" Tag ran a hand through his grey hair. "Boris, did you inform anyone—anyone at all about this?"

Boris' eyes widened. "No."

"They must be on to someone sniffing around. Hopefully, they haven't caught on to me yet. I only went in there as a curious end buyer, but never followed up."

"Wait, do you think this was on purpose?" she asked incredulously.

"Wouldn't be the first time arson was used to cover up criminal shenanigans," Tag said, pulling out his phone and texting someone. "I'll say I'm lucky that you took that risk sneaking in there a few weeks ago, even though I advised you not to. I have the hidden drug photos as evidence."

"What should we do?" Chrissy asked, putting her arm around a quaking Boris. How the hell had he gotten through the past few years involved in this kind of crime ring? The man was scared out of his mind! He must have had no choice.

Tag looked up from typing. "Boris, I need to get you somewhere safe. I have a safehouse I use in—wait, I'm not saying anything," he said to Chrissy.

"What? Why? I wouldn't tell anyone."

"It's for your protection."

Everything happened quickly after that. Tag had Boris whisked away to some safe house in God knew where. Tag ushered Chrissy out of his office, advising her to not take any calls from unknown numbers and to not answer the door from unplanned guests.

"You're scaring me, Tag."

"I'm sorry, Chrissy. But you need to watch your back. I'm calling my guy Johnnie. He'll keep tabs on you and make sure you're not made."

He sounded like an old-school gumshoe, and she marveled at it, excitement replacing fear at the way things had turned.

"Chrissy," Tag warned. "I see that look in your eyes. Don't be a hero. Lay low for the next few days until I sort this out and we get the NYPD fully on board. Do you understand me? Abbas will have my head if anything happens to you."

They were down on the curb now and he hailed a cab.

"What does Aariv know about all this?" she sniffed, both miffed and pleased that Aariv was worried about her.

"I haven't told him all the details, but he's checked in a few times since leaving town to make sure you're all right and safe."

"Oh," was all she said, her stupid cheeks heating up.

"And, Chrissy, the next time you want to wear a wire, a piece of advice—shut the damn thing off when you're done with the business portion of your conversation."

The man's ears turned bright red as a cab pulled up. He opened it and pushed her in.

"Oh," she mumbled again, embarrassed, too, but giggling that this older southern gent had heard her and Aariv together.

"Where are you headed?" he asked.

"I have to go to work."

"Nuh-uh, missy. You take the day off, or work from home, or whatever you young people do these days. Be in one place all day and I'll check in on you via text."

"But what do I tell my co-workers?"

"Tell them you're sick."

"Really? I'm supposed to hide this from them?"

"Chrissy, we don't know who we can trust. Just keep this under wraps for now. I'll tell you when it's safe to come out."

She nodded and gave the driver her address.

Now she was thinking about Aariv again, and as if his ears were burning, another text chimed in from him.

**"I'm looking forward to seeing you again."**

Sheesh, the man was relentless. Though why was she surprised, she thought as her body warmed up and her stomach somersaulted. The man was a lawyer and a good one at that.

She'd spent most of the last few days in a ping pong of sadness at letting him go, and relief that she'd sent him on his way. She needed to shield herself and her little heart, though she admitted she still loved the man. It didn't take a genius to figure that one out. He was constantly on her mind. She worried about him, missed him, and tossed and turned in fits during the night. She was haggard in the mornings, but she knew she would get through it; she'd gotten through broken hearts before, though this one took the cake.

Thankfully the investigation had developed rapidly just as he left, and she had that to focus on. And seriously, now all she could concentrate on was the shop burning to the ground. She hadn't wanted to be in charge of it, but the place being a pile of ashes was the last thing she'd wanted. It held memories of her childhood when she'd be there after school or on the weekends while her mother worked, playing hide and seek amongst the stacks of carpets with Boris, and later sitting in the office doing her homework. Who would have done something like this?

She shivered, hoping Tag could figure it out.

As the cab driver darted through traffic making their way to the Queensboro bridge, she texted her coworkers and Simran that she was sick and was staying home. She'd log on to work periodically during the day and check in.

Everyone responded in some fashion that alluded to her break-up with Aariv because it was hard to hide it from them anymore. Her mind went to different places at the oddest times of the day, filled with sadness or anger. Even thoughts of what she could have done differently.

Chrissy huffed. Aariv Abbas would be a hard man to get over, but she'd be fine—one of these days.

PRESENT DAY
dubai
THE UNITED ARAB EMIRATES

# CHAPTER 39

৩৯

ariv stared at the figure getting out of the shiny, black suburban. She was dressed in a flowy black garment and a pretty silver and pink head scarf covered her hair. Oversized sunglasses shaded her eyes from the scorching Dubai sun. She shifted her large luxury satchel over an arm and said something loudly in Arabic to the man who held the car door open for her. A teenage boy, then a teenage girl, followed closely by two more boys who looked identical and were about middle-school aged climbed out, too.

She kissed the older kids and said something to them in Bangla. He heard 'keep an eye on them' and 'be back here in an hour.' All the kids nodded in response as the teenagers pulled out their phones and began furiously texting—a behavior so like the kids in the US that it felt like he was in New York right now. When she kissed the younger boys, one of them hugged her tight—and then they were off in the opposite direction of where he sat outside in the shade of a trendy, local café.

The woman spotted him immediately, and a small smile

curved her lips as she approached the table. She adjusted her headscarf, tucking in a wayward strand that had escaped.

"Aari?" she asked, and he recognized her gentle voice.

Tag had informed him a few weeks back that he'd found her. He'd found Leila, though her last name wasn't Majid anymore but was now Hassan. She lived in Dubai with her family, in a very comfortable way. She'd been there for almost twenty years now. Through a little digging, whether lawful or not, he found her home telephone number and left it with Aariv, no questions asked.

At first, he'd been skeptical to call her, thinking that his call might not be answered, or if she wasn't in, that his message might never reach her. He had no idea what kind of home life she was dealing with. But after waffling about it for an entire day, he decided to go for it. What could he lose? When he finally did call, she was the one who'd picked up. He at once recognized the gentle lilt of her voice in the formal tone she answered with, though deeper with age.

Her shock at hearing it was him on the other end had made her ask him over and over again if this was some kind of joke. And over and over again he proclaimed that it wasn't. It truly was him. Right then, before he lost any nerve, he asked if he could come visit her. He wanted to clear some things up. She hesitated but finally agreed.

The partners at the firm weren't exactly thrilled about him taking time off after missing work during the most crucial part of their big case. But Aariv had come prepared with a doctor's note advising that he take a leave of absence due to his illness. His body had taken a toll. Granted, the note was from Zayn's doctor friend, but as he was a legit board-certified physician, Aariv couldn't complain, though he still thought the guy was questionable when it came to his best friend and his pill-popping abuse.

The partners agreed but warned that his status as the lead for the new partner position might be jeopardized. Though this irked him and given all the hard work he'd put into the firm in the years he'd been there, he wondered if they were bluffing. But for many reasons he'd finally come to realize, he couldn't buy into their bluff. He remained resolute in his decision, but, like the good arguer he was, which shot him to the top of their candidate pool when hiring him, he reminded them that he'd been a full team member from the get-go. When it came to taking a vacation, half the time he didn't take it (which was probably why he'd landed in his ill predicament in the first place), and thus unused time added up to at least two months of vacation, which he was still owed as they rolled it over every year. He reminded them that he clocked in more hours than the others, usually one of the first to arrive and the last to leave the office. Finally, he listed in order the cases he'd helped the firm win since the beginning of his career (which was a lot), along with what he'd done to push the Turner & Turner case to where they were now—settling out of court due to his findings and negotiations. He left them considering this and walked out the door. It was about as much as he could do given that more pressing matters were on his mind. He needed to close this personal case that involved Leila and move on. And he needed to move on with Chrissy Smyth if she'd still have him—he'd argue the fuck out of that scenario if he had to. They were too good together.

Now, as he scrutinized this woman standing before him, he tried to make out the girl from so long ago with the now rounded face and shapeless garment she wore. She smiled and through the laugh and worry lines, he saw Leila.

He stood up and went to hug her, but she shook her head slightly and he took the hint, dropping his arms. She lived in a Muslim world now and it was customary for those of the opposite sex to not touch when greeting. Instead, she put a hand to her chest and smiled, bowing her head slightly. He did the same in return.

"Leila, it's been so long," he said in wonder as she took her sunglasses off but didn't pull out her chair.

"Would you like to sit inside?" she asked, looking at him closely with those light brown eyes he remembered so clearly.

He was sweating in his white linen short-sleeve button-down shirt and khakis. The weather had reached the mid-nineties and it was only eleven am.

"You might be more comfortable in the air-conditioned cafe. I know I will be," she continued.

He pulled out the handkerchief from his pocket and wiped at the perspiration rolling down his forehead, nodding.

"That would be great," he said, relieved.

He didn't know how people survived in the sweltering desert heat. Though India was hot as balls in the summertime, they had some relief when the monsoon season began in June.

However, as he glanced around at the beautiful architecture with a mixture of old and modern, he noticed thoughtfully placed wide shades over the paved walkways that darted between the tall palm trees in this part of downtown Dubai. It was called the City Walk and was a bustling commercial area with the largest mall in the world, and hundreds of restaurants. It had been her recommendation to meet there, and though their meeting place was near the waterfront, it was still extremely warm.

She'd said she wasn't comfortable having him at her home because her husband wasn't aware they were meeting. This already raised a red flag in his mind, but he kept that thought to himself. He'd be ready to help her out in any way he could. He could speak to the embassy here, or whatever was needed to get her out of an abusive situation if need be.

She smiled indulgently, almost the same way he noticed that she'd smiled at the kids who'd gotten out of the car with her only moments ago as she led the way inside. As soon as they stepped through the doors, they were greeted with a blast of cool air rippling over them. People waited to be seated in the already full restaurant and they scooted through the crowd.

She turned to him over her shoulder. "Better, right?"

She didn't wait for his answer but spoke quickly in Arabic to the maître 'd who led them through the busy cafe to a table by the windows that overlooked the water in the marina. The view was stunning, with steel behemoth skyscrapers unfolding to the sky and beyond, it seemed, and reflecting in the bright turquoise water.

The Burj Khalifa—the tallest building in the world—stood out in its opulence and modern futuristic design. The rounded contours of each tower spire hugged each other tightly in what looked like a metal bundle of polished tubes. The base was wide and became less so as it spiraled up to over one hundred fifty stories. It dwarfed his favorite New York City icon, the Empire State Building, by about sixty stories. It was staggering and shone like a beacon of the wealth that surrounded this city and throughout the Middle East. With the sun's harsh glare, Aariv could barely look at it.

"It's beautiful, isn't it," Leila commented, getting settled in her seat. "Did you know that the spire design is based on Islamic architecture? It mimics some of the greatest mosques that have a similar spiral and minaret design."

Aariv didn't know that, but he could see it.

"It *is* pretty spectacular," he agreed, now looking around briefly at the inside of the café. It was a cool oasis of white brick walls with beige and grey tufted seating. The light fixtures were airy and bright with gauzy fabric shades covering them, reminding him of hot air balloons.

The other patrons were an urban mix of locals and what looked like tourists. Women wore everything from head-to-toe shapeless black coverings with headscarves like Leila, to loose, modest western attire, covering arms and legs. Some men were in an array of airy and modest western-styled pants and shirts, while others wore the long white tunic and a white headpiece secured by a circle of black rope that was the typical garb most people thought of for men in the Middle East.

Aarvi turned to Leila who'd picked up her menu, perusing it. He did the same. Everything was in English.

When the server came, she ordered for both of them—a pot of English breakfast tea, and an assortment of cakes and sandwiches to go with it.

"I hope that's all right," she said when the server left. "The high tea here is superb."

She adjusted the sleeves of her garment, pulling them lower around her wrist.

"So, Aari." She looked up at him, and again he saw the younger woman he'd known staring back at him. "How are you?" she asked enthusiastically. "It was such a surprise to hear from you. I thought I'd never see you again!"

Aariv chuckled. "Me too. But your family made it difficult to find out where you were."

Her eyes widened. "They did?" She sat back in her chair. "My parents told me you hated me and that you never wanted to see me again!"

"What!?" He leaned over to take one of her hands, and then remembered he wasn't supposed to show any intimacy and pulled it back. "Leila, no one knew what happened to you, except that you married some distant cousin. The rumors were that he was old and disgusting. Or that he beat you into submission—"

She laughed unexpectedly and he stopped, surprised. "I'm sorry. Oh gosh, I'm really sorry." She covered her mouth with her hand as her laughter shook her shoulders.

He smiled. It was good to see her joyful laughter after all of the rumors that had swirled about her disappearance. Maybe they'd been mistaken.

"That gossip couldn't be further from the truth," she said once she'd calmed down, confirming this.

"So what happened to you?"

She fiddled with the cutlery before folding her hands in her lap. She looked up at him, serious now.

"I *did* marry a distant cousin; one that I was related to by marriage, not by blood. He was older than me by about five years and had started working here in Dubai for the real estate company that had that," she pointed to the shining Burfi Khalifa, "built here."

"Wow," Aariv said with astonishment. He'd known that her husband did well, but this was another level of wealth. "And so … he's not cruel?"

She laughed again, her face pinkening. "Not at all. He's the kindest man and the best husband. We started as strangers but grew to love one another."

"But what about your dreams of going to England, or the US to become a nurse? Didn't marrying into a strict Muslim family take those dreams away from you and..." He trailed away and surprise washed over her face. Her countenance turned to sadness then, as her brows furrowed over her eyes.

"Being with you." She finished his sentence for him. She sighed. "I was already engaged to Bilal by the time I was seventeen, Aariv." She looked down at her hands.

"What? You were already engaged when we secretly dated?"

Her lips quirked up in thought. "Well, not officially, but he was my intended and what my parents were working toward once I graduated secondary school."

"I—" He thought back. Had she mentioned it? "I remember you talking about a distant relative your parents wanted you to marry."

"I did say that. And, hm." She thought for a moment. "Maybe I may not have been as clear as I should have been—in fact, I don't think I used the word engaged..."

He sat up abruptly in his chair, resting his arms on the table. Silverware clattered as the table shook.

She placed her hands on her place setting, stilling the quivering metal. "Aari?"

"Leila, why were you with me then?"

"Well." She opened her napkin and smoothed it on her lap. "I had the most enormous crush on you. I think every girl in our class did. You were handsome and smart, and such an athlete. When you started talking to me during our last year of school, I didn't want you to stop. I wanted to spend time with you while I still could."

"So, everything we discussed—a future together, your career, my career—that was all just a made-up dream for you?" He cupped his chin and ran his palm over the bristles of his beard. Had he made this entire thing up? Had he put undue guidelines on his dating life, on what his future should look like, based on lies?

She bit her lip, and it was a gesture he remembered well, even twenty years later. She'd been so young and sweet. Now she looked older, more mature, but still pretty nonetheless, with that nervous girlish tick still there.

"I had the smallest hope that it could happen. I prayed every day to *Allah* (God) that it would happen. I could see myself as your wife, as the mother of your children. But he had different plans for me. I don't know if you were aware, but I was so torn when everything was happening. Did I follow my heart or was I to obey my parents? In the end, *Allah* decided for me. My parents found out and took me away."

Aariv was silent, his jaw working as he thought about all of this.

The waiter pushed a cart over with tiered trays filled with bite-size sandwiches, pastries, and other goodies. Another came around to the other side of the table and placed the delicate tea service down, preparing and steeping the tea for them.

When they'd left, Leila picked up one of the cups. "Do you still take milk and sugar, Aari?"

He nodded wordlessly and she put in five lumps of sugar and a hefty dose of milk before pouring the tea in.

When she was done preparing her cup, she took a sip,

staring at him over the rim of the delicate porcelain. He made no move to drink his tea or to take food.

"You're mad," she stated, setting her cup down gently.

"No, Leila. I'm fucking *pissed*," he said, louder than he intended and other patrons glanced their way. He swallowed the foul language he wanted to spew out—not at her—but at the situation and the miscommunication and the years he lost believing he'd been the one to create her altered path.

"Why?"

"Because I've spent the last two decades wondering if you were unhappy and wondering if I was the cause of all of it," he said bitterly. "I didn't let myself enjoy other women, get to know them, or create a relationship with them because I thought I had failed you, and I needed to punish myself."

"Aari." She gasped, putting a hand over her mouth. Her brown eyes became watery. "I'm so sorry," she whispered. "If I had known, I would have tried to get in contact with you. But as I mentioned before, I was told you hated me—that your family now mistrusted my family, and to never get into contact with anyone who had anything to do with this back in India."

Aariv shook his head at the absurdity of the way she lived her life—to blindly obey her parents, her family, and most of all, her husband, and the lies they'd fed her. But it was no better than how his father treated him now, was it? Viraj had kept his mother's insanity a secret and continued to keep the family jute business financials under wraps though everyone knew things weren't looking so great.

He filled his plate with pretty pastries and took a few sandwiches. Then he silently sipped his tea.

"Who is she?" she asked, taking a small bite of a delicate cucumber sandwich.

"Who do you mean?" he asked pulling apart a crustless sandwich, eating being the last thing on his mind.

"The woman who has finally made you come and look for me, call me out of the blue; to find out if I had ended up happy."

He forgot how astute she was. A corner of his mouth lifted. "She's a ray of sunshine," he said truthfully.

"She sounds perfect for you," Leila said gently. "I hope she knows how lucky she is to have your heart. You were so hard to give up. I *did* truly love you back then."

He nodded, understanding her dilemma hadn't been easy. Her religion, combined with her strict family duty, and on top of that, being a woman, left little for her to make any of her own choices. All she could do was find happiness in those decisions that were made for her.

He found out during their lunch that she had six children. He'd seen the four eldest just now who were hanging out around the City Walk area, shopping and grabbing snacks. Her eldest, Aadil, was finishing high school and wanted to become a lawyer. Her next, Yasmin, was just sixteen and wanted to be an architect. She had no intention of making her marry before she got to explore her own life and career, though, in true South Asian form, they had a husband in mind for her when she was older. Then her twins, Maalik and Mahfuz, were incredible football (soccer) players, turning twelve this year. And she had two more at home and was pregnant with another.

Aariv was astounded. Here she was building a big family while he'd been wasting away, not pining for her, but repenting for what he'd thought he'd done to her.

Her husband worked for the real estate developer who had been behind the major developments in downtown Dubai, so they lived extremely well. He treated her with respect and kindness but insisted they start their family immediately, once she'd finished her secondary school education with a private tutor after being whisked out of India. Hence, how she already had two teenagers while still in her thirties.

"But do you miss it? School, education? The idea of any career, or even freedom?"

"Freedom? I'm not a prisoner," she said confused by his choice of words. "And I can't think of harder work than being the mother of my family, Aariv. I am the managing director of my household. My husband might make the rules, but I ensure they are followed, and bend them when he's being obstinate." She shrugged. "Sure, I would have loved to explore a career as a nurse, but this is what *Allah* intended for me—to be a good wife, and homemaker, and to raise our children to be good Muslims. I can honestly say I am more than happy with my life, and except for the few weeks of tears after leaving you without saying good-bye, I never looked back."

She never looked back and he believed her. She was calm and steadfast when she said all of this, and her eyes shone with humor and warmth when she spoke about her husband and children.

Later, in his hotel room, after he promised to advise her eldest son about going into law sometime in the future, and they exchanged addresses to send holiday cards, he mulled over everything. She'd moved forward, and despite the knee-jerking way they'd been separated, she'd had the courage to go on and create a life for herself.

Did he feel like an idiot? Not precisely. It seemed he'd been the one more invested with how their relationship could become reality, whilst she saw it for what it was—young love that could go nowhere because of all the insurmountable obstacles. She'd enjoyed it while it lasted, then faced the future that was foisted on her.

He had to admit, the initial fury he experienced at finding out that she'd known all along she would end up with her husband had completely dissipated. Instead, he felt a gaping hole where his angst had been living. It was gone now, and he felt different. He almost didn't know what to do with himself … almost.

He reached for his phone. He'd sent Chrissy messages sporadically throughout his trip, needing to feel connected to her somehow, though she didn't answer back. He smiled thinking about her anger and how she'd practically thrown him out of the club herself a few weeks back. She was the one for him, he was surer than ever now, and now he could be everything to her.

He smiled as his fingers flew across the keys, his chest expanding with warmth, his body feeling weightless. That warmth slipped into that gaping hole, filling it. And he felt more carefree and yet more complete than he'd ever been.

But he had just one more obstacle he needed to tackle—his parents.

Pepsi Cola

THREE DAYS LATER

new york, new york

# CHAPTER 40

# 80

"Estimated Time of Arrival: I'll be back soon, Sunshine. I have a lot to share."

She glanced at her phone, scanning the text that had come from him a few days ago. She looked at it more closely to read it again. Was it just her, or was Aariv texting her messages that were similar to the last few she'd sent him when he'd unintentionally stood her up? She couldn't help herself, she smiled.

A few days had gone by between this text and the one before that, and regardless of their uninvolved status, she'd been on the edge of her seat waiting in anticipation for his next text—wondering if he'd even message her again. The air had left her body in a loud whoosh as she heaved a sigh of relief staring at his message bubble.

Reading it again only made her stomach tumble, and her head swim at his simple words, making her want to collapse onto her bed with a silly grin pasted on her face for the rest of the day. Her body trembled in anticipation at the thought that he'd be back soon. But, did she feel any different? Did he? He'd called her 'Sunshine' indicating that he still saw her like that. But the part about having a lot to share made her nervous in a less than positive way. Dull pin pricks traveled up the base of her neck to her scalp. And she had to physically shake herself out of it.

*Stop it. You aren't even sure you want him anymore.*

Yeah right.

She rolled her eyes and made herself stop thinking about him. She had a lot to do and needed to get moving.

She was meeting with surfer computer nerd, Taylor from California, today, to show him around her beloved Long Island City neighborhood of Queens. Her friend Shana would be joining them.

As it so happened, she'd sent Shana in her place to meet him for coffee when he first arrived in town a few days ago. She was still playing it safe, staying clear of going out and about, unless necessary. She'd canceled on him twice already because a certain Russian mafia smuggling ring had burned some of her property to the ground (Tag had confirmed this), and she was sorting through *that* insurance mess now. So she asked the only friend she knew who was available to meet him for a quick coffee in place of her. Surprisingly, she didn't have to wheedle and whine too much, just promise to buy dinner for her somewhat testy friend soon.

What happened during that coffee date couldn't have been more perfect. Sparks flew between Taylor and Shana, and they wanted to get to know each other further. Chrissy was more than happy—relieved actually—of this occurrence. Her feelings for Aariv would make attempting to date someone else a miserable effort, for both parties involved. She'd been there before—as the rebound and it sucked. She'd never put anyone in that position if the opportunity ever arose.

She told the both of them to meet her in front of her apartment building that Saturday morning. It was finally (finally!) a clear sunny day with temperatures warmer in the mid-seventies. Chrissy didn't hesitate, craving the warm weather from the dreary on-and-off chilly rain, and she dug one of her favorite sundresses out of her closet. It hit her just below her knees and was white with a woven eyelet pattern in the fabric. Thick straps crisscrossed in the back with a sweetheart neckline in the front. A cute bow of the same material sat in the middle of the bodice and there was a triangle cutout at the bottom that hit right at her ribcage. It was perfect for a day like today because it was airy and light, and the cutout design would cool her off after walking around for hours in the warm weather.

She paired them with a knock-off pair of Swedish-style clogs that had a pretty tan woven strap detail, excited to show off her new pedicure in a happy cherry red. She threw on a sheer yellow pastel cardigan and grabbed her purse, eager to get outside.

Once she got downstairs, she saw Taylor already waiting in front of her building. She waved through the glass doors and went out to meet him.

The guy was a hugger it seemed, and he leaned in to embrace her, smiling and saying that Shana was just a block away and would be there shortly. But just as he stepped back, still holding her hands and thanking her profusely for taking the time to show him around, a delivery truck started up that was parked in front of her building. As soon as it moved, she saw a burgundy Porche parked on the other side, and a tall, broad figure stood leaning against it. He was in jeans and tan loafers, and a light blue button-down linen shirt that was rolled up to his elbows, displaying strong wide forearms. His shirt was unbuttoned because why not taunt her with that chest hair of his that she loved so much? His ankles were crossed, and his arms were folded over his chest. His sunglasses glinted in the sun as his gaze stayed frozen in their direction. No smile emerged across his face. She'd be mistaken if she didn't think that he looked practically livid; his jaw was so sharp from clenching that she could make out the slight movement under his beard even from across the street.

And yet, her heart stopped, and her lungs forgot how to function. She needed oxygen, stat, because her breath had literally been taken away. He was so hot that she found herself fanning herself stupidly while Taylor continued talking animatedly, her eyes only on Aariv Abbas as he stood motionless across the street.

*Well, fuck. This probably didn't look so good.*

She felt her cheeks flame up as she tossed her head. But why should she care what he thought? They weren't officially together—had never been in the first place. And hadn't her last words to him been that she wouldn't wait for him?

But here was the problem with that entire scenario. Of course, she would wait for him. She'd wait until she took her last dying breath, an old and single, wrinkled woman pining for her grumpenhunk because if he could just figure his shit out, she'd throw all caution to the wind and jump into his arms.

Just then he stood up straight and grabbed something that had been sitting behind him on the top of the car. And as he headed across the street toward her, all she could think of was that last scene in *Sixteen Candles*, when Jake (that hunky love interest) meets Sam at the church after her sister's wedding. He'd been leaning on his Porsche waiting for her, too.

Just as Aariv stepped onto the curb in front of her, Shana arrived. She barely said 'hello' to Chrissy before she threw herself into Taylor's arms and surprised him with a passionate kiss. But Chrissy didn't have time to register that those two had just met days ago and were already tongue-tangoing, because Aariv held the most beautiful bouquet of fluffy daisies in his hands. It wasn't huge, but stunning and happy as they gazed out at her.

"Hey," he said gruffly, his gaze registering the two kissing behind her before lifting his sunglasses off and staring at her, his eyes bright and fiery.

Despite the warm weather, goosebumps spread out along the surface of her skin, and her nipples, those stupid sensitive buds, perked up in reaction to his sexy voice. Of course he would notice, as his gaze dropped to her breasts but flickered back up to her face with that lazy grin of his that she'd been dreaming about since their club altercation.

"Hey yourself," she said a little more breathlessly than she wanted. She cleared her throat. "What are you doing here?"

"I heard you were here," he responded, his smile widening.

She laughed. He'd been thinking the same thing as her. *"Sixteen Candles,"* she nodded appreciatively at their play of words.

He chuckled and cupped his chin, his gaze raking her over. "It's good to see you, Sunshine."

That's when she noticed that Taylor and Shana had stepped away, arms around one another watching them. She distinctly heard Shana say, "I think they're having a moment."

She looked down bashfully as Aariv stepped closer to her.

"Are those for me?" she asked, wide-eyed.

He chuckled. "What do you think, Sunshine? They're your favorite, aren't they?"

God, the man was good. He'd remembered that daisies were her all-time favorite flowers. She took them and pushed her nose into the delicate white petals, inhaling their slight, fresh scent.

"These are my favorite now, too." He hiked a pant leg up to display his daisy-printed socks—the ones he'd worn that first time they'd been together.

Her jaw dropped. "I knew it. I knew you had to have some romance in there. You couldn't have a birthday on Valentine's Day for nothing—" She realized her mistake when his brows arched high on his forehead. But he tilted his head back and started laughing. A sound that both soothed her and made her insides liquify.

"And guess what, I was aware you may have seen that *Vedic Cosmic Calendar* document in my office that night."

"How—" she began curiously.

"I did nothing to hide it. I wasn't afraid of you finding it." He shoved his hands into his pockets.

"So, the C is—"

"You, Chrissy."

And out of all the things she thought she would have done at that moment—throw herself into his arms and kiss him passionately or laugh in happiness and joy and love—big fat tears ended up rolling down her cheeks. It was so unexpected she tried dashing them away quickly, but they only came faster.

"Chrissy," Aariv said concerned. "What—" He laid his big warm hands on her shoulders hesitantly.

"I'm just *so* f—fuck—ing relieved, Riv," she whispered, mortified that she was stuttering and couldn't stop crying.

"That, my man," Shana interjected, one arm still around Taylor, the other on her hip, "are tears of joy. You've cracked the Chrissy code. Only the most romantic gesture will do that to this one." Shana stepped closer examining her as Chrissy laughed and cried at the same time. "I think you've overwhelmed the shit out of her."

"Hon, why don't we let these two have some privacy," Taylor said, ushering Shana away.

All Chrissy could do was look stunned at the retreating figure of the uber-new couple as they left, then up at Aariv in disbelief. She just could not wrap her head around what was happening. It was like a rom-com movie.

A hand glided down to her waist, squeezing, as another reached up to wipe away her tears.

"Can we go up to your place, Chrissy? I'd like to talk."

She sniffed and nodded, and they wordlessly headed inside, his arm around her waist. They silently took the elevator up, as she continued inhaling the blooms, unable to look at him right then.

When she unlocked her front door and they both stepped inside, she'd barely put the flowers down before he hugged her tightly from behind, burying his face in her hair and breathing deeply.

She heard the door shut and he breathed a 'Chrissy' before he started nuzzling her neck, his warm thick lips caressing her overheated skin.

She turned and wove her arms around his neck, pulling him down to her lips, crushing his into hers as she opened her mouth for him.

"Riv," she murmured huskily against him. And he shuddered at that name, having wanted to hear her say it again for weeks.

His hands gripped her waist, his thumbs gliding into the opening at the front of her dress, grazing her exposed flesh. And she pushed her body closer to his as if gluing herself to him while her sighs of pleasure reverberated against his lips.

His desire for her was growing by the second. He wanted to take her now, right on the kitchen counter until she screamed bloody murder and groaned out her love for him.

But he had so much to get out before he could let himself fall into that inexplicable joy.

He pulled his lips from hers, and she stood there, eyes closed, mouth apart. When her lids finally opened, he was staring into her look of delirium and wonder. The blues of her glassy eyes were almost black.

"I want to tell you what I found out, Chrissy."

She blinked slowly, her eyes coming back into focus. "I don't care, Riv. I love you. I'm sorry I made you leave. I'm sorry—"

He put a finger to her lips, quieting her. "I love you, too," he murmured. And her eyes welled up again. He sighed, shaking his head, and engulfed her in a hug. His romantic little sunshine had such a soft little heart. And he'd do his best to protect it if she let him.

He led her to the couch and sat down, pulling her onto his lap. She rested her head on his shoulder as he continued speaking. "You *do* care, Chrissy. I'm glad you did what you did. You are so much stronger than I could ever be." He caressed her back and she sighed, content in his arms. "I wouldn't have gone and found out the answers unless you kicked my ass into gear. It was good for me. So, thank you for your strength, your fury, and your passion."

"You're welcome," she whispered against his shoulder, and he smiled.

"Now, do you want to hear what I found out?"

She lifted her head, her rounded cheeks damp with tears. He wiped them with his fingers as he waited for her response.

"Will I like it?"

He chuckled and considered this, leaning back with her still in his lap. She went with him, leaning her head on him again.

"I think so. I know I did. But I found it extremely infuriating, too."

"Well … go on then. What kind of mess did you find Leila in? Is she that unhappy? Are you going to spend the rest of your life trying to make things right?"

She was resigned to this fate, it seemed.

"Actually, she doesn't need any rescuing." He considered his next words carefully but decided what the hell, she should know. "She's kind of like you, Sunshine. She takes what's given to her and crafts a life that works out for herself. She's happy, has a house full of kids, and hadn't thought of me for years until I called her up out of the blue."

"Sounds like my type of person—making lemonade out of

lemons and all that crap," Chrissy said. "But how was she able to let you go so easily? I was finding the task extremely difficult…" she said knowingly, fingering his shirt.

"Are you sure about that? You seemed pretty good at kicking me to the curb that night at the club," he teased.

"I fucking hated it!" she said petulantly. "But I needed to protect myself."

He nodded and hugged her tight. Self-preservation was a driving force in many of his past decisions, too.

"Leila knew from the get-go that we weren't destined to be together. She always knew that she intended to marry another, to have a different life than the one we dreamed about. She was far more level-headed at that age than I could have ever been."

"Seems like you've always had a little bit of romance in you."

"I guess so," he said, realizing she was right as he fiddled with the little bow on her dress.

"So … what do we do now?"

His hands slid up and down her back, finally landing on her ass and squeezing. He groaned as the firm and soft flesh filled his hands perfectly. "I can think of a few things."

She smiled but smacked him on the chest. "I mean, about your parents and us."

In his relief at seeing Chrissy, then his jealousy at seeing some long-haired guy hugging her (had she really not waited for him?), and then feeling relief again realizing the guy was with her other friend, he'd forgotten about his parents. Which oddly told him that their opinion didn't matter that much to him anymore. Did it really ever, though?

"My parents will get over it." He pulled her closer to him, nuzzling her neck again.

"Wait, that's it? Are you serious?"

"Yeah. But in the meantime, they've disowned me." He trailed kisses down to the swell of her breasts and nuzzled his nose in her cleavage.

"Wait, wait, wait." She pulled away from him. "Stop with that. I can't think straight."

He smiled, pleased to hear her say it.

"Stop it, Riv. Tell me exactly what happened."

He groaned and leaned back, spreading his arms along the back of her couch as he recalled that conversation with his parents. He'd had the entire flight from Dubai to think about what he wanted to tell them and had talked to them right before he'd come over here.

# CHAPTER 41

8১

"So you found her," Huma said. "I never doubted you could, Aari."

He'd just arrived home and was unpacking his suitcase, sorting through his dirty clothes, throwing things haphazardly into his hamper before he gave up. It could wait. Instead, he sat heavily on his bed.

"Why had you never encouraged me to find her before, Aunty? You saw me suffering and yet, you asked me to move on."

"Aari, I never knew what happened to her. Your father didn't either. What is the point in circling a truth that shouldn't matter to your future?"

He grunted. "It did matter, though. I felt guilty for her disappearance. I thought she was in a shitty situation. You heard the same rumors I did!" He distinctly remembered Huma trying to do damage control when it had all happened, trying to place blame on the other family, not him, and talking about how the girl was most likely married to a backward old man now.

"*Heh*, I did. But I was trying to protect you the best way I knew how."

"The same way you protected me from knowing about my real mother?" he asked bitterly.

She gasped. "Aari! How can you say that? I knew nothing about that either, though your father has revealed that he knew all along that she ran away, that she was a *pagal*—"

"Don't say that!" he said sharply. She inhaled quickly, not used to him using this kind of tone with her. "I'm sorry. It's just that she wasn't crazy. That's such a negative way of thinking. She had some kind of mental issues that my *abba* refused to help her with."

"*Eesh.*" Her tone was disgusted, and he knew it wasn't directed toward him. "But he cannot be changed, *Beta.*"

He sighed, very much aware of that fact.

She switched the topic to his search for a wife and he stopped her.

"I'm not pursuing that anymore."

"*Ki*? But why?"

"I've already found someone perfect for me."

He heard her clap in delight. "*Atcha*! Finally! Pinky never said anything, so I assumed we were starting again—"

"I fired Pinky."

"What!? She's still working for us, finding new matches for you. And I just received her recent bill. When did you do this, Aari?" She sounded hurt about not being aware of his decision.

"I can't work with that woman. She's sneaky and meddlesome."

"Oh, Aari. I was so worried when I didn't hear from you.

How was I supposed to know you were sick? You never get sick. Thank goodness Mimi checked on you, and I had Pinky go over there for good measure."

"I *hate* that woman. Please do not ever involve her where it concerns me again."

"But she told me she found that girl at your place." She sounded befuddled. "Aari? I thought we discussed you getting her out of your system to focus on your marriage."

"I'm not ready to get her out of my system." He tried to keep his patience.

"When will you be ready? No good woman will be left for you to choose from."

"I don't see her ever getting out of my system, Aunty. I'm in love with her."

Silence stretched between them until he heard her murmuring to someone on the other end.

"Are you out of your damn mind, Aariv!?" his father bellowed on the phone now in place of Huma.

"Probably, considering I'm my mother's son. But man, does it feel great!" he said with feigned excitement.

He chuckled as he heard his father curse him on the other end.

"Are you marrying this girl?"

"We're not quite there yet, but I'm sure a wedding will be in our future." And he meant it when he said that.

"What about your career? Will you decide to leave the law world, too?" Viraj sneered.

And Aariv didn't know why but revealing that his life plans were shifting felt fucking exhilarating. "I'm still an attorney, but I may not have made partner this year."

The older man scoffed and lamented, "What have we not done for you in this life to make you act out like this?"

"This has nothing to do with you. This has everything to do with me."

"Aariv, what did you not do at work? Did they pass you over for a more hard-working person?"

Always his fault—never being good enough was *always* his fucking fault. Aariv shook his head. "I'm sure they had their reasons, and you know I'm a damn good lawyer. I'll make partner someday, but it's not my time, yet."

"*Uri Baba* (my God)! I cannot control your big New York City law firm, but I am disappointed, especially if you think you will marry this girl and I will be fine with it. If you go through with it, I will disown you. You will not inherit the factory and the business. You will not see a penny!"

Aariv laughed outright; a heavy burden lifted off his shoulders. "That's fantastic, *Abba*. I don't want that mismanaged operation anyway."

"*Bas*! You will never be able to speak to your stepmother again."

That sobered him up. "I hope you don't mean that, *Abba*. You would keep her from seeing her stepson happy? From celebrating his life and love with another? Even if grandchildren were involved? You truly are a cruel man."

"She will do what she is told."

"Then I feel sorry for you both. To live your lives in such a box, where rules can't be bent." His exhalation was heavy as he realized he had to say something about how his father was destroying his own life. "No wonder you drink so much. You've created such a tight framework to live by that alcohol is your only reprieve. *Abba*, I say this with the utmost respect—you need to get help."

"Enough!" the older man shouted. "I will take your advice only when I ask for it. Right now, you are nothing to me." And he hung up.

Aariv stared at his phone, but the dejection didn't overtake him. He felt jubilant, and he knew that was fucked up.

CHAPTER 42

# 8২

"It's not that fucked up," Chrissy said now slowly in thought. "He's burdened you all your life with responsibilities that you never created for yourself. I think you feel free."

How she came up with these ideals, he had no idea. He looked at her closely, wondering if her and all her positivity were real.

She was, and he was the luckiest asshole he ever knew.

"But you aren't making partner?" She looked at him worriedly.

"Chrissy, I don't need to, at least not now. I'm ok with where I am with my career."

She looked at him suspiciously. "Who are you and what have you done with Grumpenstein?"

He guffawed, having hated that name in the past, but not so much now. He could be grumpy, or cranky, but that was just his nature. He was fortunate that he had people in his life who loved him for all of his sides, good, bad, and cranky.

"So, you're using me to get out of some failing family

business?" She shook her shoulders, acting peevish. He reached in and tickled her, and her giggles burst forth, merrily. "It's ok, Riv. I get it. Failing family businesses are the *worst*."

He chuckled. "God, I love you," he said, pulling her close against him again, inhaling her sweet perfume until he was dizzy with her.

She giggled again, and murmured, "Say it again."

He did and he kissed her with as much feeling as he could muster behind those words, hoping she felt it.

"So," she said breathlessly as they came up for air. "You really think marriage is in our future?"

"No. I know it is."

"Wow, you're one confident guy."

"Hey, when I know, I know."

Her cheeks turned bright red as she lowered her eyes bashfully. But she nodded. She fingered his wrist, then stopped, picking up his other hand and examining that wrist, too.

"Where's your bracelet?"

"I'm not wearing it anymore."

"I see that, but why?"

"I don't need all those superstitious charms. I just needed the chance to carve out my own destiny to feel like I was living up to my potential."

"And when did that all start?" she asked softly, poking a finger in the opening of his shirt.

"When I watched you all night at the wedding after being a dickhead to you. Then danced with you for way too short of a time, before leaving to go rescue my drunk cousin."

Her blue eyes peered up at him. "Seriously?"

"Yep. You have been on my mind ever since then. I can't tell you how many times I jerked off thinking about you—"

She covered his mouth, her face scrunching up, but her playful smile was hard to contain. "You were so close, Counselor. So close to being all about the romance. Then your dirty mouth got in the way."

"You love my dirty mouth," he whispered devilishly.

"I do," she agreed.

"So, let's go remedy that, shall we?" He stood up abruptly, making her squeak, but she held on as he lifted her bridal style and walked to her bedroom.

"Wait, Aariv. I need to tell you something."

He paused after laying her gently on her mattress, his body lying beside hers. He propped his head up on an elbow.

"What's wrong?" he asked, his concern rising as he noticed her serious expression.

"The rug shop caught on fire. Tag did a little digging and found out it was linked to the Russian crime syndicate that was doing all the smuggling before."

"Wow. Are you okay? That's a crazy new development."

"I'm fine," she said, distracted by his buttons, her fingers gliding lightly over them. "I never wanted it in the first place."

"Okay," he said slowly, trying to understand where she was going with this. "What about Boris?"

"He's in hiding at a safe house until we have a court date. Then he's leaving New York for good."

Aariv considered this. "I'm sorry about that, Chrissy. I know you'll miss him."

She shrugged. "I will. But his safety matters more to me than anything. Maybe one day, many years from now, we can be reunited."

He pushed her hair behind her ears. She seemed fine with

everything, her expression placid, but it was a lot of change all at once.

"The rug shop burning down—you know that can only be a positive thing. Now you don't have to worry about selling it and running into roadblocks in case the bad guys don't want to let it go."

She nodded and he continued, his hazel eyes searching hers in concern. "You don't have to work two jobs anymore. You could quit dancing—"

"I'm going to keep dancing," she said, her chin raising slightly, but she kept her eyes on his chest. She heard his sharp inhalation.

"Why?" he burst out, the irritation in his voice evident. She hid her smile. The man was jealous. But he didn't need to be.

"Because I'm a dancer, a performer at heart. My mom may have been wrong about me being destined to be a prima ballerina, but she was right about my passion for dance."

He sighed. The frustration was evident. "Chrissy, I'm not about to tell you what to do but—"

"But you're about to tell me what to do, aren't you?" Her eyes met his and she couldn't hide the smile dancing on her lips.

He huffed, rubbing a hand over his bearded jaw. "I hate that you dance almost naked in front of horny men."

"Hmm." She batted her eyes and caressed his chest, feeling the heavy thud of his heart. "You'd rather that I just danced in front of one horny man?"

"At the risk of sounding like an asshole—hell yes! That horny man being me."

"You're already an asshole, and I love you for it." She put a finger to his lips quieting the response he began to give. "I'm not dancing at the club anymore. I'm going to continue working at the dance studio I rented rehearsal space from, but only on the weekends. They had an opening to teach a little kids' dance class."

Aariv was surprised. Then he closed his eyes and huffed out a loud relieved breath. "That's great, Chrissy. With your experience, you're going to be fantastic at that." He hugged her. "Congratulations."

"Thanks," she murmured against his chest. "Everything is falling into place and I'm so happy."

"Fuck. Me too, Sunshine." He sounded humbled, and her heart melted.

"There's just one other thing," she said a little coyly.

He leaned back to look at her, his eyes squinting in question. She undid his buttons, not bothering to close them back up.

"And what's that?" he asked curiously, watching her undo more buttons until she reached his jeans.

"I'm knee-deep in insurance paperwork," she pouted. "And I have no idea what I'm doing when it comes to filing claims," she lamented, trying her best to cover her giggles.

He rolled her over onto her back, his hard body pressed into hers, and her giggles turned into a sigh of appreciation.

He stared at her intensely, his hazel eyes burning bright. She felt his love, adoration, and respect with that one look.

"So, what do you need, Little Girl?" he asked, his voice gruff and tender.

She bit her bottom lip and her hands dove into his shirt,

caressing his warm chiseled chest and abs. "I think I need a lawyer."

He leaned down to brush her nose with his, a smile playing across his thick lips. He was lighter, less somber, and more relaxed. Did she dare to believe that it was their love that made him so? Yes, yes, she did. They were free to fall into happiness together and her entire being felt joyful, never expecting that a future for them could ever be a reality.

And would they live happily ever after? If she had anything to do with it, yes, yes, they would.

His breath tickled her cheek as he murmured, "You're in luck. Thankfully, I know a really good one." And then his mouth covered hers in a fiery and tender kiss.

**THE END**

# ACKNOWLEDGMENTS

ধন্যবাদ –
Dhanyabad –
Thank you

Thank you so much for reading Free Fall. If you loved it, please leave a review on Amazon and/or Goodreads. Indie authors like myself appreciate it, and appreciate readers like you!

This was by far the hardest book for me to write. I have to thank my editor, Jessica Gang, for being so patient with me and helping me get to the third and final round of this story (the third time's a charm, right?). I grew up with men like Aariv, those who straddled both cultures and pushed themselves to be good men with a responsibility to uphold and the need to care for their families. They were smart and bright and good at everything it seemed. It was peripheral for me, though as I am one of three daughters. So getting inside a modern male South Asian's head took a lot of effort and research, along with thinking back to what my male cousins had to face when they came of a certain age. But I didn't want to give up. I wanted to tackle this story and show a male point of view. What's interesting is so often they can do no wrong but are still viewed as helpless, and need help to find a wife, or even do their laundry, cooking, and cleaning. Aariv has a bit of that, but he's also strived to be independent, thus showing that he has a more modern take on life than say how his father lives.

I hope I did Aariv's character justice. He's a grumpy a-hole with a gentle soul. What he thinks is a failing in him when he can't help his attraction for Chrissy, becomes a strength pushing him to find his own path in life. So I hope you can cheer him on the way I did throughout their story.

Also, my editor will tell you that he started even worse and it was a lot of finessing to get him to be more relatable and human. Thank you again, Jessica, for working with me on him, and for being honest—that you just couldn't like him in the first round 😊.

And Chrissy—she's every romantic, soft-hearted, funny, naïve girl we've probably all been once in our lives. She has an inner strength that Aariv admires and what pulls him to her. Her dating history comes from some of my dating mishaps when I lived in New York. It was fast-paced, exciting, and more often than not, ended quickly with no rhyme or reason, and a lot of disappointment. Are men fickle f*cks? In New York City where there are more single women than single men in the population? Absolutely, and I wanted to write a character who experienced the hazards of dating in a crazy competitive city like NYC, but still maintains a positive, sunny attitude, because fiction and one can dream can't they?

Also, the recipe for Chrissy's mother's health remedy is an amalgamation of a few different Russian tonics that I researched. So try it at your own risk if you dare.

Lastly, many, many thanks to my husband and my boys for understanding that writing is my therapy and that sometimes I need to hole up with my laptop at the library or local coffee shop for hours. I love you guys!

Stay tuned for more books coming soon (can we say ultra spicy love between a chef and a doctor with secrets of her own?)!

XOXO,

Khushi

# ABOUT ME

I love romance, travel, and not only exploring the South Asian identity, but personal transformation. As a South Asian woman, I write about what I know, having grown up in the US and living coast to coast. When I'm not toiling away on my computer writing about love and self-discovery, I'm teaching crafting classes, hanging with my guys, and playing with my pup.

# WANT TO STAY IN TOUCH?

Visit Kushi T. Saha at …
https://www.ktsromance.com/
ktsromance@gmail.com
Monthly newsletter sign-up: https://subscribepage.io/PG9p3a
https://www.facebook.com/KhushiT.S
https://www.instagram.com/ktsromance
Khushi T. Saha (Author of Desire's Unravelling) | Goodreads
Khushi T. Saha Books - BookBub
Amazon.com: Khushi T. Saha: books, biography, latest update